DAVID LAFFERTY

A PLACE OF

VENGEANCE

Tales from Windward Cove

ISBN: 979-8-35092-651-4 (paperback)
ISBN: 979-8-35092-652-1 (ebook)

Dedication

This tale is dedicated to my father, David Lee Lafferty, 1933–2004. A writer, musician, actor, and healthcare professional, his greatest gift was instilling in my sister, brother, and I a love of books and movies. Most of my fondest childhood memories are of him reading aloud to us—*("Read on, Dad…read on!")*—and inviting us to sit up late with him on Saturday nights, watching old horror films. If you're very lucky, some gifts you get to keep forever, and I wouldn't trade those memories for the world.

Thanks, Dad. This one's for you.

ONE

"WHICH GHOST IS THIS ONE, AGAIN?" LES ASKED.

"The scary one," I muttered, a little nervously. Okay, maybe more than a little.

"Dude…they're ghosts. They're *supposed* to be scary."

I gave him a raised eyebrow, but he only grinned at me. Leslie Hawkins, the un-ruffleable. Seriously, nothing ever seemed to bother the guy. He had hung around with us the whole summer long, taking charge of the Common Sense Department while Ab did the hardcore research and provided all the ghost expertise. Abigail Chambers had been studying the paranormal most of her life (if you could even call it studying—raging fangirl would probably be a better description), and she had emerged as our unofficial leader.

And me? I was just the guy who could see and feel things no one else could.

We were gathered at the end of the third-floor hall in front of Suite 324—the only locked door inside the Windward Inn. I stood a little to one side, avoiding the cold spot I remembered from the day my mom and I had first explored the old, boarded-up hotel. The spot still lingered, a space of maybe three square feet where the temperature dropped fifteen or twenty degrees. But that wasn't the part that bothered me. The feeling of detached, brutal menace that emanated from whatever lurked on the other side of the door bothered me a lot more. I swallowed, feeling sweat gather on the back of my neck.

I didn't want to be there.

"This should be Frank Delgiacco," Ab reported when I didn't answer. She consulted her stack of notes, most of which were copies of old newspaper columns downloaded from the internet, and I watched as she flipped through the pages. Lean, with a narrow face and high cheekbones, her hair matched the dark brown of her eyes, longer on top and cut short on the sides, and even in the dim hallway I could make out the purple highlights. The line between her eyebrows smoothed out when she found the right page. "Aha—here it is. Frank was a gangster from the nineteen-thirties with connections to crime families in both New York and Chicago."

"So how'd he end up here?" Les asked.

"As the story goes, he hooked up with his boss' girlfriend—a woman named Martina Russo. They ran away together when they were discovered, but the mob caught up to him here a little over a year later." Ab frowned down at the page. "The article doesn't say if Martina was with him or not."

I reached out mentally, immediately finding the brief vision I had seen earlier that summer: the muzzle flash of a gun, a spray of blood, and the body of a woman in a red dress being buried in the desert. "She wasn't," I told them, my mouth going dry. *What happened?* I wondered offhandedly. *Did they have a fight? Did Martina have second thoughts and want to go back?* I shook my head, realizing that I would probably never know.

"Anyway, on the night of April 14th, 1933, two mob hit men showed up and knocked around eleven p.m.," Ab went on. "When Frank asked who was there, one fired a shotgun right through the door, and then kicked it in. Delgiacco took most of the blast in his chest and stomach, but he must've been a big guy because as soon as the door swung open, he shot one of the mobsters in the face, and dragged the other one into the room. They must have both dropped their guns in the fight, because the second mobster was found strangled to death. Frank bled out before the police got here."

"And you want *me* to go in," I said. "Am I the only one who thinks this is a really stupid idea?"

"*C'mon*, Wolfman," Ab prodded, sounding impatient. "All we want to find out is if this ghost is aware of people, or if he's only stuck reliving the past. And anyway, we've been through this place from top to bottom and nothing has hurt you so far, has it?"

I sighed, realizing she was right, and it made me feel like a wuss. After all, you'd think after a summer of investigating the spirits in the old hotel I'd be used to it by now. But then again, each case had been a little different: from Myra Lang down in room 209, who killed herself in May of 1926 by taking a whole bottle of sleeping pills; to William "Willie" Boyd, who got drunk off his ass during a New Year's Eve party in 1949, and died after wrestling the third-floor elevator door open and falling down the shaft. There were ghosts who stuck around for reasons known only to them, others who didn't even know they were dead, and pretty much everything in between. No two were exactly alike.

My friend Lisette Gautier had spent a lot of time over the summer trying to teach me how to reach out to them, hoping I'd be able to *"help move 'em on."* So far, though, my batting average stood at zero. Sure, under the right circumstances I could experience mind-blowing visions of past events. I could sense emotions too, both from the people around me and any strong feelings that were sometimes imprinted on places and objects. Once in a great while I could even foretell events, though far less specifically or reliably—more like having a touch of Peter Parker's spider sense. But despite Lisette's patient coaching and all the ghost hunting we'd done over the summer, I still had not been able to form any sort of connection by which I could genuinely communicate or interact. I dunno…maybe I just sucked at the whole psychic thing. Sensing and watching was the best I could manage, which sometimes made me feel like I brought the least of all of us to the party.

Ben Wolf, useless psychic.

Moe nuzzled my hand, as if sensing my uncertainty, and I ruffled his black, shaggy fur. The puppy I had found and taken in the previous June had grown a lot during the last couple of months. His shoulders now stood above my knees, and he wasn't even close to done yet. The vet in Silver Creek had identified him as a Black Russian Terrier; a dog originally bred for military and police work, and if what I'd read from the internet turned out to be true, he could end up weighing upwards of a hundred and thirty pounds. Good thing he was so mellow.

"Wolfman…? You still with us?"

"Yeah," I said, bringing my thoughts back to the present. "Sorry." I dug the hotel passkey out of my hip pocket and inserted it into the lock. I had to twist hard before the old key began to turn, and I wondered how many years had gone by since it was locked. At last, though, something inside gave way with a grind and a snap, and the bolt rolled aside.

My heart began thudding in my chest. Ab's research had included pouring through boxes of old, leather-bound hotel registers we had discovered in a small office behind the front desk, and we'd found out that the last guest to stay in Suite 324 had checked out a little after midnight on September 12th, 1934. In the seventeen months following Frank Delgiacco's murder, the suite had been rented only twenty-eight times, with no one making it through a single night. Five of the guests had switched to other rooms, but the rest had all left the hotel anywhere between 7:00 p.m. and 3:15 in the morning. From the night the last recorded guest fled the room until the Windward Inn finally closed its doors for good in October of 1958, no record existed of Suite 324 ever being occupied again.

Knowing that wasn't exactly comforting.

I twisted the knob, holding my breath as a crack of semi-darkness appeared between the door and the frame.

Before I could think, I found myself stumbling awkwardly into gloom, yanked inside as the door flew savagely open! I had barely a second to realize they hadn't even bothered to clear out the room's furniture before I somersaulted over the back of a sofa, my legs landing hard on a coffee table on the other side and breaking it in half. Dust from the upholstery rose in a cloud and I could hear Moe barking as I scrambled to my feet. The cracks between the boards that covered the windows allowed the late afternoon sunlight to penetrate the room, the narrow beams looking like lasers as they cut through the billowing dust.

I found my bearings again, and was looking back to where Ab and Les stared in from the hallway, wide-eyed with shock, when something hit me hard in the chest. I flew through the air, my back slamming against a wall and shattering a big mirror that hung there. I had barely landed when what felt like a huge hand closed around my throat, smashing me back against the wall and pinning me there with my feet dangling a foot above the floor. Panicked, I flailed at the towering, man-shaped shadow figure that merged into view in front of me. It formed from bits of darkness all over the room, coming together into something nearly solid—blacker than the blackest midnight and freezing cold. My punches and kicks sailed right through it, though, like fighting smoke. I struggled to breathe, but the icy hand holding me had completely closed off my windpipe. My vision dimmed to gray around the edges…

Then suddenly, the hand released me as Moe tore into the room, his bared teeth glinting in the dimness and barking furiously as the shadow appeared to retreat in surprise. I landed hard on my hands and knees, inhaling ragged gulps of air as Les skidded to a stop beside me, hauling me back to my feet and half-dragging me to where Ab waited, ready to pull the door shut.

"Moe!" I managed to choke out, my throat burning, and he turned and scrambled out into the hall half a step ahead of us. Ab slammed the door shut as soon as we were clear, and it rattled in its frame as something heavy hit it from the other side.

The thud echoed hollowly down the empty corridor, fading away until only the sound of our labored breathing remained.

After a long moment, Les turned away from the door, his pale eyes glinting mischievously in the half light. "Well," he remarked, "ol' Frank seems pretty aware to me. What do you guys think?"

I chuckled. It made my throat hurt, but I couldn't help it. Ab and Les joined in, and we shared a laugh that was part hysterical relief, part lingering shock and terror, but mostly the laugh of good friends finding the moment freaking *hilarious.* We kept going until a second, louder thud rattled the door, as if the ghost inside resented the sound, and we all jumped a little. "Lock that, will you?" I asked.

I watched as Les strained to turn the key. "It won't budge," he said at last, giving up and handing me the key. "Something inside must've broken when you opened it."

That made me nervous, but I told myself that if the ghost of Frank Delgiacco wanted to get past the door, he would have done it already. Just the same, I figured we shouldn't press our luck. "So," I asked Ab, "do you have any more near-death experiences you'd like to put me through, or can we get out of here?"

"Nah," she replied, grinning. "I guess that's enough for today."

We made our way down to the lobby, and I left the passkey on its hook behind the front desk before following Ab and Les out to the porch.

"Have you and your mom ever thought about reopening the Windward?" Ab asked, watching as I locked the front doors behind us.

"Not really," I admitted. "I mean sure, it's come up, but we only got all the wiring fixed at the house last month, and Mom has a lot of other stuff planned. It'll be a while before this place makes it that far up the To Do list."

I watched Moe as he loped ahead of us, and we shared a companionable silence as we ducked under the chain stretched across the entrance to the grounds and began our hike down the steep drive. Although the sun warmed me through my shirt, a cool wind off the ocean reminded me of the waning summer. The afternoon light had been turning a deeper gold as autumn crept near, the sunsets ticking steadily southward and giving way to twilight a minute or two earlier each evening. Thinking about it made me a little sad. The last day of summer vacation always did.

"You guys all ready for tomorrow?" Ab asked, as if reading my thoughts.

"Yep," said Les.

"Nope," I answered at the same time, and we laughed.

"C'mon, hombre," Les offered good-naturedly, ruffling the lingering dust from his light, almost colorless hair. "Tomorrow you're officially a Silver Creek High Buccaneer. What's not to like about that?" He stood a little taller than me, though thicker in the chest and shoulders in a burly kind of way that sometimes reminded me of a mountain man, or maybe a lumberjack. He was a year ahead of Ab and me—a junior—and had shown us around the campus the week before.

I shrugged. "Nothing, I guess. I just like summer better. You know, staying up late watching movies, getting to sleep in whenever I want, hanging out on the beach... Now we have to trade it all in for boring days in class, homework and all the rest."

"Don't forget football games and dances," Les countered.

"Halloween, Thanksgiving and Christmas," Ab added.

"Knock it off, will you?" I complained, smirking. "Can't you just let a guy feel sorry for himself?"

From there our conversation drifted to other subjects like which teachers were cool and which weren't, what to definitely stay away from in the cafeteria, and other random bits of intel Les thought we might need. It kept us busy until we made it to my house, a rambling Victorian ringed by elm trees about halfway down the hill from the inn. It sat in a meadow fifty yards south of what had been a private vineyard back in the 1940s, maybe ten square acres of abandoned grape vines that had grown into a great, tangled jungle of green that stretched twelve to fifteen feet high in some places. The house and vineyard had both been haunted when Mom and I moved to Windward Cove back in June, but they weren't anymore. And anyway, that's a different story.

"You guys want to stay for dinner?" I asked. "Mom's making her enchilada casserole. It's awesome—one of my all-time favorites."

"Can't," Ab said. "I probably should have been home an hour ago. My Aunt Abby is visiting, and if I don't go and pretend that I'm a girlie-girl for a while, I'll never hear the end of it."

"I should go, too," Les replied. "I need to shove some clothes in the washer—you can only turn your underwear inside-out so many days in a row."

That got us to laughing again, and afterward we agreed to meet early at Tsunami Joe for coffee in the morning so we could ride to school together. I sat on the porch step, feeling sad again as I watched my friends get on their bicycles and pedal away. End-of-summer blues, I knew, so I tried to shake it off. I entwined my fingers in Moe's fur, turning my gaze through the gap in the western hills where a coppery sunset glowed above the Pacific. Pretty, and as good a way to end my last day of freedom as any, I supposed.

"*Benny!*" My mother's call drifted faintly through the screen door from somewhere in the back of the house. "*You around? Dinner's almost ready!*"

"Be right there!" I hollered back, but I stayed put for a few moments longer, watching a black spot out over the ocean glide south against the backdrop of shimmering water. It was a bird—either a seagull or a pelican; it was too far away to tell for sure—skimming a foot or so above the waves, as if enjoying the last flight of the day.

I knew exactly how he felt.

TWO

"OH, *LOOK*...IT'S THE FREAK'S COUSIN!"

My hearing zeroed in on the sound, and I glanced up from where I was locking my bike to the rack. Students flowed in from the school parking lot—some talking cheerfully with friends, others looking like they weren't quite awake yet—and I had to crane my neck around before I finally found the source of the contemptuous tone.

A heavyset girl with blond, greasy-looking hair and bad acne lingered with a couple of friends just outside the campus fence, passing around a cigarette before the first bell. She wore camo pants, flip-flops, and a black T-shirt advertising somebody's bar or restaurant (I was too far away to read the lettering, but the logo showed a blue dolphin jumping through the handle of a beer mug.) I noticed that the bottom hem of the shirt was cut four or five inches above her waistband. It wasn't a good look for her.

"Darlene's starting early," Les remarked.

Ab looked over, scowling.

"What's her deal?" I asked.

Ab shook her head. "Nothing. Just a mean streak a mile wide."

I turned back toward the scene, frowning automatically. I hate bullies.

A slender girl in a long skirt and a loose, zippered hoodie was trying to squeeze past them through a narrow pedestrian gate. Darlene moved to block her way. "How can you stand to even be in the same house as him?" she challenged. "Or maybe you're a freak, too—is that it?"

The girl in the skirt just stood there, hugging a binder to her chest with one arm while holding an insulated lunch bag in her free hand. The hood of her sweatshirt was up, and she looked at Darlene through dark hair that partially obscured her face. I could just make out pale skin and brown eyes that were wide with fear. Her expression reminded me of a small animal caught in a snare, and before I even realized it, I was weaving my way toward them.

"What...are you *deaf*, new girl?" Darlene taunted as I drew near. She reached out and yanked the binder out of her grasp, flinging it casually behind her and evoking tribal laughter from her friends. It landed open and face down inside the chain link fence, a handful of loose pages floating lazily to the asphalt like leaves. "You *answer* me when I'm talking to you!"

"Leave her alone," I called out as I drew near, and Darlene turned toward me, her eyes narrowing. "What's your problem, anyway?" I asked. "Was she trip-trip-tripping over your bridge?"

It took a second or two before her expression registered understanding, and I began to suspect she might not be the brightest crayon in the box. "Mind your own business, asshole!" she snarled, but I wasn't fooled. She was making a pretty good show of being tough, but the eager aggression I had initially sensed from the big girl was mostly gone.

"Wow...you kiss your mother with that mouth?" Les asked, stepping up beside me.

"*Screw* you, Hawkins."

He chuckled. "Not in a million years, princess."

"If you want to push someone around, how about me instead?" Ab challenged from my other side. "It didn't work out for you last time, but hey, I'm up for a rematch if you are."

Darlene's friends exchanged a glance and moved tentatively to back her up. One was tall and pear-shaped, wearing a green and yellow tie-dyed shirt and jeans. The other was skinny and had spiky hair. She wore a gray sweatshirt with the sleeves cut away and the poo emoji on the front. Classy.

Their combined feelings only amounted to nervousness and fear, though, so I decided to end our little standoff before it got any uglier. Staring Darlene in the eyes I stepped calmly forward, moving right into her personal space. Just as I figured, she scuttled back, bumping into her friends as all three retreated. "Come on," I said, turning to the girl they had been picking on. "Let's go get your stuff." I gestured toward the gate and she hurried through.

"There goes the big man!" Darlene called after me as we walked away, but there wasn't much conviction left in her tone. We ignored her, so she pitched her voice to carry over the crowd. "SOMEBODY NEEDS TO TEACH *YOU* THE RIGHT WAY TO TREAT WOMEN!"

Conversations fell silent as everyone in the immediate area paused to see what was going on.

Ab turned. "Yeah?" she fired back. "Well, somebody needs to teach *you* the difference between a bare midriff and a *beer-gutriff!*"

Laughter erupted all around and I could hear Les chuckle behind me as I squatted, helping the girl pick up her scattered papers. "I don't know about you," I confided, "but much more of that and Darlene will lose my vote for prom queen."

She raised her head slightly, looking up at me through dark bangs as I handed the pages over. I didn't need my gift to sense her wariness—I could see it in her eyes.

"That was a joke," I explained, hoping that being friendly would make her feel better. "I'm Ben, by the way."

Her wary expression eased a little. "Gina," she murmured, sounding either shy or reluctant, I couldn't tell which. Then, as if in afterthought, "Thanks."

"No problem," I said, rising. "And don't worry about…"

But she was gone, scurrying away head-down through the crowd.

The bell rang, and Les waved as he veered off toward his first class while Ab and I headed for the sophomore assembly at the gym.

"Beer-gutriff?" I asked after a moment.

She grinned at me.

We parted ways as soon as we stepped inside, Ab heading toward a table with a paper banner reading *Last Name A–F* while I fell into a shorter line on the opposite side with the rest of the U through Zs. Their system turned out to be pretty efficient. The line moved quickly, and less than five minutes after I reached the front I was headed back outside again with my schedule for the semester, hall and gym locker assignments, campus map, and a photo ID that was still warm in my hand. They hadn't noticed I'd crossed my eyes.

I hiked across campus, which consisted mainly of rows of flat-topped, rectangular buildings connected by sidewalks beneath aluminum awnings. The sprawling, three-story Victorian that had been Silver Creek's first high school still stood on a rise at the eastern side of the grounds, frowning down on the rest like an old, disapproving matriarch, and was now just used as the admin building. A gymnasium big enough for an aircraft hangar had been added in the 1920s, and was the only other original structure. Ab had told me during our first visit back in June that the rest had been built in the early 1950s as part of a major expansion project. Rather than rebuilding Windward Cove High, which had burned down in the summer of 1946, the two towns had decided to stick with a combined school, and it had remained that way ever since. The place was now definitely showing its age, the bricks rounded at the edges and cracks in the concrete walkways, and had been further expanded by a theater that also housed the fine arts department. As I passed, I could hear the band running through its first scales of the year. Lots of flutes, saxophones and trumpets, I noted, wincing at how out of tune they were. *Give them a chance,* I reminded myself. *It's only the first day—they're bound to get better.*

Room 19 was in the next building over and I opened the door, stepping tentatively into my first-period geometry class. The teacher— Miss Gillman, according to the name written on the ancient-looking blackboard—was still going through her expectations while a couple of volunteers passed out books, and she waved me in without stopping. The only desks left open were toward the front *(thanks a lot, sophomore assembly)* and I dropped into the second seat back in the row closest to the door. Math was my least-favorite subject, but at least I'd be getting it out of the way first thing. I watched as other kids came trickling in, hoping to see Ab or someone else I knew, but by the time Miss Gillman began taking attendance I had decided I was out of luck.

Gina walked in when the teacher was about halfway through calling out names, and she hurried over and slipped into the last open seat, just to my left. I brightened a little, relieved to see someone I recognized, but then I gave an inward sigh when she just stared at the desktop after giving me barely a glance. When Miss Gillman called "Gina Lynch?" she replied a soft "Here" without looking up.

So much for finding allies, I decided gloomily. Geometry was going to suck.

Second period was English, which I had with Ab, followed by third period U.S. History with both Ab and Gina. I was also glad to see Vern Ashley, a guy I had first met a few days after moving to the area, and who usually joined our Saturday night fire circle on the beach. He had ebony skin and muscles that made him look like he'd been carved from granite, and even though we sometimes talked about him teaching me to lift weights, it hadn't happened yet. Phys Ed came right before lunch, and there at least I got to hang out with Les (major score!) along with Monica, one of the other girls from Windward Cove. She was lean and athletic from long days on her surfboard, and based on her hair and skin tone I took her for Native American, though I hadn't gotten around to asking her yet.

I checked my schedule as I left the locker room, noting that all I had left after lunch was Biology 1 and then a drama class—my only elective. I had taken Beginning Drama back in junior high, and while I wasn't much of an actor, I was fine with building sets, hanging in the background and helping out as a stage hand. It would be a pretty chill way to end the day.

All in all, I figured things weren't looking too bad as I exited the lunch line in the cafeteria, holding my back pack in one hand and balancing my tray in the other. I scanned the room, looking for someone I knew, and I recognized a familiar cascade of dark auburn hair on the far side. Kelly Thatcher sat at a table by the windows, along with three or four of her cheerleader friends and some guys from the football team. She brightened when she saw me, and I could see there was an open space to her left, but I kept my gaze moving, pretending I hadn't noticed her. I knew that sooner or later she and I would have to talk, but it took me all of half a second to decide today wasn't that day. Then, from the corner of my eye I saw Alan Garrett walk over to claim the open spot, and the pressure was off.

I figured everyone else was lagging behind, so I made my way to a large, round table near the wall that was mostly open. "Mind if I sit here?" I asked the table's only occupant, but then I almost immediately wished I hadn't. The guy was large—six-two, maybe six-three, I estimated—though round shouldered and kind of pudgy. He wore a dark, long-sleeved tee with a dragon on it. He glanced up as if annoyed, regarding me with large eyes over the top of thick, horn-rimmed glasses, and then turned his attention back to the open book in front of him. He turned the page, ignoring me.

"Ben...?"

I turned to see Gina standing a couple of steps behind me holding her lunch bag. "Oh, hey," I said. "Just looking for some space."

She chewed her lower lip, looking uncertain. "You can sit with us if you want," she offered at last, moving cautiously around me to the table. That earned her a scowl from Mr. Cheerful but she ignored it, sliding into the chair next to his.

"Thanks." I set my tray down in the place across from them, and then hung my backpack on the chair before dropping into it.

"This is my cousin Darren," she told me. "Darren, this is Ben."

Now that they were side by side, I could make out the family resemblance. They both had the same eyes and cheekbones. "Hi," I said.

"You know this guy?" he asked Gina, still ignoring me.

I guessed he wasn't the welcoming type.

She nodded. "Some girls were giving me a hard time before school. Ben and his friends made them stop."

"What girls?" he demanded.

"It doesn't matter. It's over now." She began unpacking her lunch, and I watched as she arranged a yogurt and a plastic spoon next to a sandwich made of a single slice of processed turkey on wheat bread.

No wonder she's so slender, I thought.

Darren looked like he was going to press her further, but then just shook his head. "I *told* you the people around here suck," he muttered, and then turned his attention back to his book.

"Oh, I don't know," I countered, and then took a sip from my water glass. "Darlene's got some issues, but pretty much everyone else has been cool so far."

He looked over at me with a sour expression, and then glanced down at the meatloaf and mashed potatoes on my plate, wrinkling his nose in disgust.

Maybe he was vegan.

Gina's expression darkened. "Darlene's a…" She paused, as if looking for the right word. "A *witch*," she finished awkwardly, as if she had said something crude. She looked down at her food, blushing.

"Yeah," I agreed, picking up my fork. "We just pronounce it differently where I come from."

She looked back up, her brown eyes momentarily wide, and then offered a tentative smile.

"There you are!" Les said cheerfully, setting a huge sack lunch beside my tray and pulling out the chair. Ab was half a step behind him, along with Monica and Vern, and they all took places at the table. They were followed a second or two later by Nicole and Kim, two more girls we knew from Windward Cove, and the conversation brightened as we exchanged hellos. Across from me, Darren's scowl deepened as the table filled up, and I wondered if it was his go-to expression. Gina just retreated into her own space, staring at the tabletop.

"Hi," Ab said from the chair next to her. "You're new, right? You took off before we had a chance to meet this morning."

As she began making introductions, Darren rose abruptly and stalked away, obviously in a state of high piss-off. I wasn't sorry to see him go.

"Don't worry about Bubbles," Les confided, pitching his voice low so Gina couldn't hear. "He's always that way."

I shrugged, turning back to the conversation at the table.

"…and you've already met Ben," Ab finished. "He's new, too, and just moved here at the beginning of summer. So where are you from?"

Gina hesitated, but I could see Ab's friendliness superpower was already working its magic. I hadn't met anyone yet she couldn't get to like her, and the new girl smiled shyly. "Rome," she answered in a soft voice.

"*Italy?*" Nicole asked excitedly, moving into Darren's vacant seat so she could better hear.

The girl shook her head, blushing. "New York. Upstate. My family has…" She paused. "We had a farm there."

"So what brings you to California?"

Gina frowned, looking down again. "There was an accident. I had to come live with my aunt and uncle."

It grew quiet as a brief, awkward silence fell over our table. "So, have you tried surfing yet?" Nicole asked, grinning.

That salvaged things, and the conversation was off and running again. I relaxed, working on my meatloaf and chiming in every now and then as everyone did their best to make the shy girl feel welcome.

It looked like Gina was already part of the crowd.

THREE

TSUNAMI JOE WAS MORE CROWDED THAN USUAL WHEN
I strolled in at a little after 7:00 the next morning, with most of
the tables taken and eight or ten customers lined up waiting at the
counter. I frowned, wondering if I would have time to order anything, but then I noticed Ab and Les waving at me from where they
were already seated near the back wall, so I headed over to join them.
I wove around people relaxing in assorted armchairs with steaming
mugs beside them, others caffeinating or eating pastries at the mismatched tables that were scattered randomly across the room.

The coffee house was one of Windward Cove's most popular spots,
and since Mom and I had moved there it had become one of my favorite
places in the world. It was set up in a building that had started out as
the Redwood Empire Hotel in the 1890s, but a fire in 1946 had pretty
much gutted the place. The brick walls were still dark with soot, and the
rafters two stories above charred at the edges. But the blackened interior
had been left untouched, decorated by framed, mostly black and white
photos that covered the walls with the same disregard for order as the

furniture. The place served a reliable morning crowd, and a lot of the kids from the area were regulars too, ducking in after school to hang out, do their homework or surf the net using Tsunami Joe's free wifi.

"Wow, the place is really slammed this morning," I remarked, raising my voice slightly to carry over the murmur of conversations. I dropped into the open seat between them, smiling gratefully as Ab slid a mocha in front of me.

"The coffee machine at Brenda's Café died this morning," she explained, grinning. "Rotten luck for her, but we're happy to take the extra customers."

Ab had every right to be pleased. Her family owned the building, as well as Pirate Pizza next door and the coin-op laundry down the street, and her folks had involved her in their family businesses since she was in grade school. Just the same, Mr. and Mrs. Chambers had been skeptical a year and a half before when Ab suggested they turn the unused space into a coffee house. She had eventually won them over, though, between a mixture of determination and a business plan she'd put together herself, so they loaned her the startup money and let her run with the project. She had outfitted the place with secondhand equipment and furniture, and while her parents were the official owners and managed the paperwork, the rest had been all Ab's doing—from the menu, to managing the inventory, to employing the small staff of part-timers who kept the place open while she was at school. With everything else she had going on, I sometimes thought Ab's life had to be like juggling chainsaws and rattlesnakes, but somehow she made it look easy.

"So, what do you have stuffed in there?" I asked, nodding at Ab's backpack. Its sides were bulging.

"Oh, just some things for Gina," she replied. "We have sixth-period P.E. together, and yesterday when Coach Camarillo was talking about the dress code, Gina started looking really uncomfortable. I had to nag her before she finally opened up and admitted she doesn't have any real gym clothes—or much in the way of clothes, period—so I threw together a bunch of stuff I outgrew last year. Gina's smaller than me, so they should fit her just fine."

I frowned, feeling sorry for the new girl. "You'd think her aunt and uncle would take care of that."

"The Lynches never have had much money," Les explained. "Tim works off and on for a few of the fishing boat captains when they need an extra deck hand, but the rest of the time he fixes cars in a shed behind their house. His wife Roxanne has some kind of health thing…"

"Migraines," Ab inserted.

"…so all she can do is wait tables at Hovey's when she feels up to it. They've always just kind of scraped by. Kids used to give Darren a lot of crap about his thrift store shirts and how his Mom buys a lot of their groceries with a government card." He shrugged. "It's part of the reason he's such a ray of sunshine."

I thought about Darren and his sullen, almost hostile attitude. *Maybe if I'd been treated that way, I'd be kind of a dick, too.*

"Finish up, guys," Ab reminded us, glancing up at a clock on the wall. "It's time to go."

We pedaled the three or four miles over to Silver Creek, arriving at the high school a little over fifteen minutes later.

"…although I thought the ending was the best part," Les was saying.

He had read *To Kill a Mockingbird* in English class the year before, and had spent most of the ride trying to convince Ab that it wasn't going to be as bad as she thought. I had seen the movie a few times (it was one of Mom's favorites), so I was good with the assignment, and I listened without comment as we joined the sluggish flow of kids making their way onto campus.

It had rained sometime during the night—one of the short, heavy downpours that were common along our part of the Northern California coast—but it had moved on before dawn, leaving the grass glistening and numerous puddles scattered across the concrete. I had gotten used to the frequent changes in the weather since moving to the area, and I liked the cool, clean smell of the morning air.

"So anyway, there's this guy Boo Radley who lives just down from the Finch's house..."

"Hold on," Ab interjected, scrunching up her face. *"Boo?"*

"Yeah, you'll need to just roll with that. See, everyone is scared of him because..."

I tuned out of their conversation when I noticed Darren and Gina Lynch walking maybe fifty feet ahead of us. They passed close to where Darlene and her friends were clustered around one of their open lockers, and Gina flinched when Darlene called out something I was too far away to hear. Darren spun, pivoting surprisingly fast for his size and marching toward them with a furious expression. I heard the open locker slam just before the three girls scattered.

Way to go, Darren, I thought, still not liking him much, but glad to see him stick up for his tiny cousin. Maybe deep down he wasn't such a bad guy after all.

"Ben...hey," called a voice.

I stopped at the sound of my name, glancing to my right where Kelly Thatcher stood near her own locker a few steps away. She looked good in faded jeans and a loose, cream-colored sweater. Of course, that wasn't exactly surprising—she could wear a garbage bag and still look amazing—but I liked the way her dark auburn hair contrasted with the sweater as it spilled over her shoulders, the color reminding me of smoky firelight. Les and Ab halted a couple of steps later, their conversation trailing off as they glanced first toward Kelly, and then back at me. "We'll, uh...catch you later, Wolfman," Ab said after a second or two, and she drew Les away.

I gave them a distracted wave, swallowing back a knot that had lodged in my throat as I made my way over to Kelly. My feet seemed to have gained twenty pounds each, and I hoped I didn't look as nervous as I felt. "Hey," I said at last. My hands were sweaty, so I stuffed them into my jacket pockets and leaned my shoulder against the locker next to hers.

"Hi." She smiled tentatively, and I could sense her apprehension without even trying to. Then I realized that something was different. Normally, all I could pick up from Kelly was a jumble of conflicting emotions, too scrambled for me to understand. But that seemed to have smoothed out a lot since the last time I had been near enough to sense her, and I wondered what was up with that.

"I haven't seen you around much."

"No, I guess not," I said. "How are you?"

She shrugged. "Okay, I guess. I've just been wondering over the last couple of months if we're still friends." She looked up, meeting my gaze. "Or if you even want to be."

I had forgotten how green her eyes were, like spring leaves, and a few seconds ticked by before I remembered she was waiting for an answer. "I'd really like that," I managed at last, feeling like a dork. "Last summer was pretty crazy, and things sort of went off the rails, didn't they?"

She studied my face for a moment before speaking. "What happened, Ben?"

I shook my head. "Jeez, where do I even start? See, there was this whole thing with my aunt…"

"Oh, I know about all *that*," she interrupted. "There was that big story about it in the news. How *awful* that must have been for you. I just…" She paused, a slight blush coloring her cheeks. "I've been thinking…about that night."

I knew which night she meant, and my heart began thudding in my chest. I'd thought about it, too. *A lot.* I didn't know how many times I'd lain awake in the darkness, turning the details over and over again in my mind.

"You said you were going to call me, but you never did."

I sighed, dropping my gaze. "I'm really sorry about that. It's just that everything started happening so fast and it took forever to get it all sorted out. And by then…" I paused, swallowing. "Well, by then I'd heard that you and Alan were back together. I didn't know what to think about that, so I figured I should leave you alone."

Kelly shook her head. "And there *I* was, waiting for you to call. And the longer I went without hearing from you, the more I began to think you weren't going to."

"So you patched things up with Alan."

"I was just so mixed up, you know?' she said, a pleading expression on her face. "When I didn't hear from you, I thought you *hated* me. And Alan kept calling and calling, so after a while it seemed like the best thing to do was just put things back the way they were before." It was her turn to sigh. "I guess that sounds pretty dumb, huh?"

I thought about it, and then shook my head. "Not really. I get it."

"You do?"

"Sure. Call it bad timing, crossed signals, whatever…things just didn't work out." I offered her a smile. "It doesn't *have* to be anybody's fault." It wasn't how I really felt—it just seemed like the right thing to say. The truth was, just seeing Kelly had rekindled the monster crush I had on her, and all at once the fires were burning as high as they ever had. *But what does that matter now?* I realized. She was back with the quarterback and I had missed my chance.

She smiled, and I sensed her apprehension fading, replaced by relief. "You know, right now I just wish…"

The first bell sounded, and she paused while waiting for the loud jangling to stop. After it did, she opened her mouth as if to go on, but then closed it again, seeming to think better of it. "So…friends?" she asked instead, raising her eyebrows.

"Friends," I agreed, wondering what it was she had almost said, and feeling a stab of disappointment that the bell had cut her off. *Then again*, I thought, *maybe I'm better off not knowing.* "I guess I'll see you around, then."

She smiled briefly. "Yeah...see you." And then she was gone, merging into the flow of kids starting to make their way to class. I watched her retreating back until she disappeared.

I was headed to Room 19, thinking that my talk with Kelly had actually gone pretty well, all things considered, when I heard the scream. It cut through the morning air like a rusty knife, a cry of horrified anguish that sent a shiver up my back and brought everyone within earshot to a standstill.

I looked over, noticing a crowd that was quickly gathering on the far side of the quad. I veered that way, curious, and began to catch snatches of conversations as I drew near:

"...patch of ice..."

"...split right open! Did you see all the blood?..."

"...went down *hard*..."

"...already called 911..."

I had just arrived when the crowd suddenly parted and a male teacher I didn't recognize emerged, helping Darlene as she walked unsteadily beside him. Tears ran down the girl's red, blotchy cheeks as she moved past me, biting her lower lip while making soft mewling sounds in the back of her throat. She cradled her right elbow in her free hand, and two or three kids went pale as they saw blood dribbling from between her fingers.

"Alright people, the excitement's over," called Coach Barbour, arriving to wave kids away with burly arms. "Get to class."

I was about to leave when I saw Les standing in place a few paces off, frowning at the concrete. I stepped up beside him, following his gaze to a six-inch pool of Darlene's blood glistening bright red next to a frozen rain puddle. No wonder she had slipped—the ice was so clear it looked like glass. Kids still milled around despite the coach trying to chase them off, and I caught the scent of some girl who must have been standing there right before I arrived. It was an earthy smell, but sweet and kind of spicy, too—more like incense than perfume—and I wasn't sure if I liked it or not. Then I forgot about it as I offhandedly began picking up bits of emotion from the lingering crowd:

Disgust…

…Horror…

…Sympathy…

…Unease…

And then I caught one I wasn't expecting:

…Satisfaction.

My head snapped up in surprise and I glanced around, wondering whose feeling I was sensing. There was a sharp, vindictive quality to it that stood out among the rest. It seemed to be coming from somewhere off to my left, so I looked past Les and tried to read the facial expressions of the kids in that direction. There was still a handful in that area, but only one that I recognized:

Darren Lynch.

He stood a little apart from the others, scowling at the bloody concrete. But he wasn't the only one making some sort of face, and anyway, scowling seemed to be his default look, so it was hardly what I could call a smoking gun. Then his expression softened when Gina stepped up to tug gently at his sleeve, so I kept scanning the crowd, trying to pin down the source of the disturbing emotion. Coach Barbour shooed off the stragglers before I could, though, and the feeling drifted out of my range.

Les still hadn't moved, so I returned my gaze back to the concrete. "That's a lot of blood," I remarked.

"Uh-huh," he replied, nodding. "But that's not what I'm looking at."

"What, then?"

He raised his head slightly to point with his chin. "The ice. It shouldn't be there."

"What do you mean?"

He looked at me. "How chilly did it get last night? Fifty-five degrees? Fifty, maybe?" Les shook his head. "That's not anywhere near cold enough. And take a look...do you see any other puddles frozen? Even one?"

A feeling of vague unease settled over me as I looked around, realizing he was right. "Weird," I said. It was all I could think to say.

"Hawkins!" Coach Barbour called over. "You and your pal get a move on—you've got about two minutes to the tardy bell!"

Les and I exchanged a final glance, and then went our separate ways.

FOUR

THE AFTERNOON FLOOD OF KIDS LEAVING SCHOOL FOR the day had lessened to a trickle while Les and I lingered near the parking lot, waiting for Ab to join us for the ride home. Between her having to change after P.E. and the gym sitting way over on the far side of campus, I figured that waiting for her in the afternoon was something we would have to get used to.

Then she appeared, straggling a step or two behind Nicole, Monica, and Kim, who were talking excitedly as they clustered around a reluctant-looking Gina. They stopped at the curb, waving over at us while Monica started across the parking lot toward her truck. Ab veered off to retrieve her bike from the rack, and then headed our way. "You go on ahead, guys," she said, looking annoyed. "I'm going to be a while."

"What's up?" Les asked.

She indicated the other girls with a sideways motion of her head. "They all saw me giving those clothes to Gina after lunch, and when they found out why, they decided they all had hand-me-downs they wanted to give her, too."

I smiled, remembering how they had all been so cool and welcoming when I first moved to the area. It occurred to me just how lucky Gina and I both were to have such nice friends.

"One thing led to another," Ab went on, "and by the middle of fifth period Kim and Monica had decided it was *Makeover Day*." She exaggerated the last two words, rolling her eyes in exasperation.

I held back a smirk, knowing how Ab hated that sort of thing. *Good thing they didn't think of that when I was new.* "So what? Just tell them you already had plans with us."

She shook her head. "Can't."

"Why not?"

"Because all the attention was starting to freak Gina out a little, and she looked at me with those big doe eyes of hers until I said I'd come." She sighed. "So now we're all going to Kim's to help Gina try on clothes."

"Oh, come *on*," I teased, snickering. "You'll have an awesome time! The five of you all giggly, talking about boys, doing each other's toenails…"

She looked stricken. "Ugh. Someone *please* shoot me."

"*Ab-by's a prin-cess… Ab-by's a prin-cess…*" Les crooned softly, grinning at her.

Ab swept us with a glare. "Okay, you two. This *princess* still runs the place where you drink your coffee, remember?"

Les' grin faded. "I take it back," he said solemnly. "Ab Chambers is a total badass."

"The baddest," I agreed. "Guys want her, girls envy her, and ghosts tremble at the sound of her name."

The corners of her mouth turned slightly upward. "Better."

We laughed, and I glanced past Ab's shoulder, noticing movement on that side of the parking lot. Alan Garrett, wearing stained football pants and a ragged Buccaneers jersey, stood with his arms crossed beside his car, a yellow mustang convertible. He frowned down at Kelly, who motioned widely with her hands while saying something I was too far away to hear. Then Alan made a slashing gesture, interrupting her in a tone that sounded angry. When he finished, she said something back, her voice rising at the end like she was asking a question, but Alan just stepped past her, making his way back toward the school in the direction of the football field. She called out after him, but he just kept walking, finally saying something loud enough for me to hear: "*Whatever, Kel!*"

Hmm.

As he stormed off, Alan passed Jessica Tanner headed the other way, wearing workout clothes and her blonde hair in a ponytail. She asked him something as he went by, but he ignored her, so she turned back toward the parking lot, gazing around until she found who she was looking for. "Kelly!" she shouted. "Come *on*—you're late for practice!"

Kelly hesitated, and then started toward her. She didn't look happy about it.

"Hey, Ab—let's go!"

We all turned to where Monica's truck, a silver, crew-cab Toyota Tacoma, idled at the curb with the doors open, and Les and I walked over with her. We had just finished helping load her bike in the bed when a voice called Gina's name, causing everyone to turn.

Darren marched over, wearing his all-purpose scowl. "What are you doing? It's time to go home!"

She took a couple of steps that way, meeting him. "You go ahead. Monica said she'd drive me home later. I already called Aunt Roxie and she said it was okay."

Darren stood there for a second or two, glancing between Gina and the other girls as if unsure what to do.

"Relax, Darren," Nicole assured him, stepping up to pull Gina away. "We'll take good care of her. I promise."

His face clouded. "You'd better be nice to her!"

Nicole frowned in exasperation. "Oh, chill *out*, will you?" She followed Gina into the back seat, pulling the door closed behind her.

He remained still, glaring after the truck as it pulled away.

Feelings of unease and abandonment pinged my mental radar from where he stood, and a sudden thought occurred to me. "Hey, Darren." I called over. "We're headed over to Hovey's for something to eat. You in?"

His head pivoted toward me, and I could read distrust and resentment in his expression. Then he turned, stalking away without a word.

No loss, I thought, feeling annoyed. But I felt a little sorry for him, too.

"It's a shame he's not coming," Les said drily. "Seriously...I'm all choked up."

I snorted laughter, and then we mounted our bikes and pedaled away.

I thought about Darren during the ride out of town, wondering why he seemed to get so uncomfortable whenever Gina was out of his sight. You'd think a guy who hated people so much wouldn't care one way or another. *But Gina isn't the only one, is she?* I remembered. I had been surprised the day before to see Darren in my sixth-period drama class, thinking that a course where you had to interact with people so much would be his last choice for electives. But then I had noticed him glancing repeatedly over toward a pretty Latina girl on the other side of the room. Her name was Celeste Ramos—Cece to her friends—and by the time the final bell rang I was pretty sure she was the reason he was there.

My thoughts returned to the present as we arrived at Hovey's and swung our bikes into the gravel parking lot. The old drive-in sat on a back road midway between Silver Creek and Windward Cove, the low, cinder-block building looking like it should have 1950s Chevys and Pontiacs and Buicks parked out front. I sighed gratefully, my mouth starting to water as soon as we came into range of the good smells coming from inside. I'd given up on lunch after only my first couple of bites, the cafeteria's chicken and rice casserole tasting like paste, and I'd been starving since the end of fifth period. Hand-lettered signs in the windows advertised the week's specials, but I ignored them as I led the way inside. I had a date with one of the place's monster-sized cheeseburgers.

The interior was totally retro—all chrome and red Formica—and it always reminded me offhandedly of that old movie *American Graffiti*. Mike Hovey, the retired Army Master Sergeant who owned the place, took our orders as soon as we sat at the front counter. Between his deep, gravelly voice and the way he stood roughly the size of Mount Kilimanjaro, he had made me nervous when Ab had taken me in there the first time, but it hadn't taken me long to discover he was actually a good guy.

"So, what was with inviting Darren along, anyway?" Les asked after Mike dropped off our Cokes.

"I dunno. I just felt bad for him, I guess—at least for a second or two. I figured maybe treating him like one of the guys might make him mellow out a little." I shrugged. "It seemed worth a try, anyway."

"Yeah, well, nice thought, but I could've told you it was a waste of time. Darren's issues run deep."

"What *is* it with that guy?" I asked, a little exasperated. "So his folks don't have a lot of money. So what? Mom and I didn't, either—not until Aunt Claire died and left us set up—but we were never angry about it, or went around with a big chip on our shoulders. Is that really his problem?"

"Oh, no. Being poor is only part of what makes Darren so… Darreny."

"So what's the other part?" I asked. "Darlene called him a freak. What's that all about?"

Les snorted. "He earned that one a long time ago. It happened when he and Rick Hastings got into it back in the fifth grade. And get this—it wasn't even Rick's fault."

I raised my eyebrows. "Wow...this should be good."

"Now, I didn't see any of it myself, so I might not have the story right," Les cautioned. "But the way I heard it, Darren liked this girl Riley Chase. You know her?"

I shook my head.

"Yeah, well you'll meet her sooner or later. She's kind of a big deal around here. Anyway, as the story goes, he slipped her some kind of love note. Now, obviously Riley wasn't interested. But she was cool even back then, and she did her best to let him down easy. Darren got mad, though, and said some ugly things. Rick stepped up and told him to knock it off, but then Darren turned on *him*, and was so hurt and pissed off that he just kept running his mouth."

I winced, remembering what it was like to face off against Rick. He was Silver Creek's starting wide receiver, with a high-and-tight haircut like a Marine and the aggression of a mountain lion. He also looked like he could bench-press about a thousand pounds, and I knew from experience he was the last guy you wanted to have mad at you. "Bad move."

Les nodded. "I know, right? Of course, by the time Rick cornered him after school, Darren had cooled off enough to know he was in real trouble. So at the last minute, he threatened to put a curse on him."

"A *curse*?"

"Yeah. Crazy, huh? Said his family had Gypsy blood, and that he'd put a curse on Rick if he didn't leave him alone."

I choked back laughter. "And he thought Rick would *believe* him?"

"I guess. But maybe he didn't know any better. Darren was always awkward around people. Hair-trigger temper...no friends to speak of... kind of a douche. You know, like now."

"So, what happened?"

Les shrugged. "About what you'd expect. Everyone who came to watch the fight started laughing, and Darren still got his ass kicked. The worst part for him was that by the next day the whole Gypsy thing was all over the school. It would have died off sooner or later if he'd just kept his head down, but no—Darren just got more pissed off and obnoxious, so nobody ever let it go. Sucks to be him, but it's his own fault."

Our conversation trailed off as Mike set our burgers in front of us and we got to work. I immediately started plowing through mine, relishing all the meaty-cheesy goodness of a half-pounder piled high with lettuce, onion, tomato, and smoked cheddar. Seriously…if they serve food in Heaven, then Hovey's burgers will definitely be on the menu. I made myself stop at the halfway point through, reminding myself that Mom would have dinner on the table around 6:00. Her feelings would be hurt if I was too full to eat, so I asked for a piece of foil and wrapped up the other half of my burger patty for Moe. Then I settled back, sipping my Coke and feeling tons better while waiting for Les to finish eating.

He was down to the last few bites when I felt my phone vibrate in my back pocket. I dug it out, blinking in surprise as I read the caller ID on the screen:

KRYPTONITE

I didn't recognize it at first, probably because she had never called me before. But then I remembered the code word I had entered for Kelly Thatcher, back during summer when getting within fifteen feet of her would make me feel like Superman when all his powers failed him—sort of like mine were failing right then. But I swallowed back my nervousness, answering just after the third ring. "Hello?"

I heard only silence for two or three heartbeats, followed by a muted beep as the call was ended.

FIVE

BY LUNCHTIME ON FRIDAY, I WAS READY FOR THE WEEK-
end. I had more or less settled back into the rhythm of school, but the
afternoons were still warm, the beach would be crowded Saturday
night, and I was looking forward to enjoying a couple of days of freedom while I still remembered what summer felt like.

I was feeling pretty good by the time I dropped into my customary
seat in the cafeteria and nodded across the table toward Darren, who
was eating a fried-egg sandwich while reading a Robert Jordan novel.
He ignored me, which was *also* customary, but whatever—I was used
to it. And anyway, everyone else would be along any minute. Lunch
was the only time we could all hang out together, and even though the
cafeteria's food was hit or miss (I'd say more miss than hit, but maybe
that was just me) it was still a good time. While I waited, I took a closer
look at the chili-mac on my plate, gave it a sniff, and decided maybe I
was in luck. To top it off, sixth period was going to be cut short so we
could all go to the pep rally in anticipation of the Buccaneers' opening
game that night.

All in all, things were looking up.

"Hi, Ben," Gina said softly as she arrived with Kim and Monica.

"Hey," I answered, and could just make out her shy smile and a hint of a blush before she glanced away. She had been doing that a lot lately, and I wondered how long it would be before she would feel comfortable enough to speak above a murmur. I probed her emotions mentally, not really surprised to find that the hints of more positive feelings I'd been starting to pick up since Wednesday were still mostly concealed beneath an overwhelming, timid nervousness. But she was getting better—the good stuff was starting to peek through more and more.

And that wasn't Gina's only change. Ab and the rest of the girls had set her up with a pretty nice wardrobe—better than nice, actually—and the combination of new friends and clothes seemed to be slowly building her confidence. Of course, they hadn't gotten her to ditch the hoodie yet, but it was only the first week and I figured she'd get there. Gina just seemed to feel safer beneath the hood, where the shadows and her hair partially obscured her face. I felt badly for her, wondering how long she had been hiding out under there and what had happened to make her do it, as well as curious to see what she'd look like when she finally came out into the sunlight.

I scanned the room, noticing that Ab, Nicole and Vern were headed over, but then my gaze found Kelly Thatcher as she exited the lunch line carrying a salad on her tray. I watched her, liking the way she looked and moved in her white, maroon, and green cheer uniform. I probably should have tried not to stare, but the whispers around school were that Kelly and Alan were fighting and might even be headed for a breakup. Much as I didn't have any use for idle chatter and gossip (I'd figured out a long time before that most rumors turn out to be crap when the facts finally roll in), relationship trouble between the starting quarterback and head cheerleader was apparently prime-time entertainment at Silver Creek High. And since it was all everyone seemed to be talking about, it was impossible to shut it out completely. Then on Thursday Kelly had surprised everyone by stepping down from cheer captain and handing the squad over to Jessica, which *really* threw the rumor mill into overdrive. Still, I had done my best to ignore it, but I'd be lying if I said the news hadn't left a few what-if's rattling around in my head.

I watched as she crossed to the table with the football and cheer crowd, and then stood patiently, waiting for someone to notice her and make some space.

No one did.

Long seconds ticked by, and I would have bet real money that Kelly and I realized it was all fake at exactly the same moment. They knew she was there all right, but they all just kept talking and laughing, pointedly ignoring her. Instead of heading somewhere else, though, Kelly seemed frozen in place, and I wondered why. Then I followed her gaze to the far end of the table, where Alan Garrett seemed to be paying a lot of attention to a cheerleader with short brown hair. She sat close—any closer and she would have been in his lap—and was smiling at something he was saying in her ear. I halfway recognized her (Brittany or Brienne or something) and she was one of Kelly's friends. Or she had been, anyway—I had a feeling that was about to change.

This isn't good, I thought.

Everyone else in the cafeteria must have been thinking the same thing, because the longer Kelly stood there awkwardly waiting, the quieter it grew. The hum of conversation quickly died down to whispers as all eyes shifted between Kelly standing there alone and Alan and the brunette getting all chummy ten or fifteen feet away.

Without thinking, I rose to my feet just as Les arrived to stand beside me. "That's not going to end well," he observed after a moment, and then set his lunch down beside my tray.

"No, it's not."

He turned toward me. "Rescue mission?"

"Good idea." We began making our way across the room.

Before we got there, though, Jessica arrived and took in the scene at a glance. "Guys, tune *in!*" she scolded, her voice carrying in the nearly silent hall. "Make room for Kelly and me!"

I had always thought Jessica was cool, even though we had never actually talked much. She and Les went out sometimes, and though it didn't appear to be serious for either of them, she was well liked enough that no one gave her any grief about dating outside her crowd. Now there she was, fearlessly sticking by Kelly when nobody else would, and I liked her for it.

At her command, uncomfortable glances were exchanged as the kids reluctantly shifted aside. A couple of empty chairs were dragged over and squeezed in at the end of the table opposite from where Alan and the girl still sat with their heads together. At last Jessica offered Kelly a smile that was probably meant to be reassuring, but ended up looking strained instead. "Here we go—lots of room now." There wasn't, really, but she looked determined to make the best of it.

"Hey, Wolf…you lost?" called out a voice. I looked over to discover that Alan had noticed Les and I standing there. His smile looked almost friendly, but his gaze didn't. He pointed in the general direction of Ab and the rest of our friends, calling out loudly, "The *loser* table is that way."

Even without my gift, I could have predicted he would say something like that. He and I had started off on the wrong foot back in June, and the handful of times we had run into each since then had just made things worse. It was dislike at first sight, and I was pretty sure that wasn't going to change any time soon. As nearly as I could tell, Alan was all about appearances—everything from his designer clothes to shunning anyone he thought was below him on the social totem pole—and his status had made me an automatic reject from the popular crowd. Not that I was losing any sleep over that. All in all, I thought he was about an inch deep, so I ignored him while turning my attention back to Kelly and Jessica. "Actually," I offered, "since it's so packed over here, we thought you might like to come sit with us."

Alan called out again, his smile disappearing. "Take a *hint*, asshole. Get lost!"

Everyone else seated there watched us silently, looking anywhere from uncomfortable to mildly amused. The only two who stood out were Brittany-or-Brienne, who was beaming up at Alan like he was some kind of hero, and Rick Hastings, who was seated behind him. Rick frowned slightly at his friend, and then met my gaze, nodding almost imperceptibly in…what? Acknowledgment? Greeting? I didn't know, but I didn't have time to think about it right then.

Turning my attention back to Alan, I said, "Or else."

His eyebrows came together as he looked confused. "What?"

"You forgot to say, 'or else,'" I explained. "Like you were actually going to *do* something if I say no."

Nervous whispering rose and fell while Les chuckled. Alan came to his feet, his face growing red. "Are you getting smart with me?" he demanded.

I shrugged. "If I was, how would *you* know?"

Jessica stepped between us, first shooting me a warning look, and giving Les the hundred-watt smile she seemed to save just for him. "Thanks, guys. It's nice of you to invite us, but…"

"We'd love to," Kelly announced loudly.

The tide of low muttering and whispers rose again as Kelly moved past me. Outwardly she was holding it together, and walked with her head held high, but a quick read of her emotions told me she was humiliated, hurt, and angry. Kelly's sudden decision must have surprised Jessica, but she followed after only the briefest of hesitations and my liking and respect for the pretty blonde climbed another rung.

Les winked at me as he turned to follow them, and I brought up the rear, feeling a prickling sensation between my shoulder blades from all the stares boring into my back.

We were halfway across the room when a brittle silence descended again, and I sensed Alan's fury even before he came up behind me. "You got some kind of death wish?" he snarled.

The voice in the back of my head—the one that always suggests far better decisions than the ones I usually end up making—was suggesting right then that the smart thing to do was keep walking. So naturally, I stopped and turned. "No," I said, making sure my voice carried. "I'm just not going to stand by and watch some douchebag treat his girlfriend that way. Seriously, if you don't want to be with Kelly, don't rub her nose in it while you hook up with someone else. That's a dick move. Grow a pair and break things off like a man."

He flushed, glancing self-consciously around at all the faces watching us. I sensed most of his anger bleeding away in the space of about two seconds, replaced by uncertainty. Uncertainty…and maybe just a little guilt, which served him right. "That's none of your business," he said at last. It sounded lame, and he probably knew it.

"No, it isn't." I agreed. "But maybe it ought to be." And with that, I turned my back on him and walked away. I braced myself, more than half expecting him to jump me, but he didn't. By the time I made it back to my table and looked over, Alan was back with his crowd, everyone talking in low voices and casting occasional glances our way.

More drama, I thought, shaking my head. *Awesome.*

Darren must have left in his typical huff when everyone had arrived, because Kelly was now seated over beside Gina. Les pulled an empty chair over and held it for Jessica, sliding her in between him and me, and I dropped down in front of my tray, smiling while everyone stared at me in silence. "Well," I said cheerfully, "*that* wasn't awkward at all. Who's hungry?"

Everyone laughed, which took the edge off the tension. Still, things were a little quiet and strained for the first minute or so, the sudden addition of Kelly and Jessica making everyone feel a little uncertain.

Finally, Ab saved the day by saying, "How about that, guys? Looks like the loser table is getting cooler all the time!" Jessica joined in the laughter and even Kelly managed a small smile as conversations resumed, the atmosphere returning to normal.

I tried my chili-mac. Not awful, but it had gone cold. Then I noticed Kelly casting a glance my way, the corners of her mouth still turned upward, and I decided it didn't matter.

Totally worth it, I thought.

SIX

THE LARKSPORT BEARS NEVER KNEW WHAT HIT THEM.

To be fair, they had probably expected an easy win. Les told me while we were waiting for the football game to start that the Buccaneers hadn't beaten them in seventeen years, and the school, which drew its players from a town with nearly twice the population of Silver Creek and Windward Cove combined, had always been a powerhouse. Silver Creek had gotten creamed 31-0 early the previous season, before the varsity quarterback was injured the following week and Coach Barbour took a chance on Alan Garrett.

But times had changed. By the end of the first quarter, the Bucs had put 17 unanswered points on the board, Alan calling the plays with confidence and authority. Much as I didn't like him (and was secretly hoping he'd get sacked at least once), I had to admit he was really good. Our lead increased to 24-0, but then Larksport pulled off a long field goal attempt just before halftime to make it 24-3. It turned out to be the only time they scored the whole game. By the close of the third quarter, we had picked up another touchdown and a field goal and were completely dominating them. The score was 34-3, with Alan having thrown four touchdown passes—three to Rick Hastings—and Emilio "Dozer" Vasquez running the ball for over 160 yards.

It was a lot of fun. The stands were overflowing, with nearly everyone wearing maroon and green—including a cluster of guys who were shirtless and decked in body paint—and a lot of others adding pirate hats and waving plastic cutlasses. The band was still a little out of tune, but played the fight song with enthusiasm every time we scored. The roars from the crowd were loud enough to make the stands vibrate, with people blowing horns, throwing confetti, and sitting close together under the stadium lights as the smell of hot dogs, nachos, and popcorn drifted tantalizingly in the air.

"I'm going to take off," I announced at last, standing up from where I had been crowded in between Les and Nicole. It was halfway through the fourth quarter and the game had paused while the Bears used their last time out.

"What…*now*?" Les asked. "Dude, there's less than eight minutes left!"

I smiled. "I'm pretty sure Larksport isn't coming back from this."

"But we're all going for pizza afterward. It's tradition!"

"Don't worry," I assured him. "I'll be there. There's just something I want to do first."

"Oh, let him go," Ab advised, smiling knowingly from his left. "He has other things on his mind."

She was right. As much fun as it was, my attention had not been totally on the game. We had found space in the stands near the 35-yard line, and I had spent a lot of the time glancing over to where the cheerleaders were going through their routines, wondering if Kelly was going to show. She hadn't, and even though I had kept an eye out, I'd realized early on that she wasn't going to.

I had not seen her at the pep rally, either, though part of me hoped it was because it had gotten off to such a rotten start. Everyone had milled around the center of the gym for the first ten minutes or so before Coach Camarillo and Coach Barbour finally showed up with the keys to a control box mounted adjacent to a side door. Unlocking it, they activating the switches that made the folded bleachers on either side clatter and clank as they extended outward, driven by ancient electric motors. By the time everyone was seated, that left only enough time for Principal Powell to introduce the team and talk briefly about last year's league championship before the final bell rang. Most of the cheerleaders had managed to sit together, but not all of them, and I had not finished scanning the crowd for Kelly before everyone was on their feet again and moving for the exits.

When she hadn't shown at the game, though, I knew that something was definitely up, and I wanted to find out what.

I left the stadium, listening as the sound of cheers and horns and the almost unintelligible drone of the man calling the game over the loudspeaker faded behind me, replaced by the cool, peaceful night. I moved through the shadows, hooking around the two lines of people waiting to use the restrooms and weaving my way between students or adults talking in small, scattered clusters. Less than five minutes later I was on my bike, following my headlight's beam past the overflowing parking lot and the lines of cars that were crammed nose to tail along the sidewalks for two or three blocks beyond the campus.

A little over a mile later, I swung onto a wide avenue that was part of Silver Creek's only upscale neighborhood. Custom homes sat well back from the street on half-acre-plus lots, separated from one another by carefully trimmed hedges or decorative split-rail fences that were supposed to look rustic, but didn't. The neighborhood seemed out of place in a town so small and off the beaten path, and I wondered what the people who owned them did for a living. *Reclusive lottery winners, maybe,* I thought. *Or Spectre agents hiding from James Bond while plotting a world takeover.*

I had only been to Kelly's once, back in June at her birthday party, but I found the place without much trouble. It was one of the biggest houses—two stories of herringbone-patterned brick with ivy climbing the north wall. It was centered on a parklike acre of lawn with artfully arranged trees and a couple of decorative ponds. There was a big swimming pool out back and a detached four-car garage off the drive, all of it connected by meandering, lit pathways.

Oh, yeah, I thought as I rolled to a stop at the mouth of the driveway. *A Bond villain hideout if there ever was one.* I smiled in the darkness, imagining the roof swinging open while a giant laser rose up from inside.

I dug out my phone, then found Kelly's number and sent a text: [HEY. U MISSED A PRETTY GOOD GAME.]

I waited, diving my time between keeping an eye on my phone and gazing over at the house. Most of the downstairs windows were showing lights, but only one on the second story. I wondered idly if that was Kelly's room, and whether all her stuff retracted into secret compartments when they brought out the laser.

Then I smiled as I noticed three dots appear at the bottom of my screen, blinking on and off in series as she typed a reply. The dots disappeared after a few seconds, then reappeared for a few seconds more. Then they stopped again, and I wondered if Kelly was pausing to think, or if she kept deleting her replies and starting over. Finally, the dots appeared briefly again and her text popped up: [HI. DID WE WIN?]

I tapped a reply: [WE WERE KILLING THEM WHEN I LEFT.]

[UR NOT THERE?]

[NOPE]

[WHY NOT?]

[GOT WORRIED. R U OK?]

A long pause. [IDK…NOT REALLY. BAD DAY.]

[…?]

[QUIT THE CHEER SQUAD]

I blinked. *That* came as a surprise. I hesitated, not knowing what to say to that, and then went with the only thing I could think of: [COME OUT 4 PIZZA]

[NO THX]

[WHY NOT?]

[EVERY1 WILL BE AT DEMOS. NOT READY TO FACE THEM YET]

[NOT GOING TO DEMARINO'S. GOING TO PIRATE IN WC]

Another pause. [THX, BUT NOT DRESSED]

[GET DRESSED…I'LL WAIT]

I counted seventeen seconds while she thought it over.

[HOW FAR AWAY R U?]

I smiled, looking over to gauge the distance to her front door. [150 FEET, GIVE OR TAKE]

[??!!]

[CHECK UR DRIVEWAY] I looked up, and a second later a silhouette appeared in the lit window upstairs. It disappeared almost right away, and another text hit my phone:

[BRT]

I chuckled, tucking my phone away and pedaling up the drive. I reached the house just as Kelly came out the front door, shoving her arms into a sweater and then holding it closed in front of her. She was barefoot, wearing flannel pajama bottoms with pictures of seals on them and her hair pulled back and secured with an elastic band.

"Hey," she said, giving me an uneasy smile. "What are you doing here?"

"Taking you to pizza," I said. "Though you'll have to drive, unless you don't mind riding on the handlebars."

"Ben…"

"*C'mon,*" I interrupted. "We're friends, right? So what kind of friend would I be if I left you to wallow all by yourself on a Friday night?"

Her eyes widened as she did her best to look indignant, but I could detect the humor that was starting to elbow her other feelings out of the way. "*Wallow?*" she asked pointedly, her lips twisting as she tried not to smile.

"Oh, yeah…I know all about how you girls wallow," I said, grinning. "If I don't drag you out of here, you'll end up eating a gallon of ice cream and binge-watching old *Gilmore Girls* episodes all night long." I shook my head. "Not on my watch, lady. Now, do you want to put on something else, or go as you are? It's all the same to me."

Kelly did smile then, shaking her head as her eyes looked suddenly moist. "You know what? You really *are* a good friend."

How can someone do all that at once? I wondered, and then shooed her toward the door. "This is no time to spring a leak. Pizza's waiting, and pizza makes *everything* better."

"Alright…you win. Give me five minutes!"

It took her closer to twenty, but that was okay. I used the time to relax on her front step, enjoying the night and feeling pretty good about myself. After all, how often did you get to be a hero twice in the same day? Then I frowned, sensing conflict a second or two before the sound of angry, muffled voices rose from just inside. I got to my feet, turning.

"…just need to go clear my head for a while, that's all," Kelly was saying as the door swung open. She emerged wearing jeans and a short, black leather jacket over a T-shirt, and I decided the wait was worth it.

"What you *need* to do is figure out a way to fix this!" her Mom shot back hotly. "I can't imagine why you would intentionally ruin…" Then Wendy Thatcher's voice trailed off as her gaze fell on me. As I watched, her expression registered first surprise, then confusion as she tried to remember where she had seen me before, and then finally annoyance when it came to her—all of it happening in the space of two or three heartbeats.

"You remember Ben Wolf, don't you, Mother?"

The woman's face rearranged itself into a tight smile. "Of course. How are you, Ben?" But no amount of politeness could conceal her disdain. It was coming off her like a bad smell.

Oh, yeah…she remembers all right, I thought. She had not liked me from the start, though I never figured out why. "Hi, Mrs. Thatcher. I'm good, thanks. How are you?"

She ignored me. "Kelly, I really think you should stay in tonight."

"Some friends are getting together for pizza, and Ben dropped by to ask if I wanted to join them," Kelly told her. "I already said yes."

"I see," Wendy replied, shooting me a hooded gaze. "How…*considerate* of him."

I could tell they were both playing nice in front of someone who wasn't family, but underneath it all was a tightly constrained antagonism, and I couldn't help wondering what it was all about. I kept my mouth shut, though, doing my best imitation of a flowerpot while waiting for them to work things out.

"We won't be too late," Kelly announced, pulling her keys from her purse.

"Of course, dear. So long as you come back with your *head clear.*" Wendy returned, emphasizing the last two words. Maybe I was wrong, but I had a hunch they had something to do with me.

"See you, Mrs. Thatcher," I called back over my shoulder as Kelly pulled me in the direction of the garage.

"Goodbye, Ben," she replied with a note of finality in her tone.

Yep, I thought. *Spectre all the way.*

My bike fit easily in Kelly's Jeep Liberty after she folded down the back seats and I took off my front wheel, and we were headed toward Windward Cove less than five minutes later. We drove without speaking for the first minute or two, listening to Pat Benetar sing *Treat Me Right* on the local oldies station. I thought about making a joke about it, but after sensing that Kelly's tension was still cranked up to eleven, I decided not to. "You want to talk about it?" I asked instead.

She shook her head, her features bathed in the glow of the instrument lights.

Fair enough, I thought. After all, it was none of my business.

She didn't say a word until we pulled up to the curb three or four doors down from Pirate Pizza, and she sat there for a long moment after switching off the engine. "Thanks," she said at last, staring into the darkness beyond the windshield. "For what you did at school today, I mean. *And* for getting me out of the house."

"Sure." I didn't know if that was the answer she was looking for, but her tension was starting to ease, and I figured the less I said right then, the better.

Kelly hesitated briefly, as if she were going to say something else, but then opened her door and got out instead. We walked together toward the entrance, keeping a careful separation between us that had nothing to do with physical distance, and I held the door open for her as a blare of music from the jukebox and the smells of spicy sauce and Italian sausage welcomed us in.

Kelly paused just beyond the threshold, looking around, and I wondered if she had ever been inside. The place served up incredible pizza, even if the interior was kind of cobbled together. It definitely had a nautical theme going on, but aside from a giant Jolly Roger flag painted on the back wall, the rest of the decorations really weren't all that pirate-y. Fishing nets hung from the ceiling, a stuffed marlin was mounted on the wall behind the bar, and a surfboard advertising Foster's Lager was hung vertically between the restroom doors. Sure, the door for the men's room was labeled *Sea Dogs* and the ladies' was for *Wenches,* but it didn't help much. Heavy plank tables with benches stood in long rows, interspersed by smaller round ones for groups of two or four. I finally spotted Ab and the rest jammed into a back corner and I pointed them out to Kelly. "Over there."

It looked like they had gotten there maybe twenty or thirty minutes ahead of us, because they were all dragging their first slices off a couple of extra-large pizzas and didn't notice us when we arrived at the table. "There you are!" Les said, causing everyone to look up.

Conversations trailed off when they noticed Kelly standing beside me, with Monica exchanging a quick glance with Kim, and even Vern raising his eyebrows. Gina was seated beside him, and looked around uneasily as she detected the shift in the atmosphere, and I saw Darren look up from where he sat alone at a small table to one side.

Two or three seconds ticked by.

"I *love* your jacket, Kelly!" Nicole said suddenly, breaking the silence. "Here…come sit next to me!" I smiled gratefully at her, and she winked back while scooting over to make room on the bench. Nicole was awesome that way, always one to reach out and make people feel welcome. She was pretty, with shoulder-length dark hair and a slender gold ring in one nostril that added just a touch of spice. I sometimes wondered why I wasn't drawn to Nicole the way I was to Kelly, but there you go.

I reached out mentally, taking a quick read of the table. Aside from Gina's unease and Darren's standoffishness, everyone else was already recovering from their mild surprise, so I relaxed. "Sorry we're late," I said. What was the final score?"

"41-3," Vern reported, grinning. "We *slaughtered* them!"

Talk around the table was off and running again, so I squeezed in between Ab and Les and reached for a slice.

"So…you and Kelly?" he asked quietly, eyebrows raised.

"Just friends."

He grinned. "Uh-huh."

"Shut up and pass the pepper flakes, will you?"

SEVEN

"I ALWAYS THOUGHT I WAS MORE CLINT EASTWOOD," LES objected, frowning.

"In your *dreams*," Kim shot back, her almond-shaped eyes crinkling at the corners as she grinned. "You *maybe* have a little Luke Perry going on, but you smile too much for Eastwood."

Over the last two hours, we had eaten both the pizzas we had started out with, as well as most of a third one that I had bought after that, and the restaurant's other customers had trickled away until it was down to just us. Ab's father had called it a night maybe twenty minutes before, leaving with the two employees who had stuck around to help with the cleaning, and asking Ab to lock up behind her when we were done. Conversation had meandered everywhere—from school, to music, to everyone's favorite movies by category—until finally we were down to which celebrities each of us looked like.

"Well, *you* look a lot like Grace Park," Ab said to Kim.

"Who's that?"

"She was in *Hawaii Five-0*," I offered, agreeing with Ab.

"Lots of other stuff, too," Vern added, "Grace Park is *smokin'* hot!"

Kim blushed, obviously pleased. "Who's next?"

We had already decided that Ab looked a little like Catherine Parker, especially around the eyes, Vern could have been Wesley Snipes' cousin, and Monica was sort of a Native American Jennifer Connelly. Nicole had called over to Darren a couple of times, trying to draw him into the conversation, but all she got for her trouble was a shake of his head. He seemed to only be there to keep an eye out for Gina, and while I got that he was protective of her, I really wished Captain Buzzkill would lighten up a little. That, or decide that we weren't going to hurt her and quit hovering so much. When Gina's turn came, we gave her some gentle teasing, trying to get her to pull back her hood. She wouldn't, though, and Les finally said that until she did, she looked like a Jawa from *Star Wars*. That had made Darren glare over from his table at first, but when Gina just giggled, he looked back down at his book.

"How about Ben?" Ab suggested, grinning at me.

"Lon Chaney?" I suggested. "When Mary Philbin pulls his mask off?"

That earned me only blank stares, so I guessed none of them had seen *Phantom of the Opera*.

"Ian Somerhalder," Nicole decided suddenly.

"Hmm…*sort of*," Monica conceded, frowning thoughtfully. "A younger version, anyway. Only softer in the face, and Ben's eyes are gray."

"Ian who?" Vern asked.

"He played Damon Salvatore in *The Vampire Diaries*."

He frowned. "That wasn't the one where the vampires were all sparkly, was it?"

"Oh, no…you're thinking about the *Twilight* movies. *Vampire Diaries* was a TV show."

Vern looked relieved. "Good. That whole sparkly vampire thing was *lame*."

I agreed with Vern, but then all the girls dogpiled on him to argue, so I decided to keep my mouth shut. *Ian Somerhalder...I'll take that,* I thought instead, and smiled to myself. Damon Salvatore was a badass.

Just then a wisp of cool air brushed against my cheek and I glanced over, my smile fading as I saw who had come in the front entrance.

Alan Garrett stood just inside, his arm draped across the shoulders of Brittany-or-Brienne, with Rick Hastings and Dozer Vasquez crowded in behind them. His gaze swept briefly across the empty tables before zeroing in on us in the back corner, and he began leading the others our way. Conversation at our table trailed off as everyone noticed that we were about to have company.

I took a quick read of their emotions as they approached, frowning as I sensed vindictive anger from Alan, a kind of eager aggression from Dozer, and something that felt like triumph from the girl. Rick Hastings, though...he was just feeling uncomfortable, which surprised me a little. Even so, my mouth went dry as I got the feeling that things were about to get ugly.

"Great game tonight, guys," Vern said affably when they arrived. "I bet the bus ride back to Larksport was pretty quiet."

Alan ignored him, his gaze finding Kelly near the opposite end of the table. "*There* you are," he said a little louder than necessary, and I noticed that he was swaying a little, his eyes slightly glassy. "I knew if we looked long enough, we'd find you slumming somewhere." His smile widened, but not in a good way.

The girl under his arm smiled too, looking over at Kelly with a smug expression. She was wearing Alan's letter jacket open over a T-shirt that looked sort of stretched out and rumpled, and when she reached up to tuck her hair behind her ear, I saw a good-sized hickey below her jaw.

"Sorry, guys," Les said. "Private party."

"And anyway, we're closed," Ab added.

"Oh, don't worry," Alan assured her. "It's not like I'd ever eat here—especially looking at the size of the roaches in this dump." His gaze moved to me when he said it.

Nice.

"You're not driving, are you Alan?" Les asked mildly. "You look like you've had a few, and I can smell your breath from here."

Behind him, Rick Hastings held up a key fob bearing the Ford Mustang emblem. He was the only one who looked sober, and part of me was relieved to see at least the sheriff's son was thinking.

Vasquez snorted, and then spoke up for the first time. "Yeah, well you'd know something about *that*, wouldn't you, Hawkins?" His face was flushed, and I guessed Alan wasn't the only one who'd been celebrating with a beer or three.

Nobody said anything for a long moment, with Ab and Vern trading a nervous glance as the tension at the table coiled like a spring. Les smiled, narrowing his eyes, and said in a low tone, "I don't think you want to go there."

Dozer grinned. "Your Mom ever decide to come home? Or is she still stuck in rehab?"

Les was on his feet faster than I would have thought possible, moving to stand in front of the running back with their noses inches apart. "Say that again, *Hondo*," Les invited, still smiling, but with a dangerous undertone that was both impressive and a little scary. "Say it *one* more time. I dare you."

Vasquez was taller than Les by a good two inches, and outweighed him by maybe thirty pounds, but right then I wouldn't have traded places with him for the world. The same thought must have occurred to him, as both his smile and his confident aggression faded, sweat beading on his upper lip. I rose, stepping clear of the bench as I sensed that things were about to go south.

"Why don't you just leave us alone?" came a murmur, and everyone turned in surprise to look at Gina. Her expression was unreadable as she gazed at Alan from under her hood.

Brittany-or-Brienne shrugged out from under Garrett's arm, moving past where Les and Dozer had squared off to stand right behind Gina. "You sit there and be *quiet!*" she snapped. Gina hunched her shoulders, staring at the tabletop as the cheerleader loomed over her, jabbing her shoulder with a finger. "Open that mouth of yours again and I'm smack you *stupid!*"

"Get away from her!" Darren snarled, coming to his feet while shooting an apprehensive glance toward Rick.

"Brianna."

The single word brought everything to a halt again.

The brunette looked up, flinching a little as Kelly pinned her with a look of cold fury I'd never seen her wear before.

Brianna, the part of my brain that was taking notes recorded. *I was close.*

"Step back from her," Kelly ordered. "Do it now."

"*Everybody* step back," Alan cut in, reclaiming the focus and Brianna retreated to his side. "This isn't about any of you. This is about me...and her." He returned his attention to Kelly. "You're nothing but a *quitter,* Kel, you know that? What's *wrong* with you? You quit your team, your friends, and you even quit on *me* after this asshole came to town." He jerked a thumb my way as he said it. "We're *done,* you hear me? I just came by to say that...and to make sure you knew what you threw away. I'm going to take Silver Creek to another championship, and you can just think about *that* while you're stuck hanging out with these losers." He looked her up and down contemptuously for a moment, his mouth twisting as if he tasted something bitter. "*Bitch!*"

"Okay, everybody out of the pool," I said, my face feeling hot. I was trying to contain my own anger, but not doing a very good job of it.

"You said what you came here to say, and showed everyone what a class act you are. So, if you're all done, the door's *that* way."

"Oh, I'm all done with *her* alright," he seethed, turning his gaze to me. "But not with you. Not by a long shot." He smiled, pushing Brianna aside. "You've been asking for this since you came to town, Wolf, and now I'm going to give it to you."

Something inside me snapped, and an eerie calm settled over me as I had the familiar feeling that I was about to lose control of my mouth. "Fine," I told him, offering a smile of my own. "I've got *nothing* better to do."

My answer must have struck him as funny because Alan straightened, barking a short, ugly laugh. "What…you think you're gonna kick *my* ass?"

"No," I told him, feeling my smile widen to a grin. An idea had occurred to me, and I went with it. "I think I'm going to break your hand."

A crack appeared in Alan's sneering expression as uncertainty flashed in his eyes, but he did his best to recover. "Oh, is that right?" he said after a pause.

"Oh, yeah," I said, sensing the ripples of fear in his emotional water, and I knew at once I had pushed the right button. "Do you know how many bones are in your hand, Alan?"

He shook his head, probably without even realizing it.

I shrugged. "Me neither. But there are *lots*, and they're all pretty small. It shouldn't be too hard. A finger will do. Your thumb would be even better." I let my grin widen as I sensed his growing dread, and I took a step closer to press my advantage. "Hell, maybe I'll get lucky and get your elbow or shoulder. But I'm not greedy—I'll take what I can get."

Alan wet his lips.

"Kind of hard to be the football stud then, don't you think? I figure that'll put you out for the rest of the season—maybe longer if it doesn't heal right. Hell, if it's bad enough, you could be done for good. What are you going to do *then*, Goldilocks? Get by on charm?"

He glanced nervously toward Dozer, but the running back was still being faced down by Les, so his gaze returned to me.

"What are you waiting for?" I pressed, stepping up to close the last of the distance between us. "We gonna do this or not?"

At that moment, Rick Hastings put a hand on Alan's shoulder, pulling him back. "Let's go," he said softly.

Garrett shook him off, trying to make a good show of it, but he didn't fool me for a second. He was scared.

"*Bro,*" Rick pressed. "Coach'll bench you if he hears you got in a fight."

I could sense the relief washing through him, and I figured Rick had picked the right thing to say. It gave Garrett the excuse he needed to back down. "Let's get out of here," he said, taking a cautious step backward. Dozer followed his lead, edging away from Les, and the tension in the air began to ease. "I'll find you later," Alan promised.

"I'll be around," I told him, and then watched them leave. I let out a breath as the door swung shut. I was trembling with lingering adrenaline, but I didn't want anyone to see, so I stuffed my hands in my jacket pockets until the shaking passed.

"*Dude...*" Les sounded surprised—maybe even a little impressed. "That was stone-cold. Awesome, but freaking *cold.*"

"You wouldn't really have tried to take out his hand, would you?" Vern asked.

I thought about it, but then shook my head as the tension in my shoulders and neck began to ease. "No, probably not."

He relaxed. "I *knew* it."

"Yeah, but Alan didn't," Ab said, grinning. "C'mon, guys—it's after midnight. Time to go home."

We all pitched in to clean off the table and wash our dishes, and then stood in a group just outside while Ab locked the front door. We said our goodbyes, with most of us agreeing to meet the next night down on the beach, and I watched as Gina and Darren followed Monica over to her truck while everyone else drifted away.

"Ready?" Kelly asked.

I nodded, and followed her to her Jeep. Neither of us spoke during the short ride out of town, and as she turned through the gap in the low stone wall and began to climb the switchback drive up to my place, I suddenly realized how tired I was. "Long day," I said, yawning.

"Yeah...long day." She didn't have time to say more as we emerged into the meadow and my house came into view. It was dark except for a light showing in the kitchen windows on the back corner, and I wondered if Mom had waited up for me.

Kelly pulled up near the front porch, and stood to one side as I pulled my bike out of the back and put my front wheel back on. After that, we just lingered for a moment, neither of us knowing what to say.

"Thanks for coming out," I offered at last.

"Thanks for asking me."

"I'm really sorry about Alan showing up," I went on. "It never even occurred to me he'd do something like that."

She offered me a wan smile. "You don't need to be sorry. It's not your fault. Or even your problem."

"Yeah, but if you change your mind and want to talk..."

"I don't," she interrupted. "At least...not right now."

"Your call," I said, and then turned when I heard a muffled bark behind me. The Jeep's headlights were angled toward the porch, showing Moe looking out the front window, his paws on the sill and tail wagging furiously.

"Looks like someone's glad you're home," Kelly said, smiling as she closed the back and headed for the driver's side door. "Good night, Ben."

"See you tomorrow?" I called after her, but just then her door shut, and she swung the Jeep around in a U-turn, heading back out the way we had come.

I shrugged. She probably hadn't heard me.

EIGHT

THE ROCKS WERE STILL WARM FROM BAKING IN THE SUN all day, the heat seeping through the back of my denim jacket and feeling good in the twilight chill. It wasn't going to last much longer, though, and I crossed my arms over my chest.

A few feet away, Les sat on his knees beside the kindling he had carefully arranged in a depression in the sand, shielding it with his body from the light breeze that was coming off the ocean. The sun had disappeared into the Pacific a few minutes before, the sky darkening from a coppery band on the horizon to purple and finally a deep blue where the stars were emerging overhead. As I watched, Les struck a wooden match, protecting the flame with his cupped palms as he touched it to the combination of dryer lint and petroleum jelly he used for fire starter. Bright yellow flames blossomed at once, smoky at first, but then burning clean as the kindling caught and grew hot. Patiently, he added increasingly larger pieces of wood until a fire two feet high crackled cheerfully before us, spitting occasional swarms of embers that floated upward into the night, and I began to feel warmer right away.

We were the first of our friends to arrive, purposely getting there early so we could claim a good spot. We had timed our arrival about perfectly, manhandling Les' single-wheel bike trailer full of wood down the trail from the cliffs to the prime real estate at the north end of the cove where the angle of the rocks cut most of the wind. Not that it looked like it would be much of a problem that night—the breeze was just enough to send tendrils of ocean fog drifting lazily onshore, haloing around the other fires that were springing up all over the beach as more and more people arrived.

The cove just south of town didn't have a name—not as far as anyone knew, anyway—but it was the most popular Saturday night gathering place for kids from all over the area. From spring through late fall, everyone from young teens to groups of college students wearing the green and gold of Humboldt State University would come down with snacks and armloads of firewood, hanging out with their friends from shortly before sunset often until one or two in the morning. On any given Saturday there would be at least a couple of volleyball games being played by the light of tiki torches thrust into the sand, glow-in-the-dark Frisbees zooming back and forth, and couples dancing to music from Bluetooth speakers, and never once had I seen things get out of control. Sure, there was generally a fair amount of drinking going on among the older kids, and once in a while even a little weed being passed around, but the unspoken rule was to keep things mellow. Sheriff Hastings or one of his deputies would occasionally stroll through, not being obvious about it, but nevertheless sending the message that things would be fine so long as everyone behaved, and no one wanted to be the first to mess up the good deal.

Les leaned contentedly back against the rocks beside me as I watched Moe and a German shepherd down by the water. They were playing tug of war with a piece of driftwood while four or five other dogs circled and barked, trying to get in on the fun. The shepherd's name was Chloe, and she was usually able to steal and keep whatever toy she wanted, but that was starting to change as Moe grew bigger.

"Now *that's* going to be a cheery little blaze," Les remarked, and I turned to see him watching a crowd of fifteen or twenty college kids setting up a little over fifty yards away. Some of the girls were arranging beach chairs and coolers in a big circle while the rest slowly assembled a big stack of wooden pallets and scrap lumber, tirelessly carrying them down from the cliffs like a trail of ants. They must have brought a whole truckload, and as the pile grew, I wondered if they were building a bonfire or trying to signal the Romulan Empire. Either way, it was going to be awesome.

"Hey-*hey*-hey!"

We looked up as Vern emerged, grinning, from the deepening gloom into the firelight. He carried a couple of blankets over one arm and a small cooler in his free hand. Ab and Nicole were right behind him carrying bags from the market, with Monica, Kim and Gina trailing maybe twenty feet behind them. An annoyed-looking Darren brought up the rear. Everyone but Darren arranged themselves on blankets around the fire and soon began passing around sodas and bags of chips, while he hung back in the shadows, sullenly watching over Gina with his hands buried in the pockets of an old field jacket.

One thing you can say for Darren, I thought, *he's consistent.*

We had been talking for about fifteen minutes when a large group of the football and cheer crowd arrived and picked out a spot between us and the waterline. They were bringing more stuff than usual, I noted, with half a dozen of the football players lugging big armloads of wood and everyone else carrying plastic food containers, coolers, and folding camp chairs. *Must be a victory party for last night's win,* I mused.

"Hey, Wolf."

I turned the other way to see Rick Hastings standing in the gloom between us and the cliffs, and the conversation around our fire trailed off as everyone looked at him with uncertainty. I didn't detect anything threatening, though, so his appearance only made me curious. "Yeah?"

"Talk to you for a minute?"

I shrugged. "Sure."

He glanced over our fire to where his friends were still getting settled, and then beckoned me back into the shadows with a sideways motion of his head.

"You good?" Les murmured as I got to my feet.

"Yeah, it's fine," I told him. "I'll be back in a minute. Don't eat all the Cheetos." I followed Rick back away from the firelight and out of earshot. "What's up?"

My question was left hanging in the air for a second or two before he answered. "I wanted to say sorry," he said at last, sounding either uncomfortable or reluctant, I couldn't tell which. "About last night, I mean. Alan said he wanted to tell Kelly they were done, but I didn't think it would go down that way. It was out of line."

My irritation flared, but I managed to keep most of it out of my voice. "So…what? The rest of you were just along for backup? Or did Alan need an audience for all that drama?"

He shifted his weight uneasily. "When we got there, I thought the rest of us would be staying in the car. But Brianna said she didn't want to be left behind, and Dozer… Well, he can turn mean when he gets a couple of beers in him."

"I hadn't noticed."

Rick must have picked up on my sarcasm. "Yeah, well he *said* he just wanted to watch, but I decided to come in case he was looking to start something. I didn't want that to happen."

That surprised me, and my irritation slipped a notch. "Why are you telling me this?"

"Because you did my family a huge favor last summer, even after my brother and me had been total dicks to you. I just wanted to let you know that none of what happened last night was my idea."

I thought it over, and then nodded. "Okay."

"So…we're cool?"

Who are you, and what did you do with Rick Hastings? I almost asked, but then decided it wouldn't be helpful. "Yeah, we're cool," I told him instead. "Thanks for letting me know." I stuck out my hand.

Rick hesitated briefly, then shook it—another first. "Okay. See you around." He paused, frowning, and then added, "You probably want to watch out for Alan. Even though he and Brianna are going out now, he's still pretty messed up about Kelly. When she broke up with him last summer, he figured it was because of you. He probably still does."

I didn't have an answer for that, so I settled for a nod. After a few seconds, Rick walked away.

"What was that all about?"

I turned in time to see Kelly emerge from the darkness, frowning as she watched Rick's retreating back. "Hey, you made it!" I said. "I wasn't sure you were going to."

She smiled. "I wasn't sure either—not until I got in the car, anyway. But you didn't answer me. What did Rick want?"

I grinned at her. "He wanted to *apologize*, if you can believe it. Said he didn't know that Alan was going to be such a jerk last night."

Kelly raised her eyebrows. "Well how about that? Maybe I'm not the only one who's getting tired of the great Alan Garrett."

I was curious what she meant, but decided not to ask. *If she thinks it's any of your business, she'll let you know,* I reminded myself. "Did you come for their victory party?" I asked instead.

"Victory party?"

I waved in the general direction of the football-cheerleader fire. "Looks like they brought quite a spread."

Kelly looked over, and then frowned. "Oh, *great.*" I must have had a questioning look, because she went on. "Don't let them fool you. That isn't for the team—it's for me. They figured I'd be here, and I'll bet you any kind of money I'm supposed to be jealous. They're trying to make me sorry for quitting."

"So, you're not going over?"

She shook her head. "Wasn't planning to. I was hoping to hang with you guys. Can I?"

"Absolutely."

She hesitated, biting her lower lip. "Um, can we walk a bit first? They picked a spot awfully close to yours, so someone is sure to notice me and say something. I don't know if I'm ready for that just yet."

I shrugged. "Sure...no problem." Neither of us spoke as we began strolling along the base of the cliffs, which arced in an irregular crescent for quarter-mile or so until meeting the surf at the south end of the cove. We kept to the shadows, Kelly steering us clear of the scattered beach fires, and I shivered a little as the wispy fog caressed the back of my neck.

"He never used to be like that, you know."

I had been looking up at the stars, lulled by the easy rhythm of our footfalls while my mind idled in neutral, and her statement caught me by surprise. "Who...Rick?"

"Alan."

I didn't know what to say to that, but Kelly seemed to be waiting for an answer, so I said, "Mm."

That's me: Mr. Articulate.

"We used to be able to talk about everything," she went on. "Music, TV shows, what we wanted to do when we grew up, whatever. Then in the eighth grade he started getting really good at football, and at that point everything else took a back seat." Kelly stopped and turned toward me, her face faintly illuminated by the glow of a nearby fire. "Did you know he was the reason I went out for cheer in the first place?"

I shook my head.

She resumed walking. "I thought it would bring us close again, but all it did was make things worse—like I was only doing what I was supposed to. After last season, all he could talk about were which colleges he might want to play for, and he started hinting that we should just skip the dorms and get a place together. It's like he just *assumed* I'd be coming along to wave whatever color pom-poms he decided on."

"Mm," I said again. When in doubt, stick with what works.

"So we were having problems even before you moved to town," she finished. "I just wanted you to know that—in case you're wondering if I'm someone who throws herself at every new guy I see."

I remembered the first time I had seen her, the day after Mom and I came to Windward Cove. Ab and I had ducked into Hovey's for lunch, and Kelly and Alan had been the only other customers in the place. I had picked up on some pretty intense emotions, and assumed at the time we'd interrupted an argument. Now it looked like maybe we had. "Okay," I said at last.

We reached the southern tip of the cove and turned right, walking along the firmer sand by the shoreline. Gazing ahead, I saw that the college crowd had gotten their bonfire going, the flames crackling ten or fifteen feet high and lighting the whole northern end of the cove. I smiled, appreciating the way the firelight reflected on the sea foam as the waves slid up the beach.

I took a quick mental read of Kelly's emotions, sensing an overall calm mixed with just a little uncertainty—probably because she was wondering what I was thinking, I assumed. It occurred to me again that it was a far cry from the jumble of feelings that had made her so hard to figure out back in June, and it made me like her even more. "You're a lot different than you were last summer," I said.

"Different how?" She sounded dubious.

I hesitated as I tried to figure out a way to describe it. Kelly still had no idea about my mental abilities (and the jury was still out on whether I would ever tell her), so I had to be careful. "I dunno," I said evasively. "Not *Invasion of the Body Snatchers* different, but there's definitely a change in you. It's like you're…quieter, I guess. More sure. Like you have things figured out a lot better than you did before."

Kelly laughed. "Maybe…but if it's true, I probably have you to thank for it."

"What do you mean?"

She paused, considering her answer. "I think it started that last night at your house. By the time we ran outside, I was scared out of my mind, remember? All I could think about was getting out of there, but you wouldn't come with me, even when I begged. You said you wouldn't leave your mom in there alone, and sent me away. I'll always remember watching in the rearview mirror, seeing you go back inside that dark house in spite of everything. It was the bravest thing I ever saw."

I felt my face flush. "It wasn't *that* big a deal…"

"It *was*," she insisted. "To me, anyway. I had the rest of the summer to think about it, and somewhere between then and now I realized that you're the only person I know who always tries to do the right thing. You're really special that way, Ben." Kelly stopped, placing a hand on my arm to turn me toward her. We had made it most of the way back up the beach, and the bonfire blazing behind her made it hard to see her features. "At some point," she said, "I realized I wanted to be…a better person, I guess. More like you."

An unexpected movement beyond Kelly's right shoulder caught my attention, and I looked past her in time to see a black shadow swoop down into the firelight, snatching at the hair of a girl walking across the sand maybe forty yards away. It looked like she had been making her way back from the cliffs, where tall bushes offered some privacy for anyone who needed to pee. For a crazy second I thought a bat had flown past her, but as it banked to fly between me and the bonfire, I recognized the silhouette of a large crow. "Hey!" shouted the girl, staggering a couple of steps as she spun around in surprise. As she turned toward the light, I recognized Brianna. She touched her fingers to her head and then inspected them, as if looking for blood, and then stood in place for a moment, rubbing her upper arms while scanning the darkness where the bird had disappeared.

A shrill cry then sounded behind her, and she half turned just as a seagull flapped out of the gloom, landing on the back of her shoulder and upper arm. Brianna screamed as the gull beat savagely at her with its wings, the yellow beak snapping at her ear and cheek. My brain was still trying to process what I was seeing when all at once a whole flock of different birds—seagulls, sandpipers, crows, and at least one pelican—descended upon her in a cyclone, their shrieks and caws drowning out Brianna's screams as they flew around her, darting for her face!

I was sprinting across the sand before I even realized I was going to, pulling off my jacket as I passed clusters of people who either had not yet noticed what was happening, or who stood frozen in place, gazing open-mouthed in shock and horror. A detached part of my brain realized that it was just like that old Hitchcock movie, *The Birds*, and I craned my neck around as I ran, wondering if the rest of us were going to come under attack, too. But no…as nearly as I could tell in the seconds it took to reach her, the assault seemed limited only to Brianna.

"GET AWAY!" I shouted as I reached her side, and the flock scattered briefly as I swung my jacket in circles over my head. It hit one of the crows, sending it sideways into the sand with a squawk, and with my free hand I batted away the seagull that was still latched onto her shoulder. One of its wings smacked me in the face as it flapped awkwardly away, the feathers smelling like brine and dead things, and I had just enough time to cover Brianna's head with my jacket before the birds swooped back in, all beaks and talons and beady, black eyes in a wall of beating wings and screeches.

Brianna flailed in panic as I wrapped my arms around her, ducking my head and squinting as I half-pulled, half-dragged her toward the bonfire. *Maybe it's her perfume,* I thought offhandedly, wondering if the scent had attracted them. I couldn't imagine why, though—the spicy-sweet-earthy smell was strong enough to nearly gag me. *Jesus, Brianna,* I thought, *what did you do—soak in it?* Just the same, something about it tugged at a memory that I couldn't quite place. Then Moe was there, barking furiously and leaping in circles around us to snap savagely at the attacking flock, and I yanked my thoughts back to what I was doing. An opening appeared in the circle of college kids as we drew close, most of them retreating in fear, but a few of the guys following my example and rushing over to wave the attacking birds away with jackets and burning chunks of wood. Kelly joined them a second or two later, with Les and Ab arriving in time to help as I pulled Brianna as close as I could to the fire—close enough to feel the heat baking my clothes and exposed skin as I squinted against the bright, golden light. Only then did I risk a glance upward, watching as the birds circled warily, crying out in frustration, and occasionally trying to dart in, only to be driven back by the heat and flames.

The flock continued circling for probably only thirty seconds or so—though at the time it seemed like a lot longer. But at last, the birds reluctantly dispersed, their cries fading away as they disappeared into the night.

Brianna was crying hysterically as she shuddered against me. I pulled my jacket off her head, and then sucked in a shocked breath when I saw her face was covered in oozing scratches, the blood mixing with her tears in a crimson mask. Blood spotted her gray hoodie as well, the droplets scattered among rips in the fabric and white splatters of bird crap. She wrapped her arms around my neck as she sagged against me, her breath hot against my skin and her face wet as she sobbed helplessly into my neck and shoulder. "Shh…it's okay…I've got you," I told her. I was doing my best to sound reassuring, but inside I was wondering which one of us was trembling more.

"Bri? *Bri!*…Are you okay?" Alan Garrett ran up with Rick and four or five of their teammates, followed by a couple of the cheerleaders. I let Brianna go as he shouldered his way between us, and he shot me a brief, resentful glare that I was pretty sure I didn't deserve.

Really, dude? I thought.

"It's okay, I'm here," he said, half supporting her as they started for the cliffs. "Are you alright? C'mon…we need to get you to a doctor!"

"We'll be right behind you!" one of the cheerleaders called after him, and then led the rest back to their fire.

Just then Ab and Kelly nearly knocked me off my feet, pulling at my arm and shoulder to turn me toward the firelight. "Oh my God, Ben! Are you alright?"

"Yeah, I'm fine," I answered, "Just…"

"There's so much *blood!*"

"How bad is it, Wolfman?" Ab asked, reaching up to pluck a stray feather that was stuck in my hair. "Tell us where you're hurt!"

"I'm *fine,*" I insisted, shrugging free of them and retreating back from the bonfire. A few seconds more, and I'd be medium-well on that side. Moe trotted up, dropping a dead gull at my feet before whining up at me with his head cocked, as if asking if I was okay. I ran my hands experimentally over my face, head and neck, and then inspected my arms for wounds, and was both surprised and relieved to find nothing. "I'm good," I assured them at last. "All clear."

"But the *blood*…"

I shook my head. "Not mine."

At that moment, one of the Humboldt girls walked over and handed me an open bottle of water and a wad of paper towels. "Here—clean yourself up."

I accepted them gratefully. "Thanks."

"No problem," she said, smiling tentatively. "You did good. I hope your friend is okay."

I was going to tell her that Brianna and I weren't friends, but she stepped back as Ab and Kelly ganged up on me again, taking the towels and water and using them to scrub away the dirt and semi-dried blood. I squirmed at first, uncomfortable with all the attention, but at last just gave up and took it, letting them satisfy themselves that I wasn't going to die.

My attention began to drift as my heart rate returned to normal, and I realized that quite a crowd had gathered around the bonfire. It looked as if nearly everyone on the beach had come over to see what all the commotion was about, the murmur of conversations drowning out even the pounding of the surf. Most everyone cast at least one nervous glance toward the sky, and after a brief, muttered exchange, the bonfire crowd began packing up their stuff.

Without thinking I took a mental sweep of the crowd, and was nearly overwhelmed by the emotions pressing in around me:

Confusion…

…Terror…

…Skepticism…

…Apprehension…

…Panic…

…Satisfaction.

I frowned. There it was again. That same feeling I had sensed the morning Darlene shattered her elbow, this time tinged with a kind of cruel glee. Both its intensity and the way it stood out in contrast made me uneasy, and I looked around, trying to pinpoint its source even though I knew it wasn't any use. It was lost in the flood of other emotions. Just the same, I turned my head slowly, sweeping the faces I could make out in the firelight's glow. Some were people I recognized, but most weren't. Then, not far from where the football and cheer crowd were hurriedly gathering up their stuff, I spotted Vern, Gina, and Nicole, their heads together in conversation while casting occasional glances our way. Turning, they made their way back to where Kim and Monica were shaking out the blankets and kicking sand over our fire. My gaze drifted past them, but then froze when it landed on Darren.

He stood well back from the bonfire's light, where the crowd had thinned considerably as people scattered to go gather their things or just hurried for the trail. I couldn't be sure, but it seemed as if our gazes met for a second or two, just before a cluster of five or six kids crossed between us.

By the time they had passed, Darren was gone.

NINE

BY MIDMORNING ON SUNDAY, WORD HAD SPREAD ABOUT the bird attack. Luckily for us, since most of the officials who came to town ended up spending a lot of time at Tsunami Joe, Ab was able to keep us on top of events by having her employees ask questions or just listen in.

Sheriff Hastings kept the beach closed for the next two weeks, stationing a deputy at the trailhead to keep away the curious while a team from the California Department of Fish and Wildlife investigated the incident. A lot of us were questioned, and even though our accounts were pretty consistent overall, I got the feeling the officials were skeptical. Apparently, it's rare for any of those birds to fly at night, let alone flock together or attack a human. Just the same, they conducted a lot of tests—soil, water, the birds themselves, what have you—but found nothing. Then they called in a group of veterinary experts all the way from UC Davis who tested everything all over again, but they didn't find anything, either. After that, the two teams got together and spent a day comparing all the nothing they'd found, as well as brainstorming what to do next, but at the end they just packed up their gear and left. None of the investigators were happy with how things had turned out, with the Fish and Wildlife folks writing it off as a freak occurrence, and the university people getting all huffy and declaring the whole thing a hoax.

Maybe they should have called in Mulder and Scully.

Brianna stayed home from school the whole first week. We heard that she had been treated at the Silver Creek Urgent Care Clinic for scratches, minor lacerations, and an abrasion to her left cornea, but that was the worst of it. A rumor that she might have caught rabies briefly made the rounds at school, but a quick Google search revealed that birds are immune, so that died off pretty much right away.

Of course, the scene from the beach was all over YouTube the same night, captured by ten or twelve cell phones at different angles and distances. Most of them were just shaky clips of my silhouette against the backdrop of the bonfire, running into the attacking flock while flailing my jacket around and shouting "*GET AWAY!*" in a voice that sounded a lot more panicked on playback than it had seemed to me at the time. Sure, it earned me some claps on the back at school for a couple of days, but it was embarrassing just the same.

Even more embarrassing was when one of the videos went viral and a dozen or so angry protesters rolled into town a few days later, waving signs out by the trailhead and demanding the arrest of the young man who had cruelly attacked a flock of sea birds. The protesters left a day or two later when no one paid them any attention, only to be replaced by seven or eight representatives from the state assembly. They arrived with a caravan of news people and spent an afternoon filming interviews and insisting the "avian attack" was a side-effect of manmade climate change. Last of all was a guy who camped out in his van for nearly a week, asking around if there had been any reports of strange lights in the sky, and telling anyone who would listen that unusual animal behavior was linked to UFO activity (which sounded like tinfoil-hat stuff to me, but what did I know?)

In the meantime, the Silver Creek Buccaneers won their next two games (both of them out of town), Brianna returned to school the second week wearing dark glasses and a lot of makeup but only a couple of bandages, and I'd decided that maybe geometry wasn't so bad after all—the proofs were sort of like logic puzzles. Best of all, the attack on Brianna had taken the spotlight off Kelly, the rest of my friends had welcomed her as part of our circle, and she had started sitting next to me every day at lunch. Neither of us had made any move to take things beyond that—not yet, anyway, although I thought about it sometimes and suspected that maybe she did, too. All in all, life definitely didn't suck.

The most interesting thing to happen was Gina finally came out from under her hood. It happened the day of Les' birthday party. He had made the mistake of mentioning that he didn't have any plans, so naturally Ab and the rest of the girls decided *that* couldn't stand, and set about organizing a party for him at Tsunami Joe.

For me, that day started a little after 7:00 while I was trying to sleep in. It was a great plan in theory, anyway, but when forty-something pounds of growing puppy stands with his forepaws on your chest, licking your face because he needs to go outside, staying in bed isn't an option. Staying grumpy about it isn't, either.

"Okay, okay," I said, giving in and laughing, and I gave Moe's ears a good scratching before pushing him back and throwing the covers aside. I pulled on a pair of sweatpants and my T-shirt from the day before, and then followed him downstairs and let him out the front door. I leaned against the porch rail post while he took care of business, shivering in the chill air with my arms crossed over my chest. The nights were getting cooler as September waned, the dew heavy on the grass, but I smiled when I looked at the sky and noted that the morning marine layer was high and already thinning. We were in for some sunshine. The last couple of days had been breezy and overcast, and I had already figured out that I needed to make the most of any nice weather that came my way. Back in Vacaville, where I had lived before moving to Windward Cove, the days would still be bright and hot, with temperatures in the mid to high 80s. I was beginning to realize, though, that fall fell a lot sooner on the north coast.

"Morning, Benny!" Mom called, hearing the door close when Moe and I came back inside, and we followed the smell of bacon through the family room to the kitchen. She stood at the stove wearing athletic tights, grass-stained Nikes and a gray, long-sleeved shirt that was sweat-darkened into Vs on her chest and back, so it didn't take a genius to figure out she'd already finished her morning run. Mom pounded out five, sometimes six miles at least four times a week, as well as yoga classes on Tuesday and Thursday evenings, and it showed. Her cheeks were still flushed under her tan, with perspiration lingering in the roots of her ash-blonde hair. She was thirty-eight but could have passed for ten years younger. She looked over her shoulder at me, smiling in that way of hers that lit up her face. "French toast, bacon, and melon okay with you?"

"Sure. Sounds great," I said, and gave her a hug before picking up Moe's bowl and heading toward the pantry to get his breakfast. I mixed some canned food into a scoop of kibbles before setting it on the floor, and then got myself a glass of juice while Moe sank to his belly, crunching away with his bowl between his forepaws.

Sunday was housework day, so after breakfast we flipped a coin to see who had bathroom duty. I lost, and spent the next hour or so scrubbing both the big bathroom we shared on the second floor and the half bath tucked under the stairs just off the family room. Moe did his version of helping, which mainly consisted of sticking his nose curiously into whatever I was working on, and occasionally batting at me with a paw, trying to get me to play. Mom had the kitchen sparkling by the time I was finished, and then we double-teamed the rest of the downstairs rooms, her dusting and polishing while I damp-mopped the hardwood floors and ran the vacuum over the area rugs. After a quick sweep and mop of the second-floor hall and stairs we were all done, everything was in order, and the house smelled of Lemon Pledge and Murphy's Oil Soap.

After taking turns showering, we got into the '69 LTD station wagon that had been our car for as long as I could remember, and Mom let me drive us to the Home Depot in Silver Creek (we were a little over a month out from my sixteenth birthday, and even though I'd had plenty of practice behind the wheel, I was determined to ace my driving test). Mom had scheduled a couple of local painters to come by and give estimates on doing the house inside and out, and she wanted to decide on colors before they arrived. We agreed on an off-white for the interior, but negotiating an outside color took us a while. I thought a brick red would look cool, but she was set on yellow. After a lot of back and forth, we finally compromised on a pale green with white trim, which didn't exactly thrill me, but by then I was tired of talking about it. Mom was the artist, after all. And anyway, it wasn't as if I really cared all that much, and almost anything would look better than the dreary, chipped gray.

By then it was early afternoon, and once we got back to the house, I was free and clear at last. Even better, I had some time to kill before the party. As Moe and I headed for the front door, a voice in the back of my head suggested I would be doing myself a favor by getting my homework out of the way first, but after one look at the golden afternoon, the voice was nice enough to mind its own business.

We hung out in the yard for an hour or so, working on Moe's fetch skills. Mom had bought me a book on dog training, and so far we'd figured out "sit," along with "lie down," "stay," "come here," and "leave it," with Moe eager to learn and picking up on everything quickly. He still wouldn't roll over, though, and walking on a leash was still giving us some problems (he'd stick right beside me without it, but once I put the leash on, he pulled like a freight train), but I figured we'd get there sooner or later. Fetch, though…that's where Moe really dug in his paws. He'd get all bouncy and excited when I brought out a tennis ball, and would reliably bring it back the first two or three times I threw it, but after that all he wanted to do was play Keep Away while I chased him around.

We lost track of time, and when Mom came out of the house carrying a large, covered pot and a bag of toasted baguette slices, it took me by surprise. "Ready?" she called, heading for the car.

I looked at my watch: 3:34. "Be right there!" I hollered, and trotted back to the house for the present I had picked out for Les—a Shimano fishing reel he had been eyeballing at Silver Creek Sporting Goods for the last couple of months. My wrapping job was typically awful (I could never get the folds right and always used too much tape), but it wasn't like Les would care, and it was too late to redo it even if I'd wanted to.

We drove into town with the smells of garlic, onions, and beefy tomato sauce filling the car and making my mouth water. Mom had made her sloppy Joe dip for my contribution to the party, and it was guaranteed to be a hit. It was driving Moe crazy too, and I kept having to push him back as he leaned over the front bench seat, sniffing in the direction of the pot resting on my lap.

Even though the coffee house officially closed at 2:00 on Sundays, half a dozen customers still lingered inside when Moe and I walked in just after 3:45, so I figured Ab must have relaxed the rules. The next thing I noticed was that Kim and Nicole had been hard at work. They had volunteered to decorate, and had hung an intricate pattern of streamers across the ceiling in different shades of blue. They had also cleared a wide space for dancing and rearranged some of the furniture to create a long table for the guests. In the center was a monster-sized carrot cake—Les' favorite—but the rest of the food was arranged on a couple of tables on the far wall where they had set up a buffet. *Wow... nice!* I thought.

I was headed over to drop off Mom's dip when a voice challenged me from off to my left. "Yo! Get that dog outa here!"

I paused, looking over to where two guys maybe a year or two older than me were seated at a table littered with drink cups that were mostly empty and some wadded-up sandwich and chip wrappers. I didn't know either of them, though I had seen both around school. The one scowling at me was a white guy with pale, pockmarked skin. He had dark brown dreadlocks and wore a Che Guevara T-shirt. His buddy had thick black hair and a slightly olive complexion, like maybe there was Italian or Spanish in his family, and wore a scuffed leather jacket despite the pleasant day outside. "Did you hear me, fucktard?" Dreads snapped. His buddy's gaze flicked between him and me, smiling like he was mildly amused and curious to see what would happen next. "Get that mutt outside—people are trying to eat in here!"

Maybe he was a cat person.

Moe lowered his head, growling, and I figured he didn't like them any more than I did. I couldn't help smiling when I saw their eyes widen slightly, but I bumped him gently with my knee, quieting him. "He's legal," I said. "Service dog."

He didn't appear convinced. "You don't look blind to me."

"Therapy," I explained. "He keeps the voices from making me do bad things."

His buddy snorted laughter, but the scowl on Dreads' face just deepened. He didn't say anything else, though, so I ignored him and crossed to the other side of the room to join Ab, who was holding a big tray of finger-sandwiches while Nicole made room for it on the buffet table. "Nice guys," I muttered.

"Yeah, well we get all kinds in here."

"You know them?"

They both glanced over. "The one in the jacket is Tony Cruz." Nicole reported. "He pretty much lives in Auto Shop."

"And Milo Waters is the one with the hair," Ab added.

"*Milo?*" I asked, handing Mom's pot over to Nicole. "Wow…his parents must not like him, either."

"It's a family thing. Named after his Dad and Grandpa. His Dad is a carpenter here in town and built the shelves behind the service counter for me." Then Ab's face registered shock as her attention was drawn to something beyond my shoulder. I turned, following her gaze.

A girl wearing jeans and a lavender, scoop-neck top stood just inside the front entrance, looking around shyly while holding a plastic tub of what looked like vanilla ice cream. She was short—five feet, maybe a little more—with a slender build and skin the color of polished ivory. A mass of thick, dark hair framed a heart-shaped face, falling well below her shoulders in a tumble of loose curls.

"*Gina?*" Ab exclaimed, and I felt my eyes widen as I recognized her at last.

Just then Darren shouldered his way in behind her, carrying a couple of paper grocery sacks and looking like he wanted to be anywhere else. He was followed by Monica, who said something to him while pointing toward the buffet behind us. He passed us as we hurried the other way, joining Kim to crowd around his cousin.

"O-M-G is that *you?*"

"Gina, you're *gorgeous!*"

"I *love* your hair! Where did you have it done?"

"Monica," she answered softly, blushing, and then glanced at the girl beaming beside her.

I hung back, listening to them gush while more and more guests arrived, branching around us as they made their way in carrying food and presents. It was almost time for the party to start.

"Sorry folks," Ab called out, and I turned, noting that she had peeled off to address the handful of customers who remained. "Thanks for coming in, but we're closing now for a private event. We'll see you next time, okay?" She watched as the diehards slowly gathered up their stuff and headed for the door.

Milo shot me a hostile glare as he and Tony passed, but then he pulled up short when he noticed Gina. "Check *you* out!" he said, pushing his way between me and Nicole to stand in front of her.

"Back off, man," Tony countered, crowding in beside him. "I'm calling dibs on this one!" His gaze traveled appreciatively down from her face, but then stopped, and I realized I wasn't the only one who had noticed that not *everything* about Gina was small. She crossed her arms self-consciously over the ample swell of her chest, her gaze darting around as if looking for an escape route.

"Aw, don't be shy, baby," Milo said, grinning. "You need to show them off. Damn girl, you're *fine!*"

"Leave her alone," I ordered, feeling annoyed, and both turned around just as Darren stepped up behind me, glowering. I didn't know if he'd be any use if things went badly, but at least he had size, and that alone made me glad for the backup.

"You got somethin' to say, shit-stain?" Milo challenged.

Just then Moe glided in to stand between us, growling and showing teeth, and both the older guys took a nervous step backward. Moe has *really* big teeth. I was still trying to think up a cool comeback when Les and Vern came through the door behind them, smiling at first, but then sobering as they took in the scene at a glance. "These guys giving you some trouble, Ben?" Vern asked. He was wearing a tight, dark red tee, and all those muscles made him look nearly as dangerous as Moe.

"Nah," I said, my gaze still locked with Milo's. "Just putting out the trash."

"Time for you girls to run along, don't you think?" Les prodded, and then stepped aside as the two of them exchanged a glance, and then left without another word.

Cheers broke out for Les as he and Vern moved past me into the crowd, and I relaxed, feeling pretty satisfied with how things had turned out.

"Hey," said a voice, and I turned to see Kelly standing beside me. She balanced a platter of hot wings in one hand and held a gift bag topped with a lot of foil ribbons and sparkly stuff in the other. "Did I miss anything?"

"Nope," I said, grinning, and I reached out to help her with the platter. "You're right on time."

We mingled for a while, and then fell into line when Ab announced it was time to hit the buffet. Someone got the music going before we found chairs at the big table, and I found myself glancing repeatedly at Gina, who was seated seven or eight places down on the opposite side.

"She looks really pretty, doesn't she?" Kelly asked, reaching out to give my hand a squeeze. I thought she would release it afterward, but she didn't.

"Yeah, she does," I admitted, and squeezed back as I turned to her. "Not as pretty as you, though."

She smiled mischievously. "Nice save."

TEN

SPIRIT WEEK WAS A BIG DEAL AT SILVER CREEK HIGH.

The days leading up to homecoming each had a different theme, and I was amazed by everyone's level of enthusiasm. An online link for homecoming king and queen nominations was posted on the school website, with the finalists to be announced during Thursday night's pep rally, and lunchtime discussions were pretty much split between who the winners might be and gossip over who was going with who to the dance that Saturday night.

The week started off with Pajama Monday, which featured an all-you-can-eat pancake breakfast before school that Ab told me was one of the music department's annual fundraisers. Spending the day in flannel lounge pants was fun—though kind of weird—and even though the pancakes weren't anything special, they were still a step up from most of the food served in the cafeteria, so I counted it as a win. Next came Tie Dye Tuesday, which turned into an unofficial contest to see who came wearing the brightest or ugliest shirt. Personally, I think Les took the gold on that one—his neon yellow, purple, green and orange combination was loud enough to make your eyes bleed, but earned him lots of attention and envious glances all day long.

Windward Wednesday was interesting, too. Everyone was encouraged to wear blue and white in remembrance of Windward Cove High. The library even put out a display of old memorabilia—year books and school cardigans, flyers for dances and plays from back in the day, and even full football and baseball uniforms emblazoned with the Sea Lion mascot. It was a nice nod toward our half of the school population.

Torchlight Thursday, though...that turned out to be the best.

The event was hosted by the Silver Creek Chamber of Commerce and took place at 8:00 in the big park at the center of town. The handful of restaurants that bordered the park stayed open late, and I noticed the chamber had also set up a couple of stands selling hot cocoa and cider, along with popcorn, nachos, and fresh pretzels. Mom and I joined the throng moving across the grass, exchanging hellos with people we knew as we made our way toward town hall, where a couple of portable fire pits blazed to either side of the wide concrete steps. Pretty much everyone carried some kind of light. Mom and I were among a few who held camping lanterns, but apparently anything would do. Looking around, I saw kerosene lamps, flashlights, candles, and even three or four toy light sabers as people chatted with friends or stood in line at the food stands. Little kids raced around everywhere, wearing necklaces and bracelets made from colored glow sticks, or waving sparklers left over from the Fourth of July. I had not expected the homecoming rally to be anywhere close to this cool, and I grinned, soaking up the excitement in the air and feeling almost as if we were taking part in some forgotten pagan ritual.

We joined the crowd by the steps just as the Silver Creek High drum line marched into the firelight and ran through a series of intricate cadences, followed by Jessica and the rest of the cheer squad, who performed a dance routine to a hip-hop tune I halfway recognized from the radio. They were really good, and the cheers that rose up when they finished were nearly deafening. After that, Jessica introduced Mayor Hahn, a pretty Korean woman whom I'd only recently found out was Kim's Mom. She must have been popular, as she had to wait fifteen or twenty seconds for all the applause to die down before welcoming everyone to this year's homecoming week. The mayor then introduced the chamber of commerce chairman, a silver-haired guy who looked about two-hundred years old, and who droned through a list of thank-yous so long I thought he'd crumble away to dust before he finished. The chairman then introduced Principal Powell, who introduced Coach Barbour, who bragged about the Buccaneer's winning season so far before finally starting to introduce the football team.

Clearly, folks in Silver Creek were big on introductions.

The coach was halfway through the defensive line, the players walking into the firelight one by one to stand on the steps before the cheering crowd, when I felt someone edge up beside me. "Hi, Ben."

"Gina!" I said, turning. I was happy to see her. "Have you seen anyone else?"

"Vern and Monica are over there," she replied, gesturing vaguely northwest. I looked, but couldn't see them. Of course, Gina's wave could have placed them anywhere from over by the gazebo to somewhere up in Alaskan tundra, so I figured maybe I would run into them later. "How are you?" she asked.

"Good, thanks. How about this rally? It's really something, huh?"

"Yeah, it's...fun."

I caught the hesitation in her voice and reached out with my gift for a quick read of her emotions. We had not really talked much since Les' party, although several times during the previous few days I had noticed her watching me, and then looking away and blushing when our gazes met. I hadn't thought much about it at the time, writing it off as standard Gina shyness, but now I sensed a nervous anxiety in her that was totally off the scale, and it worried me. "*Hey,*" I said, reaching out to touch her shoulder, and I frowned when I felt her trembling. "Are you okay?"

Gina smiled, relaxing slightly. "I'm fine."

"Are you sure? Has Darlene or one of the others been giving you crap again?"

"No, nothing like that. I just…" She cleared her throat. "Can I ask you something?"

"Sure. Ask away."

She wet her lips. "Would you…like to go to the homecoming dance with me?"

I straightened. *Oh,* I thought, feeling incredibly flattered and like the world's biggest dork at the same time. *Is* that *what's been up with her?* It took a second for my thinking to rearrange itself as the memory of all those shy glances suddenly took on new meaning. I shifted my weight nervously. "Gee, I'd love to…" Her expression brightened so I pressed on before it got any more awkward. "…but I can't. I'm going with Kelly."

Gina's smile dimmed, and I sensed her trying to control her disappointment.

"Sorry," I said, and I offered her what I hoped was a reassuring smile. "I'd totally go with you, but…"

"It's okay," she interrupted. "No big deal. I waited too long, and I didn't know you'd already asked her."

I frowned, feeling a little dishonest because that wasn't exactly how it had gone down. The truth was I had *meant* to ask Kelly, but kept chickening out, and she'd ended up asking me on Tuesday just as I was working myself up to it. I supposed it all amounted to the same thing, though, so I just shrugged.

"So…are you guys, like, *dating* now?"

I chose my next words carefully, not wanting to lead her on, but not wanting to say anything that wasn't true, either. "I'm not sure," I told her honestly. "Not yet, I guess, but we might be headed that way. We haven't exactly talked about it."

"Oh," she said, and relaxed a little more. "Okay."

"Okay," I answered, and hoped that I had said everything well enough that things wouldn't get all weird between us.

"So…I'll see you around, I guess." She took half a step back, as if to leave.

"Just a sec," I said. "I'm here with my mom, and I'd love for her to meet you." Gina's eyes widened in alarm, but I had already half-turned to see that Mom was chatting with Barbara, the lady from the arts and crafts store, so I turned back. "Hang on…I'm sure she'll…"

But Gina hadn't waited. I watched her go, scurrying off in the direction of a large silhouette that was probably Darren. *Crap*, I thought. It looked like things were going to be weird after all.

"And last but *certainly* not least," Coach Barbour announced, and I turned my attention back to the gathering on the steps. The coach paused, grinning into the microphone as the sound of cheers and whoops rose even before he finished, and he shouted out the final player. "*YOUR* SILVER CREEK STARTING QUARTERBACK AND LAST YEAR'S MVP, *AL-AAAAAN GARRETT!*"

The crowd went nuts, and even though I didn't like the guy, I found myself cheering too. The band blared out the school fight song as people jumped up and down in place, waving their lights around and exchanging hugs and high-fives.

Small-town pride. It was hokey. It was funny.

And it totally rocked.

The high spirits carried over all through the next day, in fact, with nearly everyone wearing maroon and green and talking excitedly about not only the game but Saturday's dance as well. Lunch was especially fun, as Principal Powell had ended Thursday's rally by announcing the finalists for homecoming king and queen, and it turned out that Kim was one of the contenders. She would be going up against Jessica Tanner and Riley Chase for the crown, and even though Riley was the odds-on favorite (she was a senior on the swim team, Ab told me, and had made it to Sections as a sophomore, and then gone all the way to State as a junior), we were all super excited about Kim. I secretly wondered if Kelly would have been up there too if she hadn't quit the cheer squad. She didn't seem bothered by it, though, so I figured it didn't matter. *Besides,* I thought, *she's only a junior—there's always next year, right?* I had expected Alan to be on the ballot for king, but the contenders were Vern and two guys I didn't know. None of us had seen that coming, especially Vern, and even though Les and I gave him a hard time about it, we were both totally in his corner.

The excitement level was still running high at game time, and even though a fine drizzle had started falling around dusk, the stands were overflowing with fans wearing rain gear or sitting close beneath umbrellas or sheets of plastic.

Everyone was in a great mood…right up until the Bucs took the field against the Ranier High Mountain Men.

It started with our first possession, right after kickoff. Alan took the snap at the twenty-yard line, faked a handoff to Dozer, and then faded back to pass. Then the ball just popped out of his hand—like a wet bar of soap when you squeeze it too hard. It fell to the ground right behind him, and Alan accidentally kicked it as he whirled around to recover the fumble. The ball bounced toward a Mountain Man who had made it past the offensive line, and he changed course, plucking it off the ground and running it in for a touchdown.

The enthusiastic roar of the crowd became an *"Oooh!"* of disappointment.

Ranier made the extra point, and then kicked to us again.

As Alan and the team lined up for their second possession, Jessica and her squad did their best to get the crowd fired back up, leading them in a rallying cheer that alternated with a clapping pattern:

"LET'S GO BUC-CAN-EERS!"

Clap-Clap-ClapClapClap!

"LET'S GO BUC-CAN-EERS!"

Clap-Clap-ClapClapClap!

Dozer took Alan's handoff and plowed into the defenders, taking a hit only a couple of yards past the line of scrimmage. The ball popped loose, and a Ranier lineman fell on it.

I turned my head, looking one row behind me and three places down to where Darren sat just beyond Gina. While his cousin watched the game with a somber expression, Darren's lips were turned upward in what looked to me like the barest hint of a smirk. I reached out with my gift, curious to see if I could detect that feeling of satisfaction I had sensed twice before, but there were too many people around experiencing too many strong emotions—mostly frustration and disappointment—and if it was there, the other feelings drowned it out. *Or maybe I'm wrong*, I reminded myself, directing my attention back to the field. *Maybe it isn't there at all.*

The game continued that way, with our defense at least making Ranier High work for it, but Alan and the offense struggling to gain even a few yards. Coach Barbour called a time out a couple of minutes into the second quarter, calling both Alan and Dozer to the sidelines. He yelled at them for a few seconds, but then Alan interrupted him, looking angry and gesturing with his arms widespread. The coach turned away before he finished, though, calling out to a couple of second-stringers who trotted onto the field to replace them. The two starters pulled off their helmets—Alan wearing a furious expression and Dozer just looking dejected—and made their way to the bench.

By midway through the third quarter, Ranier was destroying us. The score was 31-6, and the crowd had thinned considerably. Maybe it was the rain, but I wouldn't have bet on it. As the fans grew more and more quiet, both vocally and emotionally, I began to catch faint, occasional pings of that familiar, cruel satisfaction on my mental radar. I kept glancing back toward Darren, trying to see if I could narrow it down to him, but then stopped when he caught me looking a couple of times. Maybe it was him, but maybe it wasn't. There was definitely something off about the guy, though I wasn't sure exactly what. Maybe he had been a social outcast for too long and was enjoying watching someone else eat dirt for a change. Maybe he just didn't like football. Or maybe he was every bit as mean-spirited as he seemed.

Hmm, I thought. *Maybe it's time someone found out.*

ELEVEN

IT WAS MIDMORNING ON SATURDAY WHEN IT SUDDENLY occurred to me that I should probably figure out what I was wearing that night. I went through my closet, feeling a rush of near-panic when I realized I didn't even know if the dance was a formal kind of thing, informal, or something in between. I'm generally just a jeans and T-shirt kind of guy, so my choices beyond that were kind of limited. There was my suit, of course, which I had last worn to a funeral during the summer, but when I looked more closely, I noticed there was a layer of dust on the shoulders of the jacket.

Not good.

Then the obvious occurred to me and I flopped onto my bed. Grabbing my phone from the nightstand, I tapped out a text to Kelly: [HEY... WHAT R U WEARING 2NITE?]

I set my phone down on my chest, and was reaching out to pet Moe when it buzzed with a reply almost right away. [HA! WOULDN'T U LIKE 2 KNOW? ;-)]

91

It wasn't helpful, but I smiled anyway. [SRSLY...JUST WONDERING HOW FORMAL IT IS.]

[LOL...UR ONLY THINKING ABOUT THIS NOW?!]

My grin widened. [CAN'T DECIDE BETWEEN THE HAWAIIAN SHIRT OR MY TUX.]

I wondered if Kelly would tease me some more, but she must have decided to take it easy. [GO WITH NICE, BUT NOT 2 DRESSY. COLLARED SHIRT. JEANS ONLY AS A LAST RESORT.]

I figured I could manage that. [WILL DO. THX.]

I was reaching over to set my phone back on the nightstand when it buzzed again.

[MOTHER WANTS U 2 COME 4 DINNER.] My eyebrows went up, but Kelly texted again before I could reply. [I KNOW IT'S LAST MINUTE, SO OK IF U ALREADY HAVE PLANS.]

[NO...NO PLANS. JUST DIDN'T SEE THAT COMING. THOUGHT UR MOM H8ED ME.]

After a long pause: [CHG OF HEART.]

My stomach knotted as I thought it over. As much as I would have preferred to keep some distance between me and Kelly's Mom—ideally, a midsized state with a mountain range—maybe this would be a chance to show her I wasn't such a bad guy. And it would sure make things a lot less strained if Kelly and I ever started officially dating, too. *Probably need to suck this one up, big guy,* I thought.

My phone buzzed again. [...?]

[SRY. SURE, I'LL BE THERE. WHAT TIME?]

[6:30?]

[OK. TELL HER I PREFER RAT POISON OVER DRAIN-O IN MY SOUP.]

[HA-HA. SEE U L8R.]

[OK]

[XO]

I grinned at her last text. Maybe it was worth being poisoned at that.

Ten minutes later I had decided on what seemed my best option: a pair of khaki pants and the white shirt that went with my suit. The shirt had been a little tight across the chest and shoulders the last time I'd worn it, but would probably still be okay, and the pants would be fine after a few minutes in the dryer to knock out the wrinkles.

"You're kidding, right?"

I turned to see Mom leaning in the doorway, surveying the outfit I had selected with her arms crossed. "What?" I asked, a little defensively. "You think I need the tie, too?"

She chuckled, rolling her eyes with a shake of her head. "Come on…let's go."

She drove us to Silver Creek, and we got out in front of a tidy-looking shop that was tucked into a side street just off downtown. I hadn't noticed it before, and paused to read the sign posted above the entrance: *J. Grant, Haberdasher.* "What does haberdasher mean?" I asked.

Mom smirked, holding the door open for me. "It's Latin for 'no Levis here.'"

Everybody's a comedian.

An older man looked up as we entered; stepping out from behind a mannequin dressed up in a three-piece suit he had been dusting with a soft brush. He looked like a college professor, wearing a tweed jacket over a shirt, tie and sweater vest, and he offered a polite smile as he regarded us over the top of his reading glasses. "Good morning. May I help you?"

"I sure hope so," Mom replied. "We have what you'd call a wardrobe emergency. This guy has a hot date to the homecoming dance, and… well, just *look* at him. Is there anything you can do?" She was grinning as she said it, and I could tell she was having fun.

So this is how it's going to be, huh? I thought, and steeled myself to be a good sport.

The man made a show of looking me over, and then made a tsking sound. "Hmm…an unfortunate case, but I'll do my best. Did you have anything in mind?"

Unfortunate. Nice.

Mom's smile only got wider. "I'm thinking classic: something in a mid-70s polyester leisure suit, maybe."

"Always a popular choice," he replied, eyes twinkling. "Ruffles or pleats on the shirt?"

"Ruffles, of course. Go big or go home, right? But only if it comes with the white, patent-leather belt and shoes."

"Can I go outside while the two of you work this out?" I asked. "There's probably a truck I can throw myself in front of."

"Ah," said the man, ignoring me. "Sadly, I sold the last set this morning."

Mom frowned. "That's a shame. What else have you got?"

He smiled, pulling a cloth measuring tape from his jacket pocket. "I'm sure we can find something that will do."

Forty minutes later I was standing in my socks on a little raised dais with three angled mirrors behind me. Mr. Grant (he had finally introduced himself once he and Mom were all done joking around) made some marks on the sleeves and waist of a gray sport coat that had met with Mom's approval, and then he had me step into a pair of unlaced dress shoes so he could pin the cuffs of the matching slacks. "Alright, Ben," he said, helping me out of the coat. "Go ahead and change so I can get to work on the alterations."

"How long will you need?" Mom asked as I headed for the dressing room.

"Not long. Why don't you and Ben go have lunch, and then come back in an hour or so?"

"That would be perfect."

I waited until we were out on the sidewalk before speaking. "Thanks, Mom…thanks a lot. This is really great." She slid an arm around my waist, smiling up at me, and in that moment I could not imagine anyone having a better mother.

We found a Chinese place just around the corner and worked our way leisurely through pot-stickers, Mongolian beef, and mu-shu pork. Mr. Grant had everything altered, pressed, and ready to go by the time we got back, and Mom had me put it all on, including a black dress belt, shoes, and a cobalt blue shirt she said brought out the color of my eyes. "Look at *you*," she said approvingly. "All ready to go out and break hearts!"

"*Quit* it, Mom," I said, embarrassed.

"*They come runnin' just as fast as they can*," she sang, "*'cause every girl's crazy 'bout a sharp-dressed man!*" Mom waited, and then laughed at my blank expression. "*C'mon*, Ben….ZZ Top?"

I could only shrug.

"Oh, God. I'm a complete failure as a Mother."

"It happens to the best of families," Mr. Grant said solemnly.

Kelly opened her front door at 6:27 just as I was about to knock, so she must have seen Mom drop me off at the mouth of her driveway.

"Wow," we said at the same time, and both of us laughed.

Kelly wore a short, dark green dress that went well with the auburn of her hair, making me think of a forest in autumn when the leaves are just starting to turn. "You look amazing," I said.

She smiled. "I was just thinking the same about you. You know, I think this is the first time I've seen you in anything other than…"

"Ben!" her Mother cried, stepping up behind her and pulling the door wide open. "You're right on time—and *my*, how handsome you look! The two of you are going to outshine everyone at the dance!"

"Uh…thanks, Mrs. Thatcher," I managed, feeling my face flush. I didn't know what sort of welcome I'd been expecting, but it sure wasn't this. I took a quick read of her emotions and was surprised to find none of the disdain that was usually directed my way. It had been replaced by a sort of eagerness mixed with anxiety, and I wondered why.

"Please—call me Wendy," she said, and reached past Kelly to grasp my arm, pulling me inside.

I shot Kelly a questioning look as I passed, but she just shook her head and whispered, "*Later*," softly enough so her Mother couldn't hear.

Wendy set a brisk pace and I had to hurry to keep up. She wore white designer jeans gathered close at her ankles and a loose top that was almost the same color as Kelly's dress. I wondered if that was just coincidence, or if she had intentionally dressed to match her daughter—like some sort of accessory—and then felt guilty for thinking it.

"I know the two of you don't have much time," she said, leading me through the sprawling living room, "so I hope you don't mind that I have dinner on the table already." The dining room was just beyond, and I blinked when I saw the amount of food laid out. Only three places were set, though, and I wondered what was up with that. "What can I get you to drink, Ben? Soda? A beer, maybe? Kelly told me she's driving, so feel free to relax."

This is just too weird, I thought. "A soda would be great, thanks."

"Kelly?"

"Just water, please."

"Take a seat—I'll be right back."

At the head of the table was half a glass of red wine beside a bottle that was maybe a third empty. "Yours?" I asked Kelly.

She smiled. "I had red for breakfast." She moved to the place on the far side of the table, and I remembered my manners in time to get her chair for her. "Such a gentleman—thank you."

"Only the five-star service for you, ma'am." I was in the chair opposite hers by the time Wendy returned with our drinks, but she waved me back down when I moved to stand.

"Please, Ben—we're very casual here." She began ladling soup into bowls. "I hope you're hungry, because along with the Tuscan vegetable soup we have two kinds of pasta—sausage tortellini and mushroom ravioli in case you don't eat meat. There's also salad and bread."

I smiled politely as she placed my steaming bowl in front of me, and silently mouthed, *"Drain-O"* to Kelly when her Mother wasn't looking.

She pressed her lips together, trying not to smile.

"So," Wendy said, seating herself and reaching over to top off her wine glass, "it's nice that we finally have a chance to talk. Kelly tells me you're originally from the San Francisco area." Her voice rose at the end, turning it into a question.

"Closer to Sacramento," I told her, "but yeah."

"And what brought you and your parents to Windward Cove?"

I had just tried a spoonful of soup, and I swallowed before answering. "It's just my mom and me. My great aunt passed away and left us the house."

"Oh, yes…I heard about that. I'm sorry for your loss, Ben. Your aunt…I understand she was Claire Black?"

The conversation went on that way all through dinner—less of a talk, and more like a polite interrogation. I guess if I had a daughter like Kelly, I would want to know all about the new guy too, so I answered her questions and tried to make a good impression. It was a good thing I'd had a big lunch, though, because there wasn't much time to eat between answers. I managed to sneak in a few bites of pasta here and there, but stuck mainly to salad. The only thing I left alone was the bread—it smelled extra garlicky, and I had been toying with the idea of trying to kiss Kelly before the night was over. She passed on the bread, too, which I took as a hopeful sign.

Wendy didn't eat much either, although she did kill the rest of the wine bottle.

At last it was over, and she walked us to the door when it was time to leave. "It was wonderful chatting with you, Ben," she said, and then surprised me by stepping forward to give me a quick hug. "I hope you'll come back soon."

"Thanks for everything, Mrs. Tha—*Wendy*," I amended. *That* was going to take some getting used to. "I'll see you later."

"You two have fun," she said, and closed the door behind us.

I exhaled a thankful sigh as we made our way to the garage, feeling the tension in my neck begin to ease.

"How about that? You survived."

"That was…different," I said. "Dinner was good, though."

"You don't think she cooked all that, do you?" Kelly shook her head. "That was for show. Take-out from DeMarino's."

"I thought the tortellini tasted familiar." Then I frowned when I sensed her irritation. "Are you okay?" I asked, pretty sure I hadn't done anything wrong.

"Yeah, I'm fine. Mother can just be so *exasperating* sometimes. I'm sorry you had to go through all that."

"It wasn't so bad," I said, opening the driver's side door for her, "though she did kind of catch me by surprise. Both times I met her before, she acted as if she'd like to skin me and nail it to the wall as a warning to other guys. Now she's treating me like I'm her favorite son."

Kelly waited until I closed her door and got in on the other side before answering. "Yeah, well there's a reason for that. It's why we've been fighting so much lately." I waited for her to continue, and after she backed out of the garage and turned right onto the street, she did. "Mother was mad enough to chew nails when she heard I'd quit cheer, and absolutely *furious* when I told her Alan and I were over. It killed her dream that Alan and I would get married one day and give her a bunch of pretty grandkids."

"Wow. She has that all figured out, and you're not even a senior yet? She doesn't waste a lot of time, does she?"

Kelly shrugged. "It's not really her fault. She just has this thing about security. See, she grew up with parents who were really bad with money, and between cheer and studying her ass off, she got into college on a couple of scholarships. That's where she met my dad. He's this total software genius who wrote a program that handles pretty much everything related to professional accounting. All sorts of businesses use it, even a few of the Fortune 500 companies. Anyway, it made him a lot of money. He moved here with my mother and older sister because he liked the quiet."

"Where's your dad now?"

Kelly shook her head. "He's not around much. Spends most of his time near his office down by San Jose. Things between him and Mother have been strained ever since my sister went missing."

"*What?*"

She nodded. "Anne inherited Dad's brains, but Mother's headstrong side, too, and she used to get into trouble a lot. After she was expelled from Silver Creek High, Mother and Dad were finally able to get her into this private boarding school. She had only been there a few months when she disappeared, and no one has heard from her for nearly three years." Kelly glanced over at me. "I'm telling you this so you can understand why Mother is the way she is. Dad makes a good living, but it's not like he's Bill Gates or anything. And while I'm not dumb, I don't exactly have Anne's brains *or* Mother's drive, so colleges aren't going to trip over each other trying to get me to enroll. Alan, though…his family comes from fairly big money, and Mother saw me marrying him as my best chance for a good future. So, when *you* came along…"

"She thought I'd spoil everything," I finished for her, finally understanding. "I'm the other guy. The bad boy from the low side of town."

"Except you're not," Kelly said. "*Are* you?"

I shrugged.

"After Alan and I broke up, she started asking around about you. When she found out you and your mom were Claire Black's heirs, her jaw just about hit the floor. *That's* why she invited you to dinner."

I rolled my eyes. "So now I'm Future Husband 2.0? Awesome."

"Don't take it personally—it's just the way she's wired. She says your family is 'fabulously wealthy.'"

I shrugged again.

"*Are* you?" Kelly pressed. "Not that I care…but just so I know who it is I'm dating."

I grinned at her. "So…we're *dating?*"

There was just enough sunlight left to show her blush. "You didn't answer my question."

I chewed the inside of my cheek while thinking about what to say. "Well, we don't swim around in a money bin like Scrooge McDuck, but yeah…we're pretty loaded, I guess. Does that change anything?"

"Between us? Of course not—I liked you before." She shook her head. "And what's the big deal about money, anyway? It doesn't define what kind of person you are."

"It's a big deal if you don't have it. Six months ago, Mom and I were living in a tiny apartment while she worked two jobs. Looks like your mother and I may have more in common than I thought."

Kelly glanced at me, smiling. "I had no idea. Maybe that's why you don't go around acting like Richie Rich." She put on her turn signal, and then pulled into the school parking lot and found a space.

"Well, I've been practicing, but it's harder that you think," I told her as we got out. "Next week I'll start lighting cigars with hundred-dollar bills."

She laughed, and we walked with our shoulders nearly touching as we joined other couples heading for the gym. "So…" she said after nearly a minute, "we're *dating?*"

"I thought you'd never ask."

Kelly laughed, stopping and turning toward me as her arms encircled my neck. Her lips were just as soft and warm as I remembered, and my arms slid around her waist as I pulled her against me. The press of her body made my heart beat faster, and I felt dizzy as I inhaled the subtle scent of her perfume.

"Hey, you two…get a room!" someone called out, and we broke off the kiss to join in the scattered laughter.

"Well then," Kelly said, beaming as she pulled me toward the gym doors, "now that the pressure's finally off, let's go have some fun!"

TWELVE

MUSIC ISSUED INVITINGLY FROM THE OPEN DOORS, AND Kelly and I exchanged smiles as we joined the line of people making their way inside.

Ever since the first day of school, I had felt drawn to the Silver Creek High gym. The building wasn't just old, it *felt* old, which I thought really added to its cool-factor. Mostly, though, I couldn't help but wonder what it would be like to spend some time in there alone. Like a lot of places where emotions tended to run high, all those feelings over the decades had seeped into the wood, the paint, and even the concrete of the foundation, and I could sense that there were any number of visions I could tap into if I tried. The problem was that opening myself to my gift was like this total 3D, surround-sound experience where the real world faded away completely and I would find myself immersed in the past, walking around unseen while forgotten events played out all around me. Not the best idea if I didn't want the whole school thinking I was a total nutjob, so I ignored the whispers and flashes of vision that tugged seductively at the back of my mind. *Someday,* I thought.

But tonight wasn't that night.

The arched ceiling started from a height of around 30 feet where it met the east and west walls to a shadowy 50 feet at its apex. Dozens of banners and pennants dangled from the high trusses like flags from forgotten battles, from last year's football championship all the way back to when the Silver Creek girls' archery team took the silver at the 1925 state finals. Foil streamers had been added for the occasion, winking almost magically as they swayed on wisps of breeze and reflecting beams from a disco ball that rotated in the glare of colored spotlights. Tables and chairs had been brought over from the cafeteria, surrounding a wide space at center court where a sea of dancers rippled and swirled, and a portable stage had been assembled at the far end of the gym near the doors to the pool center, where larger tables were loaded with punch bowls and refreshments.

"Kelly!" called a voice, and I looked over to where a girl with cropped brown hair was waving to us with what looked like a stack of three-by-five note cards. Kelly pulled me along as she veered in that direction, and I had time to notice that the girl was pretty, with an open smile, a scattering of freckles across her nose, and a black dress that was cut to show off her lean, muscular figure. "Who's this?" she asked, looking at me as we joined her.

"Oh, you haven't met? This is my boyfriend Ben. Ben, this is Riley Chase."

I glanced sideways at Kelly, feeling a dopey smile tug at one corner of my mouth. *Boyfriend.* Then I remembered I should probably do something other than stand there like a doofus. "So *you're* Riley," I said, shaking her hand. Her grip was firm, the muscles in her forearm clearly defined. "The swimmer, right?"

"That's the story going around," she said, smiling at me, and then turned back to Kelly. "Did you say boyfriend? How long has this been going on?"

Kelly glanced at a clock on the wall, and then smiled radiantly. "Officially? About three and a half minutes."

"That's fantastic! I'm so glad you moved on from Alan—he's *way* too full of himself." Riley made a show of looking me over, and then leaned close to Kelly. "He's *cute!*" she whispered conspiratorially. "Will you share?"

"Ask me in a week," she replied, grinning as she took my arm.

Riley laughed, and then changed the subject. "I almost forgot," she said, handing each of us a card. "I'm supposed to pass these out."

I looked at mine, realizing it was a ballot for homecoming king and queen. There was a space to write my name, followed by blank check boxes beside the names of the contenders, then a warning at the bottom that any duplicate cards would not be counted. Democracy in action.

"Trolling for votes?" Kelly teased.

The girl laughed, shaking her head. "Like I even *care.* It's not my fault I got nominated. If it weren't for that, I probably wouldn't even be here—I had to give up my afternoon workout for this. Anyway, there are pencils everywhere and a box on the refreshment table where you can turn in your ballots."

"Great. We'll see you later, okay?"

"Nice meeting you," I called out as Kelly led me away.

Riley waved, and then turned her attention to someone behind us. "Sherrie Sova! Sue Lum! You both look *gorgeous* tonight!"

We made our way further into the gym, and almost right away I could sense emotions all around us starting to shift. For a second or two I thought the music had gotten louder, but then I realized that it hadn't—it was just that the voices competing with it had died off. Conversations trailed away as faces turned toward us wearing expressions of surprise, mild confusion, or appraisal, and I could feel my face grow warm. "Um…there's, like, lots of people watching us," I muttered sideways to Kelly. My mouth had gone dry, and I squirmed inwardly at all the attention we were receiving.

"Uh-huh," she replied softly, giving my hand a comforting squeeze as made our way through the crowd. "Just go with it."

I swallowed, following her lead and hoping to God my fly was zipped.

A few steps later Kelly chuckled, bumping me with her shoulder. "It's okay to *smile*, Ben!"

I did, letting out a breath, and even managed to exchange heys with some of the kids I recognized from class. After what seemed like a long time (but was probably only twenty or thirty seconds) conversations resumed as everyone's surprise at seeing us together started to wear off, and I began to feel less like a bug under a magnifying glass.

I spotted Kim talking with Ab and Vern on the far side of the room, so I steered Kelly in that direction. Kim was facing away from us, but I could tell who she was right away—the shimmery, dark red dress she wore didn't have much of a back, and showed a lot of the tattoo of cherry blossom branches that climbed from just above her left hip all the way to her right shoulder blade. On anyone else it might have been over the top, but somehow Kim made it look elegant. Before we got there, though, I felt a tug at my sleeve.

"Hey…"

I stopped, turning, and was surprised to see Brianna standing next to me. Looking past her shoulder, I could see Alan two or three paces back, glaring and looking like a sulky five-year-old, and I held back a grin. Despite my not liking his new girlfriend, the fact it bugged him that we were talking made me that much more inclined to be friendly. I gave Kelly a questioning glance, but she only shrugged, so I turned back to Brianna. "Hey," I answered.

"It's Ben, right?"

I nodded.

"I just…" She paused, biting her lower lip as she looked over her shoulder at Alan, and then turned back toward me. "I wanted to say thanks for what you did. That night at the beach, I mean."

"No problem," I said, and then looked more closely at her face. Her makeup was still a little on the heavy side, but the scratches were mostly healed, and it didn't look like she'd end up with any scars. "I'm glad you're okay," I told her, and was a little surprised to discover that I actually meant it.

The girl offered a half-smile in return, and then looked past me. "Hi, Kelly."

"Brianna," Kelly answered, nodding. Her tone was a little distant, but not as frosty as it could have been, and I idly wondered if that meant the two of them might eventually patch up their friendship. You can never tell with girls.

Brianna must have found it encouraging, though, and she gave a tentative smile. "You look really…"

"*Bri*," Alan called over, interrupting her.

He was looking even more annoyed, and I thought about waggling my eyebrows at him, just to see if his head would explode. But I didn't. Sometimes you have to take the high road.

"Are you done?" he complained. "I wanna get a punch."

You've got that coming, at least, I wanted to say, but somehow managed to keep that inside, too.

Ben Wolf, master of self-control.

"Okay…bye," Brianna said, and then hurried back to Alan, who drew her away with a final glare toward me. It was probably supposed to make me feel all kinds of threatened, but it didn't.

I shook my head as I watched them go. *Weird*, I thought. Never in a million years would I ever have imagined feeling sorry for her.

Les had joined Kim and the rest by the time we made it over, and I was surprised and pleased to see him standing with his arm draped loosely over Gina's shoulders. She wore a sapphire-colored dress one of the girls must have passed on to her, and I was careful not to react when I noticed how well she filled it out. She frowned briefly as we stepped up, her gaze zeroing in on Kelly's and my clasped hands. She returned the smile I offered, though, so I figured we were mostly okay. I turned to Les. "*Dude*," I said. "Look at you!"

He laughed, releasing Gina and turning a slow three-sixty to show off his jacket. "You gotta have a party coat, right?" One sleeve was a blue pinstripe, while the other was a solid black. The four front and back panels consisted of a hunter green, a paisley design on salmon, a blue-and-gold plaid, and a blood-red silk, none of which even remotely went together.

I wished I'd thought of it.

Monica arrived with an African-American girl named Jasmine that she dated off and on, just about the same time that a tall Asian guy came from the refreshment table with a cup of punch for Kim. She introduced him as Phu, who had graduated the year before and was now a freshman at Humboldt State, and the open smile he gave me when we shook hands made me like him right off. Nicole showed up last of all with a guy she had brought to our beach fires two or three times, but whose name I could never remember. I thought he was kind of a douche—one of those superior types who had an opinion about everything and got his panties in a bunch if you disagreed with him. Personally, I thought Nicole could do a lot better, but I figured that was none of my business. We had all just begun talking when the music swelled into a song Ab liked, and she excused herself as she pulled Vern toward the dance floor. The rest of the girls followed her lead, and soon we were all crammed together under the disco ball, moving as much as we could in the tightly packed crowd.

It was a great night. Even taking periodic breaks, we all must have averaged five out of every seven songs on the floor. I thought Kelly and

Vern were probably the best dancers of all of us, but Ab moved with a joyful abandon that was fun to watch. Kelly kept me busy for the most part, but we all traded partners as the hours went by, and I got to dance with all the girls at least once. When the DJ announced that the voting for homecoming king and queen was about to close, we had to scramble to get our ballots in. The timing was good, though—it gave us all a chance for a water break while the votes were tallied up. I was sweating like crazy, and probably sucked down at least a quart by myself. As most people had predicted, Riley won by a landslide, and even though we had been rooting for Kim, we all clapped and cheered while she and Jessica presented a grinning Riley with a tiara and a huge bouquet of roses. Then Vern was announced as king, and we all yelled our heads off as he led Riley to center court for the traditional dance.

Good times.

"So...you finally sealed the deal, huh?" Les asked.

It was an hour or so later, and the crowd had thinned by about half. We were the only ones at our table, Les slouching with his legs stretched out comfortably in front of him while I straddled my chair backwards with my chin resting on crossed arms. We had taken a breather while Kelly and Vern danced together at center court, where the crowd had drawn back to give them space and several couples had stopped to watch. I shifted my gaze to Les, raising my eyebrows.

"You and Kelly," he explained, and then snorted. "About freaking time. *And* you gave the whole school something to talk about."

"Yeah, I wasn't sure we'd ever get together, but here we are," I said, smiling. "But hey, we're not the only ones surprising people. You and Gina...who saw *that* coming? I figured you'd be here with Jessica."

He shrugged. "I would have, but Matt Case got to her first."

"Sorry, man. Bummer."

"Nah…Matt's a good dude, and it's my own fault for taking too long to ask. And anyway, Gina asked me about an hour later, so it's all good. She's really cool."

"Not to mention easy on the eyes," I added.

He grinned. "Yeah, that too."

"So are you guys just here as friends? Or is this a date?"

"Dunno," he said, shrugging. "I'd say friends to start. We'll see how it goes."

I smiled. "Either way, it's nice to finally see Gina out having some fun without Darren hovering all the time."

Les chuckled. "Look again, amigo."

I glanced at him questioningly.

"Visitor's bleachers, far left, five rows up. Gina asked him to stay home, but he followed us anyway. He's been there all night."

It took me a few seconds to find Darren, seated with his elbows on his knees and gazing down to where his cousin was chatting with Monica and Jasmine by one of the mostly depleted refreshment tables. Then I frowned as I watched Milo Waters and Tony Cruz drift past. One of them must have said something to Gina, because Monica and Jasmine closed ranks in front of her, with Monica snapping an angry retort I was too far away to hear. The two boys moved off; Cruz walking backward with his middle finger raised. Jasmine didn't hesitate, flipping him off in return, and it made me smile.

The whole thing was over almost as soon as it started, and I looked back up at the bleachers to see Darren making his way down, glaring after Waters and Cruz. He stopped when he reached the bottom, glanced back at Gina, and then just watched the two guys disappear through a side exit as he seemed to realize there was nothing for him to do.

Always on duty, I thought, and I wondered what it felt like for him to sit there by himself all night. Finding things to like about Darren was uphill work, but it was hard not to feel sorry for him just the same.

"*Last dance!*" came the voice of the DJ as the music faded away and the lights dimmed. I glanced down at my watch, surprised to see it was nearly midnight. "*Last dance, everyone!*"

Kelly and Gina both hurried over, arriving at almost the same time to pull us to our feet, and both Les and I groaned in mock protest. My thighs and upper back had begun to stiffen, and I had a feeling I was going to be sore in the morning.

We were nearly beneath the disco ball when Kelly turned toward me, moving in close as her arms encircled my neck. She pressed herself against me, her face snuggled against the base of my neck, and we began to move our feet slowly to a ballad, not dancing so much as simply holding one another as we rotated in place. I could just detect the clean smell of her sweat beneath her perfume, and right then I couldn't imagine anyplace I would rather be.

Gazing idly toward the edge of the crowd, I noticed Darren looking uncomfortable, wiping his hands on the thighs of his pants as he seemed to be trying to decide something. At last, he walked purposefully to a couple of girls who lingered on the sidelines, and I could see his mouth move as he addressed them, a hopeful expression on his face. *Good for you, Darren*, I thought, glad to see him break character and at least try to have a little fun. Then the good feeling passed as I watched one of the girls give a dismissive shake of her head and then step over to a random guy and pull him onto the floor. Her friend looked at Darren like he was something smelly she'd just stepped in, and then turned her back and walked away, heading for the restroom.

Really? I thought, irritated by their treatment of him. *Couldn't you at least have been nice about it?*

Then the scene slowly swung out of my field of vision as Kelly and I kept rotating, and I found myself looking at Gina as she danced with Les. From her scowl I figured that she had also witnessed Darren's rejection. Then she met my gaze, and her expression softened as she regarded me silently, her head against Les' chest. I offered her a smile that I hoped looked consoling, but really, what else could I do? Darren would have to figure out girls on his own, just like the rest of us.

"Are you okay?" Kelly murmured. Her breath was warm on my neck, and it brought my mind back to what I was doing.

"Better than okay," I said, pulling my head back to smile down at her.

"Good," she said, her eyes twinkling. "'Cause if you don't kiss me pretty soon, I think I'm going to go crazy."

I grinned, leaning down toward her…

And then the overhead lights started to explode.

It started with a spotlight off to our left. It went with a *Pop!*—like an inflated paper bag when you smash it between your hands, only about three times as loud. Startled cries followed as sparks, embers, and shards of glass rained down on the dancers below. A light behind me blew right after that, and then three more in rapid succession—*Pop!…Pop!Pop!Pop!*—as shrieks rose all around us. I hunched over Kelly, trying to shield her with my body as the rest of the spotlights all blew at once, the combined explosion nearly drowning out the surprised screams of the crowd. The gym went black for a few seconds as panicked cries rang out from the darkness all around us. Then, just as someone found the light switches and started turning on the overhead fluorescents, there came a cracking sound almost directly above us. I risked a glance upward, and then swung Kelly out of the way just as the disco ball dropped from the rafters! It plummeted to the gym floor, exploding with a boom and sending shards of mirror everywhere like shrapnel. Looking back, I could see the falling sphere had barely missed the girl who had turned down Darren. She stood there shrieking and flailing, her arms and legs bleeding from a dozen tiny cuts as she tried to fish out a hot ember that had fallen down the front of her dress. The guy she had been dancing with stood frozen in place for a moment, and then stepped forward as if to help, but she pushed him away.

The *fwoosh* of fire extinguishers sounded irregularly around us as a few resourceful kids and chaperones began putting out the fallen embers that still smoldered on the floor. The slightly acrid odor of the chemical was strong, almost covering the smell of...

Of what? I wondered, looking around suddenly. There it was again... that sweet, spicy scent. In all the confusion, I'd almost missed it. *What the hell is that?* I reached out with my gift, trying to see if I could detect the cruel satisfaction that always seemed to go with it, but if the feeling was there, all the fright and confusion around me was drowning it out.

Kelly pushed me gently away, first checking herself for cuts and then looking me over. "Are you alright?"

"Hmm?" I asked, still distracted. "Oh, yeah...I'm good. You?"

"I'm okay—just shaken up a little. What *was* that?"

"Probably a power surge," Les answered, stepping up behind me. "The wiring in this place is about a million years old. Either of you hurt?"

We shook our heads just as the rest of our friends clustered around, and I was glad to find out that everyone else was okay, too. Our initial fright turned into nervous relief almost right away, and scattered applause and even a couple of cheers rose above the tense murmuring that was quickly replacing the sounds of general confusion and fear. It didn't last long, though, as chaperones starting ordering us to get outside, sounding borderline panicky even as they kept shouting at everyone not to panic. The faint sound of a siren rose in the distance, and I realized that someone had called the fire department. "Nice save, Ben," Nicole said, smiling at me. "I thought that disco ball was going to drop right on top of you two!"

I smiled in reply as we began moving toward the exit as a group, but I didn't think Nicole was right. Someone else had been even closer. I felt Kelly take my arm, only half-listening as everyone started talking about heading to Hovey's for something to eat, and instead glanced uneasily back over my shoulder.

The girl by the shattered disco ball had calmed down, so I figured she must have gotten the ember out of her dress. Her friend rejoined her, and the two inspected her injuries even as one of the adults tried to herd them toward the door. The cuts looked minor—barely more than scratches—and had already stopped bleeding, but still…

Twenty feet beyond them, couples steered clear of the broken glass as they made for the exits, veering around Darren as he stood like a rock in a stream. I watched as he stared at the two girls, his face bearing an expression that I could not read.

THIRTEEN

DESPITE MY WORKOUT AT THE DANCE, THE TWO CHILI dogs and milkshake I had pretty much inhaled at Hovey's, and not crawling into bed until nearly two in the morning, my brain wouldn't let me sleep. I dozed some—twenty minutes here, half an hour there—but even those brief periods were plagued by disturbing images and snatches of nightmare that made me jolt awake, gasping raggedly in the darkness while my gaze darted around the room. I had already forgotten most of the scenes within a few seconds after waking up, but the last one stayed with me: Darren Lynch, standing in the middle of the gym while flames erupted all around him, like Chloe Moretz in the remake of *Carrie*.

Screw this, I thought irritably, at last throwing the covers aside and swinging my legs out of bed. Even though my alarm clock only read *04:43*, I knew I was done sleeping for the night. Moe's tail gave the bedspread a couple of halfhearted thumps as soon as I switched on the nightstand lamp. He yawned, his tongue curling like a question mark before he cocked his head, regarding me with a curious expression on his face. Or maybe he was annoyed—it was hard to tell.

"Go back to sleep," I told him. "There's no reason you should have a rotten night, too."

He didn't, though, and was standing on the bed with his tail wagging by the time I finished pulling on jeans and a hoodie. He jumped down when I grabbed my shoes and turned off the lamp, moving beside me like a darker patch of night as I crept past Mom's room in my socks, heading downstairs.

Moe trotted out ahead of me when I exited the front door, probably to go sniff out the perfect spot to pee, while I sat on the porch steps to lace on my hiking boots. An overcast sky blotted out the stars and all but concealed a sliver of moon that peeked through a gash in the clouds out over the ocean. Moe came back just as I stood, and he fell into place beside me as we moved out into the darkness. A wind that smelled like rain was blowing from the northwest, chilly but not really cold, and the restless gusts matched my mood about perfectly.

We wandered around aimlessly for a while, eventually ending up by the vineyard's dilapidated fence line. I leaned my back against what had been a gate post, listening to the vines creak softly, rubbing against one another as the breeze rustled through the overgrown tangle. The sound was oddly soothing, and I thought about how the deep green of the leaves was steadily giving way to copper and rust, brown and gold as autumn came to Windward Cove. Of course, at that lonely hour the vineyard was just a black, undulating mass, and I found myself missing the soft laughter that had sometimes drifted out from it back when Mom and I had first moved to town. I wondered idly if the vines missed it, too, but then realized that was stupid—sentimental nonsense from a brain that needed sleep. *Get a grip, big guy.*

Instead, I turned my mind to what was keeping me awake in the first place: the weird things that had been happening lately. *All just freak occurrences, right?* I thought, and then shrugged. *Yeah, probably.* After all, absolutely none of the events were related. Darlene's shattered elbow and the ice that shouldn't have been there. That flock of birds attacking Brianna. Lights exploding and a disco ball falling from the ceiling for no reason. Even the game against Ranier High, with Alan and Dozer flailing around like they had never handled a football before. Odd? Sure, but there wasn't a single thing to connect any of them.

Except Darren, the voice in the back of my head reminded me. *After all, each of those events happened to someone who had pissed him off, and Darren was there to watch it every time.*

I shook my head, dismissing the thought. That wasn't fair, or even realistic. How could anyone do those things? And even if it were possible, just because I had noticed Darren hanging around didn't mean that he was to blame. After all, Silver Creek wasn't that big a school, and there were probably any number of people who'd been nearby at the time—me included. Did that make me Colonel Mustard in the ballroom with the lead pipe? Nope. So, what was more likely? That Darren was channeling his inner Carrie and taking revenge for a lifetime of being picked on? Or that he was a social outcast and an annoying douchebag, and I was unconsciously tying him to all those events because I didn't particularly like him and he had just been in the wrong place at the wrong time?

I knew the answer to that...and it made me feel dumb for even considering Option A.

Then there's the smell, I remembered. Cloyingly sweet...spicy... earthy. I had been close to Darren lots of times, and the odor from whatever laundry detergent the Lynches used (along with the faint, sour whiff of Darren's underlying B.O.) was nothing like that. For all I knew, the presence of the smell was just coincidence, too—perfume worn by some girl who happened to be in the vicinity, just like I had been.

So, we're back where we started.

The darkness was deepening as the gap in the clouds slowly closed over the moon, so I turned to make my way back toward the house while I could still see. I was nearly there when I paused, halfway remembering something Les had said. What was it? Something about Gypsy blood? And curses?

I stood there, the chilly wind at my back blowing my hair into my eyes while Moe whined, looking up at me curiously. *No*, I thought, shaking my head. *No…that's just crazy.* The idea made me flash back to the classic film *The Wolf Man*, where the old gypsy Maleva tells Larry Talbot, "*Even a man who is pure of heart, and says his prayers by night… may become a wolf when the wolfsbane blooms and the autumn moon is bright.*" I smiled, trying to imagine Darren with gold earrings and a silk kerchief on his head, telling fortunes and riding to school in a brightly painted wagon. What a pile of crap.

Still, the voice in the back of my head mused, *it would explain a lot.*
I snorted. C'mon…was that *really* what I was thinking?
No.
No, of course not.
Are you freaking kidding *me?*
(…)
…Maybe?
I started walking again, shoving the thought aside. It was way too early in the day for ideas that stupid.

Just the same, the notion stayed with me, wiggling around in the back of my mind and trying to get comfortable. It was annoying, like an itch in the middle of my back that I couldn't quite reach. I thought about going back to bed, hoping that a few hours' sleep would restore my common sense, but I was still far too restless. I wandered around the house for a while before it finally occurred to me that I could kill some time by getting an early start on Mom's and my weekend chores. Not my first choice for fun-filled activities, but what the hey—it wasn't like

I had anything else going on at oh-dark-thirty on a Sunday morning, so I started in.

Having something to do with my hands gave me time to think, too, although since my brain kept circling back to the whole Gypsy curse idea, I wasn't sure if that was a good thing or not. Surprisingly, though, instead of talking myself out of it, the longer I considered the idea, the less outrageous it began to seem. After all, what did I know about curses…or even Gypsies? About as much as I did about nuclear physics, which was zilch. And who the hell was I to just arbitrarily dismiss it as bullshit, anyway? After all, most people scoffed at the idea of mental abilities like mine, and yet there I was, proving them wrong every day. So, just for the sake of argument, what if there actually was something to it? Not in an Amazing Bela, Master of the Crystal Ball kind of way—that was too far in left field, even for me—but something else? Some underlying truth beneath all the folklore, stereotypes, and Hollywood crap?

What *if?*

And even if it all turns out to be just as silly as it seems, I thought, *it wouldn't hurt to look into it, right?*

Hmm.

No…no, it wouldn't.

So I kept working. And thinking.

Everything was pretty much done by a little after 8:00 when Mom came down for her coffee, and after she finished gushing about how wonderful I was, I took a break from my thoughts to tell her about the dance—and Kelly's and my new status—while she made breakfast. Of course, she teased me some (which I had expected) but overall, she didn't give me too hard a time about it. She couldn't resist the chance to pass on some relationship advice, though, which I supposed I should have seen coming. I probably rolled my eyes three or four times, and said, "I *know*, Mom," at least twice, but inwardly I realized she was offering some good pointers. Don't brag, don't take Kelly for granted, don't forget to keep the primary focus on being friends, that sort of thing—total dick mistakes that I hoped I would have avoided all on my own, but part of me was glad to have her point out just the same. After all, if I was going to be a boyfriend, there was no sense in screwing it up before the first week was out, was there?

At last Mom was finished, and she even said she would take care of the dishes. Between that and the fact that all my teachers had gone easy on weekend homework assignments—probably because of the dance—I was free and clear for the day.

Does life get any better than that?

I was on my bike and pedaling for town less than ten minutes later, Moe trotting tirelessly alongside me. The wind still smelled like rain, gusting insistently beneath dark, sullen clouds that hung low in the sky. I had gotten used to reading the coastal weather, though, and was pretty sure I had until at least midafternoon before it started dumping on me. Plenty of time.

Ab lived in a green, craftsman-style house on McKennedy Street, and as I coasted up the walk it occurred to me that I probably should have called first. Neither of her parents' cars were in the driveway, and I hoped I hadn't come all that way for nothing. Stepping into the shadows under the deep front porch, I leaned my bike against the railing and rang the bell. Fifteen or twenty seconds went by and I rang it again, starting to think I was out of luck. Then I heard footfalls from inside and I smiled when Ab opened the door, squinting up at me through the screen with her hair mashed and corkscrewed from her pillow. "Wolfman...hey," she said, her voice raspy. "What's up?" She was barefoot, wearing blue flannel pajama bottoms and a matching tank shirt, and she crossed her bare arms over her chest as the breeze ghosted inside.

"Can I talk to you about something?"

"In the middle of the night?"

I grinned. "It's almost 9:30 in the morning."

She yawned, scratching her left armpit, and then shrugged. "Okay… in that case, you can come in."

She stood aside as Moe and I stepped into the entry hall, and I heard an angry hiss from my right. Looking down, I saw Goblin, Ab's orange-and-black calico, glare at Moe with her ears folded back. The cat then turned and glided up the stairwell, growling.

"Great…now *she'll* be pissed off for the rest of the day," Ab said. She didn't sound all that bothered by it, though, and we followed her through the family room to the kitchen at the back of the house. "Juice?" she asked.

"No, thanks—I'm good." Moe curled up on a rug by the stove while I moved to the table, and I watched Ab pour herself a glass of OJ before dropping into the chair next to mine. She folded one leg, sitting with her left foot up on the seat bottom, and I noticed a tiny silver ring on her second toe. It surprised me a little, though I wasn't sure why. Maybe I had just never noticed it before.

Ab swished a little of the juice around in her mouth before swallowing. "Okay, so what's on your mind?"

"Have you thought much about the stuff that's been going on lately?" I began. "You know, like that flock of birds going after Brianna…or last night, with all the lights?"

Ab shrugged, drinking more juice.

"Don't you think it's weird?"

She grinned. "It's Windward Cove, Wolfman. Weird is our normal." Her grin faded, though, replaced by a thoughtful expression as I told her about the feelings of vindictive satisfaction my gift had picked up, as well as the musky smell that so often seemed to accompany the strange events. "So…what? You think they're all connected somehow?" Ab frowned, shaking her head. "I don't see it."

"Just go with me on this for a second. What if…" I hesitated, pretty sure I was about to make a fool of myself, but pressing on before I had time to talk myself out of it. "What if someone is *making* these things happen?"

"Yeah? How?"

I wet my lips. Talking about this stuff would have been *so* much easier if I could gauge Ab's feelings, but I had never been able to. She was one of those rare people I couldn't read. It was like her emotions ran on a slightly different frequency, or a sound pitched just a little too high or low to be within my range of hearing. It felt weird to me sometimes— almost like she wasn't really there—but I had mostly gotten used to it. "You're, uh…probably going to think I'm out of my mind."

"I think that a lot."

I gave her an annoyed look, but let it go. "This morning I remembered something Les told me. You know that story about Darren threatening to put a curse on Rick Hastings?"

Ab snorted. "*Everybody* knows that one, Wolfman."

She was looking at me expectantly, but I just stared at her.

Her smile faded again. "C'mon…you can't be serious."

"I know it sounds stupid…"

"You *think?*"

"…but what if there's something to it?" I insisted. "What if it's like a lot of legends that seem silly to us now because they've been exaggerated and blown out of proportion? What if, underneath it all, there's some truth to it?"

Ab sighed. "Let me get this straight. Are you telling me you actually believe in this stuff?"

"No," I told her. "But six months ago, I didn't believe in ghosts, either."

That got her. Ab opened her mouth, then closed it again as she settled back with her eyebrows raised, thinking it over.

"Maybe it's all crap," I went on. "Hell, it's *probably* all crap. But it doesn't cost us anything to find out, right?"

Ab held my gaze with hers for a few seconds. She still looked dubious, but her resistance appeared to ease. At last, she shook her head. "*Gawd*, the things you do for your best friend. Fine…you want me to play *Nancy Drew and the Gypsy Curse*, I guess I can do that." She stood, picking up her glass and heading back out into the family room. "Come on. Let's do some research."

Moe and I trailed along as she went upstairs, and I was three or four steps from the top when I suddenly realized what Ab had said: *best friend.*

I paused long enough to smile.

Cool.

FOURTEEN

I HAD NEVER BEEN UPSTAIRS AT AB'S HOUSE, SO I ASSUMED hers would be one of the bedrooms on the second floor. Instead, she ducked through a narrow doorway in the upstairs hall, and Moe and I followed her up a second flight of stairs to the attic. The space was huge, probably twenty feet wide and spanning the whole length of the house, with high, gabled windows and no walls—just a ceiling that peaked in the middle and slanted down to the floor as it followed the roof line. Mismatched bookshelves lined both sides, along with an antique dresser, a paper-strewn table with a big Hewlett Packard all-in-one computer, and a free-standing wardrobe that looked big enough to send you to Narnia. A futon bed was centered against the chimney where it climbed the far wall, the sheets and blankets all twisted and bunched up like a couple of bears had been wrestling in there, beneath a framed, black-and-white poster that stood out against the bricks. The poster caught my attention right away, showing a ghostly apparition descending a wide, old-fashioned flight of stairs. "That's cool," I said, pointing.

"My dad had that framed for me," Ab explained. "It's the Brown Lady of Raynham Hall. The photo was taken back in the thirties, and is still one of the most famous pictures ever of a real ghost." Then she pushed me toward the table with the computer while she headed toward the dresser. "But don't get distracted. Get online and open up the storehouse of all human knowledge."

"What…the Library of Congress?"

"Wikipedia."

Sitting down, I noticed that the computer was already on, so I wiggled the mouse to wake it up from standby mode. Immediately her desktop image filled the screen, and I smiled when I recognized the photo: Ab, Les, and me in our swimsuits up at Hermit Springs. Les was grinning beside me as we stood waist deep in the water. Ab was seated on my shoulders, her mouth open as she had been caught in mid-whoop, her hands raised over her head and curled in Hang Loose gestures. That had been in early August, and I remembered Nicole had taken the picture with her phone.

A good day.

The photo disappeared as I opened up Ab's web browser, and I saw that Wikipedia was on her shortcuts menu. "You know all this stuff is unverified, right?" I asked, waiting for the page to load.

"Oh, I know," she answered behind me, and I could hear her opening and closing dresser drawers. "But it's a good way to get a head start, and most of the time there are links to source material. We have to begin somewhere, right? So instead of searching the whole internet, why not start where somebody has already done some of the heavy lifting?"

I shrugged, typing *Gypsy Curses* into the search field, and then frowned when the results popped up with suggestions for different links rather than a specific article. Scanning the page, I saw that a lot of the suggestions were for various horror movies (most of which I had seen), but then my eye finally landed on *Romani Mythology*, so I clicked on that and started to read. "It says here that Gypsies are actually the Romani people," I reported after a few seconds. "They're thought to have originated in India and migrated to Europe during the Middle Ages."

"Yeah?" Ab asked, leaning over my shoulder to look at the screen. She was finishing pulling a sweatshirt down over her midsection while she did it, and I realized that she had been getting dressed while I sat at her computer. The thought that she had probably been naked right behind me made feel a little weird, but I shoved the idea aside before I had a chance to dwell on it. Best friend status must come with a lot of trust attached.

"'*Romani people*' in that first sentence is a link," Ab said, dragging over a second chair. "Click on it, and let's see where it goes."

I did what I was told, and that started us down the rabbit hole. A couple of hours and who knows how many web sites later, though, and we didn't know anything more about Gypsy curses than we had starting out. We had skimmed dozens of articles about Romani culture, learning that they had been historically persecuted wherever they traveled and were even among the people targeted for extermination by the Nazis. We had also learned that the first Romani immigrated to the United States somewhere in the 1850s, and even now they were still largely misunderstood as a people. It was all interesting stuff, just not what we were after. The closest we came was finding out that a curse was defined as "*An appeal or prayer for evil or misfortune to befall someone or something.*" There were also a number of new-age web sites offering advice or practical steps on how to *remove* a curse, but none of the pages we found—none that seemed credible, anyway—really got into how they were supposed to work.

"I guess you were right," I said at last, feeling frustrated. "This *was* a stupid idea."

"Oh, I don't know," Ab mused, sitting back in her chair. "Maybe we're just going about it all wrong."

"How do you mean?"

"Instead of sorting through all this stuff about the Romani, maybe we'd have better luck sorting through Darren. After all, we don't even know if he's really descended from Gypsies, or if he just made it up."

That deflated my mood even more. "Yeah, that occurred to me, too. After all, if he could curse people, you would think he would have done it long before now."

Ab shook her head. "Actually, that's the part I *don't* have a problem with. I read somewhere that it's common for a lot of paranormal stuff to only begin happening to kids once they hit their teens. Something to do with hormones, I think."

"Okay, so what do we do?"

"Maybe it's time Mr. Peabody and Sherman took a ride in the Wayback Machine." Ab reached over to pull the keyboard in front of her and typed *myfamilyline.com* into the web address field. A page opened up with a graphic of a big tree, with little round photos of people hanging from the branches like fruit. "I use this site a lot when researching a haunting," she explained. "It's not as good as a lot of the bigger genealogy web sites, but there are links to all kinds of government census and birth record data. Best of all, since it's free, every family tree is open for anyone to look at." Ab clicked on a menu item at the top that read *Find Family*, which took her to a page where she entered *Lynch* into the *Family Name* field, and Silver Creek's zip code in the box marked *City/ State or Zip*. Last of all was a dropdown menu marked *Search Radius* where she selected *50 Miles,* and then clicked a button marked *Find*.

A little hourglass graphic turned over three or four times before *NO RECORDS FOUND* appeared in the results field.

"Crap," I muttered.

"Oh, quit whining," she replied, clicking on the *Area* field again. "All that probably means is that Darren's family hasn't been around here long enough for the census data to be released as public record yet. So, relax…if it were easy, it wouldn't be fun."

I sat back and kept my mouth shut, realizing that Ab was in her element. I watched as she typed *Rome, NY*, and my interest piqued again. It never occurred to me to try Gina's home town, and I admired Ab for thinking to link Darren's family through her. Ab also increased the search radius to *200 Miles* before clicking *Find.* The little hourglass spun even longer before the screen lit up with a long list of people beneath *1138 RECORDS FOUND.* Each entry included a little graphic of the part of the state that person lived, and as Ab skimmed through the results, I realized that the search engine had sorted the hits by distance, starting with *Lynch, Charles E., 1972—Present* in Rome, and ending up with *Lynch, Susannah (née Szymanski) 1847—1902* all the way up in Buffalo.

"Jackpot," Ab said.

"That's a lot of Lynches," I remarked, and then I grinned. "In fact, you could say it's a whole Lynch *mob*."

She shot me a disgusted look. "This is going to take a while. Why don't you make yourself useful—like finding me something to eat while I go through this? I'm starving."

Still snickering, I got up and left her to it, heading for the stairs with Moe trailing behind me. Down in the kitchen, I rummaged around in the refrigerator until I found some eggs, an open package of bacon, and some sliced cheddar. None of them looked like they were doing anything important, so I hunted around until I found a skillet and started cooking her up a breakfast sandwich. I was waiting for the bread to finish toasting when my phone chimed with a text from Kelly: [HEY…R U ALIVE?]

Smiling, I leaned back against the counter while tapping out a reply: [YEP. U?]

[TIRED, BUT GOOD. SLEPT UNTIL ALMOST 11, LOL. WHAT R U DOING L8R?]

[No plans.]

[Good! Want to see you! :-D]

I felt a warm, tingly rush. [Where and when?]

[Still need to shower/dress, so give me an hour? I'll come get u.]

That seemed more sooner than later to me, but I shrugged. [Cool. C u then]

[xo]

I grinned as I stuffed my phone back into my jacket pocket. Having a girlfriend was already awesome. Then I noticed that smoke was billowing from both toaster slots. *Crap!* The slices ended up blackened beyond repair, but on my second try I managed toast a couple more without burning the place down and carried Ab's sandwich up to the attic. "You could have told me your toaster doesn't work right," I said, sliding the plate next to her.

"The toaster doesn't work right," she replied absently, never taking her eyes off the screen, and then took a bite of the sandwich. "Mm—not bad. Thanks, Wolfman."

"How's the search coming?"

"Great. The very first hit turned out to be Gina's dad. And we're in luck—Charles has a second cousin named Emily up in Rochester who put together a pretty good family tree, so once I figure out how their families are related, I might be able to pin down where Darren fits in and see if there are any Gypsies back on his woodpile."

"How long will that take?"

Ab shrugged. "Depends. Lining up ancestors is the easy part. Finding out who they really were takes a lot more digging. Sometimes you can find something on Google just by entering a name, but most of the time not. Luckily, more and more libraries and local newspapers have old back issues saved online, so there are all kinds of ways to find bits of information—birth and marriage announcements, obituaries, society pages, what have you. It's even easier if they had actual articles written about them. The trick is to pick one name at a time and chase it down. Sometimes there's a lot out there, but most of the time there's little or nothing. You never know until you look, and it takes time."

"Oh."

I must have sounded disappointed, because Ab turned her head to look at me. "What? You have something else to do?"

I grimaced in embarrassment. "Yeah, Kelly texted me while I was in the kitchen. I'm supposed to meet her in…" I glanced at my watch "…just over forty-five minutes. Sorry. I didn't know this would be so involved." I started to dig my phone out of my pocket. "I'll let her know I can't make it."

Ab rolled her eyes, shaking her head. "You're such an idiot, Wolfman. *Go*—get out of here. Girlfriends need care and attention. Besides, there's nothing you can really do here anyway, and it'll go a lot faster if you're not hovering."

I frowned, feeling guilty. "Are you sure? I don't want to leave you hanging if there's some way I can help."

"I'm sure. You've got me interested now, so I want to see if there's anything to this." She made a shooing gesture with one hand. "Now take off. I'll text you if I find anything."

"Thanks—you're the best!"

But she had already turned back toward the screen. "Why, yes… yes I am," she murmured, her fingers typing rapidly on the keyboard.

The wind had really picked up, gusting almost directly in my face and making the ride home take forever, and I had just put my bike away and let Moe into the house when Kelly pulled up out front.

"Hey," I said, sliding into the passenger side, and then leaned over to give her a quick kiss. I was reaching for my seatbelt when Kelly grabbed a fistful of my shirt and dragged me back over, her mouth finding mine in a long, deep kiss that left me short of breath and feeling twenty degrees warmer all over.

"Better," Kelly said, grinning as she released me at last.

"*Much* better," I agreed, smiling back. "Wow…looks like I need to bring up my game."

"You just need practice."

"Show me the ways of The Force, Obi-Wan."

She laughed, pulling her Jeep in a U-turn, and we headed back toward town.

Kelly was hungry, so we grabbed some tacos at Chuy's, a Mexican place across the street and just three or four doors up from Tsunami Joe. We sat there for a long time after we finished, holding hands across the table, and talking about all sorts of things we'd never gotten around to. I found out that her favorite color was green, that snakes scared her but spiders didn't, and that she loved Mel Brooks movies because she used to watch them with her dad—stuff like that. I also learned that for years she had dreamed of being a TV news anchor, but had recently started thinking that maybe nursing or physical therapy might be better, and that while she used to love Thanksgiving and Christmas, she now dreaded the holidays because they reminded her of her sister.

I told her about my life before moving to Windward Cove, and shared some of my likes and dislikes as well, but in the back of my mind I was wondering when the right time would be to tell her about my mental abilities—or even if I should. I knew that trying to keep it all secret forever was not the right choice, but I wasn't ready just yet to open up and let her know I was a freak, either. Finally, I gave up and tossed the question on the Too Hard pile, deciding that I didn't need to decide right away.

That's me: Mr. Decisive.

Finally, after the late lunch crowd was long gone and our waiter had stopped by half a dozen times or so to ask if we were *sure* he couldn't get us anything else, we finally took the hint and got out of there, running to Kelly's Jeep through the lashing rain that had finally rolled in to pummel downtown.

"Where to next?" I asked.

Kelly only smiled in answer, and then drove us up a narrow, potholed road just south of town to where Windward Cove Cemetery sat on a bluff overlooking the Pacific. The wind was a lot stronger out in the open, and as we approached, I could see the scattering of eucalyptus trees sway, their heavy boughs nearly brushing the headstones and sending dead leaves winging through the air. The afternoon was growing more and more gloomy as we pulled through the rusted, wrought-iron gate, and Kelly turned right, following a ribbon of asphalt to the west side of the grounds. At last she pulled off the pavement, stopping well back from the cliff's edge, and turned off the engine.

Our vantage point gave us a sweeping view of the ocean. The water was almost the same slate gray as the sky, with big swells rolling toward shore and wind-driven whitecaps sending spray high into the air as they crashed against the rocks below. I was about to say something about it when I felt Kelly's hand on my neck. I looked over as, smiling, she pulled my face toward hers.

It turned out she hadn't brought me there for the view.

FIFTEEN

"*ALL RIGHT, FELLAS, HERE'S YOUR STORY,*" I QUOTED. "*North Pole, November third, Ned Scott reporting. One of the world's greatest battles was fought and won today by the human race. Here at the top of the world a handful of American soldiers and civilians met the first invasion from another planet…*"

Squinting past the stage lights, I could barely make out the faces of my drama class in the darkness of the auditorium. A few were watching me—some attentively, others wearing vaguely confused expressions—but the rest were either staring at their phones or just looking bored. I didn't know which was worse: their indifference, or the impatience I could sense from those behind me as they waited for me to finish. Our assignment had been to deliver a short monologue from a play or movie to get us used to performing in front of people, and I had picked the final scene from *The Thing from Another World*. Judging by everyone's reactions, though, it didn't look like I was exactly wowing them. That, or it was just one more example of an old movie no one else had seen but me. Either way, there was nothing to do but get it over with, so I pressed on:

"*The flying saucer which landed here and its pilot have been destroyed, but not without causalities among our own meager forces. I would like to bring to the microphone some of the men responsible for our success, but senior Air Force officer Captain Hendry is attending to demands over and above the call of duty, and Doctor Carrington, the leader of the scientific expedition, is recovering from wounds received in the battle. And now before giving you the details, I bring you a warning: Every one of you listening to my voice, tell the world, tell this to everybody wherever they are. Watch the skies. Everywhere. Keep looking. Keep watching the skies!*"

There was an awkward silence for three or four seconds before anyone realized I was done, followed by a few snickers mixed with a round of scattered, polite applause. I turned and slunk back to my chair, feeling like a total dweeb.

"Nice job, Ben," Mr. Davis called up from the front row. "A little slower next time, though, and remember to *project*—like your grandma is in the back row and she forgot her hearing aids. Darren Lynch… you're up!"

Darren rose and moved to center stage. He stood there, looking nervous and uncertain for a few seconds before suddenly roaring, "*HOLD YOUR GROUND!*" A couple of kids jerked back in their seats, startled, as everyone else looked up in surprise. "*Hold your ground! Sons of Gondor, of Rohan, my brothers! I see in your eyes the same fear that would take the heart of me…*"

I recognized it right away: Aragorn's speech from the third *Lord of the Rings* movie. The scene where he rallies his army just as the orc horde comes marching out the black gate of Mordor. I felt a stab of admiration, wishing I'd thought of it.

Most of the class had delivered their monologues over the previous couple of days, leaving the last nine of us seated in a semicircle on stage.

I had been third from the last. Cece Ramos would follow Darren, and then we were done. I glanced at my watch as Darren bellowed on, glad to see we only had a few minutes left before the bell. It was warm under the lights, and besides, I was going to see Lisette after school.

I had woken up that morning feeling a need to go see her. It was one of those special intuitions I get every now and then, a vague but insistent feeling that wouldn't leave my brain alone—like an annoying kid in the back seat who keeps asking *are we there yet?* over and over until it was hard to think of anything else. It was the part of my abilities I experienced only once in a while, and even though sometimes it turned out to be nothing, it was right most of the time, and I'd learned to pay attention to it. *I just hope nothing's wrong,* I thought, but then shook off the idea. I would find out soon enough, and anyway, I needed to pay attention.

"*By all that you hold dear on this good Earth,*" Darren cried, coming to the end, "*I bid you stand, Men of the West!*" His voice cracked on the last word, causing most of the class to chuckle, and Darren flushed. Turning, he paused when he saw Cece giggling into her hand. Even though she didn't look mean-spirited about it—not as far as I could see, anyway—I could sense his embarrassment deepen to humiliation as he slunk back to his chair.

That had to suck, I thought. Nobody wants to see the girl he likes laugh at him.

"Settle down, people," Mr. Davis called out. "Don't sweat it, Darren—it happens to everybody sooner or later. But you did alright. Great on volume, but you need to work on your inflection to put some emotion into it, okay? Celeste Ramos…care to finish us up?"

Cece rose and moved forward. "*Welcome to Hogwarts,*" she quoted, doing a pretty fair Professor McGonagall. "*Now, in a few moments you will pass through these doors and join your classmates, but before you can take your seats, you must be sorted into your houses…*"

I leaned back, grinning. She was really good! Just then the final bell rang, interrupting her, but afterward she picked up again right where she'd left off. The sound of students leaving school for the day rose faintly from outside, but we all kept our seats, continuing to watch her with interest.

I guess we know who the Harry Potter fans are, I thought.

She was getting to the part where the first-year witches and wizards could gain or lose points for their houses when I caught a whiff of the familiar odor…earthy and cloyingly sweet. I sat up straight, frowning in sudden alarm as my gaze swept the hall. Then I noticed Cece's shadow wavering back and forth at her feet, and I looked up at the high ceiling in time to see the lighting rig sway alarmingly, as if pushed by a gust of wind. Then, with an audible snap, the cable attaching it to the rafters on the far side suddenly broke free! Startled shrieks rose up as the metal rig swung downward, heavy with a dozen or so big stage lights. I was closest, and leapt from my chair barely in time to tackle Cece out of the way. We landed hard, her head bouncing against the stage as her elbow slammed into my gut, knocking the wind out of me. The free end of the rig crashed into the stage right where she had been standing, the impact shattering the old wood and leaving it partially imbedded. One of the lights broke loose, clattering to a stop less than three feet from us, and I turned my face away as it lit us up in its hot glare.

Then we were surrounded as everyone rushed over, veering around the wreckage, or climbing onto the stage, and I rolled off Cece just as someone killed power to the rig and brought up the house lights. I took my time, looking up at the ceiling while trying to get my breath back, and then Mr. Davis moved into my field of vision. "Oh my God!" he said, looking terrified. "Are you two alright?"

"I…I think so," I heard Cece say weakly, and I rolled my head to look over as a boy and girl helped her to her feet. Her right cheekbone was reddening where it had smacked against the floorboards, and it looked like it would probably turn into a pretty good bruise. *I bet that hurt*, I thought offhandedly as hands reached down to haul me up. I stood for a second or two, swaying with momentary dizziness, and then noticed Darren in my peripheral vision. His face was pale as he backed toward the semicircle of chairs, and then grabbed his backpack from beside his seat. As he snatched it up, a book tumbled from a pocket he had left unzipped, landing on the floor behind him as he crossed the stage and made his way down the stairs. I followed him with my gaze, watching him brush past Gina where she waited for him at an open side exit, a questioning expression on her face. Then the door swung shut and they were gone.

Hmm.

"Ben? Are you alright?" Mr. Davis asked again, turning toward me.

I nodded. "Yeah, I'm good. Cece…you okay?"

"I'm fine," the pretty girl said, her voice still sounding a little shaky. "Thank you *so* much!"

I nodded, smiling at her.

Mr. Davis clapped me on the shoulder. "That was quick thinking, Ben. Ten points to Gryffindor!"

Everyone else laughed in relief, but I only pretended to while my gaze drifted back to Darren's book lying beside his chair.

A little over twenty minutes later I was pedaling my bike slowly, hanging back maybe a hundred yards behind Darren and Gina as I followed them up a potholed street on the northern edge of Silver Creek. The neighborhood was the exact opposite of the one where Kelly lived, with tired-looking houses that needed paint and most of the yards overgrown with tall weeds. Some of the porches had been halfheartedly decorated as we entered the beginning of October—pumpkins and dried cornstalks, fake spiderwebs and even a scarecrow here and there—but mostly not. The homes had become more widely spaced the farther we got from downtown, and I began to worry that Darren or Gina would glance back and see me before they got home. At last, though, they turned into the yard of a white frame house that looked even more tired than the rest, and I coasted to a stop as I watched them disappear inside.

Okay big guy, I thought. *So, what now?*

I didn't have much in the way of a plan. Ever since the homecoming game, I had been trying to decide whether the feelings of vindictive satisfaction I'd been picking up whenever something weird happened were coming from Darren. After all, he still seemed to be the most likely suspect. There was no way of knowing without getting closer to him, though, and so far, that had turned out to be even tougher than I had thought. I had tried a number of times to strike up casual conversations with him, but even when he didn't ignore me completely, the best I'd gotten were a few single-syllable replies. The thing was, when he wasn't watching over Gina like a hawk, all he seemed interested in were the fantasy novels he kept reading one after another. So I had followed them home, hoping to use the book he had dropped as a way to finally break the ice.

Besides, I needed something to do. Ab was still spending most of her spare time climbing around in the Lynch family tree, and had told me a couple of days before to quit pestering her for updates. I had given in and left her alone to work, but having no way to contribute was making me feel useless. Even so, I probably could have sucked it up and waited, but the near-catastrophe in the auditorium had made my need to get to the bottom of things a lot more urgent. I still couldn't see how it was possible, but if the weird events really did have something to do with Darren, I wanted to find out sooner rather than later—before someone *really* got hurt.

And what then? the voice in the back of my head prodded. *Even if Darren turns out to be responsible somehow, what do you expect to do about it?*

I didn't have a plan for that, either.

Ben Wolf, master strategist.

I gave them five minutes or so to get settled in, and then rode the rest of the way up the street. The Lynch home was shaded by a tall, crooked pine that had choked the rain gutters and covered nearly a quarter of the roof in a deep thatch of dead needles. Three old cars and a pickup truck were parked out back beside a shed where the sound of AC/DC's *Thunderstruck* drifted out a set of double doors. Only the truck and one car looked like they had been driven in a while. I leaned my bike against the stair railing and climbed onto the porch where an old sofa sagged beneath the front windows. One of the window panes was cracked and had been mended with clear tape.

I didn't see a doorbell, so I knocked instead.

The door opened after a few seconds to reveal Gina. "Ben…*hey!*" she said, brightening as the initial surprise I had sensed from her was quickly replaced by excitement. That, and a feeling of tender longing that I did my best to ignore as she offered me a smile. "What are you doing here?"

"I came by to see Darren," I told her. "I hope that's okay."

"Sure! Come on in." She stepped back, pulling the door open, and I moved past her into a narrow entry hall. "He's down in his room. I'll show you the way, but you'll need to take your shoes off first. Aunt Roxie doesn't want anyone tracking dirt on the carpet."

I kicked off my sneakers, adding them to the line of family shoes arranged neatly to one side, and then followed Gina past an intersecting hall that I assumed led to bedrooms in the back of the house. "Nice place," I said as we passed through the family room, noting that while the inside of the house was showing its age, it was spotlessly clean. I supposed I had been expecting the interior to be as neglected as the outside, and I suspected that Gina's aunt and uncle had different areas of responsibility.

Gina led me through the kitchen and opened a door on the back wall to reveal a set of stairs leading into darkness. "Darren!" she called. "Can we come down?"

"Who's *we*?" he called back.

Gina took that for a yes, and after smiling back over her shoulder, led me down the bare wood steps to the basement. The space was cavernous. A water heater, furnace, and a washer and dryer were lined up beneath the stairs, but the rest of the room was clearly Darren's territory. Rough wooden shelves ran along the far wall, crammed with books, comics, models, and assorted guy-stuff, beneath a row of narrow windows that ran along the low ceiling at ground level. A pulled-out sofa bed sat opposite a console TV that was probably older than all three of us put together, a cluster of ancient video game systems and controllers crowded on top amid a snarl of wires. There was also a worn recliner and a table with mismatched chairs. Posters were taped to the cinder block walls, mostly split between fantasy scenes and Marvel superhero movies, along with a couple of hot-looking models wearing seductive expressions and not much else.

It was awesome.

"What's *he* doing here?" Darren asked suspiciously. He sat at a rust-scarred metal desk that was roughly the size of a navy destroyer, lit by a combination lamp and magnifying glass on the end of an adjustable arm. He held a narrow brush in one hand, with assorted paints in tiny jars arranged on a sheet of newspaper in front of him.

"Oh, quit being rude," Gina admonished, looking embarrassed. "Ben's our *friend*, Darren!"

"Check out the Batcave!" I said admiringly, ignoring his attitude as I made a show of gawking around. I wasn't sure what I had been expecting, but it wasn't this. It didn't look like the hideout of someone able to throw curses, but what did I know? "You have all this space to *yourself*? Dude, I'm totally jealous!"

He just stared at me, but I could sense Darren's suspicion begin to ease grudgingly. I pulled his book from the inside pocket of my jacket. "You dropped this on your way out of class," I told him, strolling over, and then I glanced at the cover. It showed a teenage boy in jeans and a flannel shirt surrounded by a company of fantasy dwarves. The dwarves were staring at a blue amulet about the size of a hen's egg the boy wore around his neck. "*The Dance of the Ocurrie,*" I read aloud. "Any good?"

Darren glanced at Gina, as if for reassurance, and then back at me. "Yeah," he admitted, reaching out to take the book. "It's one of my favorites. I've read the whole series twice."

"Maybe you'll let me borrow it when you're done?"

Darren hesitated, still studying me with uncertainty, and then surprised me by handing it back.

Progress.

I looked past his shoulder, grinning as I recognized some books on a shelf above his desk—worn editions of the Dungeons and Dragons *Player's Handbook, Dungeon Master's Guide,* and *Monster Manual,* along with several notebooks and an impressive number of adventure campaigns. "Hey! You never said you were into D&D." Then I looked at his desktop, noting that he had been painting one of the tiny figurines players used when setting up game combat. His brush work was detailed, showing that Darren had a steady hand. "Wow, you're really good. I suck at painting, so my figures are all plain."

"You *play*?" he asked, sounding surprised.

"Are you kidding? A couple of years ago I used to play like a madman. Back in my old town there was a group of us who got together just about every week, with an all-nighter at least once a month. My buddy Steve was an awesome DM, and my other friends Chris, Rich, and Bill were just as hardcore as I was."

"Maybe you can play with us," Gina volunteered hopefully, stepping forward to touch my arm.

Darren frowned at her. "Since when are *you* interested? You never want to play."

"Only because I keep getting killed," she argued defensively, and then turned back, giving me a shy smile. "Darren tried to teach me, but I'm *terrible.*"

"Solo games are rough," I told her. "Unless you're used to managing several characters at once."

"I just have one. An elf ranger named Summerfox. Maybe *you* can help keep her alive."

I shrugged, giving her Mr. Casual, but inwardly I was excited by the opportunity. This was exactly the sort of thing I had been hoping for. "Maybe, but we'll probably need my wizard, Ralph the Terrific."

Gina giggled, but Darren just frowned. "Ralph the *Terrific*?"

"Yeah," I said, grinning. "Seventeenth level. Totally deadly with fireballs and lightning. He also has a staff that can cast an explosive diarrhea spell once per day."

Darren snorted. "That's not a real spell. And it sounds stupid."

I shrugged. "Not when you get hit with it. Or if you don't like him, I can bring Krobar the Barbarian."

"*Crow-bar?*"

"With a K."

Gina laughed that time, but Darren just rolled his eyes. "You're such a retard."

"Okay," I said, grinning, "final offer. There's my paladin, Elmer Fudd."

"*Elmer Fudd*?"

"Yeah. He has a speah and magic helmet, a cwossbow, and wots and wots of awwows. *Huhuhuhuhuhuhuh!*"

Gina rolled her head back, cackling, while Darren shook his head, one corner of his mouth curving ever so slightly upward.

Gotcha! I thought, feeling triumphant. Maybe it wasn't much of one, but it was still a smile.

Just then I remembered I had somewhere to be, so I checked my watch: *3:27*. I needed to get a move on. "Whoops…gotta go," I said. "Let me know if you're serious about playing, 'cause that sounds like a total blast." Gina beamed at me in a way that made me feel absolutely horrible—like I was taking advantage of her crush just so I could gather intel on her cousin.

…Which, whether I wanted to admit it or not, was pretty much the truth.

SIXTEEN

THE PLACE WHERE LISETTE GAUTIER LIVED WAS NOT far, so there was still plenty of daylight left when I swung my bike onto a short access drive past a sign that read *Autumn Leaves Residential Care Home*. The architecture was about as interesting as your average brick; a wide, flat-roofed structure laid out in a big U shape that I always thought looked more like a bunker than an old-folks home. In the center of the U was a lush flower garden that was carefully tended by some of the staff and residents, but you couldn't see it from the front. The cinder block building squatted behind a row of ancient poplar trees that had stretched out their roots far enough lift the concrete sidewalk in places and ripple the patched asphalt of the parking lot. The poplars shaded the grounds nicely in summer, but had since dropped most of their leaves and now looked skeletal with the dying year.

While half a dozen older-looking cars and a pickup truck were nosed into spaces on the side of the lot marked *Staff Parking*, the *Visitors* side was empty. Seeing that made my insides twist with another pang of guilt. All through July and August, I had made a habit of coming by to see Lisette a couple of times a week, but since school started, I hadn't made it out even once. It wasn't that I'd forgotten about her or anything, but between school and homework, and now Kelly—not to mention all the weird stuff that had been going on—there had just been too many distractions, and the time had gotten away from me. As I locked my bike to the awning post by the front entrance, I promised myself silently that I would do better.

Charlotte looked up from an issue of *McCall's Magazine* as I entered and strolled down the short entry hall. Tall, angular, and with a mole on her left cheekbone that was *really* hard not to stare at, Charlotte was one of four or five ladies who usually worked the reception desk. I liked Nancy best because she was always cheerful and seemed glad to see me, but Charlotte was okay, too. "Hello, Ben," she said. "Haven't seen you in a while. Lisette said you would be coming by this afternoon."

I smiled, half in greeting and half in silent admiration of Lisette's abilities. I never had to tell her I was coming. She always just *knew*, and I wondered for the hundredth time if my own gifts would ever be as strong as hers. The fact that she had told Charlotte to expect me was also a good sign that nothing was wrong, and my heart felt lighter with the news. "Hi, Charlotte. Is it okay to go on back?"

She gave a sideways nod of her head, indicating the hallway to my right, and raised her magazine again. "You know the way."

I thanked her and moved down the hall, passing open doors to either side where bedridden folks watched the news or afternoon talk shows, and smelling the faint odor of urine and antiseptic cleaner that always lingered in the air like the Ghost of Accidents Past. Ab had first brought me to Autumn Leaves the previous summer when we were researching the mystery surrounding my house and family, and Lisette's abilities had been a big help. Since then, she had worked with me to further develop my own gifts—Yoda to my Luke Skywalker, I guess you could say—and we had become close friends. The last time I had seen her was a few days before school started, when we had brought her out to the house for a visit and she had spent the afternoon teaching Mom, Ab, and me how to make jambalaya (well, Mom and Ab, anyway—I think I mostly just got in the way.)

Lisette's room was at the very end of the hall, with a big window overlooking empty fields dotted here and there with clusters of redwood trees and big snarls of blackberry. At night you could see the headlights of cars traveling north or south along U.S. 101 a couple of miles away. Most of the residents at Autumn Leaves were doubled up, but Lisette was one of the very few who lived alone. For whatever reason, people were uncomfortable having a roommate who could make scary-accurate predictions about pretty much everything, and somewhere along the line the management decided it was best to let her fly solo. Lisette had taken advantage of the situation, asking that the second bed be taken out and filling the space with a small table tucked between an overstuffed rocker for her and an imitation leather armchair for whoever came to visit. On the north wall was a picture of an old man saying grace over a bowl of soup, while on the south was a big tapestry of dogs playing poker. The first time I had seen it, Lisette made sure to point out that one of the bulldogs was passing an ace to his buddy under the table, laughing like she thought it was the funniest thing ever. Personally, I didn't see what was so hilarious, but was I...an art critic?

She was facing her closet with her back to me when I arrived, so I rapped on the open door frame. "Excuse me," I called out. "Publisher's Clearinghouse—you're our grand prize winner!"

The tiny Creole woman turned slightly to look back over her shoulder. "Does everybody think you're funny?" she asked, her deep-South accent as rich as warm honey. "Or jus' you?" She smiled as she said it, though, her eyes standing out against the chocolate color of her skin and glinting playfully. A pair of thick glasses swung low on her chest, suspended by a string of purple beads around her neck, and between the beads, the bright yellow of her housedress and a scarlet kerchief tied over her hair, she brightened up the room. "Now get in here, boy—I want my hug!"

I smiled as I crossed the floor, realizing just how much I had missed her. I leaned down and held her gently, careful of her brittle bones. Lisette hugged me fiercely in return, her thin arms surprisingly strong, and she kissed my cheek before stepping back to hold me at arm's length, looking me over. "Mercy, *cher*! You gettin' taller every time I see you!" Her gaze shifted momentarily as she seemed to study a spot somewhere in the air between us. Then her smile brightened as her focus returned to me. "And tha's not *all*, is it? You got all kinds of girls chasin' after you these days…and you even let one catch up, didn't you? She treatin' you right?"

Her reference to girls made me feel weird again about Gina, but I did my best to ignore it. "Oh, yeah," I answered. "Kelly treats me better than I deserve."

"Then you'd best get to work deservin' it, boy," she said, winking, "and everything will be jus' fine." She started for her rocker, waving one arm absently toward the closet. "Before you sit down, reach me that suitcase from the top shelf, will you?"

I did as she asked, pulling down a boxy suitcase that had probably been new back when Kennedy was President, its rigid sides covered in a faded, plaid-patterned cloth. Lisette pointed toward the bed and I set it down, opening the brass latches and swinging it open to release the scent of old mothballs. "Taking a trip?" I asked.

Lisette nodded as I dropped into the armchair. "Baton Rouge," she answered. "My gran'son Paul is a lawyer there, and he an' his wife are havin' their third baby. Fern wasn't expectin' her for another week an' a half, but turns out that li'l girl is of a mind to come early. Yolanda Lisette Lanier—ain't that a nice name?"

It was, and I told her so. "When did they find out?" I asked.

Lisette's gaze briefly lost focus again, but then returned to mine almost right away. "Won't be long now." A hint of a smile deepened the lines around her mouth, and I grinned, trying to imagine how her grandson and his wife would react if they found out Lisette knew their baby was coming before they did.

"This'll be their firs' girl, an' Paul gonna be so excited he'll send his brother Joe out to collect me. That'll be tomorrow—maybe the day after—an' I need to be ready to go meet my new great-gran' baby."

I was happy for Lisette that she was getting a break from Autumn Leaves for a while, but a selfish part of me was sad that she wouldn't be around. Then I remembered that I had zero right to feel that way, and the pang of guilt I had felt earlier was nothing compared to what hit me then.

"It's alright, *cher*," she said, leaning forward to pat my knee, "You got a lot goin' on, so you just come when you can." Her reassurance wasn't surprising at all. There was no way I could hide my feelings from her, and I never even bothered to try anymore. "Seems to me you got somethin' *else* on your mind, too," Lisette went on, "though I'm not real clear on what it is. You wanna tell me?"

I realized that I did, although I wasn't sure how much help she could be. "Not unless you know anything about Gypsies," I answered. "Do you?"

She settled back in her rocker, regarding me silently with an expression of mild surprise. Uneasiness rippled her emotions—something I had never sensed in Lisette before—and it roused my curiosity. At last, she reached over and pulled a tissue from the box on the table between us, frowning thoughtfully down at her glasses as she used it to wipe the lenses. "I know..." she began, her voice trailing off as she seemed to consider how to answer me, and then her gaze met mine again. "Well, let's jus' say I know all I *want* to."

Something in her tone made an icy tingle creep up my spine, but I kept my mouth shut, waiting for her to continue.

Lisette finished cleaning the left lens, and then the right. Then she held her glasses up to the light, inspecting her work, and rubbed at a spot on the right lens again before putting them on. "I only met me a Gypsy once," she began at last, "though Gypsy ain't what they called themselves—leastways, not back then. When I was a girl, they called themselves Roma or Romani, an' I 'spect they still do."

That much I already knew, but I didn't interrupt her.

"I don' know for certain, though, 'cause like I said, I only met the one…and the one I met scared me." She frowned. "You *sure* you want to hear about this?"

She sounded reluctant, but I nodded anyway.

"It was the spring I turned fourteen," Lisette began. "I remember that clear, 'cause I'd just met my Calvin the night before at a school dance." She paused, her expression warming as she relived the memory. "Lord, I was over the *moon* about that boy, *cher*, an' I guess I still am. We got married right outa high school…did I ever tell you that? Got married, and stayed together for the next fifty-four years. He was a fine man, an' I 'spect I'll be seein' him again before too long."

I must have looked alarmed because she leaned forward, chuckling as she patted my knee again. "Now, now…don' you fret. Ol' Lisette got a few more years left in her. An' anyhow, here I am wool-gatherin' when I should be tellin' you about Lavinia."

"Lavinia?"

Lisette nodded. "*Ms.* Lavinia is what everyone called her. She had a last name, surely, but I never knew anybody who'd heard it. As the story goes, her husband had been leader of their group of families for years an' years, but it was Ms. Lavinia who really decided where they'd go, how long they'd stay, and what kind of business—and trouble—they'd be up to when they got there. 'Course, after he died, the normal Romani way would be for the next oldest man to take charge, but Ms. Lavinia stepped up instead, an' no one said boo about it. They'd caravan into New Orleans every two, three years—a line of old trailers, campers on pickup trucks, station wagons an' a couple of converted school busses— an' they'd always find some farmer needin' money who was willin' to rent them space to camp.

"Aside from that sorta gossip, I didn't know much else," she continued. "We lived out on the edge of the city, so I saw 'em around every now and again, but *ma mere et ma gand-mere* always tol' me to stay away from the Romani when they was in town. Told me stories about how the boys was handsome and wild and would get a nice girl into trouble. Jus' the same, it was awful hard not to be curious. Folks said Ms. Lavinia could read the tarot deck or people's palms, tellin' fortunes like nobody'd ever seen. Girls at school said she could sell you a love potion that really worked…and if it worked *too* good, an' a girl found herself in a family way, well, she had a potion that would fix that, too. Again, I don' know how much of it was true, and how much was jus' tall tales, but that was what folks whispered about whenever Ms. Lavinia's caravan rolled into town.

"Like I said, I was fourteen the day I met her. *Ma gand-mere* had passed the summer before, so it was just Mama an' me. *Ma mere* worked for one of those rich families in the Garden District, cookin' and keepin' house, and she was there from eight in the mornin' to six at night, Sunday through Friday, with more'n half an hour on the bus each way gettin' there an' back. We wasn't exactly in high cotton, but the job paid enough—especially in those days when hirin' a woman with a child and no husband wasn't somethin' folks talked about in polite comp'ny. But *ma mere* could cook like nobody's business, and once they gave her a chance, you can bet they was glad to keep her on!" Lisette laughed, her dentures glinting in the lamplight.

"Now, we had us a washin' machine on our back porch," she went on. "It worked good enough for small loads of clothes, but anything heavier and it would just make a squealin' noise and refuse to budge. That meant our sheets and towels went to the laundry-mat, which was my job on Saturday mornin's while Mama had her feet up. I'd load our laundry basket into my old Radio Flyer, and pull that wagon six blocks to the coin-op. I had a good forty-five minutes to pass while the wash was in, so I'd gen'rally go across the street to a little local bakery where I could get two beignets an' a cold glass of milk for fifteen cents. Lookin' back, there was always an extra dime an' a nickel in the change Mama gave me for the wash, though I never thought about it at the time." She paused, smiling fondly at the memory. "So that was my Saturday mornin'. I'd sit at the counter eating my beignets while lookin' at the morning funny papers an' feelin' all kinds of grown up."

The old woman's rich voice was pulling me deeper into the story, and I settled back, letting my imagination paint pictures from her words.

"That mornin' my head was full of Calvin, though—so much I nearly forgot to put soap in the wash!—and when I walked into the bakery a few minutes later, the last thing in the *world* I expected to see was a white woman." Lisette must have read something in my expression, because she paused long enough to smile. "Yes, *cher*, it was *that* far back. New Orleans was still segregated, and different folk mos'ly kept to their own.

"Anyway, she sat at a corner table in a cloud of smoke, her ashtray spillin' over as she smoked unfiltered Camels like my daddy used to, one after another. Just then Mabel, who owned the place, came out from the back and asked, *'More coffee, Ms. Lavinia?'* and that's when I knew who she was. I was shakin' a little as I sat down at the counter—I won't lie to you—though I can't say if it was excitement or fear I was feelin'. Likely a little of both.

"There was a big mirror on the wall across from me, and I used it to watch her as I started into my first beignet. I tell you she was nothin' like any grown woman I ever seen. Her hair was mostly white and hung in frizzy curls nearly down to her waist. She was heavy, wearin' a man's tan work shirt untucked and patched blue jeans. She had rings on every finger and God only knows how many chains and strands of beads around her neck, along with a couple of leather cords holdin' little pouches." Lisette shook her head, chuckling nervously. "My lord, *cher*...talkin' about this sure does take me back. I can almost smell the smoke from them Camels and the chicory in her coffee.

"Ms. Lavinia was workin' the crossword puzzle—the crossword at the bottom of the funny pages *I* wanted to read—and the longer she sat there, the less scary she seemed and the more irritated I got. I remember thinkin', '*Who does this woman think she is, anyhow?*' I was fourteen, and was proud I had the sight, jus' like all the women in my family. I had it strong, even then. Lookin' back, I s'pose I was right full of myself—too big for my britches by half. So I picked up my milk glass, actin' like I wasn't payin' her any attention at all, and reached out to Ms. Lavinia." Lisette paused, meeting my gaze. "Now, *cher*, understand that I didn't mean any harm. I thought I'd just take me a little peek, to see if there was anything at all to the stories folks told, an' maybe prove to myself that she wasn't so much after all."

The old woman drew a long, shuddering breath, her bony hands gripping the arms of the rocker, and even without my gift I could see that the memory made her uncomfortable. That icy tingle crept up my spine again, this time prickling my scalp and making my chest feel tight.

"Ms. Lavinia caught me right away, though. She had the sight, sure enough—stronger than anyone I *ever* run across, before or since. I tried to pull away, but she latched on and wouldn't turn me loose. She took hold of my mind and shook it like a hound dog shakin' a *rat!*" Her voice had become tremulous, a bead of sweat appearing just below her kerchief and channeling its way downward along the dark wrinkles on her forehead.

Without thinking, I moved to squat in front of her, placing my hands over hers in concern. "Lisette…hey…you don't need to…"

"Then the bakery jus' *went away*," Lisette went on, as if she hadn't heard me. "One second I was sittin' on my stool at the counter, an' the next I was in a place full of smoke and shadows. That woman, she…she *showed* me things, *cher*. *Dark* things…things I never tol' a livin' soul about, an' never will. Things that haunted my dreams and lurk there sometimes still, even after all these years."

Her gaze returned to the present, refocusing on me. "I tried to scream, thinkin' for sure she was jus' gonna *leave* me there, but then I heard the sound of glass breaking." She exhaled, seeming to relax a little, and I got the feeling that she had gotten past the worst part. "An' jus' like that, I was back in the bakery. I'd squeezed that milk glass so hard it plumb shattered in my hand! Milk was all over the counter, mixed with blood from where I'd cut myself. I still got the mark to prove it, see?"

Lisette withdrew her right hand from mine and showed me her palm. Just below the V between her index and middle finger was a jagged, puckered scar maybe an inch and a half long. Without thinking, I reached out to touch it, and was surprised when a strong vision filled my mind:

I stand in a tiny storefront, little more than a long counter with six stools and three or four small tables spaced along a narrow strip of worn linoleum. Behind the counter is a glass display case full of pastries, pies, and loaves of bread. Morning sunlight streams in from big windows behind me while music issues from somewhere in back. It sounds like something from the fifties or sixties, but I don't know for sure:

If we could start anew, I wouldn't hesitate
I'd gladly take you back, and tempt the hand of fate
Tears on my pillow, pain in my heart, caused by you…

A young black girl sits alone at the counter, staring in disbelief at her open hand. Broken glass lies scattered on the countertop in front of her, centered in a widening pool of milk that is tinged pink from the blood dribbling from her palm. A little to one side is a plate with a couple of square, puffy pastries covered in powdered sugar, one partially eaten. In the back corner of the room sits a dumpy woman looking just as Lisette had described her, staring unconcernedly at the newspaper lying on the table in front of her…

"Now, now, *cher*…that's enough."

And just like that, the vision was gone.

Lisette's gaze held mine for a long moment. "You *saw*, didn't you? You *went there*."

I nodded.

The old woman shook her head. "Boy, you are a wonder, an' that's the plain truth."

"What happened then?" I pressed.

"Well, Mabel came out to see what was wrong, and looked at me with eyes as big as hubcaps. All I could do was turn on my stool, starin' at Ms. Lavinia, who was finishin' the last of her coffee like nothin' at all had happened. I can't be sure, but I'd bet you anything she'd never even looked up the whole time. I sat there so scared I was froze solid, watchin' as that ol' woman got up and started headin' for the door just as calm as you please. She stopped as she passed me, though, jus' long enough to stub her cigarette out in my other beignet. '*That'll teach you to keep yourself to yourself, girl*,' was all she said. An' then she was gone."

For a minute or so, all I could do was sit there, soaking in everything Lisette had told me. She watched me closely for the first ten or fifteen seconds, then nodded and pushed herself slowly to her feet, seeming to sense I needed time to digest her story. With slow, deliberate movements, she stepped over to pull open the top drawer of her dresser and began transferring underclothes to her suitcase.

Moments passed.

"Do you think Ms. Lavinia was…evil?" I asked finally as I watched her pack.

Lisette paused, considering the question. "Maybe at first I did," she said, "but not now. She might've had some mean in her, but that ain't the same thing. Like as not, she was jus' a grumpy ol' woman with no patience for a young girl stickin' her nose where it didn't belong."

"But you said that Gyp…that the Romani scared you."

"No," Lisette corrected. "I said *Ms. Lavinia* did. Scared the bejesus out of me that mornin'. But I think she was jus' someone with gifts like you an' me." She paused, seeming to give the issue more thought. "What I *will* say is I think maybe the Romani are gifted more than most. They almost always marry their own people, so their blood heritage stays strong. But in the end, they jus' folk—no better or worse than anyone else."

"Can they…*curse* people?"

The old woman shook her head. "I don't know, *cher*."

I had not expected that, and it made me sit up straight. "So you think it's *possible*?"

Lisette pursed her lips while she thought it over. "What *I* think," she said at last, "is there's a lot of things in this ol' world that ain't been explained yet—or can't be—an' I think it's best to treat 'em all with respect." She turned to watch me with a somber expression. "Growin' up in New Orleans back in my day, I seen my share of things. I seen ghosts walkin' around Lafayette Cemetery, an' heard screams comin' from the LaLaurie mansion when no one was s'posed to be inside. In my time I run across Vodou priests and priestesses, Shamans and Wiccans, and people who can tell you all about past lives they lived. I even heard tell that back in the eighties there was a Satanist group down in Ranier that was up to all kinds of no good. Ms. Lavinia was just one more example. Jus' the same, if you gettin' mixed up with the Romani, *cher*, I want you to promise me one thing.

"What's that?"

"Be careful, boy. Be very, very careful."

SEVENTEEN

MILO WATERS USED A TAPE MEASURE TO MAKE SURE THE fence on the table saw was lined up square on both ends of the blade, and then dropped the lever to clamp it in place. His current wood shop project, a short bookshelf he would be giving his mom for Christmas, was nearly finished. All that was left was to trim a sheet of eighth-inch plywood for the back, and once that was glued and tacked on, he could start the sanding. He glanced at the clock on the wall, surprised to see that the class period was nearly over. Okay, sanding tomorrow, he thought. Stain and a couple of coats of varnish the following week, and an A on his report card—probably his only A, the way things were going so far that semester—was a sure thing.

Milo was so done with this high school bullshit. He would be eighteen at the end of May, the semester would be over a week and a half later, and then diploma or not, he was out of there. His Uncle Jack had promised him a job with his construction company—just a laborer to start, but he would move up fast enough. Come June he would be helping to build tract *homes in a new development just outside Las Vegas, making good money and never wasting another thought on Silver Creek.*

Smiling to himself, Milo's gaze traveled idly to where Darren Lynch hunched over a workbench a few feet away, trying to attach the roof to a bird house. Milo studied the project with a critical eye and then snorted in contempt. The dipshit hadn't beveled the peak right, so there was no way the edges would come together flush. And the whole thing kept rocking as he tried to hold the roof in place, which meant one of the walls wasn't square. As he watched, Darren finally lined up the roof as close as it was going to get, and then tried shooting one corner with the nail gun.

"Ugh!" The boy's frustrated snarl rose half a second after the ta-chok! *of the gun, and Darren flung the birdhouse against the back wall of the bench.*

Milo snickered. The dumbass had used too big a brad too close to the edge and had split the board. Could the guy be any more stupid?

"Problem back there, Lynch?" Mr. Martin called over from where he was helping George Pope at the router table.

Darren glanced at the teacher, flushing as the most of guys in class paused to see what was going on, and then shook his head.

"It was shit anyway," Milo muttered just loud enough for Darren to hear. The big boy glared, taking a breath to say something back, but just then Milo hit the power switch and pointed to his ear, mouthing "I can't hear you" as the table saw whirred to life beside him.

Darren turned abruptly away, scowling in fury, and Milo snickered. Sometimes, giving Lynch crap was the best part of his day. The only thing the loser had going for him was that hot cousin of his. What was her name? Jenny...Jill? Something like that. Milo had seen the two of them while crossing the quad between second and third period, and had told her "Nice rack!" as they passed—partly to see her blush, but mostly because he knew it would piss Darren off. He wondered offhandedly if Lynch had ever tried seeing her naked...maybe sneaking a peek while she was in the shower. Milo definitely would have if she lived at his *house, but aside from that she really didn't interest him much. Too mousy. And anyway, come summertime he could have all the hot girls he wanted—hookers were legal in Nevada.*

Milo picked up the thin sheet of plywood, butting the right edge up against the fence guide and starting his first cut. He was most of the way through when he abruptly paused and looked up, wrinkling his nose.

Jesus…what's that smell? *he thought.*

He glanced around, thinking one of the other guys must have walked past wearing some kind of cheap-ass cologne, and then his head snapped back around when he felt something seize him! Milo sucked in a gasp, watching in horror as a patch of darkness floating around his wrist seemed to solidify into the vague shape of a hand. Just as it occurred to him to pull away, the black fist tightened, dragging his right hand into the saw blade. Blood sprayed in a crimson fan, splattering his face and safety glasses as the fine-toothed steel tore into his hand between his middle and ring fingers, slicing diagonally through meat and bone and exiting just below his wrist. For a couple of heartbeats, all he could do was stare uncomprehendingly at the missing third of his hand, the severed fingers twitching reflexively beside the whirring blade.

Then the pain hit just as the end of period bell rang, and Milo Waters began to scream.

EIGHTEEN

DARREN STOOD, REACHING OVER THE DUNGEON Master screen to rotate the orc figure on the combat grid, turning it to face the elf ranger. "The orc guard stumbles in surprise, then turns and takes a swing at you with his battle axe."

"Why *me*?" Gina asked, looking alarmed.

Darren rolled his eyes. "You just smacked him from behind for eight points of slashing damage. What did you *think* he was gonna do?"

Gina turned her gaze to me, but all I could do was shrug, offering her a smile that I hoped looked encouraging. "This is how it works. But don't worry...I've got your back."

It was our first time playing together, and we had been at it since midmorning. Darren was a good DM—he knew the rules forwards and backwards, and he ran a lively game. I was particularly impressed by his vivid descriptions of the adventure setting, which I figured probably had a lot to do with all that reading he did. Granted, my mission was to get closer to Darren to see if I could find proof of any connection between him and the events around school. That idea had seemed even more urgent following that gory incident in the wood shop, but after the principal had called an assembly and lectured everyone about general power tool and appliance safety, I was half inclined to write that one off as an unrelated accident. Fact-finding aside, though, I was enjoying the game far more that I thought I would.

Behind the screen, we heard a die roll on the tabletop as Darren made his attack. "The orc rolls an eleven. What's your armor class again?"

Gina looked down at her character sheet, searching for the number, and after a couple of seconds I reached over to point it out for her. "Twelve," she reported.

"*Woosh*! The axe blade sails just over Summerfox's head, missing her." Darren turned his attention to me. "Krobar...you're up."

I grinned. "Since he's facing away from me, I'm going to run right up behind the orc and hack at the back of his left knee, trying to take him down."

"Go ahead."

I reached over to position my unpainted barbarian figure right behind the orc, and then picked up my twenty-sided die. "Since I'm behind him, don't I get advantage on the attack?"

Darren shook his head. "You would normally, but since you're aiming for a specific body part, I'll say no this time."

I nodded. It seemed like a fair call.

"What's 'advantage' again?" Gina asked.

"It's a modifier used for special circumstances," Darren replied. "When you have advantage, you get to roll *twice* and use the higher of the two numbers. When you have disadvantage, you have to use the lower one."

I rolled, taking the result and mentally adding my character's modifiers. "Nineteen!"

"That's a hit. Roll damage."

I picked up two six-sided dice, rolled them, then added them together along with Krobar's damage adjustment. "Fourteen."

"The orc roars in agony as you nearly hack his knee clean through, then crashes to his side and rolls onto his back."

"Woo-*hoo!*" cheered Gina, beaming as she reached out to touch me. She did that a lot, squeezing either my shoulder or forearm whenever something exciting happened in the game, and I wasn't sure what to make of it. She and Les had been spending more and more time together over the last couple of weeks, and the feelings of attraction and longing that she had been directing toward me had diminished a lot, replaced by a sense of calm that I wasn't sure what to make of. Did all those reflexive squeezes mean that she wasn't completely over her crush? Or was it that she was naturally one of those "touchy" kinds of people, and it was only coming out now that she was more at ease around me and the rest of our friends? Either way, ignoring it seemed like the best way to go.

"Your turn, Summerfox."

She turned back to her cousin excitedly. "Can I take my sword and just kind of, you know, stab it down through his neck?"

He shrugged. "You can give it a try."

Gina rolled. "Sixteen?" she asked hopefully.

"That's a hit. Roll your damage."

She paused again, and I helped her out by pointing to the eight-sided die used for her elf's rapier. The different dice and all the numbers on her character sheet still confused Gina sometimes, but she was starting to get the hang of it. "Seven...no, *nine*," she reported after she remembered her damage adjustment.

"Blood sprays everywhere as you hit an artery," Darren described. "The orc gurgles and grabs onto the blade of your sword, but between yours and Krobar's hits, he bleeds out in seconds. He slumps against the ground, dead, and the entrance to the cavern is now clear."

Just then my phone vibrated in my back pocket and I pulled it out to read a text from Kelly: [Hey. Where R U?]

I glanced at the time, discovering I was nearly fifteen minutes late, and then tapped out a quick reply: [Sorry! B there in 10.] "Whoops," I said, rising to my feet. "Looks like I just turned into a pumpkin." Gina frowned unhappily, and I was surprised to see Darren looking a little disappointed, too. But I had told them when we first sat down that I had plans with Kelly later that afternoon, so what could I do? "Can I leave my stuff here, Darren?" I asked, pulling on my denim jacket. I figured it didn't make sense to drag my dice and books back and forth when we'd just be at it again the following week.

He shrugged. "I guess."

"But you'll be back next Sunday, right?" Gina asked hopefully.

"Count on it," I replied, trying to put her at ease. "Thanks, guys—this was fun!"

They both called out "Bye!" as I trotted up the stairs from the basement, and I nearly ran headlong into Darren's mom as I emerged into the kitchen. "*Yikes!*—sorry Mrs. Lynch. I'm running late—thanks again for lunch!"

"Nice meeting you, Ben," she called after me, and I tossed her a wave as I made for the entry hall. I pulled my shoes on as quickly as I could and then exited the front door, running down the porch steps to the car.

My car!

My sixteenth birthday had come and gone the previous Tuesday (with me glad to celebrate it with just Mom—I had managed to sneak it past my friends without anyone finding out, though I knew that couldn't last forever), and I had aced my driving test a couple of days later after school. At first, I had thought it strange that Mom had scheduled my appointment at the Department of Motor Vehicles in Eureka when the Crescent City DMV office was closer, but that mystery got solved afterward when she drove us to the local Ford dealership. It turned out that she had been car-shopping off and on during the last couple of weeks while I was at school, and had made a deal on a Ford Explorer painted a nice forest green. The SUV was all ready for her to pick up, and after a few minutes while she signed some paperwork, she tossed me the keys to our old '69 station wagon.

"Happy belated birthday!" she told me. "I know you've been driving since summer, but until you've been at it a while longer, I'll feel better knowing you're in a *tank*."

She had looked apologetic when she said it, which I confirmed by a quick read of her emotions, but she didn't need to be. "Thanks, Mom!" I had cried, both surprised and overwhelmed. At that moment I couldn't care less if driving it made me look like a soccer-mommy—I had *my very own car*!

The old Ford LTD had seemed as big as the Titanic the first time I had sat behind the wheel, but I'd gotten more comfortable with practice and now I hardly gave it a second thought. I guided the car south through downtown Silver Creek and was parking in Kelly's driveway only eight minutes after her text. She opened the front door just as I bounded up the steps, smiling in a way that still made my stomach do little flip-flops. "Sorry I'm late," I said, offering her a lopsided smile. "We had some last-minute killing that just couldn't wait."

"Uh-huh," Kelly said skeptically, though I could sense that she was only teasing. "And just what needed to die so badly?"

"A badass orc," I reported. "He was guarding the entrance to the cave where they're holding the baron's daughter hostage."

"What's an orc?"

I rolled my eyes, pretending to be shocked. "You know, like Sauron's troops in the *Lord of the Rings* movies? Seriously, woman...what are you good for?"

Kelly moved out onto the porch, pressing herself against me as she drew my face to hers in a long, lingering kiss. Then she stepped back, looking at me expectantly.

"Oh yeah," I said. "Now I remember."

She giggled. "Get in here, you goof."

I followed her into the entry hall, waiting while she shut the door behind us, and then she took my hand, entwining her fingers in mine as she led me further inside. "Mother, Ben's here!"

"Hello, Ben!" came her mom's voice from the direction of the kitchen. "We've got about an hour until dinner. Can I get you anything?"

"Hi, Wendy—no thanks!" I called back. I still wasn't super comfortable around Kelly's mom, but it was a relief that she didn't see me as the Prince of Darkness anymore.

"We'll be upstairs!" Kelly announced.

"That's fine…just keep your door open."

"And I had the body oil all warmed up and everything," Kelly murmured, and I felt my face flush. I was ninety-nine percent sure she was only kidding, but I couldn't help probing her feelings as she led me up the stairs, just to make sure.

I had never been to Kelly's room before, and I paused just inside the door to look around. The space was about three times as big as mine, with a bed roughly the size of a tennis court I imagined her parents had bought for her with sleepovers in mind. There was a big desk with a monitor, keyboard, and her laptop resting in a docking station, as well as a monster-sized beanbag chair under a reading lamp in one corner. Built-in shelves dominated one entire wall, loaded with books, knick-knacks and framed photos, and a TV sat on top of a wide dresser that matched her desk. She also had her own bathroom and a walk-in closet.

"You like?" she asked.

I shrugged, acting unimpressed. "The gym at school has more floor space."

Kelly laughed, selecting a playlist from her phone, and music began to issue through hidden speakers while I wandered over to read the titles on her bookshelf. It looked like she had held onto every book she'd ever read, I realized, beginning with childhood picture books to horse stories and the *Little House* novels. I continued scanning through the *Harry Potter*, *Twilight*, *Hunger Games*, and *Divergent* series, and finally on to the thick Gothic romances like my mom read, which she usually referred to as "bodice-rippers."

Then a framed eight-by-ten caught my eye. A slender teenage girl with freckles sat in one of the Mad Hatter teacups at Disneyland. Beside her was a much younger girl, maybe only seven or eight years old, her hair an identical shade of auburn. The camera had caught them while the ride was in motion, both of them laughing as they spun the cup, hair flying in that frozen moment in time. I picked up the photo and showed it to Kelly. "Is this…?"

"Yeah," she said, her smile dimming a little. "That's me and Anne."

I stared at the picture for a moment longer, and then put it back on the shelf. Part of me wanted to learn more about how Kelly's older sister had gone missing, but I decided not to ask. It would probably just ruin the mood, and I figured it could wait for another time.

"Come here," Kelly called, and I looked over to see her booting up the computer at her desk. I saw an extra chair positioned to one side, and I pulled it around so I could see the monitor. "Have you decided what you're wearing to the party?" she asked. "It would be fun if we could dress to match." When I didn't answer after a few seconds, she looked over at me, her smile fading as she read my blank expression. "Oh, God," she said, closing her eyes. "You don't know, do you?" Then she shook her head. "Of course you don't—how could you?—and I didn't even think to mention it."

I raised my eyebrows.

"My Halloween party," she said. "I throw one every year. Sorry…I guess I just assumed you knew."

I gave her a shrug. Ben Wolf, king of the nonverbals.

"It's okay," Kelly decided, shaking it off. "We've still got almost two weeks—plenty of time." She went on to explain that her sister had held the very first one after she got bored with trick-or-treating back when she was in seventh grade; and even after Anne had disappeared, Kelly had carried on with the tradition. "Halloween and my birthday are the two parties Mother allows at the house every year, and part of me holds onto this fantasy that someday Anne will just show up to surprise me." She winced. "Does that sound stupid?"

"No, not at all," I assured her, and right then I decided I would do whatever I could to help. It was obviously important to Kelly.

For a while we batted ideas back and forth, and she showed me images she had Googled of costume combinations that had already occurred to her. It was fun, but just the same I had to veto a lot of her initial suggestions:

Cinderella and Prince Charming?

Uh…no.

A 70's disco couple?

HELL no.

Bonnie and Clyde?

With or without all the blood and bullet holes?

We went on like that for a while until an idea suddenly hit me, and I pulled her keyboard over. "You said you liked Mel Brooks movies, right?" I asked, typing rapidly in the search field.

Kelly nodded. "Daddy and I used to watch them together."

"Then how about this?" I asked, indicating the image I had called up.

Kelly's eyes widened, a smile slowly spreading across her face. "*Genius!*" she cried, and then leaned over to kiss me.

I sat back afterward, feeling pleased with myself.

Genius, huh? I thought. *Take* that, *Wile E. Coyote!*

NINETEEN

THE WEATHER TURNED MOODY THE WEEK LEADING UP
to Halloween. Gusts of bitter, onshore wind put nearly everyone on
edge, sending dead leaves winging through the air or sweeping them
into brown and gold drifts against the sides of buildings. Thunder
grumbled threateningly from dark clouds that loomed low overhead
and dropped spats of icy rain. At last, the sky opened up and rained
heavily all through the 29th and 30th, as if trying to wash our whole
stretch of coastline into the Pacific, leaving the streets eerily deserted
as everyone stayed indoors to ride out the storm.

I had woken up sometime during the black hours of Halloween
morning, still half-asleep and with the unsettling feeling that something
was out of place. It took me a few seconds to realize that rain was no
longer hammering the roof, and after that I drifted back off. When I
woke again a few hours later, I found that the wind had also moved on
sometime during the night, taking the cloud cover with it. The morning
was bright and clear above a foot or two of wispy fog that huddled close
to the ground. I smiled as I stood at my bedroom window, squinting

in the sunlight, and scratching an itch between my shoulder blades as I gazed out across the soggy meadow and green hills beyond. Kelly had been worried that the weather would spoil her party, but it looked like we were in luck.

I caught movement from the corner of my eye and looked over to see Mom running up the drive, cheeks ruddy and her breath coming out in puffs of steam. She slowed to a walk, hands on her hips as she got her wind back, her face tilted toward the sky and wearing a satisfied expression. I could have guessed that she would take advantage of the clear morning to pound out a few miles, which was sure to put her in a happy mood for the rest of the day. I was glad for the good weather too, as well as the fact that it was Saturday morning and my weekend homework was already out of the way (which almost *never* happened—I had just gotten bored after dinner the night before and had blasted it out for something to do; desperate times, desperate measures).

All in all, things were looking up.

Mom was still on the front porch when I let Moe outside a minute or two later, and she smiled at me as she leaned against the rail post, holding her left heel against her backside as she stretched the muscles in her thigh. "Morning, Sunshine," she said, smiling broadly.

"Hey," I said, crossing my arms as I started to shiver almost right away. *Dang*, it was cold! The temperature had plunged with the disappearance of the cloud cover, and was now probably in the low forties... maybe even colder. "How far did you go?"

She shrugged, switching legs to stretch her other thigh. "Six or seven miles, I guess. I looped around downtown for a while, and then finished with a sprint up the drive. It was fun!"

Running seven miles in the bitter cold sounded like a lot of things, but "fun" wasn't one of them. "You're a better man than I am, Gunga Din," I said, shaking my head in admiration. Then I sighed as I looked past her. Moe had finished peeing and was now racing happily back and forth through one of the deeper puddles, tongue lolling out the corner of his mouth as he sent great sprays of water into the air. It was a good thing we had taken to keeping a stack of old towels by the door—he was going to be drenched.

Mom looked over her shoulder. "Looks like I'm not the only one who's glad to be outside," she observed with a chuckle. "You can dry him off while I fix breakfast. Is there anything you're hankering for?"

I shrugged. "I dunno…an omelet, maybe?"

She ruffled my hair playfully on her way to the door. "You got it. See you in a few."

An hour later, fed, showered, and dressed, I exited the front door with Moe right behind me and hurried to the car. The morning had warmed by a few degrees, but it was still cold enough that I was grateful I didn't have to take my bike. The chill seeped right through my denim jacket, making me wonder just how cold the winter ahead would get, and whether I needed to ask Mom for something warmer.

We drove into town, noting that the clusters of pumpkins most of the businesses had set out for fall decorations still looked fine, but the dried cornstalks tied to awning posts and streetlamps had taken a beating from the storm. They sagged on their zip-tie fasteners, bedraggled and still dripping, reminding me of torture victims I'd seen in movies. We found an open spot at the curb just across from Tsunami Joe and headed inside. The morning crowd was light, which I figured meant that the abrupt change in the weather had caught most people by surprise, and I stopped just a step or two inside the door, looking for Ab behind the service counter.

She wasn't there.

I moved to one side, telling Moe to sit while we waited to see if maybe she was just in the back room and would come out soon. When she didn't appear after a minute or so, I crossed the floor to where

Donna, the assistant manager, was chatting with her friend Marcy over the counter. "Oh, hey, Ben," she said, noticing me.

"Hi, Donna. I'm looking for Ab. Is she around?"

"No, she called this morning and asked me to cover for her."

That was odd. Ab was always at the coffee house on weekends. "Is she sick?"

The woman shook her head. "Not that she mentioned. But I didn't ask, either—the holidays will be here before we know it, and I was happy to take the overtime. You want your usual?"

I was still full from breakfast, so I shook my head. "Thanks anyway."

"If Ab calls, I'll let her know you stopped by."

I smiled in thanks before turning and heading for the door. Moe was still sitting where I'd told him to—all that training was really starting to pay off!—and he looked pointedly at the counter, and then back at me, wagging his tail tentatively as if asking what was up. This wasn't our usual routine. "Change of plans, boy," I told him, and then pushed the door open and followed him onto the sidewalk. Pausing just outside, I dug my phone out from my jacket pocket and punched in the speed-dial code for Ab, frowning when it went right to voicemail.

Crap.

I had wanted to talk to her about the Gypsy curse idea, to see if maybe she wanted to forget the whole thing. Despite my suspicions, it was becoming more and more clear that Darren was just Darren, and since life had gone back to normal at school, I was beginning to think my imagination had just gotten way out of hand. Ben Wolf, conspiracy-theorist. How embarrassing. Sure, the football team was still only winning about half their games, but the longer that held as a pattern, the less likely it seemed that there was some dark force behind it, and the more I began to think maybe Alan Garret was just having a rotten year. All in all, I was starting to relax enough to feel stupid, but since Ab had gone radio-silent for the morning, I guessed I would have to wait and catch her later at the party.

We got back in the car and drove to Les' house, first slowing, but then driving past when I didn't see his bike on the front porch. Les had all sorts of theories about the best times for fishing, and right after a rainstorm was supposed to be one of them. I figured he was off drowning worms somewhere, so we drove down to Windward Cove's small harbor, and then past a couple of his favorite stretches of beach that were visible from the car, but didn't see him.

Strike two.

I sent a quick text to both he and Ab, telling them to let me know if they needed a ride to the party, then pocketed my phone, feeling a little lonely. I thought about calling Kelly, but then decided not to when I remembered she and her Mom were busy decorating. I had offered a couple of times to go over and help, but she had told me it would spoil the surprise. I thought about my options, but then realized that there was nothing else that I particularly felt like doing. Disappointed, I headed back home.

The low fog from earlier had burned off, the grass heavy with fat drops of water that sparkled in the sunlight. I knew the ground beneath was probably a bog, though, so goofing around outside with Moe wasn't going to happen. I wandered around downstairs for a while, feeling restless, and even turned on the TV and channel-surfed for ten or fifteen minutes. Nothing reached out and grabbed me, though, so I turned it back off.

After a brief search I finally found Mom upstairs in the cupola above the attic. She was seated at her easel, working on her latest project—a seascape at twilight—and when I looked at the canvas, I recognized a stretch of rocky coastline maybe half a mile north of the house. I tried to get her to talk, but she was concentrating on her painting and all I got for my trouble was a distracted *That's nice, Benny* and an *Uh-huh* or two. Grinning, I switched tactics, confessing to a gas-station robbery and a couple of murders, just to see if she was paying attention. It wasn't long, though, before she looked over and politely suggested that if I was so bored, I could always start on the weekend housecleaning.

I suddenly remembered something urgent and got out of there.

Down in my room, I flopped onto the bed, petting Moe as he wormed his way under my arm. He rested his head on my shoulder and sighed, his warm breath tickling my ear. At last, I reached out with my free hand, picking up the Darren's book from my nightstand. I thumbed it open, the strip of paper I had been using as a bookmark falling onto my chest. Although I was usually more into horror and sci-fi, the fantasy novel was really good, and I was about halfway through it. I settled back and got comfortable, figuring that I'd read a chapter or two while waiting for something fun to occur to me.

Nothing ever did, but that turned out to be just fine.

The light in my room had dimmed considerably when I finally closed the back cover several hours later. What a story! Moe had slept pretty much the whole time, sometimes snoring, sometimes making little whining noises and twitching in his dreams, and my shoulder had gone to sleep from him laying on it so long. I moved out from under him, wincing at the stiffness in my back and the prickle of pins and needles that ran down my right arm. Totally worth it, though.

Moe raised his head, yawning hugely as he watched me step to my bedroom window. The sky above was still clear, but the fog from earlier had returned with reinforcements, creeping out from the tree line to wrap the house in a thick blanket as the sun glared orange-red from just above the hills. I glanced at my watch: *5:17*. Less than two hours until Kelly's party.

Whatever Mom was cooking smelled good, and my stomach rumbled, reminding me that I hadn't eaten since morning. "I bet you need to go outside, don't you, boy?" I asked.

Moe got to his feet, first stretching, and then giving himself a good shake before regarding me with his tail wagging.

"Let's go, then," I said, and he jumped off the bed to follow me downstairs.

TWENTY

I LEFT THE HOUSE EARLY, DRIVING SLOWLY THROUGH the thickening fog. The headlights only managed to penetrate ten or fifteen feet beyond the front of the car, forcing me to creep along, using what little I could see of the lines on the asphalt ahead to navigate through the gloom. The reduced speed and visibility made distances hard to judge, and I had to pull over twice and get out to read the signs for intersecting roads to make sure I was still on course. It was a little unnerving, but sort of fun, too. After all, wasn't Halloween *supposed* to be creepy?

It got easier when I reached the outskirts of Silver Creek, where streetlights helped cut through the fog. Smaller moving lights began to emerge from the darkness to either side, becoming more frequent as I rolled past parents carrying flashlights as they escorted clusters of little kids out trick-or-treating. Jack-o-lanterns leered from porches and windowsills, and many of the yards had been decorated with giant inflatable ghosts or witches or black cats, and I grinned as my own excitement grew. Halloween was the *best*! I slowed down even more, just in case someone crossed in front of me, and had nearly reached downtown before I realized I had missed the turn for Kelly's street. I circled the next block, heading back the way I had come as costumed monsters and princesses and superheroes ran up driveways and rang doorbells.

My idea had been to get to the Thatcher house early in case Kelly and her Mom needed any last-minute help, but the fog had made me late, and there were already lines of cars parked diagonally to either side of their driveway when I arrived. I parked and got out, shivering as I followed the muffled beat of music toward a dozen or so jack-o-lanterns arranged to either side of the front steps.

Music, colored lights, and artificial fog spilled outward to greet me when Kelly answered the doorbell. She wore a white, floor-length gown of some shimmery material that flowed in some places and was gathered tight in others. Her hair was arranged in a loose pile on top of her head, highlighted by wide streaks the same color as her dress that began at her temples and ran up and back. "Oh, wow…you're *perfect!*" I said.

"Thanks—you look great, too!"

My costume had been easy: black jeans and T-shirt, with a dark, tattered suit coat I had found at the Windward Cove thrift store. I had pinned the sleeves of the coat up to make my arms look longer. A skull cap I had found online left me with a ring of hair above my ears, and I'd used theater makeup to turn my skin pale. Finally, Mom had helped complete the look by using spirit gum to attach short zippers to either side of my neck. Together, Kelly and I had managed a pretty good creature and his bride from *Young Frankenstein*, and I grinned, thrilled by how everything had turned out.

Kelly grabbed my hand to pull me inside, then stood on tiptoe for a kiss that left my mouth tingly and tasting like cinnamon. She took my arm, using her foot to close the door behind her before marching me into the living room. Cheers, laughter, and scattered applause erupted around us as heads turned to watch us enter, and I was both happy and relieved that we weren't the only ones who liked the old movie.

The doorbell rang again, and Kelly let go of my arm. "I need to put a note on the door telling everyone to just come in," she told me, pitching her voice to carry over the music. "I'll catch up in a few minutes!"

I nodded, watching her walk away and liking all the nice things that dress did for her. Looking around, I saw that the living room was shrouded in fake cobwebs, with banks of colored lights hung high on the wall that alternated different combinations of green, orange, purple, and red through the artificial fog. Kelly's mom was chatting with an adult I didn't recognize over by the archway to the dining room, but she didn't see me when I waved. I shrugged, and then made my way through the crowd toward the sliding doors across the room, saying hi to kids who I knew and nodding to others who I didn't, but had seen around school. Outside, a ring of propane heaters surrounded the patio, tall columns of flame that kept the fog and chill away as three or four couples danced in the firelight. Others were lined up at an open kitchen trailer parked on the grass, where a tall, bearded guy was serving street tacos. Bowls of chips and Halloween candy were scattered here and there, alongside veggie platters and stacks of cupcakes with green and orange icing. There was also a line of coolers full of sodas and bottled water, just inside a ring of outdoor chairs lined up at the edge of the concrete. Another ring of chairs surrounded a fire pit that blazed thirty or forty feet farther out in the yard.

You had to hand it to them…the Thatchers really knew how to throw a party!

I was just getting around to thinking about what to do next when I heard Nicole call out, "Hey, Ben!"

I turned to see her exit the house, and waited until she made her way over before I asked, "How'd you know it was me?"

"Are you kidding? I'd recognize you from behind anywhere. You've got a great…" she paused, winking mischievously, "…pair of shoulders!"

She wore a clingy dark dress cut high on her legs and low on top, with a voluminous black wig, purple eye shadow, and bright scarlet lipstick—a perfect Elvira, Mistress of the Dark. "*Love* your costume!" I told her admiringly. That got us to talking about the films Elvira had made after making a name for herself as a TV monster movie hostess, but we hadn't gotten far before Monica and Jasmine joined us. Monica arrived in a long black dress and pale makeup, while Jasmine wore a dark, three-piece suit with her hair slicked back, and I recognized Morticia and Gomez from *The Addams Family*. Kelly caught up to us while we were all grabbing drinks at the coolers, taking my hand as she smiled up at me. Her party was already shaping into a huge success, and getting better by the minute.

Nobody felt like dancing just yet, so we headed to the fire pit, out away from the music where it was easier to talk. Costumed guests steadily filled the patio, circulating in and out of the house, with Kelly going back and forth to greet the new arrivals. I sat where I could see the doors, keeping an eye out for Ab or Les. Half an hour or so passed, and I was beginning to wonder if I should send them a text when Kim appeared wearing zombie makeup, followed by Vern, who was decked out in a tuxedo and a cape with a high collar. We all waved, and they made their way over to join us. "Great *Walking Dead* look," Nicole told Kim, and then she turned to Vern. "So I guess you would be…"

"*Blackula!*" he finished for her, flapping his cape and smiling around a set of fangs. Everyone laughed, and I was curious if Vern had thought up the idea on his own, or if he had actually seen the old 70s movie. Then I decided it didn't matter—he looked great!

Movement at the patio door caught my eye, and I watched as Brianna walked out of the house in a really cool Tinkerbell costume, complete with fairy wings. A dour-looking Alan Garrett followed her, wearing football pants and an Oakland Raiders jersey. Brianna smiled when her eye fell on a group of friends, and she pulled Alan toward them. I was about to comment to Kelly about it when Les and Gina emerged from the house a moment later, followed by Darren. I raised my arm and waved, and after a few seconds they noticed me and headed our way.

Gina was dressed in a set of hip waders over a sportsman's shirt. She carried a fishing rod and wore a floppy hat with several lures and a bobber pinned above the brim. Les was just in his regular clothes, but wore a novelty hat made to look like a trout. "Wow," I said to Gina as they joined the circle, and then indicated Les with a nod. "Did you need the net to drag that one into the boat?"

"I put up a good fight," he answered for her, grinning, "but she finally landed me."

We all laughed, and then Kelly spoke up. "And who are you supposed to be, Darren?"

He looked uncomfortable as all eyes turned toward him. Darren wore a flannel shirt and a backpack, with a large, blue plastic jewel suspended around his neck by a strip of leather. "He's Shawn Collins!" I announced, suddenly recognizing the look he had been going for, and Darren's face lit up in surprise. "Shawn is the main character in a fantasy series Darren's into," I explained when questioning looks were turned my way. "It's a great story—I just finished the first book this afternoon." There was a brief pause, but then everyone made a point of complimenting him, and I didn't think Darren even noticed the delay. Vern went above and beyond, clapping him on the back and saying, "Wish I'd thought of it, man," and after first flushing bright red, the corners of Darren's mouth turned up in a smile.

Well how about that? I thought. *An honest-to-God* smile! The big guy even had *dimples*, if you could believe that, and I wondered offhandedly how many people had ever seen them. I smiled, feeling happy for Darren, along with a deep appreciation that my friends were so cool.

We talked for a few more minutes, but then Monica announced that she wanted a taco, and our circle broke up with most following her toward the trailer. I wasn't hungry yet, and apparently neither was Kelly, so I tagged along while she headed back to the patio, circulating and talking with the other guests. A lot of her old cheer and football crowd was there, and it looked like she was well on her way to patching up friendships.

Well…some of them, anyway. I looked over a couple of times to see Alan watching us with a sour expression, but even if I had been able to sort his feelings out from all the others around me, I didn't bother to try. Maybe losing a girlfriend and a few football games would knock some of the asshole out of him, or maybe it wouldn't. Either way, I wasn't interested—not even a little. After a while I excused myself, heading to the edge of the patio while checking my phone, hoping for a text from Ab. Still nothing, and I wondered if she was okay.

Kelly joined me a few minutes later, just as I had glanced up and caught another dark look from Alan, but then he turned away. "Does it bother you that Brianna and Alan are here?" she asked, looking concerned after she followed my gaze.

I shrugged. "No, I guess not. Seeing them just came as a surprise, that's all. I just wish he'd stop being Mr. Pouty-Face."

"Brianna called last week to apologize for being so mean and bitchy," Kelly explained, "and she's been trying really hard to make things okay between us. We've been friends since kindergarten, and even after everything that happened, I'd hate to lose that, so I couldn't *not* invite her." Then she sighed. "Of course, I knew that meant she'd be bringing Alan, but I decided to just suck it up and hope for the best."

I shrugged again. It was Kelly's party after all, and it was none of my business who she invited. Just the same, I had kept an eye on Alan off and on since their arrival. At first, he had circulated a bit with Brianna, saying hi to his friends. After that, though, he had parked himself in a chair at the far corner of the patio, mostly alternating between following Kelly with his gaze and throwing an occasional glare my way. Brianna had tried several times to get him to mingle or dance, smiling and obviously trying to cheer him up. He had pretty much ignored her, though, and the few times Brianna had stepped away to talk to friends, he had looked even more sullen until things got awkward and she returned to his side. Finally, Brianna appeared to just give up, looking dejected as she sat there in silence, scrolling through her phone. I felt sorry for her.

"Poor Brianna," Kelly said, as if reading my thoughts. "I guess inviting them was a mistake after all. *God*...can he be any more immature?"

Just then the music swelled to a slow song and an idea occurred to me. "Maybe I can fix that," I said, giving her hand a squeeze before crossing the patio to where they were seated. "Hey, Brianna!" I said, smiling down as if seeing her was the best thing that had happened to me all night.

She looked up with an alarmed expression, shooting a quick sideways glance at Alan before quickly recovering and offering a tentative smile in return. "Um...hi, Ben."

"Glad to see you're all healed up," I told her. "And your costume looks great!" Even without my gift, I could have guessed Alan's rising anger and jealousy by his smoldering expression alone. I ignored him, though, acting as if he wasn't even there. "But why are you just sitting here? C'mon—let's dance!"

That did it. Alan all but shot to his feet, taking Brianna's hand and pulling her into the crowd of dancers, bumping his shoulder against mine as he passed. I watched them for a few seconds, feeling pretty satisfied with myself. Brianna smiled happily up at her boyfriend, and after a few seconds even Alan appeared to relax a little. Mission accomplished.

Ben Wolf, relationship-whisperer.

I turned to see if Kelly had been watching, but ended up meeting Gina's gaze instead. She was dancing with Les maybe twenty feet away, regarding me with an expression I couldn't read. I felt the smile fade from my face, wondering for a second or two if she was still getting over her crush on me, and that seeing the attention I had given Brianna had stung. The air was too full of emotions from the crowd, though, so I couldn't tell. Then Gina surprised me by grabbing a double fistful of Les' shirt and pulling his face down to hers. It must have surprised Les too, as I saw his eyes widen briefly before he returned her kiss with enthusiasm, picking her up and spinning a three-sixty before setting her back on her feet. *False alarm*, I thought, feeling a huge sense of relief. It looked like the pressure was officially off…Gina was now Team Les all the way!

I smiled, veering around them as I headed toward where Kelly was sharing a laugh with Jessica near one of the blazing heaters. Then I changed course when I saw Ab emerge from the house wearing a lab coat, thick glasses, and her hair done up in spikes—a total mad scientist look. She swept the area with a quick glance, and then smiled and set off toward the food trailer like she was on a mission.

"Hey," I said, catching up to her just as she reached the folding counter. "You made it! I was starting to think you weren't coming."

"Wolfman! Just the guy I wanted to see. First things first, though." She turned to the cook. "Hey there," she said, smiling. "Taco me up—I'm starving!"

The big man smiled down at her. "Sure thing, hon. I've got spicy chicken or carne asada. How many do you want…a couple?"

"Three," Ab told him. "Of *each*."

The man eyed her lean frame, looking skeptical. "You sure?" Ab's smile only widened, though, so he shrugged and got to work.

I grinned. The poor guy had no idea who he was dealing with. Ab had a metabolism like The Flash. She could plow through a double pastrami burger at Hovey's like it was nothing, and once I'd seen her single-handedly demolish a large combination pizza, reducing it to a couple of olive slices and a streak of sauce.

"Dad drove me over," Ab said, "but I was hoping to catch a ride home with you. Can I?"

I rolled my eyes dramatically. "*Gawd*…the things you do for your best friend."

She bit her lower lip, as if holding back a smile, and I got the impression she was trying not to look too pleased. "Thanks."

"I wanted to talk to you, too," I said while she watched her plate being filled. "I've been thinking about…" I paused, feeling self-conscious as I realized we were within earshot of the taco guy. "About… you know…that favor I asked."

"What? You changed your mind?"

"Kind of, I guess. I'm just…"

"Thanks!" Ab told the cook, cutting me off as he handed her a mountain of food.

I followed her to a condiment table a short distance away, where she started loading up her tacos with onions and hot sauce. "I'm just beginning to think the whole idea was stupid."

"Yeah? Why's that?"

I went on to explain how the longer things went on normally, the more it seemed to me that the weird events had either been freak occurrences, or had rational explanations that I was just too dumb to figure out. Then I told her about how I'd managed to get closer to Darren, but so far hadn't witnessed a thing that would lead me to believe he was out of the ordinary, let alone capable of cursing people.

Ab listened politely, not interrupting even once—although that probably had a lot to do with the way she was plowing through those tacos like a machine. The first four disappeared in just a couple of mouthfuls each, after which she throttled back and put away the last couple with three or four. It didn't take long…but what I had to say didn't, either.

"Anyway," I finished, "it looks like the whole curse idea was a bust, and we should just let it go." My face warmed with a flush of embarrassment. "Sorry I wasted your time."

Ab stared at me for a couple of heartbeats, a twinkle in her eye as her lips twisted in a smirk. "Nope," she said at last, stepping around me as she headed back toward the trailer.

"Nope *what*?" I asked, hurrying to follow her.

"Nope, that's not what we're going to do," she said back over her shoulder, and then handed her plate back to the surprised cook. "Thanks—those were great!" she told him, smiling. "Hit me again, handsome. And is that sauce over there the hottest you've got?"

I snickered at the look on his face, like he was seeing sasquatch or maybe the ghost of Elvis. Thinking back, I had probably looked the same way once. Then I shook it off, reaching out to turn Ab toward me. "So, you're saying that you don't want to call it off?"

She grinned. "Not even close."

"How come?"

"Because I found your Gypsy!" Ab told me, and she winked.

TWENTY-ONE

"LATER, BITCHES!" ANGIE CALLED TO DARLENE AND ZOEY,
and then turned left on Eureka Street to walk the last four blocks to her
home alone. It was just after 11 p.m. and the sidewalks that had been
packed with trick-or-treaters a couple of hours before were now mostly
deserted. She pulled off her latex mask as she walked, refreshed by the
chilly fog on her face and grateful that she didn't have to smell her own
breath anymore. The can of ravioli she'd had for dinner hadn't mixed
well with all the chocolate she'd eaten since, and every time she burped,
the inside of the mask smelled like ass. She stuffed the mask into the old
pillowcase she used for a candy bag, which was satisfyingly heavy. The
three had given up trick-or-treating a couple of years before when too
many adults starting giving them the stink-eye, and Darlene had come
up with the idea of waiting beneath trees and in the shadows between
the streetlights to take candy from roving groups of little boys instead. It
was way more fun than ringing doorbells, and since they wore different
masks every year, nobody had figured out who they were.

Angie sucked a bloody knuckle, still pissed at the little shit in the cowboy outfit who had put up a fight, but then almost gagged when she suddenly realized that she didn't know if she was tasting her blood or his. The kid's nose had bled like a stuck pig. She spat in disgust, stopping to rummage in her bag and pulling out the first candy bar she felt. Tearing away the wrapper with her teeth, she popped the miniature bar into her mouth and rolled it around to cover the coppery taste with a layer of melting chocolate.

Much better.

She started walking again, idly wishing that the three of them had finished the night closest to Zoey's house. The fight had gotten her hot, and it would have been nice to spend some time alone with Darlene making out in the shadows somewhere. She liked Zoey well enough, but Zoey was bi, and the thought that she might have had some guy's junk in her hand (or worse—ugh!) made Angie want to puke.

Her thoughts trailed off as she caught a scent in the air—sweet, almost like some kind of exotic, night-blooming flower, but with a kind of musky undertone. That was stupid, of course. Anything that bloomed had gone dormant weeks ago.

An angry hiss rose up from the gloom at her feet, followed by a needle-like sting at her ankle just above her shoe. Angie yelped in surprise and fear, dancing nervously to the side. It was a cat, she discovered when she looked down—a big, black-and-white tom. The freaking thing had scratched her! A sudden rush of anger replaced her fear, and Angie kicked savagely at him, intending to send the goddamn thing into the next time zone. He avoided her foot easily, though, a menacing growl rising from his throat and ending in a hiss.

"Get away from me! Go on!" she snapped, still distracted by the cloying smell. If anything, it was getting stronger.

Another growl sounded and Angie whirled. A second cat—this time a fat, orange one—crouched on the roof of a car beside her, ears flat and narrowed eyes glinting yellow in the reflected light.

"What the fu..." Angie began, and then screamed as it leapt for her face! Instinctively, she ducked to the side, feeling a claw graze her cheek just below her right eye, followed by the tickle of blood. The orange cat landed badly, and then got back up to join the tom. Angie watched, feeling truly scared for the first time as they sniffed one another briefly before turning their attention back to her, separating as if to come at her from both sides. She swung her candy bag at them, causing both to shy briefly while she spun, ready to sprint away.

Instead, she froze.

A big gray cat with a scarred head emerged from the fog behind her, staring balefully at her with green eyes. Just then Angie caught movement in her peripheral vision and glanced that way in time to see a fourth cat trotting across the street, headed in her direction. Then a chorus of growls and mews rose all around her, causing Angie's breath to come in panicked gasps as she felt a sudden, almost uncontrollable urge to pee. Cats were now everywhere, she realized, looking around. Dozens emerged from under cars and spilled over fences, gliding toward her on silent paws and causing the fog to swirl all around her feet.

She shrieked as claws penetrated her calf through her jeans, followed by the sharper sting of teeth biting the back of her thigh. Half a second later, she stumbled as a weight dropped onto her right shoulder, a cat that she hadn't noticed in the tree above clinging to her hoodie and growling as it bit at her neck. Two more started climbing her legs as a third sprang up to dangle from her right breast, and Angie started to move in an awkward, shambling run, trying not to trip over the pool of cats circling at her feet. She felt a spreading warmth at her crotch as her bladder let go, and Angie screamed again, dropping her candy bag as she tried ineffectively to tear away the biting, yowling cats that clung to her. At that moment, the scarred *gray leapt onto her arm, biting her shoulder as its back paws raked at her sleeve. She flung it away, finally gaining some momentum and just trying to get the hell out of there!*

"HELP ME!...HELP MEEEE!" she screamed, trying not to gag on the sweet, earthy smell that was now nearly suffocating.

A flashlight beam appeared twenty feet away—dim at first, but then growing bright as a couple of costumed kids emerged from the fog. Angie staggered, gasping, as the cats clinging to her suddenly leapt away, and she heard the soft patter of retreating paws as she stumbled to her knees. Within seconds, they had all disappeared into the darkness. The smell dissipated as well, as if whisked away by a breeze, though the air remained deathly still.

Angie blinked through her tears, turning her head away as the flashlight beam shone directly in her eyes. "Are you okay?" asked a boy, sounding concerned.

She began to sob.

TWENTY-TWO

AB REFUSED TO SAY ANYTHING MORE ABOUT HER FIND-
ings at the party, and wouldn't even give me a hint during the drive
back to Windward Cove. The best I was able to drag out of her was an
explanation that there was just too much to share, and the story was
better told all at once. Sure, I was still leaning toward forgetting the
whole idea, but the faint, mysterious smile she offered when I tried
to press her for details left me curious just the same.

It was half past midnight when I finally let Ab out in front of her
house, and she made me promise to meet her at Tsunami Joe around
3:00 that afternoon, after they closed and everyone else was gone. I
shrugged and told her that I would. After all, the whole Gypsy curse
thing had been my idea to begin with, and even though I didn't expect
to change my mind about dropping it, the least I could do was listen to
what she had to say.

I had to soap up twice in the shower to get rid of all my Frankenstein
makeup (pulling the zippers off was the worst part, leaving me with red
marks on either side of my neck), and it was nearly two in the morning

before I finally dropped into bed. Throwing an arm over Moe, I fell asleep almost right away. If I had dreams, I didn't remember them.

I awoke late the next morning, at first looking around blearily as I tried to figure out why the angle of sunlight coming through my window seemed so different. Then I glanced at my clock: *11:27.*

Wow, I thought. It had been a while since I had crashed that hard.

Downstairs, I let Moe out the front door, and was about to call out to see where Mom was when I noticed her Explorer wasn't in the drive. I waited for Moe to finish, and then as we made our way through the family room, I discovered that Mom had taken pity on me, doing all our weekend chores while I slept in. I found a note on the kitchen butcher block saying that she would be back later, sitting next to a big ham and egg sandwich. It had gone cold, but I wolfed it down anyway while getting Moe his breakfast. After that I showered again, letting the hot water pound the morning chill and stiffness out of me, and I was dressed and feeling a lot more human by 12:15.

Realizing that I had nothing going on right away, and with plenty of time left to kill before meeting Ab, I followed Moe as he bounded out into the sunshine. The previous night's fog was long gone, and a stiff ocean breeze made the grass hiss and shiver, creating ripples in scattered pools of rainwater that had not soaked into the ground yet. It wasn't as cold as the morning before, but still cool enough that I could feel it through my jacket. The lateness of the day made me feel kind of off—even a little sad—and I sighed as it occurred to me that most of the weekend was gone already. Sundays sucked that way sometimes.

We tried working on Moe's training for a while, but he obviously wasn't into it right then, and neither was I. Abandoning the idea, we hiked up the access road instead and took a slow lap around the Windward Inn, looking for any damage it might have suffered from the storm. There wasn't any that I could see, but that didn't really surprise me. After all, the three stories of heavy, gray stone had been taking everything the coastal weather could throw at it since the early 1900's, so what was I worried about? At most, I supposed some boards could have been torn off windows, or a branch or two brought down from the wind-sculpted cypress trees that surrounded the place, but everything looked just the same as the last time I had been there.

Since all was quiet on the western front, Moe and I strolled to the edge of the cliffs to have a look at the ocean. The breeze was a lot stronger on top of the hill, causing me to blink as it blew my hair back from my forehead. I could sense the Windward Inn looming behind me, the various presences inside registering faintly at the far edge of my mental radar. The feeling had totally creeped me out the first time Mom and I had walked around the place, but as I had learned to develop and better understand my gift, somewhere along the line it had stopped bothering me. Now it just seemed natural—like the way you can be aware of someone behind you on a sidewalk without really thinking about it.

The Pacific was the color of granite beneath the pale blue sky, the wind creating rows of small whitecaps that rolled in to slap at the rocks far below. The cries of seagulls echoed faintly from somewhere in the distance, and half a dozen sea lions were sunning themselves on a rock maybe fifty yards out. Between the sea lions and the cliff face, I watched a pelican glide above the waves, scanning the water for his lunch.

Moe finally nuzzled my hand, whining curiously, and I bent over to pat him before turning back toward the road. "C'mon, buddy…let's go hang out someplace warmer."

It was a little before 2:45 when Moe and I entered the coffee house, but Ab was already waiting. She locked the door behind us, and I followed her to the far side of the room where a stack of papers rested on a small table set between two upholstered chairs. A couple of tall mochas were waiting there too, still hot and with the whipped cream just starting to melt, so I figured our timing had been about perfect.

"So, what have you got?" I asked, dropping into one of the chairs while Moe curled up on the floor.

Ab dragged the papers over in front of her, and then paused to sip from her drink. It left her with a thin moustache of whipped cream, which she absently dragged down with her lower lip after swallowing. I was *never* that neat, and always had to use a napkin so I wouldn't look like I was lathering up to shave. Then again, Ab had been practicing a lot longer.

"I thought I'd *never* figure this one out," she confessed. "It turns out the Lynches come from one of those old East Coast families that go back pretty much forever, with lots of kids and every one of them cranking out big families of their own."

"Yeah, well, they didn't have cable back then," I joked, "so what else could they do?"

Ab snorted, and then continued. "So anyway, there were Lynches spread out all over the place, from southern Pennsylvania all the way up into New Hampshire. Lucky for us, though, Darren and Gina's direct line settled in upstate New York and pretty much stayed put. Their great-great-great-great..." Ab paused, looking toward the ceiling as if counting to make sure she'd gotten the number right, but then she shook her head. "Anyway, their great-times-whatever grandfather was this guy named Archibald Lynch, who was born in Albany in May of 1888." She passed me a printed copy of an old photo. It showed a young man with dark, slicked-back hair. He sat with his legs crossed in a tall, ornately carved chair. Beside him was a table supporting a lamp with a glass, flower-patterned shade and crystals dangling from the lower rim. He was well dressed and strikingly handsome—like an old-time Hollywood leading man, maybe Errol Flynn's cousin—and looked to be somewhere in his early twenties. His formal clothes made him appear older, though, so it was hard to tell. What stood out most were his piercing eyes, which I guessed had been either gray or light blue.

"Purdy, wasn't he?" Ab asked.

I shrugged.

She passed me a second photo showing an older man seated in the same chair with a woman standing behind him, one hand on his shoulder. "These were Archie's parents, Randolph and Madeline Lynch. Randolph owned a warehouse, where goods shipped up the Hudson River were transferred to Erie Canal boats and sent on to Buffalo. But that was just his day job. Do you know what Spiritualism is?"

I shook my head, settling back and sipping from my mocha.

Ab slid over three or four different articles she had printed from the internet. "You can read about it on your own," she told me. "But the Cliff's Notes version is that it was a religious movement that was popular from around the 1840s all the through the 1920s. Spiritualists believed that when people died, they evolved into higher beings as they passed into the 'spirit world,' and it was possible for the living to communicate with them. You know…séances, spirit boards, that sort of thing. It might not have been all that big if it hadn't been for the Civil War, but after so many husbands and brothers and fathers were killed, Spiritualism really took off."

"Do you think there was anything to it?" I asked. Sure, my experience with ghosts was less than six months old, but still, the idea sounded a little fishy to me.

Ab shrugged. "Who knows? Legit or not, though, lots of people were into it, including Archie's parents. Madeline was a self-professed spiritual medium who could lead rapping sessions…"

"What's that?" I interrupted, wrinkling my forehead.

"It's a kind of séance where a medium would supposedly summon a spirit into the room," she explained. "The people there could then ask questions, which the spirit would answer by knocking a certain number of times on the table—once for yes, twice for no, like that."

"Okay. So what about the dad?"

"Randolph practiced hypnotism, believing that people could commune with spirits while in a trance state. Between him and his wife, they got to be pretty famous throughout the greater Albany area and made a ton of money."

I shook my head, confused. "What does *any* of this have to do with Gypsies?"

"Relax…we're getting there. Anyway, the only things I could find on Archie for the two or three years after he graduated high school were some mentions in the local the police blotter—four times when he was picked up for public intoxication, twice for fighting, and the last time when the cops raided an illegal gambling den. There was never any mention of him standing in front of a judge, though, and that's when I began to suspect that Archie was more than just a rich kid…he was a rich kid with family connections. What convinced me even more was when I found his name on the freshman roster at West Point the very next term."

I must have looked confused, because Ab paused her story.

"They don't hand those slots out to just anyone, Wolfman, and Archie's school grades were nothing to write home about. My guess is that Mommy and Daddy sent him there hoping that Army officer training would straighten him out, and they had to pull a few strings to do it—probably more than a few. You still with me?"

"So far, yeah."

"Archie didn't last long," she went on. "He was kicked out the following spring. Here's a copy of the letter the Army sent his parents."

I took the page she offered, skimming the brief note on faded West Point letterhead. "What do you think they meant by *repeated violations of the Cadet Honor Code*?" I asked.

"I was curious about that too, so I looked it up," Ab told me. "The code just says, *A Cadet will not lie, cheat, steal, or tolerate those who do.*"

I shook my head. "Wow. Ol' Archie must've been quite a guy."

"Oh, it gets even better," she said. "Next, his father put him to work helping to manage the warehouse, where he lasted all of seven months. Apparently, he was just as suited to the nine-to-five life as he was to the military."

"So, what did he do?"

"Why, Archibald did just what *any* self-respecting, spoiled rich kid would do when he didn't want to work," Ab told me, grinning. "He ran away to New York City and married a woman with money."

I had to snicker. "*Seriously*?"

"Yep," Ab reported, handing over another photo. "Meet Eunice Applegate. Her father was a big-time banker who was part of Manhattan high society."

The picture was of a plain-looking woman with thin hair and a pleasant, although slightly vacant expression. She was round-shouldered, with a neck that looked too slender for her head and a nose too long for her face. I imagined that picking her up probably hadn't been too tough for Mr. Leading Man. "How did they meet?"

"I'm not really sure, but since Archie had grown up surrounded by all the Spiritualism shtick, my guess is he traded on his family name to get his foot in the door of society circles. He might have been a deadbeat and a loser, but by all accounts, the guy was drop-dead charming. In less than six months, his name was appearing regularly in the newspapers, billed as a gifted medium who specialized in putting people in touch with their 'spirit guides.' He met Eunice not long after, and I figure either she or her father must have been believers—maybe both—because Archie and Eunice were married in less than a year. That would be December of 1910—a Christmas wedding, and it was big news. Archie was twenty-two. Eunice was thirty-seven.

"Now, I don't know if his parents had any actual gifts," Ab went on, "but I couldn't find anything to convince me that Archie was anything but a fake. He traveled a lot over the next couple of years, leaving Eunice at home while he went up and down the Eastern seaboard, booking lectures, conducting exclusive séances for the rich, and basically living it up. His reputation began to take hits, though, when—surprise, surprise—word got around that all those predictions the spirits supposedly shared with him almost never turned out to be right. This would have been sometime around 1912, when lots of other so-called mediums were being exposed as frauds. Here…check these out." Ab handed me a stack of old newspaper articles, and I skimmed them as she went on. "I was amazed at the lengths some of those folks would go to, rigging all kinds of special effects to convince people that ghosts were in the room—tiny wires to make objects move, sound effects, even partners in hidden rooms who would wear ghost makeup and seem to appear in mirrors that were actually one-way glass. If there ever had been anything real about the Spiritualist movement, all the charlatans ruined it for everyone else.

"By 1913, Eunice must have finally had enough," Ab continued, "because she divorced him, claiming neglect and infidelity. That cut him off from his in-laws' money, and between that and his trashed reputation, Archie was all but ruined."

"What happened then?" I asked, looking up as Ab drained the last of her mocha.

"Then," she said, smiling knowingly, "Archie met Cozanna Vale."

TWENTY-THREE

SOMETHING ABOUT THE EXOTIC NAME—OR MAYBE IT was just Ab's tone—sent a tingling sensation over my skin. I sat forward eagerly, sensing that the story was about to get a lot more interesting, but then I straightened as Ab got to her feet. "Where are you going?"

"Potty break," she said, heading toward the short hall at the far side of the room. "Can you grab me some water?"

I rose, picking up our empty mugs and taking them behind the service counter. I washed and dried them, then filled a couple of paper cups with ice water and dropped them off at our table. Instead of sitting, though, I crossed to the big picture window that looked out on Main Street. The fog was creeping back in, bringing an early twilight with it, and I watched as wispy tendrils probed blindly at windows and doorways, as if seeking a way inside. I thought about Archie Lynch and the fame he had made for himself by taking advantage of people. I thought about the genuine opportunities he had wasted—his father's warehouse business, a career as an Army officer—all because lying was easier. Then

I frowned, wondering what I would end up doing after high school, and hoping my life wouldn't turn out to be a waste, too.

"What are you thinking about?"

Ab's sudden reappearance startled me. I caught myself right away, though, and hoped she hadn't noticed. "I was just thinking about what a douchebag Archie turned out to be," I replied.

"Yeah, he was a real piece of work."

"Do you think Darren and Gina know?"

Ab shrugged. "I hope not. Who would want that kind of loser in their family history? I think the saddest story, though, was poor Eunice. I can't get over how thrilling it must have been for her when a handsome, younger man swept her off her feet, then how crushed she must have felt when he ignored her once he had access to her family money."

I hadn't thought of that. "Did her life turn out okay?"

Ab shook her head. "No."

Her answer hung heavily on the air for a moment while I decided whether I wanted to know more. I didn't want to feel even sorrier for the woman than I already was, but then curiosity got the best of me. "What happened to her?"

"I wondered the same thing, so I looked into it. According to the society pages, Eunice died of 'melancholia,' which is a kind of depression. The tabloids had a better explanation, though. A local drugstore owner told them that she had been going through bottles of this stuff called Laudanum. It was sold as an over-the-counter pain-killer back then and was, like, ten percent pure opium. The article didn't come right out and say so, but from what they hinted at, my guess is she OD'd."

I shook my head, wishing I hadn't asked.

"C'mon," Ab said, tugging at my sleeve, "let's finish up. My mom is making pot roast, and I told her I'd be home in time for dinner."

I followed her back to the table, and she took a long drink of water before continuing her story. "So, there was Archie, with Spiritualism losing popularity and his reputation trashed. One minute he's being wined and dined, all cozy with the high-society types, and the next he's all but broke, sleeping in barns and barely supporting himself by working small towns off the beaten track.

"Then, just when he'd pretty much hit rock-bottom, his luck changed. He was passing through some little farming town—one account I read said it was in Maryland, another said it was West Virginia—when he heard about a Gypsy woman telling fortunes outside the local grange hall, and he went to go see her. That was Cozanna." Ab slid another photo across the table. "Remind you of anyone?"

I looked down, then felt my eyes widen. The old black-and-white was of a slender woman leaning against a willow tree with a lake or river in the background. Dark hair fell well below her shoulders in thick, loose curls. Her head was cocked slightly to the right, with one corner of her mouth upturned in a smile that looked both mysterious and vaguely seductive at the same time. She was barefoot, wearing long skirts and a loose, white top that was unbuttoned partway down in a way that had probably been pretty racy back then. But I only noticed those details later. What drew my attention right away was her tapered chin, prominent cheekbones, and large eyes. Even though generations separated them, the resemblance was definitely there.

"It's *amazing*," I said, shivering as if I had just seen a ghost. "She could pass for Darren's older sister! Gina's, too."

"I know, right?" Ab asked, grinning. "From what I could find out, it was love at first sight for both her and Archie, and she left her people to be with him. Once they started working and traveling together, they became the new "It" couple within just a few weeks. Archie still had a few connections left—enough to open a door or two, anyway—and he knew just how to market Cozanna to put her squarely in the spotlight. They weren't major-league famous like Mata Hari or anything, but they were definitely big in the minors."

"What's Mata Hari?" I asked, frowning.

Ab rolled her eyes. "Do I have to do *everything*? Google her, Wolfman."

I shrugged. "So what made them so special as a team?"

"It was all her," Ab explained. "Maybe Archie was just a fraud and a huckster, but Cozanna...she was the real deal. By all accounts, she was a heavy-hitter as a psychic—like, on a level with you and maybe even Lisette—and wherever she and Archie went, the papers were flooded with rave reviews about her abilities. Maybe she had started out as just a fortune-teller—or *drabarni*, to use the Romani word—but Archie turned her into a star. They performed to sold-out crowds, with Cozanna able to take anyone from the audience and not only rattle off details about their personal lives, but advise them and predict outcomes with dead-on accuracy. Archie had her dress in over-the-top Gypsy costumes, and she used props like tarot cards and a crystal ball and whatnot, but my guess is all that was just for show. The woman was a natural."

"How about cursing people? Could she do that, too?"

Ab shook her head. "Not that I found any mention of. She could pick pockets like a pro, though, and perform slight-of-hand tricks, which they used to spice up her act. Oh, and get this: apparently, she could control birds and small animals."

Another shiver hit me, like icy pinpricks all down my back. In my mind I saw Brianna silhouetted against a backdrop of flames, flailing as a whirlwind of birds attacked her, and all at once my initial suspicions about Darren started creeping back. Could it be that Cozanna's abilities had been passed on to him through the generations? And if so, what else could he do? Maybe the idea of keeping an eye on him hadn't been so stupid after all.

"You're thinking about that night at the beach, aren't you?"

I nodded.

"I thought the same thing."

"But it's just a weird coincidence, though, right?" I insisted hopefully. I was not sure why I even asked, since it wasn't really what I was thinking. Maybe part of me was still looking for a rational explanation so I wouldn't have to face the crazy one. "I mean, that *had* to be just part of their act—trained birds that they used for props, like her crystal ball."

Ab shook her head. "I don't know, Wolfman. Maybe, maybe not. What bothers me is that it's the only possibility we've found so far that could explain what happened to Brianna, so even if the theory turns out to be off-the-charts dumb, I can't see writing it off just yet."

I sighed, giving in…at least for the time being. "Okay. Go on."

Ab looked back down at her notes. "Archie and Cozanna kept raking in the cash for the next couple of years, only slowing down when their son was born in 1914—Marik Randolph Lynch, named after both their fathers. By then they had bought an apple farm in upstate New York and built a big house there. After their kid was old enough to travel, though, they were back on the road every year from May through August, and they kept at it until the fall of 1918.

"What happened then?"

"That was the year a pandemic of Spanish Flu hit the country, brought over by soldiers coming back from World War I. It was huge, killing something like 700,000 people in the United States alone, and all three of them caught it. Archie and Marik ended up pulling through. Cozanna didn't."

"That had to suck for Archie."

Ab nodded. "It did. He must have been devastated, because he disappeared from the limelight for the next couple of years, and only went back on the road when his money started to run low. The problem was, without Cozanna he really didn't have anything, and trying to use his old Spiritualism tricks turned out to be a dud. He returned to Rome for a while, where his apple farm was making just enough for him and Marik to live on, but then something weird happened." She leaned forward, handing me a brief newspaper article:

26TH FEBRUARY 1921

ROME, NY: POLICE WERE SUMMONED TO ROME CEMETERY TO INVESTIGATE THE DESECRATION OF A PROMINENT GRAVESITE. THE CORPSE OF RENOWNED PSYCHIC COZANNA LYNCH WAS FOUND EXPOSED TO THE ELEMENTS, HER CASKET BROKEN OPEN AND THE LID MISSING. AS THE BODY WAS OTHERWISE UNDISTURBED, THE INCIDENT APPEARS TO BE ONE OF MALICIOUS MISCHIEF, AND NO SUSPECTS HAVE BEEN IDENTIFIED AS YET. DETECTIVES POSTULATE THE GHOULISH CRIME WAS INTERRUPTED IN PROGRESS, AS CEMETERY OFFICIALS FOUND THE GRAVE PARTIALLY REFILLED WHEN IT WAS DISCOVERED DURING THE EARLY MORNING HOURS. MR. LYNCH, THE WIDOWER, WAS NOTIFIED, AND IS OFFERING A $500 REWARD FOR ANY INFORMATION THAT MAY LEAD TO THE APPREHENSION OF THE PERSON OR PERSONS INVOLVED. THE INVESTIGATION IS ONGOING.

I looked back up at Ab, raising my eyebrows.

"Weird, right? Now look at this." She passed me another paper, this time an advertisement printed on a handbill:

BY LIMITED ENGAGEMENT: 14TH–27TH MAY 1922
ARCHIBALD LYNCH AND HIS MYSTICAL SPIRIT BOARD
PURVEYOR OF WISDOM AND VESSEL OF ANCIENT KNOWLEDGE!
PAST—PRESENT—FUTURE
WHY TRUST CHANCE? LET BENEVOLENT SPIRITS GUIDE YOU
TO SUCCESS!
MONEY! LUCK! LOVE! FATE!
BY APPOINTMENT ONLY
INQUIRE AT THE EVANS HOTEL, BALTIMORE

"So Archie found another way to bring back his Spiritualist act," I said after reading it, and then set the page aside with a shrug. "So what? No big surprise there."

"Nope," Ab agreed. "No big surprise at all...not unless the two events were connected." She sat back, staring at me.

I frowned, not sure what she was getting at. I picked the two pages back up, comparing the advertisement to the newspaper article, but nothing jumped out at me. "You must see something I don't," I said, looking up in confusion. "The two are nothing alike, and they happened over a year apart."

"*Think*, Wolfman...Spiritualists were all about communicating with the dead, and one of their beliefs was that the souls of the departed maintained connections with places or objects. C'mon...you of all people would know about *that*, right?"

Oh, yeah, I thought, nodding. Since moving to Windward Cove, I had lost count of how many times that had proven to be true.

"And the only thing missing from Cozanna's grave was her coffin lid," Ab went on. "What if—and maybe I'm going way out on a limb here—but what if it was *Archie* who dug up his wife, just to get a big enough piece of her coffin? A year would be more than enough time to have a spirit board made, as well as to let any suspicions die down. Graveyards have always been centers of paranormal activity, and grave-yard dirt is still used for rituals in some religions. Not only that, but I found a couple of articles saying that coffin wood was especially prized for spirit boards, with some makers even using a coffin nail as the pointer for the planchette."

"Planchette?"

"It's that heart-shaped thingy that moves around like a cursor. It has a little window to show which letter the spirit is pointing to. Didn't you ever play with a Ouija board?"

I hadn't, but I'd seen enough horror movies to know what she was talking about: the *Witchboard* series, *Ouija I* and *II*...it was even a Ouija board that got Linda Blair possessed in *The Exorcist*. "I just didn't know planchette was what it was called," I said. "So a Ouija board and a spirit board are the same thing?"

Ab nodded. "It's sometimes just called a 'talking board,' too. They're mostly just seen as a parlor game nowadays, although there are still plenty of people who take them seriously and consider them dangerous. They were used widely back when Spiritualism was in full swing, and Archie would have known all about them."

"Okay, so let's say you're right, and he took a piece of her coffin to make a board. Why hers, and not someone else's? I thought he loved Cozanna."

"He did, and maybe that was the point. I think Archie didn't want to channel just any random spirit...I think he wanted *her*."

"He was *that* obsessed with Cozanna?"

"Maybe," Ab conceded. "But I think it's more likely he thought he could still make money from her abilities...even if he had to reach across to the other side to get them."

"Did it work?"

Ab shrugged. "If it did, there was nothing I could find on it. Archie was shot and killed in 1929 during a card game in Atlanta. The shooter, a man named Harold Mercer, told police that he had caught Archie cheating, and Archie had pulled a knife when he accused him.

I frowned. "That doesn't really sound like Archie...does it?"

"It didn't sit right with me either, but who knows? Anyway, Mercer's story was backed up by a man named Stanley Beeman, who was the only other guy in the room, and the police wrote it off as self-defense."

"Weird, but okay."

"Oh, it gets weirder, Wolfman. Marik was fifteen by then, and he learned all the details when he traveled down to pick up his father's body and stuff. The very same week he was in Atlanta, both Mercer and Beeman died under mysterious circumstances."

"Mysterious how?"

Ab passed over a couple more articles. "Beeman was first. He lived in a boarding house and was found in his room one morning. The valve for the gas heater had been turned on, and he died in his sleep."

"So? Gas leaks used to kill people all the time."

"It wasn't a leak. The valve was *open*. Not only that, but it was July, and the windows in his room were all closed up tight."

"Suicide, then?"

"Yeah, maybe," Ab said, but she didn't sound convinced. "Mercer died two nights later. Police were called to the shack where he lived just outside of town when locals heard screams and gunshots just after midnight. They found him in a back room with four dead raccoons. There was a broken window in the kitchen and raccoon prints all over the house—investigators said there must have been twenty or more of them. There were savage bites all over Mercer's body, one of which had torn open his jugular, which caused him to bleed to death."

I shuddered. "Did anyone suspect Marik?"

"Why would they? Beeman's death was ruled accidental, and everyone assumed the raccoons that swarmed Mercer had rabies. Locals went around shooting every raccoon they could find for weeks afterward."

"Okay, so it wasn't necessarily Marik, then."

"Not necessarily, but then his name came up again a few years later in a study I found about unsolved murders. In 1937, a man named Albert Godsey was found dead in his home, pinned to the kitchen wall by every knife in the house. Marik owed Godsey a lot of money, and the two had been seen arguing. The police interviewed Marik, but he had been at a husking bee—whatever that was—at the time of the murder."

I swallowed. "Anything else?"

Ab nodded. "Marik got married in his twenties, and he and his wife had a son they named Edward. When he was seventeen, Ed was questioned by police when Betty Hanscomb, his former girlfriend who had dumped him the week before, was mauled by a swarm of rats while alone in a girls' bathroom at school. The cops suspected they had been placed there, but they couldn't figure out how. Betty's face was horribly disfigured, and she lost one of her eyes."

I grimaced, feeling vaguely nauseous. "What about Ed?"

"In class taking a geography test at the time." She looked at me solemnly. "Any way you slice it, bad things seemed to happen to people who crossed the Lynch men—at least, once upon a time. It's almost enough to make you believe in curses, isn't it?"

I opened my mouth to answer, but then closed it again when Ab's phone rang.

"Hi, Dad," she said after picking up, and then she paused, listening. "Pretty soon," she answered. "Maybe ten minutes. I'm here with Ben, and we just…what? I don't know…I'll ask." She looked at me. "Dad wants to know if you're coming over for pot roast."

I was about to say no, but then I changed my mind. "Sure. Thanks." Mom would be out with her Sunday running group, first tearing up the back roads and then hanging out somewhere for a bite, which would have left me and Moe alone at the house. I wasn't ready for that just yet. Ab's story had given me a serious case of the creeps, and sitting down with her and her parents sounded like the perfect cure. A big dose of normal was just what I needed right then.

After all, what was more normal than pot roast?

TWENTY-FOUR

THINGS STAYED QUIET FOR THE NEXT COUPLE OF WEEKS, with the weather cooling even more and the sea air tinged with the smells of damp evergreen and woodsmoke. Every few days the sun would peek through the fog for a few hours, or we would get occasional spats of rain, but mostly the world stayed wrapped in a wispy gray blanket, reminding me of a landscape straight out of Grimm's Fairy Tales.

There was a feeling of expectation around school as Thanksgiving drew near, with the top third or so of students already stressing over semester finals when they probably didn't need to, and the bottom third not worried at all when they probably should have been. (I fell somewhere in the middle, knowing that I'd have to spend some extra time in the books, but figuring it was too soon to panic just yet.) A more important issue for most was the Winter Formal, which was scheduled for the second Saturday in December and apparently was an even bigger deal than the Homecoming Dance. Couples began pairing off as early as mid-November, with the remaining guys getting twitchy as they worked up the nerve to ask someone, and the dwindling supply of girls seeming more and more anxious as the days ticked by, wondering if they'd be asked. Overall, though, the mood was festive as everyone geared up for the holidays, with Christmas decorations making an early appearance in most of the downtown storefronts, and the inside of Tsunami Joe smelling perpetually like pumpkin spice.

I was still playing D&D at the Lynch house on Sundays, although for a while there I felt a little uncomfortable. I couldn't be sure, but it seemed as if Gina's chair was positioned a little closer to mine every week. I tried suggesting that we bring Les into the game, thinking he could run interference, but I got outvoted when both Darren and Gina pointed out that we had only just gotten Gina up to speed on how to play, and bringing in another newbie would just slow the campaign to a crawl again. Since I was back to keeping an eye on Darren, and anyway, it was a lot more likely that I was just being paranoid, there was nothing to do but suck it up.

Not long after, though, I was relieved to discover I had been wrong. Gina and Les double dated with Kelly and me a couple of times—once to catch a movie, and another time to see a band that Kelly liked play not far from the Humboldt campus in Arcata. Both times Gina clung to Les like he was the only thing saving her from hypothermia, and while I didn't reach out to sense their feelings, I decided I didn't need to. It was obvious they were really into each other, so I was finally able to relax and let it go.

At last Thanksgiving Day arrived, and when a knock sounded on the front door, Mom glanced over her shoulder at me expectantly. I just smiled helplessly, up to my wrists in the wet bread crumbs she had me squishing together with veggies and spices in a big mixing bowl. The chore wasn't terrible (although working in the raw egg was kind of gross), but since her hands were clean and mine weren't, she hurried off to get the door.

It had been Mom's idea to invite the Thatchers. Kelly had told me early on that her dad wouldn't be home, and that she and her mom would probably just grab a rotisserie chicken and boxes of stuffing and instant potatoes from the market. When I mentioned that to Mom over dinner that evening, though, her face lit right up. "Oh, they are *so* not doing that!" she announced firmly, and told me to let them know that they were expected.

I suppose I should have seen that coming. Thanksgiving was hands-down Mom's favorite holiday, as it was an excuse for her to go totally bananas in the kitchen. She always made a ton of food—turkey, sides, pies, the works—and even if I couldn't see the gears already turning behind her delighted expression, the feelings of excitement and happiness that suddenly radiated out from her made me glad the subject had come up.

In light of the situation, Mom temporarily suspended her no-phones-at-the-table policy, so I called Kelly right then and there. She and her mom accepted right away, and even I picked up on the excitement when Mom suggested I invite any of my other friends who might be free as well. Ab said yes even before I finished asking, glad for any excuse to get out of her family's annual trip to her Aunt Abigail's, and Les accepted right away, too (his dad was a long-haul trucker and was already scheduled to be on the road.) He asked if he could invite Gina, and I told him sure. *Boom!* In the space of just a few minutes, the Wolf Family had gone from zero to officially hosting our first party since moving to Windward Cove. How cool was that?

Although the holiday had still been the better part of two weeks off, Mom became a woman on a mission, and it was fun watching her. Our assortment of mismatched pots and pans had worked just fine since forever, but just the same she decided to replace them with a humongous stainless-steel set that the Amazon guy left on our doorstep a couple of days later. Then she remembered that all our dishes were mongrels too, so she scoured an online auction site until she found an antique China set in an autumn leaf pattern, along with a felt-lined wooden box of vintage silverware that I got drafted to polish. (That was the only part that really sucked. It wasn't that I minded helping out, but the tarnish remover she gave me to work with smelled god-awful, and I thought I'd never get the stink off my hands.) By the Monday before Thanksgiving, our refrigerator was packed with groceries and a twenty-something-pound turkey, and on Wednesday night she set me to cleaning house while she knocked out most of the prep work and baked pies. I thought about pointing out that she was making *way* bigger a deal out of it than she needed to, but seeing as she was having such a good time, I decided to keep my mouth shut.

The faint sounds of greetings drifted in from the front of the house, and a minute or so later I looked over to see Mom leading our guests in. It turned out that Kelly and her mom had made the rounds to pick everyone up in their minivan, so they all arrived together. All but Les followed Mom into the kitchen, while he first threw me a wave, but then hung back in the family room to check the score for the Thanksgiving football game playing on our big-screen TV.

Wendy wore a beige pantsuit that looked super-formal compared to everyone else's jeans and casual shirts, and she looked a little uncertain while lingering near the kitchen archway holding two bottles of red wine and one of white. Mom came to her rescue right away, though, doubling back to draw her further in and saying how excited she was to finally meet her.

I was listening in, trying to gauge how well they would get along, but just then Ab drifted over. She gave me a half-hug while inspecting the amount of stuffing I was working together in the bowl. "How much of that is going into the turkey?" she asked curiously.

"None of it," I replied. "The turkey's already in the oven. And besides, Mom says that life is too short to cram soggy breadcrumbs up a dead bird's butt."

She snickered, but then frowned, comparing the volume in the bowl against the buttered baking dish set to one side. "You don't expect to stuff all that in *there*, do you?"

I rolled my eyes, pretending to be exasperated. "Why do women always *say* that?"

Ab cackled, smacking me playfully on the back of the head, but then she left me to it. I turned my attention back to Mom. After only a couple of minutes of awkward back-and-forth, her charm-factor quickly won Wendy over, and the next thing I knew Mom had set her in charge of monitoring the turkey in the oven, keeping an eye on the internal temp and basting it every fifteen minutes. It probably helped that the two of them immediately broke into the wine, Mom sipping at a glass of white while Wendy stuck with the red, and it wasn't long before any lingering awkwardness melted away completely. It turned out that Wendy had been an art major in college, and within ten minutes they were chattering like besties. The surest sign that Wendy was really starting to relax, though, was when Moe padded into the kitchen a few minutes later to give her a sniff. She scuttled back at first, obviously spooked by the attention of a big dog, and I hurried over to pull him away and apologize. Forty minutes later, though, no one was more surprised than me to see Wendy seated barefoot on the floor against a lower cabinet, her wine glass in one hand while stroking Moe with the other as he dozed contentedly with his head in her lap.

My man Moe!

When dinner was finally ready, everyone helped carry serving dishes into the dining room. They all gushed over the table setting and how great the food looked, and Mom positively beamed. Since we always ate in the kitchen, it was the first time the dining room had been used in who knows how many decades. Mom had batted our first holiday party completely out of the park, and I could not remember the last time she'd looked so happy. When she insisted that *I* carve the turkey, though, saying it was my duty as the man of the house, I was nervous that I would ruin the whole thing. I did my best, though, and if anyone besides me thought the end result looked like something out of *The Texas Chainsaw Massacre*, they were nice enough not to say so.

Dinner was a huge hit, and after lingering for well over an hour and stuffing ourselves until we were groaning, we all shuffled to the couch or family room rug to catch the last few minutes of the football game. Kelly sat next to me on the floor, her head on my shoulder and her left leg draped over my right, and at that moment I wouldn't have traded places with anyone in the whole world.

Next came the Wolf household's most sacred turkey-day tradition: the annual viewing of *A Charlie Brown Thanksgiving*. Wendy looked a little dubious at first, raising her eyebrows skeptically as I started the DVD, but ten minutes later she was all in. By the time Snoopy was wrestling the sling-backed chair in the back yard, she was actually snickering into her glass, obviously enjoying the show in spite of herself. We followed it with *Garfield's Thanksgiving* while eating slices of pie, and Wendy nearly choked on a pecan when one of the sillier jokes caught her off guard—another major win!

Finally, after all the traditions were out of the way, Mom led Wendy upstairs to show her the art studio in the cupola while the girls clustered around a board game at the kitchen table. "Dude…this was awesome," Les told me around a yawn. "Thanks for inviting us." We were sprawled on opposite ends of the couch, both of us still too full to move.

I shrugged, my gaze focused on the showing of *Them!* I had found on TV. It was my favorite of the big bug movies from the fifties, and we were just getting to the part where the highway patrolmen find the little girl walking alone in the desert, mute with shock because her family had been wiped out by the giant ants. "That was all Mom's idea," I told him. "If it were up to me, I would've kept it all for myself and eaten turkey sandwiches for a month."

Les chuckled.

"So how's it going with Gina?" I asked. "It looks like you two are getting pretty cozy."

It was his turn to shrug, followed by a slight frown. "Hard to tell. Some days it seems like she wants us to be together. She'll get all clingy, and we've even kissed a few times. Other days she's like one of those puffer-fish from the nature shows—I get too close, and her spines come out. I dunno...maybe she's still trying to decide."

That made me hesitate. I had only brought up Gina so I could ask Les if he'd noticed anything weird about Darren lately—weirder than usual, anyway—and so I could bring him into the loop on what Ab had found out. I had tried a handful of times at school to let him know that it looked like maybe there was something to Darren's Gypsy curse thing after all, but there was always someone else within listening distance, so I never got the chance. Right then had seemed like the perfect moment to bring it up, but after hearing that he and Gina weren't exactly working out as he'd hoped—at least not yet—I decided not to. Knowing about Ab's and my half-baked theories might make things even more awkward between them, and I figured that was the last thing he needed. "Well, she's gone through a ton of changes since September," I offered instead. "It must take some getting used to."

Les grunted noncommittally, and we went back to watching the movie. "I do like her," though," he admitted quietly after a pause. "Like... *really* like her, you know?"

I looked over at him, eyebrows raised, but didn't say anything.

"I'd like to get more serious—just to see if we'd really be a good fit—but this hot and cold thing of hers is starting to get old."

"What are you going to do?"

Les thought about it, and then sighed. "Ride it out a while longer, I guess," he said at last. "We're going to the dance together, so I'll see how that goes. If she hasn't warmed up to me by then, chances are she's not going to, and it'll be time to tap out." He looked over at me. "It'll suck, but I'll be doing myself a favor by walking away before I *really* fall for her."

I tried to think of something to say that wouldn't sound lame, but it turned out I didn't have to. The scrape of chairs on hardwood flooring rose from the kitchen, and we both looked over to see all three girls on their feet, boxing up their game. Then Kelly and Gina started carrying in stacks of dirty dishes from the dining room while Ab ran hot water in the sink. Les and I exchanged a glance, realizing at the same moment that we would look bad if we didn't get up and help, and our conversation ended there.

With all of us chipping in, everything was washed and put away in no time, and both the kitchen and dining room were more or less shipshape again by the time Mom and Wendy came back downstairs. By then it was nearly 10:00, but even so, I was disappointed when everyone started shrugging into coats and jackets. We drifted toward the front door as a group, with everybody saying what a great time they'd had, how good the food was, and thanking Mom over and over. We lingered on the front porch for a minute or two while saying our goodbyes, and Wendy surprised me again by not only giving both Mom and I long hugs, but making us promise we'd come to their house for Christmas dinner. Kelly finally pried her away, though, steering her to the van and tucking her into the passenger seat. Mom put an arm around me as we both waved, watching until the van's tail lights disappeared down the drive.

But that was only Round One. The next afternoon, the whole group was back again to help us trim and decorate our Christmas tree. It was another Wolf Family tradition—sort of the official kickoff to the holiday season—after which we all feasted on turkey sandwiches and leftover sides. Sitting at the table between Kelly and Ab, it occurred to me that big families who had get-togethers like that were luckier than they probably knew. I smiled, gazing around at the people I cared about, and I suddenly felt warm and more grateful than I could say.

Best Thanksgiving *ever*.

TWENTY-FIVE

We three kings of orient are
Bearing gifts we traverse afar
Field and fountain,
Moor and mountain,
Following yonder star!
O star of wonder, star of light,
star with royal beauty bright,
westward leading, still proceeding,
guide us to thy perfect light!

I HAD NOT KNOWN THAT SAINT AGNES CHURCH HAD ITS own choir—let alone that it would have so many members—but there they were, twenty-five or thirty mostly senior citizens arranged in a semicircle three rows deep. I stood to one side, hoping to catch Father Pete's eye as he directed them through a set of Christmas carols and hymns while shoppers either paused briefly to listen or just streamed on past. Father Pete stood roughly the size of your average grizzly, with muttonchop sideburns and a build like an NFL linebacker, and anyone seeing him for the first time would assume he would be more at home on a Harley-Davidson than in a church. So much for appearances. I had met him the summer before, when Les and I had ducked into Saint Agnes to run down a clue about my family haunting, and I had liked him right off. So, when I saw him directing the choir on the west side of city hall, I decided to hang there for a few minutes, hoping for a chance to say hi.

It was the perfect Sunday afternoon in December—sweater and jacket weather for sure, with the overcast sky dropping an on-and-off drizzle so fine it was almost like mist, but not cold enough to drive anyone inside. Even better, finals were safely in the rearview mirror, so after a stressful couple of weeks, the pressure was off at last. I'd even done better than I thought I would, and when semester report cards were passed out during the last period on Friday, I wasn't disappointed at all to see that I'd scored a C+ in geometry, a B in English, B+ in Biology, and A's in everything else. Not a personal best (and I probably wouldn't be invited to the Worldwide Genius Convention any time soon), but at least Mom wouldn't be disappointed, so that was good enough for me. Best of all, the week ahead would be all half days due to parent–teacher conferences, capped off by the dance that Saturday night, and then it was winter break all the way until January second.

Mrs. Wolf's favorite son was officially a happy guy!

The choir finished the last stanza of *We Three Kings,* and when Father Pete turned to smile and bow slightly to the scattered applause, he finally noticed I was there. He winked, and I smiled and waved in return before finally turning away to scan the crowd for Kelly.

When she had called that morning to ask if I wanted to go to the Silver Creek Christmas Fair, I had been in such a good mood that I said yes without hesitating or even cringing once—definitely out of character for me. It was not that I was against outdoor markets in general, but Mom had gone through a "crafty" phase a few years before and dragged me through probably a half-dozen of them that fall, most of which were totally underwhelming. Ever since then, whenever I heard the term "street fair" I automatically pictured a dozen or so booths selling cutesy knickknacks, table displays of homemade jelly or candles, or bins of tired-looking junk people tried to pass off as antiques. On a lucky day, you might even see a food truck. It hadn't taken me long to decide I'd rather be dragged naked across hot coals, and even Mom quit going after a while.

But it was Kelly asking this time, and since I felt like getting outside anyway, I decided to take one for the team. After all, it wasn't as if I had anything else going on, and since it would be an easy way to rack up a few good-guy points, I resolved to be a good sport and endure whatever suck factor lay ahead.

Ben Wolf, Olympic-class boyfriend.

As soon as we got there, though, all my negative assumptions were totally blown away. The Silver Creek Christmas Fair was *huge!* Town Hall Park was crammed full of tents, plywood booths, and folding canopies, with sellers overflowing into the streets on all four sides. There had to have been two or three hundred vendors at least, and I wondered how far some of them must had traveled to get there. Sure, there was plenty of the cutesy stuff I had expected, but there were also leatherworkers and glass-blowers, book sellers and woodcarvers, artists, craftspeople, fortune-tellers, and everything else in between. Street performers juggled and sang and did magic tricks, cosplayers drifted around in everything from superhero and anime costumes to Steampunk, and I even saw a pretty good Ghost of Christmas Present leading a wide-eyed Ebenezer Scrooge around, trying to shame some goodwill into him. And food? *Holy smokes!* Trucks and food trailers were tucked into spaces all around the perimeter, while inside the park itself were vendors selling pretty much anything you could want. Depending on where you stood, you could smell tamales or roast beef, kettle corn or turkey legs, roasting almonds, calzones, or any of a dozen other aromas drifting on the cool air.

Wow…who knew?

Right then, though, it was that last part that interested me the most. It was nearly 2:00 in the afternoon, and that morning's scrambled eggs and toast had deserted the war a long time before. The problem was that not only had Kelly apparently been born with the same browsing-gene as my mom, but she seemed intent on getting her Christmas shopping all out of the way at once. It seemed like she couldn't pass a single display without inspecting every shelf at least twice, just to make sure she hadn't missed anything she couldn't live without. It would not have been so bad if I wasn't starving, but every time I suggested we grab a bite, she'd get distracted by some other shiny object. There was nothing to do but trudge along behind her, dutifully carrying bags and saying things like, "Sure, that's cool" or "Yeah, I think your mom would like that" whenever she asked my opinion about something. It wasn't much of a job, and it left me with *way* too much time to wonder if I should order the clam chowder in the bread bowl, or go hit the German stand for a bratwurst.

Kelly emerged from a tent selling handmade quilts and table runners, smiling excitedly at me in a way that made me glad I was there all over again. She was wearing that loose, cream-colored sweater I liked, and I felt warm as she slid her arms around my waist and then stood on tiptoe for a kiss. "Having fun?" she asked.

"I am now."

She giggled. "Good—I was hoping you'd like it here. I look forward to it every year!"

"I can see why," I told her, happy that she was so happy. "Say, did you see the German…"

"Oh, *wow!*" she interrupted, gazing past my shoulder. "Look at that!" Letting go, she hurried around me, and I turned to watch her weave crosswise through the crowd to the other side of the aisle, where a big canvas awning covered shelves and tables of glazed pottery.

Sighing, I followed her, wondering how long the Donner Party had held out before turning cannibal.

The area inside was kind of narrow, so I hung back just outside so all the bags I was carrying wouldn't knock something off a shelf that I'd have to pay for. It was then that the familiar odor hit me…earthy and too sweet. I whirled, accidentally bumping a passerby with a shopping bag and muttering a distracted "Sorry" as I scanned the area. I wasn't sure what I expected to see—maybe Darren, maybe some weird misfortune happening to somebody—but everything looked normal. Then I noticed the next booth over, where a pretty brunette lady in jeans and a tailored suede jacket stood beside a display rack of vials and tiny spray-bottles. Above her was a sign that read *Lisa's Essential Oils*, and she had uncapped one of the vials to give a couple of older women a whiff of its contents. *That* was where the smell was coming from.

I edged closer, but couldn't hear what they were saying, so I waited until the older ladies shook their heads and moved on before I approached the seller. "Um…hi," I said.

She turned, giving me a nice smile. "Hello! Can I help you find something?"

"I was wondering what that stuff was you had open just now."

The vial was still in her hand. "This? It's patchouli oil—great for calming the mind, strengthening your immune system, relieving depression, lots of things." She chuckled, giving me a conspiratorial wink. "It's even an aphrodisiac."

I chewed the inside of my lip, wondering if any of that was helpful. Not that I had expected her to tell me *Why, it's just the thing for curses, my boy! Your enemies won't know what hit 'em!*, but then again, I wasn't sure *what* I'd been expecting. Lisa was looking at me curiously, though, so I asked the first question that came to my mind. "Where does it come from?"

"Southeast Asia, particularly southern India. Patchouli is a member of the mint family, believe it or not, and people have been using it for centuries."

India. Hmm.

"So, Gypsies would have used it, then?" I asked hopefully, not really expecting her to know, but feeling my heartbeat increase with excitement just the same.

She straightened, looking a little surprised. "Now *that's* a question I don't get every day, but yes, absolutely. The Romani used all sorts of natural oils and spices, some for everyday things, others in cultural or spiritual ways."

It was my turn to be surprised. "Wow...you really know your stuff."

She shrugged. "My grandmother was half-Romani, and we were close. In fact, she's probably the reason I do this. Selling at local fairs is the next best thing to hitching horses to a *vardo* and living on the road." She winked again, and we exchanged grins.

"Hey, you," Kelly said, stepping up beside me. "Are you getting something?"

"I don't know," I replied, and then realized that I had learned some interesting stuff, and that making a purchase was the least I could do. "I was thinking maybe some oil for Mom—she's running a quart low."

Lisa laughed. "Did you like the patchouli?" she asked, starting to unscrew the cap again.

I took half a step back. "No thanks...I'm not crazy about that one at *all*. What else have you got?"

I ended up buying a spray bottle of cinnamon leaf oil, which apparently was supposed to be good for revitalizing and refreshing, and then I stood by as patiently as I could while Kelly and Lisa discussed oils and aromatherapy in general for nearly twenty minutes.

Twenty. Agonizing. Minutes.

My stomach snarled at me, angry at being ignored for so long, and I checked my watch: 2:28. *That's settles it,* I decided. *I'm going for a bratwurst AND the chowder.*

TWENTY-SIX

THE NIGHT OF THE WINTER FORMAL WAS WINDY AND cold. Hard gusts out of the northwest tore through the intermittent rain, driving it sideways to sting eyes and skin, and carrying a biting chill that seeped down through even multiple layers of clothing to turn everyone's bones to ice. Lightning flickered threateningly behind the clouds far out over the Pacific, warning of a bigger storm that was sure to roll in sometime before dawn.

A good night to stay home.

But I wasn't staying home. At that moment, I was freezing my butt off as I headed toward Silver Creek, my wet hair dripping down the back of my neck while the car's heater failed miserably to drive away the chill. I had left the house at exactly the wrong time, just as the clouds overhead opened up and dumped on me, and even though my car was only a dozen running steps from the porch, the upper part of my sport jacket was nearly soaked through by the time I dove behind the wheel.

If this was karma, then I must have been really evil in a former life.

Kelly had obviously been watching for me, because as soon as I pulled up to her house she was hurrying over beneath an umbrella and let herself into the car before I had a chance to get out and play gentleman. *"Brrr!"* she exclaimed as she pulled the passenger door closed, and then leaned sideways to kiss me. She pulled her long coat tighter around her, and then started to reach for the heater control, but stopped when she saw it was already cranked up as high as it would go.

"A bit chilly out, wouldn't you say?" I asked blandly, backing the car into a turn, and then heading for the mouth of the driveway.

"A *bit chilly*?"

"Maybe even a trifle brisk," I went on. I was trying not to smile, but not doing a very good job of it.

She snickered. "You're a nut."

The rain tapered off just as we pulled into the school parking lot, fooling me into thinking that we had lucked out, but it started again before we were halfway across the quad. We huddled together beneath Kelly's umbrella—not that I minded *that*—and hurried among a scattering of other couples making their way to the gym.

The decorations inside were a mixture of tinsel and garland hanging in graceful arches, strings of white lights, and long artificial icicles that winked as they dangled from the roof trusses. The advertised theme had been "Fairytale Holiday," and I had to say that the decorating committee had done a nice job. Just as we entered, I caught sight of Les and Gina standing for a photo on a small raised platform in the corner, sandwiched between a couple of flocked Christmas trees glowing with lights and ornaments. Behind them was a canvas backdrop showing a snow-covered village scene, with the words *Winter Formal* across the top. At first, I thought that their smiles might have looked a little forced, but then I realized I was probably just reading too much into it after what Les had told me at Thanksgiving, so I dismissed the idea. A strobe flashed as the photographer took their picture, and then they stepped down to fill out an order form with a lady seated at a small desk set to one side.

Les waved as he saw us heading over, and Gina's expression lit with excitement when she noticed us a second or two later. She hugged his arm, entwining her fingers in his, and Les smiled down at her, looking pleased.

Maybe things were starting to work out for them after all.

"Ben…Kelly…hi!" Gina gushed, raising her voice slightly to carry over the music. She was wearing a wine-colored dress that really showed off her curves, and I wondered which of our friends had passed that one on to her. The painfully shy girl under the hoodie had come a long way since September. "You *have* to get your picture taken," she continued excitedly. "Then all of us should get one together!"

I glanced down at Kelly, who looked happy enough with the idea, so I figured *why not?* "I want to check my hair first," Kelly announced, and headed toward the girls' locker room.

Gina watched her go, and then brightened. "Hey, let's get one of us three while we're waiting!"

I looked toward Les, eyebrows raised, but he just shrugged. "Okay, sure," I said.

Only one couple was ahead of us in line right then, so after they were done, we squeezed in together between the trees. The strobe flashed, and we were about to step down when Gina asked Les, "Do you mind if I take one with Ben?"

I detected a brief sting of disappointment from Les as he moved out of the way, but it was gone almost at once. We repositioned ourselves back between the trees, and I offered Gina my elbow. She took it, and I felt a little weird when she moved in so close that the side of her left breast pressed firmly against my upper arm. I figured she didn't realize it, and was about to shift sideways, but just then the photographer said "Hold still," and the strobe flashed again.

As we stepped off the platform, I noticed that Kelly had returned and was watching us coolly from where she stood next to Les. She brightened when she met my gaze, though, and shrugged out of her coat to reveal a dark, sleek-cut dress that made Gina's fade to a distant memory.

"*Wow*," I said, momentarily frozen in my tracks. "You look *incredible*."

She stepped closer, reaching up and pulling my face to hers for a deep, intimate kiss that lasted long enough to make even me self-conscious. Blushing, and noticing that several conversations had trailed off as couples turned to stare, I allowed her to take my hand and lead me back around to the line of people queueing up for the photographer.

It took a moment or two before my heart rate returned to normal. "That was some kiss," I commented at last.

Kelly smiled faintly. "Just marking my territory," she murmured back.

I frowned. "You think I forgot who I'm here with?"

"Oh, it wasn't you I was reminding," she assured me, squeezing my hand. "Was I seeing things, or was Gina rubbing her boob up against you?"

I shrugged. "Didn't notice." I could sense Kelly's skepticism, but I gave her wide eyes—Mr. Innocent—and she let it go. After all, even though Gina *had* pressed herself close, I was still pretty sure she hadn't meant anything by it, so playing it off seemed like the best way to smooth things over. And anyway, even if I was dead wrong, I couldn't see letting it ruin the evening. I decided I would just keep my distance from her for the rest of the night, and that would be the end of it.

By the time Kelly and I finished with our photo, I noticed that Les and Gina had moved off to link up with the rest of our friends near a refreshment table a short distance away. I filled out the order form with the lady at the desk, relieved that the group picture plan had apparently slipped their minds.

Everyone was laughing at something Nicole had just said when we arrived, and Ab ended up just to my right when we joined the circle. "All through strutting on the runway, Wolfman?" she asked, grinning evilly up at me.

"The guy was just trying to get my good side," I told her. "It took him a while to figure out I don't have one." It was then that I realized that Ab was wearing a dress—an actual *dress*—which was something I had never seen before. Even at the Homecoming Dance she had shown up in slacks and a loose top, and the change was surprising. I whistled, and then grinned at her. "Check *you* out, barista-girl…it looks like coffee isn't the *only* thing served hot around here!"

Everyone laughed as Ab turned bright red, and then she slugged me in the shoulder. "Shut *up*," she said dismissively, but looked pleased in spite of herself.

I was about to tease her some more, but just then a sharp stab of jealousy pinged my mental radar. I turned to look at Kelly, wondering what had gotten into her, but as soon as I saw her smiling, I realized it wasn't her feeling I was picking up. I quickly scanned the faces of the others, and for a second thought there *might* have been the shadow of a scowl in Gina's expression, but if it had been there, it was gone before I could be sure—and the feeling with it. Then I reminded myself to quit being so suspicious. Sure, she *might* still be nursing a little crush on me (though it looked like Les was helping her to get over that) but still, she was my friend, and it wasn't fair to not give her the benefit of the doubt. And besides, the range of my gift had increased a lot since summer, and it was just as likely that I had picked up on a random feeling from someone else nearby. Either way, the moment had passed and it probably didn't matter.

We left our coats at a table no one had staked out yet, and then spent the next hour or so dancing near center court. Between the exercise and all the body heat generated by the couples pressed in around us, it wasn't long before I finished thawing out and started to really enjoy myself. We traded partners as time went on, and Gina behaved herself both times I danced with her, so I decided I had been wrong about her after all, and that I needed to stop overthinking things. I relaxed even more when I noticed she stuck to Les through every slow song, and when I saw them kissing a couple of times, I took it as a sure sign that things were looking up between them. If they weren't officially a couple by the end of the night, I figured it wouldn't be long.

After a while, Kelly announced that she wanted to sit for a few minutes and slip out of her shoes, so after dropping her off at our table, I headed for the locker room to take a leak. I was almost there when I noticed Dozer Vasquez standing not far off with a couple of his buddies. He recognized me at the same moment, and said something that I was too far away to hear, but which made the others first laugh, and then turn to stare at me as I passed.

Whatever, I thought, and pushed my way through the locker room door.

The restroom was through an archway on the left, and was deserted except for a pair of legs I could see beneath a closed stall, so I headed to the nearest urinal and took care of business. A minute or so later, I was washing my hands at the sink when I glanced into the mirror and saw Dozer and Alan Garrett standing behind me.

Neither one looked friendly.

I reached out mentally, not surprised at all to sense feelings of anger and a sort of predatory aggression. I pulled a paper towel from the dispenser—a *little* nervous, maybe, but pretty sure it didn't show—then nodded to them as I dried my hands and turned to leave.

Dozer moved to block my way.

Terrific, I thought, and I sighed, wondering just how the next couple of minutes would turn out.

"I'm going to get her back," Alan announced.

I turned toward him, raising my eyebrows, but didn't say anything.

"Sooner or later, Kelly will figure out what a mistake she made, and you'll be history," he continued. "So don't get too comfortable, asshole. Hell, I'll even leave you alone until she gets her head on straight, but once we're together again, it's *on.* You and me are gonna..."

The sound of a toilet flushing rose behind him, catching Alan off guard. I guessed he and Dozer had not noticed we weren't alone. A few seconds later, the stall door opened and Coach Barbour stepped out. He must have been on chaperone duty, and I almost smiled when Alan's feelings immediately turned to anxiety and embarrassment.

"Do we have a problem here, gentlemen?" the big man asked mildly.

There was an uncomfortable pause. "No...no problem at all, Coach," Alan said at last, obviously doing his best to recover. He offered a strained smile while Dozer looked guilty. "We were just talking."

The man didn't look convinced, so he turned his attention to me. "Wolf?"

I allowed myself to grin, thinking that things could not have possibly worked out better. I wasn't stupid—I knew that things with Alan were nowhere near settled yet, but at least it was over for now. Even better, Alan had been busted looking like a major-league dick, which was a bonus. "It's all good," I assured the coach. Then I just couldn't help myself, and gave Alan a friendly clap on the shoulder, causing his head to snap around as he shot me a glare. "Tell Brianna I said hi," I told him, and then headed casually for the exit while Dozer stepped aside to let me by.

"You want to tell me what that little faceoff was about, Garrett?" I heard Coach Barbour demand as the door swung closed behind me, and I felt my grin widen even more.

Sometimes life is just *perfect*.

A couple of hours went by, and Kelly and I were dancing to a slow song when she murmured in my ear, "Do you want to get out of here?"

It was nearly 11:00, and the night had gone so well—*after* the incident in the restroom, anyway—that I had lost track of time. When I looked at her questioningly, she said, "Mother left for San Francisco yesterday to do some Christmas shopping and to be with Dad for his company party. She won't be home until tomorrow night." Then she moved in closer—close enough that I could feel her breath on my neck. "I thought we could spend some time alone together."

She didn't have to ask me twice. We finished the song and then said our goodbyes, with Kelly making the excuse that her shoes were killing her, and we drove back to her house with the wind buffeting the side of the car and the wipers barely able to keep up with the rain.

We made it inside without drowning, though just barely, and I followed her through the dimly lit entry hall to the living room. She touched a wall switch, and a nine-foot Christmas tree lit up, elegantly decorated in red and silver ornaments and loops of ribbon. "Wow, nice," I said.

Kelly smiled. "Do you think you could start a fire?"

"Absolutely." I crossed to the fireplace, where kindling and wood were stacked and waiting. I had watched Les start fires on the beach enough times that I was pretty sure I could get one going without either embarrassing myself or burning the place down, and I was pleased when the kindling caught right away. A minute or two later, flames were crackling cheerfully as they licked at split oak logs, and I congratulated myself inwardly.

Ben Wolf, certified caveman!

Rising, I turned to see Kelly standing beside the tree, next to a thick comforter and some pillows she had arranged on the floor. My breath caught in my throat as she reached behind her to unzip her dress, and she shrugged out of it gracefully, allowing it to drop to the floor. Stepping clear of it, she held her hands out to me, smiling in a way that made my chest feel tight. I moved to her and we touched hands, then she stepped into my arms and kissed me.

After that, things starting happening quickly and it was hard to concentrate. I had not been expecting this, and I was torn between wondering if I was ready, and knowing there wasn't anything else in the world right then that I wanted more. "I've...never done this," I admitted breathlessly as she was pushing my shirt off my shoulders. I was trembling, which made my voice sound shaky.

"It's okay," she whispered, and pulled me down to the floor.

The first time it was over almost right away—totally my fault—but a little while later we tried again, and it was a lot better. After that, we lay there together for a long time, warm under the comforter and talking softly as we gazed up at the lights of the tree and the firelight flickering golden on the ceiling.

Wow. Just...wow, I thought over and over. *Did that really happen?*

After a while, I sighed and made myself check my watch. It was the last thing I wanted to do, and my heart sank when I saw it was nearly 1:00 in the morning. "I have to get home," I said reluctantly. Then I remembered my cell phone in the inside pocket of my sport coat, which I had left on silent, and hoped I hadn't missed any calls.

"*Nooo*," Kelly objected softly, sounding sleepy. "Can't I keep you?"

"I wish," I murmured back. "But I do need to get going. I told Mom I'd be late, but if I'm not there soon, she'll have everyone from the National Guard to Lassie out looking for me."

"Mmm," she said, and then snuggled closer. "Can you at least stay until I fall asleep?"

By the sound of her voice, that wouldn't take long. "Sure. I can do that."

A few minutes ticked by, and I was beginning to suspect that she had drifted off when she murmured softly, "I love you, Ben."

My heart seemed to swell in my chest, and for a moment it was impossible to speak. After a couple of false starts, I finally managed, "I love you, too," and then turned my head to gaze at her.

But Kelly was asleep, and I didn't think she had heard me.

TWENTY-SEVEN

OUR FIRST CHRISTMAS IN WINDWARD COVE WAS totally off the hook!

At least, it seemed that way to me. Until half a year before, Mom and I had never had much money, so the holiday was always more about our special traditions: almond cocoa first thing in the morning, pumpkin waffles for breakfast, hanging out in pajamas most of the day, stuff that just evolved over the years into our routine. Sure, there were never many gifts, but that didn't matter. When I was young, I would give Mom art projects I had made at school, which later got upgraded to things I could actually buy once I was old enough to mow lawns or do chores for some of our neighbors, but never anything expensive. Mom's presents to me were mostly things I needed, like clothes or school supplies, but there were always some fun gifts as well—a few toys when I was really little, a Lego set or two when I got bigger, stuff like that. The afternoon was all about hanging out together, watching old holiday movies while Mom's lasagna baked in the oven, and after dinner we would get in the car and drive around town enjoying the lights, yard decorations, and the Christmas trees we could see through the front windows of houses we passed.

Looking back, Christmas was just as much fun for us as everyone else, and even though I probably realized in the back of my mind that my friends' families made a much bigger deal out of it, I couldn't remember ever feeling like Mom and I were missing out on anything.

This year, though, came with some changes.

By the time I woke up, Mom's favorite holiday music was already playing downstairs. I could hear her clattering around in the kitchen as I let Moe out the front door, which gave me time to add her pile of presents to all the wrapped gifts she had placed under the tree sometime during the night.

We lingered over breakfast like we always did at Christmas, neither of us quite ready for the anticipation to be over. Moe sat between us, tail wagging, as we talked about how dogs *really* shouldn't be allowed in the kitchen, all the while both of us slipping him bits of bacon or waffle while pretending the other didn't notice. Then, at a certain moment when there was a longer than usual pause in conversation, we all suddenly got up and dashed from the table to the tree!

Between us, we exchanged more presents than ever before. Along with a few odds and ends, Mom gave me a couple of packs of new underwear and socks (standard Christmas fare from her) along with six thick flannel shirts that I really appreciated now that we were living on the north coast. Then she blew me totally away with a PlayStation game system, half a dozen really cool games, and a 40-inch flat screen for my room. *Wow!*

For my part, aside from the cinnamon leaf oil, I surprised Mom with a handmade olive wood paint box I had also found at the fair, a Columbia waterproof runner's jacket, one of those fitness bracelets that tracks distance, speed and all kinds of other stats, and a monster-sized box of Godiva Belgian chocolates, just to keep her universe in balance.

Last of all was a set of Dynasty sable hair artist's brushes that got a whoop of joy out of her as soon as she tore away the paper.

Moe's first Christmas, though, was the most satisfying of all. Once he understood that the paw-shaped doggie stocking was his, he stuck his nose inside, cautiously at first, and then with his tail wagging faster as he pulled out various treats and chews, a new collar with matching leash, a nylon ball that made silly noises and flashed lights when it detected motion, a soft flying disc that would float in water, and his favorite of all, a stuffed cow with long rope legs that mooed over and over as he zoomed in crazy circles around the house, shaking it.

By then it was late morning, and since we weren't expected at Kelly's until 4:00, that gave us plenty of time for our movie ritual. Agreeing that we would each pick one, we hauled out our box of holiday DVDs and poured over them. I chose *A Christmas Story*, since watching Ralphie beat the crap out of the school bully never got old. As for Mom, I would have bet real money she'd go for either *Miracle on 34th Street* or *It's a Wonderful Life* (her normal Christmas go-to's), but she picked *The Bishop's Wife* instead, which we hadn't seen in a few years. I was cool with Cary Grant, and by the time Dudley the Angel was saying goodbye to David Niven and Loretta Young, we were both slouched on the sofa with the remains of two movies' worth of snacks scattered on the coffee table, and Moe snoring between us, his new cow still in his mouth.

What a perfect Christmas!

Before we knew it, though, it was time to get ready. Mom wanted to shower first, and asked me to clean up the wrapping paper that was still all over the floor. I managed to gather the whole mess into a single huge wad, hugging it to me as I walked over and tossed it into the fireplace. On the mantel was a lighter that Mom had bought back in June, but we still had never used. I lit a shred that hung off one side, and then sat cross-legged before the hearth as flames ate slowly at the compressed ball. Like the dining room at Thanksgiving, it was the first time the fireplace had been used in who knew how long. Moe padded over to flop on the floor beside me and I stroked his fur, idly wondering if houses had some sort of inner consciousness, and if so, if ours was happy to be lived in again. Not that I would ever share dumb thoughts like that with anyone else, but there you go. It didn't take long for the wad of paper to burn itself out, and after I was sure the black ashes under the grate were cool, Moe and I headed for the stairs.

The shower was still running behind the closed bathroom door, so I went to my room, flopping on the unmade bed and grabbing my cell phone from the nightstand. There was a text from Kelly telling me Merry Christmas, followed a bunch of heart and smoochy-face emojis, and I sent back one nearly as mushy that I hoped to God she wouldn't show to anybody. There was also a group text with all our friends sharing holiday GIFs, and I added one of *Star Trek's* Captain Picard wearing a Santa hat and saying *"Make it snow."*

Just as I pressed send, I heard the bathroom door open and Mom call out, *"Next!,"* and twenty minutes later I was showered, shampooed, and deodorized. I even managed to shave without cutting myself even once—a chore I was glad I only had to do every few weeks, since it usually ended with me bleeding from an annoying number of tiny nicks and Mom calling me "Slash" for the rest of the day.

We were halfway to Silver Creek when my phone rang. It was Wendy, telling us that she hoped we were bringing Moe, and a smile stretched itself across my face as Mom turned the Explorer around. I realized that I was starting to genuinely like Kelly's mother. *Who would have seen that coming?* I wondered.

Having to double back only made us a couple of minutes late, and after we rang the bell, the front door was opened by a man I had never seen before. He was about my height—maybe an inch or two taller— and wore tan Dockers, slippers, and a red-on-black Christmas sweater showing Santa's sleigh in profile, starting just above his waist on the right side and climbing diagonally to his left shoulder. He had friendly looking eyes and a moustache like Tom Selleck. "Hi!" he said cheerfully. "Connie and Ben, right? I'm Jim. Come on in!"

Kelly hadn't mentioned that her dad would be home, but I guessed I should have expected it. Any nervousness I might normally have felt at meeting him for the first time was gone in an instant, though, as I sensed nothing from him but welcoming excitement.

He first shook with Mom, and when it was my turn, I had to shift the gift basket I was carrying to my left arm in order to clasp his hand. The balance was a bit awkward, but I managed without embarrassing myself, and matched his firm grip with one of my own. Five seconds in, and I was already pretty sure that Jim Thatcher was a good guy.

"And who is this?" he asked, noticing Moe sniffing cautiously at him.

"That's Moe," I answered. "Mom's *favorite* son."

"Can you blame her?" he teased good-naturedly, allowing Moe to sniff his hand, and then ruffling his fur.

That sealed the deal. I liked Kelly's dad just fine.

We followed him into the living room toward the kitchen, and I paused long enough to leave the gift basket by the tree. It was from one of those online gourmet places Mom liked, stuffed with crackers, summer sausage, cheeses, and whatnot, and I was straightening when Kelly's voice sounded playfully in my ear. "Mmm…that spot is *exactly* where your head was lying last time you were here."

I spun, my face immediately feeling hot, and I shushed her nervously while she grinned, eyes glinting. Kelly stepped forward, sliding her arms around my waist. "You're so cute when you blush," she whispered, and then kissed me.

I chuckled, beginning to relax again. "Don't make your father kill me on Christmas—it might upset Mom."

"Fine," she warned, "but remember, your life is in my hands." Then she took my arm and led me to the kitchen.

The adults were gathered at one end of a huge kitchen island, with Jim pouring Mom a glass of white wine while Wendy squatted in front of Moe, rubbing his ears. "What smells so good?" I asked, my stomach rumbling at the savory aroma.

"Prime rib," Jim answered. "It still has a while to go. You kids want something to drink?"

We both accepted sodas, and after ten or fifteen minutes of obligatory small talk—mostly Jim asking questions designed to give him an idea of what sort of guy I was—Kelly finally took my hand when there was a pause. "We'll be back in a little bit," she announced. "I want to give Ben his present."

"Go on, then," her father replied, glancing up at a wall clock. "He looks like he's had enough of the job interview for now, and I've got to start on the taters anyway." I looked back over my shoulder as Kelly led me away, watching as he pulled the neck-loop of an apron over his head while stepping toward a pile of washed potatoes and onions that waited beside a cutting board.

"I guess your dad is the cook of the family, huh?" I asked as we started up the stairs.

"Oh, yeah. He's *amazing*, which is why Mother and I are only okay at it. We hardly ever had to cook when he lived here all the time."

That made me think of Kelly's sister, and how her disappearance had driven a wedge between them. "Do you think your mom and dad will ever work things out?"

Kelly shrugged. "I used to, but now I don't know. I hope so."

By then we had reached her room, and the subject slipped my mind completely as she shoved me up against the door, closing it behind us. She pressed herself tightly against me as our mouths found one other, but then it was my turn as I rolled us sideways to press *her* against the wall. Kelly gasped, her hands in my hair, and I was just thinking that things were going about as well as anyone could ask for when one of us knocked an eight-by-ten photo off the wall. It crashed noisily to the floor, shattering the glass, and we both froze breathlessly, waiting for her mom or dad to call up the stairs. After fifteen or twenty seconds of silence we both exhaled. "We might want to throttle this party back a little," I murmured reluctantly, still kissing her, but a lot less intensely.

"Or take it somewhere else," she countered. "You think they would notice if we snuck away?"

"I'm in…how does Tahiti sound?"

"I'll pack a bikini; you make the flight reservations."

We kept going for another minute or so until she finally sighed, pushing me back. "Okay, we'd better stop before someone throws a bucket of water on us. Besides, we'll be busted for sure if I forget and we go back down without your present."

I grinned, stepping back. "This wasn't it? It's the only thing I asked for in my letter to Santa."

Kelly laughed, fanning her face with her hands as the flush of her cheeks slowly faded to normal. "It's all *I* wanted, too. But you must have been extra good this year, because you got a bonus."

She gestured behind me, and I turned to see a large box lying on her bed wrapped in green foil paper and silver and gold ribbons. I hadn't noticed it when we came in, but I'd been sort of busy at the time. I sat on the edge of her bed to unwrap it, releasing the smell of leather when I lifted off the top. Inside, under a layer of tissue paper was a dark brown bomber jacket with a wide collar and pockets above the waistband. I felt my eyes widen. "Oh, *wow*…" I breathed, pulling it out to hold it in front of me. It felt heavy, and the leather was soft in my hands. "Kelly… this is *incredible*!"

"Try it on!"

I did, first pulling off my Levi jacket and tossing it on the bed. It was a perfect fit. In seconds I felt ten degrees warmer, with the scent of new leather surrounding me in a cloud that was nearly intoxicating.

Kelly moved in, sliding her arms around me underneath the jacket and resting her head against my chest. "I'm *so* glad you like it. I was tired of watching you shiver under that thin layer of denim, and I called your Mom to get the size right." Then she gave a low laugh. "The only thing I had to really think over was whether to wrap it in a box, or just have you find me up here wearing it and nothing else."

Personally, I would have picked Option B, but that probably went without saying, so I didn't. I just hugged her tighter instead. "Thank you…thank you *so* much. Between you and Mom, I was spoiled rotten this year."

She didn't say anything; just hugged me back.

"Which reminds me," I said, reaching down to remove her arms from around me, "I have a little something for you, too." I turned to fish out a small box from the pocket of my old jacket. My wrapping job was typically awful, and I hoped it wouldn't bother her too much. "Merry Christmas," I said, handing it over.

"What is it?" she asked excitedly, picking at the tape.

"Forgot," I lied, and I watched as she finally wrestled the paper off to reveal a black velvet box. I grinned with satisfaction when she swung open the lid, and her surprised gasp warmed me even more than the jacket had.

"Oh, *Ben*…"

Inside, lying on a bed of pearl-white satin, was a bracelet Mom had helped me pick out. Two slender chains of silver were braided together with a single strand of gold, looking both sporty and elegant at once. I had been worried it was too over the top, but Mom insisted it was just the thing, so I'd given in and trusted her judgment. By Kelly's reaction, it had been a good call.

"Oh my God, I *love* it! Help me put it on, will you?"

I fumbled with the tiny clasp, careful not to break it. "I thought about showing up wearing this and nothing else," I teased, fastening the ends together, "but my wrists were too big."

She held it up to the light, admiring the glint, and then jumped suddenly into my arms, causing us both to fall back onto the bed in a tangle.

"Kelly?...Ben?" came Wendy's voice drifting faintly up the stairs. "Are you planning to join the rest of us?"

"Be right down, Mother!" Kelly called out, and then turned back to me. "There goes Christmas," she sighed.

I was on my back, gazing up at her through a tunnel of auburn hair that surrounded our faces. "I love you," I told her, sure that she heard me that time.

"I love you, too," she replied, beaming as she stood up and hauled me to my feet. She hurried to her bathroom to give her hair a quick touch-up, then took my hand and led me to the door. "Now, quit grinning and try to look innocent!"

Mom whistled appreciatively when she saw my new jacket, making me blush, and then she noticed the bracelet on Kelly's wrist. Looking back at me, she raised her eyebrows in a *Didn't I tell you?* kind of expression and I nodded, letting her know she was right.

Kelly stepped over to show Wendy her present while her father fixed me with a somber gaze. "It looks like you've reached an important milestone in your relationship, Ben," he said in a serious tone. "You know what it means when a woman starts buying you clothes, don't you?"

I raised my eyebrows. "What's that?"

"She thinks you have rotten taste." Then he grinned while everyone else laughed, including me.

Dinner was ready about forty minutes later, and I realized that Kelly had been right—her dad could have been a chef! The herb-crusted roast was flavorful and melt-in-your-mouth tender, and I think we all put away more than we meant to. Following that, everyone migrated to the family room, where Wendy had another surprise in store. She must have taken a page from Mom's and my book, and streamed one of their favorite Christmas movies—a musical version of *A Christmas Carol*. It was really good, and when I looked over at Mom a few times, I could tell by her expression that we would likely have a copy in our DVD collection before the week was out.

After the movie ended, we all talked for another hour or so, with the adults sipping mugs of mulled wine and Kelly sitting close and holding my hand in both of hers. I was sleepy, full, and next-level happy, and when it came time to leave, I wished I could repeat that whole twenty-four hours again like Bill Murray in *Groundhog Day*. We stood on their front porch for a while, with Mom and I thanking them for the great time and Wendy and Jim thanking us for the gift basket. There were hugs and handshakes, and Kelly surprised me by kissing me goodbye right in front of her folks. It made me a little self-conscious at first, but nobody else reacted like it was a big deal, so I took that to mean everyone was fine with us being together.

At last, we pulled out of their driveway and headed back up the street. Part of me was a little glum that the day was finally over, but then Mom put a cherry on top of the whole thing.

"Hey, Benny."

"Hmm?"

"Let's drive around and check out the lights!"

TWENTY-EIGHT

IT WAS MIDAFTERNOON A COUPLE OF DAYS LATER. I WAS standing in front of the open refrigerator door looking for something to keep me from starving to death before dinnertime when my cell phone buzzed in my back pocket.

It was a text from Ab: [HEY...WHAT R U DOING NYE?]

I thought about it, but couldn't remember any specific New Year's plans. I had assumed Kelly and I would do something—maybe just watch the ball drop on TV—but we hadn't actually talked about it. [DUNNO. U?]

[GOT A WILD HAIR & DECIDED 2 THROW A POTLUCK PARTY @ TJ. BRING KELLY]

A party sounded like fun. If nothing else, it was better than brooding about having to go back to school. [I'LL ASK IF K HAS PLANS 4 US, THEN GET BACK 2 U.]

She sent me a thumbs-up.

I was supposed to go to Kelly's house that night to hang out and stream a movie anyway, but I decided not to wait and phoned her right then while eyeing an open package of hot dogs in the deli drawer. Hot dogs make great survival rations.

She picked up on the second ring. "Hey, you!" She sounded glad enough for the call, though tired, and her voice was kind of raspy.

"Hey. Ab's throwing a New Year's party at the coffee house. Should I tell her we're in?"

"I don't know," she said in a way that made my spirits dim a little. "I woke up this morning with a sore throat. I've been holding off calling you, hoping it would go away, but now I have the sniffles, too. I may be coming down with a cold. But I'd love to go, so if I'm better by then, sure. For now, though, you should probably stay home tonight."

That sucked. I hadn't seen her since Christmas, and I was pretty sure I would be going through serious withdrawals any minute. "Can I bring you anything?" I asked hopefully.

"Mmm…a warm, steaming cup of Ben would do me good, but that'll have to wait. Thanks, though."

"Well, let me know when you're all done being Typhoid Mary, 'cause I want to see you," I told her. "Even if you're only feeling well enough for company by then, I'll be glad to blow off the party and hang with you instead, okay?"

"Okay. Call me later?"

"Count on it. Bye."

"Bye." And she hung up.

Crap. I closed the refrigerator door, not really hungry anymore.

I texted Ab with the latest, saying we were a definite maybe, and she told me that was fine. Still, I felt bad for leaving her dangling, so I promised I'd let her know as soon as I could.

Kelly only got worse over the next couple of days, though—high temperature, coughing and sneezing, the whole nine yards—so when the 31st rolled around and she was still under the weather, there was nothing to do but throw in the towel. Mom was attending a get-together with her running group, so I was on my own for the night. "What do you say, Moe?" I asked, grabbing a couple of bags of chips to contribute to the party. "Want to be my plus-one?"

He was good with that, so we headed for town.

Cars crowded every available space surrounding the coffee house, forcing me to park near the Texaco station more than a block over. All the other storefronts downtown were dark and quiet, making Tsunami Joe stand out like a lighthouse, and we followed the muffled sound of music to where the party was already in full swing.

We were fifteen or twenty steps from the front door when it opened and I saw Les emerge, one hand on the collar of Tony Cruz's leather jacket as he half walked, half shoved him out onto the sidewalk. Vern was right behind him, escorting a girl by the elbow. She was skinny and had spiky hair, and after a second or two I recognized her as one of Darlene's friends from the first day of school.

Tony stumbled a couple of steps after Les released him with a final push, and then he whirled, looking furious. The girl jerked her elbow angrily out of Vern's grasp before moving to his side. "What the *hell*, man!" Tony shouted. "You can't kick us out—this is a public place!"

"No," Vern corrected as Moe and I drew near, "this is a *private* party on *private* property, and you weren't invited. You might have been able to stay if you'd played nice, but you couldn't do that, could you? So you're out…and don't come back."

"You're kicking us out of a *public* place just because some little bitch can't take a joke?"

Les stepped forward, his eyes narrowing. "Call her a bitch one more time, Chumley, and I'll *publicly* hand your ass to you."

I swallowed as my senses were nearly overwhelmed by the sudden tension in the air. It was only the second time I had seen Les that angry, and I realized again how scary he could look when he wanted to.

Cruz must have thought so, too. He opened his mouth as if to say something, seemed to think better of it, and then closed it again and settled for a glare instead. Putting an arm around the girl's shoulders, he turned suddenly and headed up the sidewalk, purposely bumping his shoulder against mine as they passed. Maybe he thought it would make him feel tough again. Moe didn't like it, though, lunging at him with a snarl, and the two scurried quickly out of range.

I grinned. It was probably hard to scurry and feel tough at the same time. "What was *that* all about?" I asked, bending to stroke Moe. The muscles beneath his fur were hard with coiled energy as he stared after the retreating couple, and then relaxed as they disappeared into the gloom.

"Just a couple of A-holes," Vern answered. "They cornered Gina while Les was getting drinks and started giving her crap. Something about a threesome, and I guess it got pretty nasty. Then Darren stepped up, and he and Cruz were close to throwing hands, but Les and I took care of things."

"So where's Kelly?" Les asked, clearly wanting to change the subject. He still looked a little angry, but I could sense his needle had already dropped out of the red zone.

"Down with a cold. Or maybe Brad Pitt called. Could be either one."

"Sucks for you…though not so much for Brad. Glad you made it, though, hombre. Let's get inside. It's cold out here."

As Moe and I followed them through the door, I discovered that word had really gotten around about Ab's party. Instead of the twenty-five or thirty people she told me she had invited, there was probably twice that number crowded inside. I looked around for Ab, finally catching sight of her on the far side of the room. She was standing beside Gina, whose face appeared strained as she sat at a small table with Darren looming behind her. He was scowling, his cheeks red, and I wondered just how mad he was. His expression was not much different from how he looked most of the time, though, so it was hard to tell. A superstitious part of me was uneasy, dreading that some strange accident would happen at any moment, while another part of me almost wished it would, just so I'd know for sure. Moe and I hung back, watching from a distance for a while, but when the only change I saw was the color of Darren's face returning to normal, I figured I was just being paranoid.

Les joined them and squatted on Gina's other side, looking like he was trying to cheer her up. He said something I was too far away to hear, and she gave him a wan smile. She seemed to brighten, though, when she caught sight of Moe and I making our way over, and even Darren gave me a sort-of friendly nod, so I figured things were already blowing over and hadn't been such a big deal after all.

I was starting to get uncomfortably warm in my jacket, so while Moe wove his way through the crowd toward Ab, I changed course and ducked into the back room to stash it away. I hung it on one of the hooks they used for aprons, and then turned to see Ab and Moe enter behind me. "Hey," I said. "Sorry we're late. Where do you want these?" I held up the chips.

"There are tables on the back wall where everybody's been piling snacks," she answered, waving vaguely in that direction. "Les says Kelly couldn't make it?"

I tried the Brad Pitt line on her, but she wasn't much more supportive than Les had been.

"That's too bad. Listen, some people are wanting to dance—you mind helping me clear some space?"

"No problem." If I was dateless, I might as well be useful.

We spent the next few minutes shooing people out of the way so we could move tables and chairs, with other kids pitching in to help when they saw what we were up to. Ab then dimmed the lights by about half, and in no time at all the floor was packed with couples. Idly, I scanned the crowd, suddenly locking eyes with Gina as she danced to a slow song with Les. Noticing that she was distracted, he frowned, following her gaze, and I raised my chin in acknowledgment when he saw me. He nodded back, and I turned away to look for Moe.

I found him a minute later, watching me from where he sprawled beside an easy chair well clear of the crowd. The chair was empty, so I stopped by one of the refreshment tables, found a paper bowl and a bottle of water, and then joined him. Pouring half the bottle into the bowl for Moe, I settled back with the other half, happy to just chill for a while. I didn't particularly feel like dancing myself, so I settled in and had fun just talking with friends who drifted by to say hello. Nicole found us not long after, and after loving on Moe for a couple of minutes, she dragged over a chair. Kim and Vern soon followed, and we formed our own little circle, just hanging out and talking about everything and nothing at all.

The only damper on my good mood was Gina. I sat facing the crowd, and as time went by, I caught her staring at me three or four more times, twice with a slow smile that made me squirm a little. Les noticed it, too. She wasn't much for staring when Kelly was around, I realized, and I didn't want to think about what that meant. Later, I saw her and Les having what looked like a serious discussion, with Les pointing toward me from across the room. *Crap.* I shifted my gaze away before either of them noticed me watching, casting only quick glances out the corner of my eye to see what would happen. After a minute or two, Gina stepped closer, placing a hand on his arm and saying something that seemed to mollify him. Then she gave him a hug, which helped even more, and after a brief hesitation he hugged her back.

I relaxed. Crisis averted.

After a while our little circle broke up, which was fine because Moe had gotten restless—a sure sign he needed to pee. I led him down the short hallway past the restrooms and out the side door to the alley. I stood shivering while he watered the wall, and when we went back in, we nearly ran into Les heading for the men's room.

"Hey, brother," I said.

"'Sup, hombre."

As we passed, I took a quick read of his emotions. Les was annoyed—and I had a pretty good idea why—but at least it wasn't directed toward me, which made me feel better.

Just the same, I decided it might be a good idea if I got out of there, so I scanned the crowd looking for Ab so I could say goodbye. I caught sight of her at the edge of the mass of dancers just as the music swelled into a ballad. As I walked toward her, I noticed Gina standing about the same distance from Ab on the far side of the room. She glanced at her watch, and then looked around until she saw me. Smiling, she headed my way.

I glanced at a wall clock, pretending I hadn't seen her, and I was alarmed to see it was 11:58. The *last* thing I needed right then was to be anywhere near Gina at midnight. I lengthened my stride, trying not to be obvious about it, and made it to Ab while Gina was still ten feet away. "Let's dance," I said, taking Ab's arm and all but dragging her into the crowd.

I had caught her by surprise, but she recovered quickly. "Dodging bullets, are we?" she asked teasingly, putting her arms around my neck.

I showed her my confused expression—the one that comes naturally to me. "What do you mean?"

"Oh come *on*. You're telling me you haven't noticed Gina staring at you all night?"

"You're nuts." To be extra convincing, I turned Ab so she could see where Gina was now dancing with Les a short distance away. "See? A diehard Hawkins fan."

Ab snickered. "You absolutely suck at lying, Wolfman—did I ever tell you that? But never mind. I've got your back."

I opened my mouth to argue, but then decided to quit while I was behind. Ab settled in comfortably against me, allowing me to slowly put more real estate between us and Gina as we danced, and I began to relax again. It then occurred to me (and not for the first time) that Ab smelled good. Not in a perfumy kind of way, but rather just the clean smell of her skin and whatever soap or shampoo she used, along with just a whiff of coffee beans. It was nice.

All of a sudden, everyone around us started counting down: "FIVE! FOUR! THREE! TWO! ONE! *HAPPY NEW YEAR!*" Cheers erupted deafeningly all around us as couples started exchanging handshakes, hugs, and New Year's kisses. I smiled, looking around as everyone celebrated, then turned and met Ab's gaze. We shared a pause that lasted maybe two heartbeats, and then she pulled my face to hers and kissed me. *That* was nice, too. It wasn't a romantic thing, and I would have thought getting kissed by your best friend would feel all kinds of awkward, but it didn't. Then she grinned, slugging me in the arm before turning away to wish other people happy New Year.

I still wanted to go, but I didn't want to leave with things between Les, Gina, and me all weird, so I circled through the crowd, keeping out of sight as I angled to move in behind them. Along the way I scored big hugs from Monica and Nicole (which didn't bother me a bit), and I successfully surprised both Gina and Les by sneaking between then and throwing an arm over each of their shoulders. "Happy New Year!" I said, and drew them in for a three-way hug, figuring it was about as neutral as you can get. A three-way is the Switzerland of hugs.

After a second, Les pulled back to look at me warily, his eyes glinting with humor. "Dude...I love you like a brother, but I am *so* not kissing you!"

"Really?" I joked back. "You mean I wore lip gloss for nothing?" They laughed, giving me a chance to disengage and leaving them with their arms around one another. Just then I felt a hand on my arm, and

I was spun around to face Vern, who drew me in for a hug with lots of back-pounding. I used that as an excuse to move on, shaking hands with some kids I knew and others that I didn't, maneuvering my way clear of the Gina-zone.

Ben Wolf, master escape artist!

At last, I emerged from the milling crowd, and I headed to the back room for my jacket. It was time for a stealthy exit. I was just taking it off the wall hook when I heard Gina's voice: "Ben?"

I looked over, my heart sinking as I saw her just inside the archway. So much for stealth.

"You're not leaving, are you?"

"Yeah, I think I've had enough fun for one night," I said, trying to sound both cheerful and aloof as I shrugged into my jacket. Behind her, I saw Les move into my field of vision, looking around. Then he saw us alone together, and frowned.

"I wanted to wish you happy New Year," she said, reaching out as she started toward me.

I was out of options, so I did the only thing I could think of. "Hey, Les," I called, looking past her, "I'm taking off. You need a ride?"

Gina whirled just in time to see his expression go stony before he turned and walked away. She hesitated, and then hurried after him. I followed a couple of seconds later, emerging in time to see her standing halfway across the floor, watching as Les disappeared out the front entrance without a backward glance.

I'd had enough. Moe was still near the hallway to the restrooms, so while Gina was distracted, we slipped out behind her and left by the alley door. It took only a minute or so to trot up the street to the car, and then only a minute after that to catch Les in the headlights, walking fast as he headed for home.

Leaning way over, I managed to reach the crank handle and had the passenger window rolled down just as we pulled up alongside him. "Hi, sailor," I called out. "Going our way?"

He ignored me at first, taking half a dozen more strides before he finally stopped and turned. "Is Gina with you?" he asked warily.

"No."

"Good." He got in.

Silence hung heavily between us while I tried to come up with something to say. "Listen…"

"Don't," Les interrupted, and I didn't even need to try in order to sense his mixture of anger and sadness. "I'm not pissed at *you*, but you probably already know that, don't you? We're cool—I'm just not in the mood to talk."

"Want me to drop you at home?" I asked.

"I dunno. I guess. Though it's not like I'll be able to sleep."

"I've got a better idea, then," I said, and drove to my house instead. Inside, we crept upstairs to my room, closed the door, and fired up the PlayStation. We decided on an offroad racing game we could run side by side, and after a while I could sense his tension start to ease. He chose a tricked-out Jeep Rubicon while I went with the Hummer. Both of us had to finish in at least third place before we could proceed to the next level, so we raised the stakes by making up a rule that if only one of us qualified, the other had to change his truck's color to pink until he made it.

It turned out that Les was better than I was, and I ended up driving pink a *lot*, but that was okay. All that really mattered was that he started feeling better after a while. The sky was turning light in the east by the time we both had enough, and Moe and I fell asleep on my bed while Les crashed out with a pillow and a couple of blankets on the floor.

When I woke up at 10:45, Les was already gone.

TWENTY-NINE

RILEY CHASE INHALED A BREATH, KEEPING HER CHIN LOW *in the water and elbows high as she rotated her arms forward, and then noted that she was too close for another stroke. She touched the wall with hands shoulder-width apart and lifted her head. Legs together, she brought her knees to her chest and then dropped her left elbow while bringing her right arm over the top of the water. Sinking her hips, she pushed off from the wall with her feet to complete a near-perfect butterfly open turn.*

Nailed it! *she thought triumphantly.*

Riley loved the fly because it was so hard. You needed a core like iron to maintain the kick—two per every arm stroke—the turns took practice, and pulling through the water for 100 yards always left her deltoids, pectorals, and lats burning, but in a good way. Sure, the 200- yard free was her best event (she had a lightning flip-turn), but the 100 fly was her favorite. There was so much going on at once, but when you found the rhythm, it was like your whole body was a machine.

She was still feeling strong when she reached the far end of the pool, and was setting up for another turn (faster this time!) when she heard the chirp of Coach Camarillo's whistle. Riley lifted her head from the water as she allowed her momentum to carry her to the wall, and raised her goggles with one hand while catching the edge with the other. She breathed deeply, enjoying the stretched-out feeling in her lungs. "Yeah?"

"I want to see your arms out wider while pulling down and back," the dark-haired woman instructed, her voice echoing hollowly. The glow coming up from the pool bathed her in a shimmering blue, looking almost magical in the otherwise dim interior. "It's harder, but you'll grab more water that way, and we need to trim at least another two and a half seconds off your fly if you want to qualify for State this year. Also, you kicked off on that last turn with a little arch in your back. Keep it straight—you're an arrow in the water, remember?"

"Okay."

The coach nodded, and then pulled back the cuff of her maroon track suit to check her watch. "Alright, hon, that's enough for today."

"C'mon, Coach...ten more laps. Please?"

"Riley, I have a life. If I'm not home soon, my husband will try to cook dinner. That never ends well."

Riley grinned. "Eight more and I'm done. I promise."

"Do we really have to have this argument again?"

"Of course not. You can give in. It'll save time."

The woman chuckled fondly. "I'm serious. Out. I need to lock up."

"So go," Riley pressed. "I'll finish my workout, and make sure the door latches behind me. C'mon. It's not like you haven't let me stay before."

The woman pursed her lips, considering it. "I swear, if you tell anyone..."

Riley made a show of looking around. "Who would I tell?" They were the only ones in the building.

"Nobody likes a smartass, kiddo."

"Aw, you love me. You know it."

Coach Camarillo shook her head. "The problem is you know it. Fine, but promise me you'll keep it to eight laps, okay? It's only Wednesday, and we have a lot more work to do before the end of the week. I don't need you straining anything."

Riley smiled her thanks, pulling her goggles down over her eyes and pushing off from the wall. "Eight laps! No more!" she heard the coach shout after her, but she was already a quarter of the way down the swim lane and feeling too good to stop. Eight more laps.

Or maybe ten!

Four laps later she took a breather, coasting to the edge again and moving her goggles up to her forehead before reaching for her water bottle. Coach was right—pulling with her arms wider made a difference, but God her lats were screaming! She smiled, gripping the edge to stretch her upper back while enjoying the way her breathing and heart rate returned to normal in less than thirty seconds. If everything went according to plan, she would absolutely dominate *North Coast Sections that year, medal at State, and then sit back and watch the scholarship offers roll in!*

Sometimes Riley wondered how her life would be different without her training schedule. Two workouts per day, six days a week, on top of her college-prep courses didn't leave a lot of time for much else. But she was used to it...thrived on it, actually. She smiled again, remembering how annoyed she had been over having to break her routine even to go to the Homecoming Dance. At first, anyway...but it had ended up being totally worth it. Homecoming Queen...who'da thunk that would ever happen?

As good a time as she'd had, though, it only reminded her of everything she was missing out on...especially guys. She hadn't had a boyfriend in nearly two years, and hadn't even been on a date since the previous spring. Somewhere along the line, they had just stopped asking, but she supposed she couldn't really blame them. She nearly always had to say no, and even when she did say yes, she had to be home in bed by 10:00 so she could be rested for her 5 a.m. workout. She had gotten used to going it alone, and couldn't even remember the last time she had given the idea of dating more than a passing thought.

But then she had met Kelly's new boyfriend, and suddenly she was thinking about it all over again. Ben had distracted her right away. Lean... good shoulders...nice ass. Good looking, too, but without being a pretty-boy. Riley had been keeping an eye on him since the dance, and was attracted by what she had seen so far. His comfortable manner with his friends. The way he was with Kelly...not a clingy puppy-dog, and not a self-centered jerk like Alan, either. Even watching from a distance, she could tell he was comfortable in his own skin, possessing a sort of easygoing, almost offhand confidence that drew her like a magnet. And that look he got sometimes...what was up with that? Every now and then, he'd get this peculiar expression on his face while watching someone, almost like he could see right into their soul. Riley couldn't help but wonder what it would feel like if he looked at her that way...and whether or not he would like what he saw.

Quit it! *she thought. She didn't have time for boys, especially ones who were already taken. And that stunt she had pulled during lunch was totally out of line. She had gone by the table where Ben and his friends always hung out, asking Kelly a question about their English homework, but really just there to see if Ben would notice her. After Kelly answered, she had turned her attention to him.* "Hey. Ben, right?"

"That's the story going around."

She smiled, pleased that he had remembered her own words from Homecoming. "Do you swim?"

He shrugged. "Not the way you probably mean, but I haven't drowned yet."

"Well, you look pretty fit. If Kelly's ready to share you, we can always use more guys on the team."

"Careful, amigo," Les Hawkins told him, grinning. *"Riley's a beast in the water. Better men than you have died trying to keep up."*

"What...you think I couldn't be a contender?" Ben argued, grinning back. *"Ten bucks says I can take the silver in cannonball."*

Everyone at the table had laughed. Well...nearly everyone. Darren Lynch just scowled, his gaze going back and forth between them. Riley knew that Darren had once liked her—maybe even still did—and although she had forgiven him a long time before about that incident in fifth grade, she had kept a careful distance. The pretty brunette seated next to him (his cousin, she'd heard) just watched the exchange with a solemn expression on her face, making Riley wonder if he had confided to her about his crush. That, or maybe she was just picking up on Darren's mood.

"I think Riley just wants to see you in a Speedo," Kelly teased, grinning mischievously. *"Come to think of it, I wouldn't mind, either."*

"Me? In a banana hammock? Keep dreaming."

More laughter.

"Think about it," Riley said. *"The swim team, I mean. Official practice doesn't start until March, but in the meantime, I could coach you."* She grinned, deciding at the last second to throw a little flirt his way, just to see what would happen. *"I bet you'd be great at breast stroke."*

Ben had flushed a deep red—so cute!—causing the table to erupt in laughter again, and Riley had winked at Kelly to let her know she was only joking.

*Well...*mostly *joking.*

Quit it! *she told herself again.* Sections...State...lock in that full university ride...and *then* a boyfriend. In that order. *She took a breath and pushed off for her final set of laps, swimming fast to leave distracting thoughts in her wake.* And no more flirting with Kelly's boyfriend, *she scolded inwardly, promising herself that she would be good from then on.*

Of course, if down the line the two of them ended up not working out...

But she would worry about that if and when it happened. Until then, she had work to do.

Riley was more than halfway through her third lap, and had just raised her head for a breath when she was shoved violently downward from her shoulders, hard enough to make her somersault beneath the surface. She came up coughing a few seconds later, treading water while she tore her goggles off. "Hey!" she cried angrily, looking around.

She was alone.

The echo if her cry rang hollowly in the pool center for two or three heartbeats as she continued to gaze around apprehensively. The light from the high windows was fading as the mid-January afternoon deepened toward twilight, and the blue glow from the pool, which she usually found so peaceful, now just seemed to magnify the shadows. "Is someone here?" Riley called out, wondering what the hell had just happened, and then she wrinkled her nose.

What on earth was that smell?

It drifted in from seemingly nowhere, faint at first, but slowly overcoming even the strong odor of chlorine. Sweet and pungent...almost like incense.

Screw this, *Riley thought, all at once feeling unsettled and vulnerable, and she resumed swimming toward where her stuff was piled at the end of the lane. It was time to go home anyway. A nice, hot shower, then dinner with her parents and little brother. She remembered her Mother was making stroganoff—one of Riley's favorites—and the thought cheered her even as her stomach rumbled.*

She was almost to the edge when something hit her again, feeling like open palms slamming into her abdomen and lifting her completely clear of the pool! As she flew backward, Riley wondered how she had missed someone lurking below the surface before she hit the water flat on her back, one calf landing on the lane float and spinning her as she went under. She recovered quickly, coiling her legs beneath her as she touched bottom, and *then shot back to the surface, swimming hard.* Whoever the hell you are, good luck catching me! *she thought, shoving her fear aside and focusing on getting to the far end. She was in her element, the familiar rhythm calming her, and she began to feel confident again. Nobody could catch her in a freestyle sprint. Nobody.*

She was wrong.

Riley was six feet from the safety of the edge when she was shoved under again. The pool was shallower on that end, and she slammed painfully against the bottom in just five feet of water. Bubbles exploded in front of her face as she lost maybe a quarter of her air. She gathered her arms under her, straining against the hands she could feel pressing down on her back. She couldn't budge! It was like being pinned under a truck! But how could that be?

Okay asshole, *she thought, grasping at the only plan she had left.* I can hold my breath for nearly two minutes…how about you? *She forced herself to stay calm, still straining to shove herself upward while the first minute ticked by with agonizing slowness.*

After a minute and twenty seconds, her lungs were burning and Riley began to feel the first stab of genuine terror. Craning her neck around, her eyes suddenly widened and she had to struggle not to gasp.

No one was there!

No, wait, *she realized, her heart rate increasing. There* was *something—a dark shape just above her, like a cloud of black oil in the pool. As she watched, the darkness gathered itself into a shape, and it took her a few seconds to figure out what it was:*

A woman! A woman with billowy hair floating just above her… pressing her down with almost crushing force!

Panic finally overcame Riley and she scrambled helplessly in place, pinned against the bottom while her palms, knees and elbows abraded themselves raw against the rough pool floor. Sudden, bright pain in her back made her scream underwater as she felt ribs let go from the downward pressure, first on her right side, then on her left.

At a minute-fifty she was exhausted, her vision graying around the edges as she scratched weakly at the concrete. Blood oozed from beneath her torn fingernails, rising gracefully in the water like wisps of crimson smoke.

After two minutes and eighteen seconds, Riley's body floated to the surface, rocking gently as the ripples in the water slowly grew still.

Eleven minutes later, the timer for the underwater light ran out, plunging the deserted pool center into darkness.

THIRTY

THE DEATH OF RILEY CHASE HIT SILVER CREEK HARD.

The news swept through town like a flash flood. By Thursday afternoon, storefront windows across both Silver Creek and Windward Cove were edged in dark fabric, most with *In Memoriam* notices posted at the entrances. Church services for the coming Sunday were being rewritten, and everywhere you looked on Facebook, people had changed their profile picture to Riley's senior photo with a black band across the middle. Someone set up a GoFundMe account for Riley's family, and by nightfall it had already generated nearly twelve thousand dollars, and not just from local folks, either. I found out later that Riley was something of an area celebrity—known, liked, and respected among rival schools for miles around—and the donations just kept pouring in.

Kelly was waiting for us in the school parking lot when Ab, Les, and I got there, and one look at her expression was enough to tell me that something was terribly wrong. She was beside my car almost before we had our doors open, and was holding back tears when she blurted out that Riley was dead. Kelly had only heard the story herself minutes

before, and while we stood there in stunned silence, she told us everything she knew.

Riley had never come home from her after-school workout. When
a full two hours had passed with her cell phone going to voicemail, her
parents got worried and called first Coach Camarillo, who didn't pick
up either, and then around to Riley's close friends. That alone took the
better part of another hour. Afterward her mother phoned the sheriff's
office, asking if any accidents had been reported, while her father drove
around town, looking for Riley's blue Kia Soul. It didn't take him long
to find it, sitting by itself in the otherwise deserted school parking lot.

Kelly's voice began to hitch as she went on that when his loud
knocking on the pool center door went unanswered, Mr. Chase became
frantic. A few phone calls later, a deputy arrived along with one of the
school janitors and Principal Powell. The janitor unlocked the pool
center for them and turned on the lights, and that was when they saw
Riley floating face down. Her father screamed her name and dove in
after her, and even though the deputy tried CPR while Powell called
911, Riley was already gone.

A swarm of first responders were there in minutes, and the janitor
was there for most of what followed. He was interviewed by one of the
deputies, and afterward hung back out of the way, not sure what he was
supposed to do next. He was close enough to listen as Mr. Chase made
his own statement, and it was around then that Sheriff Hastings noticed
him standing there and told him to leave. The janitor went straight to
Vera's Bar and told a few friends everything. Small towns being what
they were, the news spread quickly.

Kelly got through almost all of it before she began to cry, and I held
her for so long afterward that we were almost fifteen minutes late to first
period. (Not that it mattered—lots of students were tardy that morning,
and some never showed up at all.) Tears sprang from Ab's eyes as well,
and even Les kept wiping his cheeks as we all just stood beside my car,

not knowing what to say or do. For my part, I did my best to keep my gift under control as their combined feelings all but overwhelmed it. Soaking in all that concentrated grief made my own eyes blur with tears several times, but I had known Riley least of everyone, so that was as far as it went. Still, there was a heaviness in my chest that ended up staying with me for the rest of the day. She had been nice, and I'd liked her.

What made the whole day even worse was how specifics came out piecemeal. The news that she had drowned was shock enough—totally unthinkable for most people—but when word got out later that Sheriff Hastings had opened a murder investigation, everyone was overwhelmed all over again.

The effect it had at school was devastating. Most kids suffered from at least some degree of shock, with many walking to classes in a daze, and then being unable to concentrate once they got there. Many more repeatedly broke down in tears. Almost everyone else was stunned into near silence, seemingly unable to speak above a hushed tone. It was as if Silver Creek High had turned into a cathedral, or maybe a mausoleum, and it was every bit as eerie as it was depressing. Both the school nurse and counselor had their hands full working grief management, and so many students asked to go home that just before lunchtime Principal Powell announced that classes were cancelled for the afternoon and the whole next day.

Naturally, whispered rumors made the rounds all morning long, some of them so far off the reservation that I couldn't believe how anyone could take them seriously. The pool drain had opened on its own, pulling Riley under...the water heater had gone into overdrive, boiling her alive before she could swim to the edge...stuff like that. By third period there was even a story going around that two of Riley's friends had been hospitalized and placed on suicide watch, but that turned out to be crap, too. The truth was that Riley's best friend had cried uncontrollably when she heard the news, and had to be sedated at the urgent care clinic, but she was home and in her own bed a couple of hours later. Still, it was bad enough.

It was around then that I started doing what I could to squash the rumors whenever I heard them. I reminded kids of how much of that stuff had been debunked already, that next to no real information had been released yet, and that we all owed it to Riley to chill out and wait for the official news. Did it help? I would have liked to think so—even if only a little—but I'd be lying if I said I knew for sure. Then I felt guilty, wondering if it was even my place to lecture anyone about Riley when I had only spoken to her a couple of times. I didn't know the answer to that, either. It just seemed like the right thing to do.

Just before we left, the school secretary announced that a candlelight vigil was being organized for that Saturday night, weather permitting, and that details would be posted on the school website by the end of the day.

Kelly asked me to call her later, and I said that I would. The drive back to Windward Cove was silent except for murmured thanks from first Ab, and then Les when I dropped them at home. It was lonely after that, but blessedly peaceful. My gift had been pummeled numb by strong emotions all day, and I was totally drained. All I wanted to do right then was hug my dog, then lie on my bed for the next year or so and not think or feel anything.

Mom met me at the front door, and from her expression I could see that she had heard the news. She hugged me, asking if I was okay, and I told her sure. But I wasn't, really.

Nobody was.

THIRTY-ONE

RILEY'S CANDLELIGHT VIGIL WAS HELD ON SCHEDULE AT Town Hall Park. It was supposed to begin at 6:00, but most got there early, and the place was already full of people when Mom and I arrived at 5:40. It was even more packed than it had been for the homecoming rally, and I couldn't help but compare the happy crowd from back then to the somber gathering we joined now. The sky overhead was pitch black, threatening the town with faint rumbles of thunder, but the rain gods must have felt sorry for us and held off for the time being. Stands with portable lights were set up at all four corners where everyone was invited to sign guest books, and then each received an unlit candle stuck through a hole in a small paper plate, which I figured was there to catch melting wax.

As Mom and I maneuvered through the crowd, we became separated when I stopped to talk to a few people I knew, and I was brought up to date on what had happened since Thursday. Cece Ramos told me that Coach Camarillo had tried to take full responsibility for everything, confessing that it was she who had allowed Riley to stay by herself at the pool center. Everyone knew the two of them had been super close, though, so no one blamed her.

Monica had heard that the reason Coach had missed Mrs. Chase's call was because she had left her phone behind when she and Mr. Camarillo had gone out for dinner and then caught a movie in Eureka. Plenty of people at both the restaurant and the theater had seen them, so she wasn't a suspect. Just the same, she had been placed on administrative leave pending a review by the school board, but that never happened. She resigned the next day, and no one had seen much of her since.

Finally, I heard from Kim that the sheriff's office had put together a long list of people who knew Riley, and would be calling parents to schedule interviews starting early the following week. Mayor Hahn had taken the lead in handling all the press that had descended on Silver Creek over the previous forty-eight hours, running interference so Sheriff Hastings could do his job.

Kim paused after that, and for a second or two appeared to want to say more, but then she just gave a tiny shake of her head.

I felt my eyes narrow. "Anything else?" I asked. In those last couple of seconds my gift had picked up a sudden spike of anxiety in Kim, as if she was struggling with something, and I was almost positive there was more she wasn't telling me.

Her brow furrowed. "Like what?"

"Like how Riley died."

"She *drowned*, Ben."

Anxiety pinged my gift again. *Definitely being evasive*, I thought, so I just stared at her.

Kim hesitated, biting her lip, and then looked around furtively before drawing me into the shadows beneath a spruce tree a few paces off. The boughs were droopy and wet, and we had to bend way over to get under them, but once we were close to the trunk, there was enough room to stand up straight. It put us far enough away to be out of earshot from people nearby, but she lowered her voice anyway. "Why do you want to know? I'm not supposed to say anything, and I'll get in big trouble if it gets back to my mom. She only told me because she wants me to be safe."

"It may be important."

"Important *how*?"

It was too dark to see Kim's face in the shadows, but I could sense it was her turn to stare at me, which I guessed was only fair. In that moment, I realized I was asking her to go out on a limb and trust me, so the least I could do was trust her, too. "All the weird things that have been happening since September," I said. "I'm pretty sure they're connected, and I'm trying figure out the hows and whys."

"How do you know this? And have you talked to the sheriff?"

"I can't. I don't have any evidence, so no one would believe me. The rest is a whole different story, but I promise I'll fill you in on that later, okay?"

For a second, I wondered how I would be able to manage that without telling her about my gift, but I decided I would jump off that bridge when I got to it. If worse came to worst, and I had to confess I was a freak, it would be worth the price if I could finally figure out what was going on. Someone was dead, and that was far more important. Besides, Kim was awesome, and I was pretty sure I could confide in her.

She hesitated one last time. "Okay, but you have to *swear* that if anyone asks, you'll never say that it came from me."

"I swear, Kim. Cross my heart." I left out the "*and hope to die*" part.

She let out a shuddering breath, and I could sense she was scared. "Riley was held down against the bottom of the pool," Kim told me. "Don't ask me how, because nobody knows, but they found bruises shaped like hands on her back. A person pushing someone else down in five feet of water would only shove themselves upward," she went on.

"But she wasn't just held down, Ben. She was *crushed* against the bottom, hard enough to separate three of her ribs from her spine."

I thought quickly, wanting to eliminate any rational explanations first. "Could Riley have been drowned someplace else, and then her body tossed back in the pool?" It was the only thing I could think of. Even as I brought it up, though, I was already dismissing the idea. I mean, what would be the point? I was grasping at straws, and we both knew it.

I could just make out Kim shaking her head. "No…the pool bottom is old, rough concrete, and Riley got all scratched up from it while she was dying. What's more, when they drained the pool that afternoon, they found bits of her skin still stuck to the bottom and a whole fingernail in a shallow crack, where it had stuck and been completely torn away."

I grimaced, grossed out by the thought. I was trying to decide if I had any other questions when shushing noises came from the crowd and we could hear conversations begin to trail off. "We have to go," I said, pressing the button on my watch to light up the display. "They're about to start."

She reached out to grasp my arm. "*Promise* me you'll be careful, okay?"

"I will. Thanks, Kim."

We went our separate ways.

I found Mom a few moments later and joined her. We were pretty far back from town hall's wide steps, but the organizers had set up a microphone and speakers, so when a man I didn't recognize stepped up and called for attention, his voice carried well enough that the remaining murmurs of the crowd fell silent. He introduced himself as Pastor Stenzel from the Lutheran church that Riley's family attended, and everyone bowed their heads as he began with a prayer.

Mayor Hahn followed him and spoke for a long time about the tragedy that had struck town. She promised that everything that could be done *was* being done, and asked that everyone remain respectful of law enforcement during the investigation. She also asked that everyone respect the Chase family's privacy as they grieved for Riley, and announced that Pastor Stenzel had been asked to speak on their behalf. Finally, she stressed that Silver Creek and Windward Cove were sister communities where people cared about one another, and that together we would heal and put this heartbreaking incident behind us.

All in all, I thought Kim's mom did a great job.

Pastor Stenzel took over again, going on for nearly ten minutes about Riley's life and what a wonderful, bright, and compassionate young woman she had been, as well as an exceptional athlete and friend. It was a good speech, and it made me sorry I hadn't known her better. After he finished, someone handed him a lighted candle while he invited anyone who wished to say a few words to come to the microphone. As people started lining up, a man and woman from his church lit their candles from his, and then moved down the steps to either side to share their tiny flames with the crowd. As people lit their candles, each would turn to allow the people behind them to light theirs, and the glow slowly spread across the park like a golden ripple in the darkness.

When my candle was going, I turned around and was surprised to see Kim standing just behind me. I had not realized she was there. She moved close as she touched her wick to mine, her expression beautiful and sad in the flickering glow, and we locked gazes for a moment as a reminder of our shared trust passed between us.

But she didn't say anything, and I didn't either.

THIRTY-TWO

SCHOOL WAS STILL A LITTLE OFF ON MONDAY, WITH LIN-gering shock and grief looming over everyone like the mournful clouds that hung low overhead, but all the teachers soldiered through, and the day ended up feeling more normal than I had expected it to.

Mom was waiting to talk to me when I got home. "I got a call from the sheriff's department earlier," she said while Moe welcomed me with his usual bouncy, licky enthusiasm. "They'd like to ask you some questions tomorrow."

I frowned, looking up from where I was still petting Moe. That seemed strange. I knew that many of Riley's friends had been inter-viewed already, with still more to come, but I was the last person I would have expected to be called in. "*Me*?" I asked. "How come?"

Mom shrugged. "I don't know. Probably your dazzling personality. Or maybe they're just being thorough."

"But I barely even *knew* Riley."

"Yeah, that's what you told me, and I mentioned it."

"And I was here with you all afternoon. We watched *Batman Begins*, remember?"

Mom nodded, looking thoughtful. "Good point. They'll probably need to know that."

"Really?"

She rolled her eyes.

"But…"

"*Benny*," she said, raising a hand to stop me. "Kiddo, this is totally your call. The deputy I spoke to said that they can't question you without a parent present—or at least permission from me to speak with you alone—and I can even refuse the whole thing. So, do you want to confess, or should I tell them to take a hike while we make a run for the border?"

I snorted, realizing she was right. I was wrapping myself up around the axle over nothing. The news had just caught me off guard.

Ben Wolf, overreactive doofus.

Mom's positive approach was making me feel better than I had in days, though, and I appreciated the way she was stepping back and letting me decide. "Sure," I said at last.

"Sure, as in I can greenlight the interview appointment?"

"*Pfft*…are you kidding? Let's bolt. Do you like Canada or Mexico? Personally, I'm all about the tacos."

She smiled. "I figured you would do your civic duty. Now, do you want me along for backup? My running group was going to go out and tackle some hills tomorrow, but I'll cancel if you'd like me to be there."

I waved the offer aside. "Nah, you go on. I'm sure it won't be a big deal. After all, it's not like I'll have anything much to tell them." *And besides*, I thought, *maybe I'll learn something new that will help.*

"Fair enough. Now, anything special you want for dinner?"

I grinned. "Still loving the taco idea."

Mom called the deputy back right away to say it was okay to speak with me alone, and told me afterward that I was supposed to go to the school's admin building right after lunch. My fifth-period teacher would be notified, so all I had to do was show up.

When I got there the next day, one of the secretaries behind the wide reception counter pointed toward a line of chairs in the hall to my left and told me to wait until my name was called. Three other kids were there ahead of me, one girl who was whispering to her mom while they sat with their heads together, a second girl who was reading a book, and a guy who looked either surly of bored, I couldn't tell which. He slouched in his chair, frowning at his phone, and I wondered what his connection to Riley might be. A man who looked like his father sat next to him, also scrolling through his phone.

My phone was in my car, I hadn't brought anything to read, and there was no one for me to whisper to, so there was nothing to do but look around. On the wall across from me were framed photographs of Silver Creek High principals, starting from way back in the late 1800s to the present day. I counted twenty-three of them, and was a little surprised that there weren't more. I guess when you made principal, you stuck around for a while.

A door down the hall opened, releasing a girl I didn't know but recognized from the cheer squad, and afterward a male deputy leaned out into the hall. "Randy Gordon?" he called out, and Captain Surly and his Dad got to their feet and headed that way.

It turned out that there were three deputies conducting interviews in borrowed offices, two in the hall in which we were waiting, and a third from the hall at the opposite end of the admin counter. When my name was finally called about fifteen minutes later, it was from that side, and I looked to see a woman deputy waving me over. She was tall, with dark hair in a no-nonsense cut that fell to just above her uniform collar. There were stripes on her sleeves, which the other deputies didn't have, and I wondered what I had done to deserve the heavy-hitter. *You're just that special, big guy*, the voice in the back of my mind whispered snidely, and I tried to keep my expression neutral. Sure…that was probably it.

She led me to a tiny, windowless office decorated with pictures of an older guy who smiled from docks or boat decks while holding up fish of various sizes. A monster-sized stuffed fish was mounted on the wall too, centered above the desk, and was nearly the biggest thing in the room. I didn't know what kind of fish it was, but I figured the cobwebs had probably been added later.

"Thanks for agreeing to speak with us, Ben," the woman began. Her tone was pleasant, but businesslike. "I'm Sergeant Shelton. Before we get started, can I see your ID?"

My driver's license picture was awful, so I dug out my student ID instead. She studied it for a moment, and then studied me. Her gaze focused here and there as she looked me over, and I had the feeling it was a gaze used to capturing details. My gift didn't pick up anything but professional interest, though, so I didn't worry about it.

"Your eyes are crossed in your picture."

Yep, Sergeant Shelton was definitely a detail person. "You're the first one to ever notice that," I said, offering up a smile. It couldn't hurt to be friendly.

She didn't smile back. "Noticing helps in my line of work." She handed back my ID, placed a form in front of her that had my name and info already printed on it, and then clicked open her pen. "Now, you know why we're here, right?"

"Sure. Riley Chase was drowned, and you're trying to find out who did it. What I *don't* know is why you want to talk to me."

"It's nothing personal. We're talking to a lot of kids—probably a third of the school—and it helps to know where everybody was. But you're right. According to the coroner's report, Riley died at around 4:40 p.m. last Wednesday, January 14th. Where were you at that time?"

The question surprised me, making me wonder if I was a suspect, but the sergeant's feelings didn't align with that, so I let it go. "I was home. With my Mom." For a second, I debated whether to add the Batman detail, but decided not to.

She wrote it down. "Can you tell me who Riley's close friends were?"

I shrugged. "From what I hear, pretty much everyone. She was popular."

"Do you know if anyone had it out for Riley?"

"Not that I know of. I only met her a couple of times, though, so I'm probably the wrong guy to ask."

She looked up. "Yeah, but people talk, right? Maybe you heard something?"

I shook my head.

"So, what sort of relationship did you have with her?"

"Like I said, none at all, really."

"But you were at least on speaking terms. Eleven different kids so far saw the two of you talking at lunch the day of the murder."

Aha, I thought, a lightbulb turning on in my head. *So that's what this is about.* "Riley stopped by our table to ask my girlfriend about some homework," I told her. "I can't remember exactly what. Then she asked me if I wanted to join the swim team. I thought she was recruiting."

The deputy raised her eyebrows. "That's it? People said that things looked pretty friendly between you two."

I shrugged. "There was some joking around, sure, but I didn't really think much about it. Then somebody used an ugly word, so I tapped out."

Shelton frowned. "What word was that?"

"Speedo."

She stared at me for a second or two before one corner of her mouth turned slightly upward. It was the barest crack in her carefully polite expression, but I could sense she was more amused than she was letting on, so I took the win. "So, you only talked to Riley a couple of times," she went on, back to business. "What was the other one?"

"The Homecoming Dance. That's where I first met her. My girlfriend introduced us, but I don't remember us saying much more than hi."

"And your girlfriend is...?"

"Kelly Thatcher."

"Same girlfriend as last Wednesday?"

"Yep. Amazing, huh?"

The sergeant actually chuckled then, and sensing her mood lighten put me more at ease, too. "Did Riley mention anything else she'd been up to lately?"

"No."

"Did you see any unusual behaviors in her, or maybe overhear someone else mention that they had?"

I thought about it, but nothing came to mind. "Sorry."

"Okay, final question: can you think of anything else that might point us in the right direction, or know of anyone who might?"

I paused, wondering if I should mention the story about Darren and Riley in the fifth grade. I wanted to help, and it was absolutely the only thing I had to offer that anyone else could back me up on. At the same time, being questioned by the sergeant was a face-smack of reality that left me a lot less certain about my suspicions than I had been when I walked in, and it left me feeling torn and confused. Then I tried to see things from her point of view, which only made it worse. Would she even take me seriously? Or would the whole thing sound as stupid and irrelevant to her as it did to me right then? After all, it had been just a case of puppy-love, right? Nothing had come of it at the time—other than Darren getting beat up, but that wasn't Riley's fault—and it was five or six years in the past. Sure, I knew Darren could carry a grudge, but God...could he really be *that* grudgey? And what if the sergeant started asking more questions? Did I really want to end up having to get into the Lynch family history and whole Gypsy curse thing?

Bad idea, big guy, my inner voice warned. *Stories like that will land you in a room with soft walls somewhere.*

Finally, I shook my head. When it came right down to it, suspicions and wild-ass theories were all I had. So, even though Sergeant Shelton had been pretty cool so far, I decided not to risk it and chose my next words carefully. "Sorry, but I just don't know anything." It wasn't a lie, technically speaking. It sure felt like one, though, and it sucked.

She nodded, looking a little disappointed but not really surprised as she finished making notes. "Well, if you remember something else later, even if it doesn't seem important, please give me a call." She held out a business card with her contact info. "Thanks for your time, Ben."

I took the card, told her goodbye, and headed back down the hall. I hadn't learned anything useful, and neither had she. It was raining again when I left the building.

The rest of January trudged onward, with everyone's mood as mournful as the dark sky that wept endlessly on the Northern California coast.

THIRTY-THREE

THE LAST BELL OF THE DAY FINALLY RANG, AND MOST OF *the guys who had been clustered around the open car hoods stepped away, laughing and talking as they headed toward the front to check in their tools. An impact wrench purred a couple more times from over by the lift, but then it too went still as whoever was finishing his brake project tightened the last of the wheel lugs.*

Tony ignored them, making sure the new gasket was sitting flush against the intake manifold before sliding the carburetor he'd spent the last two class periods rebuilding down onto the mounting bolts. He took his time, spinning the nuts down with his fingers before snugging them with a box wrench, all the while listening to the volume of conversations fade with distance as his classmates joined the flow of wood and metal shop students out in the hall.

"You about done there, Cruz?"

"Getting there, Mr. Dumas," he replied, looking back over his shoulder and seeing that only the two of them remained. "Just hooking up the fuel line now. Gotta connect the vacuum hoses and the throttle linkage after

that, and then see if it'll start up." He watched, smiling inwardly as his teacher frowned up at the clock on the wall, just as Tony knew he would.

The old man lived by the clock. In the four years he had been in Mr. Dumas' class, the short, wiry man had never once been late. He expected the same of his students, and anyone caught wandering in after the tardy bell was in for an ass-chewing. Most of all, though, Dumas hated hanging around after school. The old man's hands generally started getting shaky an hour or so after lunch, and by sixth period he would be short-tempered, his gaze traveling to the clock more and more often the closer they got to the end of the day. What's more, Tony knew why. Ever since Dumas' wife had croaked from brain cancer the year before, the man had spent as little time at home as possible. School let out at 2:45, and by a minute or two after 3:00, Ray Dumas would be perched on a stool down at Vera's bar, putting down the first of a long line of bourbons paired with whatever draft beer was on special.

"Hang it up, son. It'll still be there on Monday."

"You wanted me to help Evans pull the water pump out of the Chrysler next week, remember? If I'm stuck doing this, he'll just be hanging around waiting for me."

The man's frown deepened, and he raised one shaky hand to push back a lock of silver hair that had fallen across his forehead. His gaze drifted automatically to the clock, and then back to Tony. "Okay," he said at last, "but I gotta go. You can stay and finish hooking up, but I'm not about to give you the keys unless I'm here. You can start her up on Monday."

"Good enough, Mr. Dumas. Thanks." He watched his teacher cross to the bank of light switches by the hallway door, turning off all but the hooded fluorescent directly above where he was working. He then locked the door, and Tony even exchanged a wave with the old man before Dumas pulled it closed behind him, leaving Tony alone in the garage.

"*Drunk,*" *he muttered, and then quickly attached the lines and linkage, finishing just as a he heard a furtive knock. Perfect timing! He strolled over, wiping his hands on a rag before pulling open the door.*

Zoey Markham grinned. "I just saw him leave. Is everything cool?"

"I said it would be, didn't I?" She moved past him into the garage, and Tony stuck his head out, checking both ways down the hall to make sure it was deserted. Zoey was right behind him when he turned back, and jumped up to wrap her legs around his waist as her arms encircled his neck. She kissed him hard, her tongue darting into his mouth, and she moaned softly as he squeezed her ass with both hands.

"How much time do we have?" she asked as he carried her across the concrete floor.

"We've got at least an hour before the janitor comes to mop out the bays." He stopped, turning partway so Zoey could see under the hood. "That's the carb I just rebuilt."

"Cool."

Tony frowned as he studied her face, pretty sure she was looking at the alternator, but then decided it didn't really matter. After all, that wasn't what Zoey was there for.

She slid out of his arms, grinning at him, and pulled him toward the rear of the car. "What is this thing, anyway?"

"'67 Dodge Polara," he answered.

"Mm. You know what I love about old cars?"

"What?"

Zoey giggled. "The huge back seats!" Turning, she opened the door, casting a sultry look over her shoulder before disappearing inside.

Tony followed her, and Zoey was all over him almost before he even sat down. She straddled his waist, her mouth hot and wet against his as she moved her hips, grinding on his crotch. She was wearing that sweatshirt he liked—the one with the funny crap emoji—and she made a whimpery sound as he ran his hands up under it, unhooking her bra. Before he could bring his hands around to the front, though, she rolled off him, quickly kicking off her shoes and breathing hard as she slid out of her jeans. Tony grinned, unbuckling his belt. If she wanted it right away, that was totally cool with him!

The car's back door slammed shut.

His head snapped around as Zoey gave a little squeak of fear, but there was no one there. Looking through the windows, Tony could see that the auto shop was still deserted, and after a few seconds he let out a breath as his heartbeat began to slow.

He looked back at her. "Scared the shit out of me!" they both said at once, and then shared a laugh of relief. Then Zoey wet her lips, staring at him as her hands moved to the waistband of her panties.

The Polara's motor coughed, the whole car shuddering slightly as they heard the distinctive whine of an old Dodge engine trying to turn over. Then it stopped.

Tony felt his eyebrows come together. He leaned forward, looking over the front seat, but the key slot for the ignition was empty. Then he ducked his head slightly to glance through the wide crack between the bottom of the open hood and the engine bay, looking for someone standing in front, but no one was there.

"Tony...?"

The motor whined again, longer this time, and then sighed back into silence. It whined a third time after that and then finally caught, the car trembling as the engine revved twice before settling into the low, powerful rumble of eight cylinders and 383 cubic inches.

"Tony?" she whispered again, starting to pull her jeans back on. "Should it be doing that?"

Zoey sounded scared but he ignored her, wishing she would just shut up for a second. He needed to think, and it was hard when she kept asking questions. Maybe the ignition switch was stuck on, and all the rocking from the back seat had jiggled the corroded battery cable enough to make a connection. But Tony knew it was a stupid idea even as he thought it. Someone had to be screwing with him. Maybe Evans or Till or Bradley—they were the only ones who knew enough to rig some kind of switch. One of them had probably heard that he was sneaking Zoey in after school and was waiting out of sight, thinking he was funny. Well, whoever it was, his ass was gonna get kicked. Turning, Tony reached for the door handle.

All four doors locked at once.

"Hey," he said, pulling up on the old-fashioned post. It was frozen in place. Then Tony tried the window crank, but that wouldn't budge, either. "Try your door!" he snapped, and felt sweat dampen his armpits and the back of his neck as he watched Zoey try unsuccessfully to get out from her side. The smell of exhaust was growing heavy inside the car. Exhaust, and something else. Something musky and too sweet.

A second engine started, and Tony's eyes widened as he looked to his left. It was the old Army five-ton Dumas used to teach them about diesels, the stack above the truck's cab belching black smoke into the air. No one was behind the wheel!

"Climb over!" Tony ordered, trying not to sound as scared as he felt while grabbing the back of Zoey's sweatshirt and shoving her roughly over the bench seat. "See if one of the doors will open!" He coughed, rubbing at eyes that were starting to sting from the fumes, and then looked over as another engine started. It was the VW Baja buggy parked to their right, its rear-mounted four-banger sounding like an angry sewing machine as it spewed blue exhaust from the single tailpipe that was thrust upward behind it.

"They're both...locked..." Zoey slurred, her words beginning to sound thick and disoriented as she swayed in her seat, trying to remain upright. Tony figured the fumes were getting to her already. Funny...he'd always hated Mr. Dumas' first week lecture about carbon monoxide poisoning, but right then he could recall pretty much every word. "What's...going on...?" she asked.

He barely heard her, fear constricting his chest like a fist closing over his heart, making it even harder to breathe. Then the '78 Cordoba on the other side of the Baja started up, too, followed by the '97 Mercury Tracer that was still on the lift. Last of all was the '63 Caddy parked out of sight on the other side of the five-ton. Its pipes were disconnected from the exhaust manifolds, and the chugging roar of the engine was loud enough to drown out all the rest.

A fog of bluish-brown fumes now filled the shop, causing the light to slowly dim as the air thickened, but even the acrid odor wasn't enough to overpower that god-awful sweet stench that had grown every bit as strong.

"Tony...?" Zoey sounded barely conscious now.

Eyes burning, he squirmed around to lie on his back, bringing his foot up to stomp repeatedly at the rear window. He swallowed back bile, nauseous and fighting the urge to vomit with each jarring impact. Why wasn't it working? Even if he didn't bust the glass, the frame was the weakest point, and the whole window should have come free already.

Then Tony realized why...he'd grown too weak and dizzy to do it.

He managed to drag himself back up to a sitting position just before his stomach let go, dark brown puke ejecting from his mouth and nose onto his lap. He clutched the driver's headrest, gasping as the world seemed to spin like a carousel. "Zoe...?" he managed.

Just then the girl slumped forward, her head landing on the steering wheel and pressing against the chrome ring for the horn. WHAAAAAAAAAH!

It was the last thing Tony heard before darkness closed in around him.

THIRTY-FOUR

"I DUNNO," LES SAID. "BILL SKARSGARD WAS AWESOME AS Pennywise, but I remember the first time I saw a rerun of the old miniseries on TV. Tim Curry scared the *crap* out of me."

"And how old were you then?"

He shrugged, thinking it over. "Five…six, maybe. I caught it late one night when my folks were sleeping."

"Well, there you go," I said. "Hell, when I was five, even the witch from *Snow White* was scary."

Everyone laughed.

It was a warm for a February afternoon, with the cloud cover thin enough to let the sunlight penetrate, but just thick enough to hold in the heat. Better still, the mood at school had lightened a lot, especially after Riley's funeral, which seemed to give most people closure. Sure, whoever killed her hadn't been caught yet, and there still weren't any suspects that I'd heard of, but time had been chipping away at the gloom, and overall, things could have been a lot worse.

We stood in a cluster while kids heading home streamed past us—Les and me, along with Kelly, Gina, and Kim (not to mention Darren, who sulked a few steps away, so I guessed he sort of counted, too.) Les and Gina were still keeping a careful distance from one other, but their awkwardness had faded a lot since New Year's, and I was starting to believe they would be back on friendly terms before long. Valentine's Day was just over a week off, and Les had already been out with Jessica a couple of times, so things were looking up for him. In a perfect world Gina would get interested in someone else, too, but at least it no longer felt like she was circling me anymore. All I sensed from her was a sort of wary friendliness, as if she was embarrassed and wanted things to be okay between us again, so I was happy enough to let it go and keep pretending to be oblivious.

Looking oblivious was one of my more finely honed skills.

We were talking about the movie I had badgered them into seeing with me that afternoon. Windward Cove's theater drew in just enough of a crowd to stay in business, and could only afford to show films long after they'd already gone to video, but when I'd seen that they were having a special showing of *It Part 1,* I couldn't resist seeing it again on the big screen. Ab had gone back to her locker for the history book she had forgotten, and as soon as she returned, we planned to all load up and caravan over together.

"Ben's right," Kim agreed. "Bill Skarsgard's Pennywise is a *lot* scarier."

Les opened his mouth to argue, but just then the faint blare of a car horn rose up behind us: *WHAAAAAAAAAH!*

Our conversation trailed off as we all idly scanned the parking lot, looking to see who had accidentally set off their car alarm, and after a moment I realized that Les was no longer beside me. Turning, I saw him sprinting toward a potholed strip of asphalt that led to the school's shop building. Brownish smoke was oozing from around all six of the roll-up doors that were lined up facing the parking lot, drifting lazily upward in the gray afternoon, and I realized the sound was coming from inside.

"Pull the fire alarm!" I shouted to no one in particular, and then took off after Les. He was maybe fifty yards ahead of me, and I watched as he darted into the hall entrance on the west side of the building, reemerging just as I arrived.

"The door's locked!"

"Do you think someone's in there?" I could hear the sound of engines running even through the cinderblock wall, so it was probably a stupid question.

"Let's find out!"

I followed Les around to the roll-up doors, and the jangling of the fire alarm rose behind us as we tried lifting each of them in turn. They wouldn't budge.

"Boost me!" Les said, and I laced my fingers into a stirrup, catching his foot and lifting him so he could look through the line of windows high on the door. "There's no fire," he reported after a second or two, his hands cupped around his eyes as he peered inside. "But all the cars are running, and the whole place is full of exhaust!"

"Do you see anyone?" I asked, grunting as I strained to hold him up.

"I dunno," Les reported after a few seconds more. "It's hard to see… no, wait! I think there *is* someone! There's a shadow inside one of the cars!" He jumped down, and we looked back toward the main part of campus, where teachers and students were merging into a crowd as they headed our way, followed by Coach Barbour and the basketball team as they trotted over from the gym.

"You boys get back from there!" a male teacher I didn't recognize hollered over. "The fire department is on the way!"

We both looked automatically toward the parking lot entrance, straining to hear the sound of sirens in the distance, but there was nothing but the continued blare of the horn and roar of engines inside.

"I don't think we have that much time," Les said, sounding uneasy, and we exchanged a worried glance.

Then an idea occurred to me. "Stay here!" I told him, and began sprinting back to the parking lot, dodging my way through the thickening crowd while digging my keys out of my pocket. I was going too fast when I reached the car, skidding past the driver's side door, and had to scramble back before throwing myself behind the wheel. Stabbing the key into the ignition, I started the engine and threw the transmission into reverse, blaring the LTD's horn as I backed up the access drive toward the shop. Kids and teachers scattered out of the way until I was through the crowd, and then I floored the accelerator, aiming the rear end for the door next to Les. *Mom's gonna be pissed,* I thought, and then faced forward just before I hit, the impact first throwing me into the seat back and then bouncing me against the steering wheel just as the engine sputtered and died.

Scrambling out of the car, I turned to see the back third of the station wagon was now inside the shop. The big door had buckled inward on my side, breaking free of its track to form a high, narrow triangle from which thick exhaust fumes billowed outward in clouds.

A hand seized my shoulder, turning me around, and I found myself face to face with the teacher who had tried to call us away from the building. "What the *hell* do you think you're doing?" he shouted, glaring at me from behind thick glasses.

I didn't have time to get into it right then, so I shoved him away, barely noticing as he stumbled backward before falling down hard on his butt, and then I turned and followed Les into the breach. I started coughing immediately, blinking against the acrid sting as I wormed my way through the wreckage of the door. The smoky fumes were so thick I could barely see, and I stretched my arms out in front of me as I moved tentatively into the shop. After only a few steps I touched metal, and I felt my way along what was probably a big truck, the cool steel vibrating under my palm. Then, all at once my heart began to beat faster as I was hit by the thick, sweet smell of patchouli that combined with the fumes to nearly make me gag. I reached out mentally, not at all surprised to detect a feeling of cruel satisfaction that was nearly overwhelming.

Is this Darren's doing? I wondered, trying to remember if he'd been acting at all strangely a few minutes before. But there wasn't time to worry about it as I reached the front corner of the truck and saw a shadowy form to my left. "Les!" I shouted, trying to make myself heard above the roar of the engines. I headed that way, feeling lucky to have caught sight of him. Between the thick smoke and the tears that were nearly blinding me, he appeared to be barely more than a darker spot in the air.

"Dude!" Les called from the darkness behind me, and I spun around, looking for him. "Over here!" he coughed out. "Hurry!"

I switched directions, casting a glance behind me as I moved across the concrete, but the form I thought I had seen was gone. Had I imagined it?

"This way!" Les called out, guiding me, and at last I was close enough to see him tugging at the door handle of an old Dodge. "There's a girl locked in here! Go find something to break the window!"

Already dizzy from the concentrated fumes, I moved toward the front wall until I found a workbench, and felt around until my hands landed on something I thought would work—a socket wrench extension maybe eighteen inches long. Turning, I realized that the clouds were finally starting to thin as they escaped through the wrecked door, and I hurried back to Les.

"You get her out of there while I shut these things down," he ordered, and I watched long enough to see him run around to the open hood and yank the coil wire from the distributor cap, causing the engine to die. Turning back, I could see the girl was too close for me to break in the driver's side so I smashed in the window behind her instead. I was reaching around to unlock her door when I noticed a second figure lying half on the floor in back.

"There's a guy in here, too!"

But Les didn't answer, hurrying along the line of cars and killing the engines one by one. By the time I had the girl halfway out of the car, he had shut them all down and had unlocked the big door directly behind the Dodge, rolling it up to release the rest of fumes. He was beside me a second or two later, and between us we carried the unconscious girl (at least, I *hoped* she was just unconscious) out into the fresh air. The teacher I'd pushed down was there when we emerged into the daylight, and we shoved her into his arms before turning and running back inside.

It took us longer to drag the guy out of the back seat, and even though the exhaust was rapidly clearing, my eyes were burning like crazy and my stomach felt ready to turn inside out from what I'd already breathed in. Thankfully, the sweet stench seemed to have dissipated altogether, which helped a lot. The sound of sirens finally reached us as we wrestled the guy out of the car, and it was then that I recognized Tony Cruz. His face was pale, his chin splattered with puke that was all down his front and peppered with bits of broken glass. Les got him under the arms while I lifted from behind his knees, and a few seconds later we were clear.

A fire truck and ambulance were just pulling up out front, with a sheriff's department SUV not far behind, and as soon as we laid Tony down on the asphalt, Les stumbled a few steps to the side, falling to his knees and vomiting on the grass. I nearly did the same, but managed to keep it down while the teacher stepped to my side.

"Is anyone else in there?" He didn't sound like he was mad at me anymore.

I was still coughing, trying to clear my lungs and tasting bile in the back of my throat, so it was a few seconds before I could answer. "I… don't think so," I managed at last. "Les…?"

He looked over at me, shaking his head as he wiped his mouth with the back of his hand, and I noticed his eyes were bright red with irritation. I figured mine probably were, too—they felt like two holes burned in a blanket. Looking over, I caught Kelly's worried gaze and tried to reassure her with a wink as teachers pushed the crowd back, making room for half a dozen firefighters wearing oxygen masks. They dashed past us into the building while a few others hung back to help a couple of EMTs lug cases of gear and a gurney over from the ambulance. I bent over with my hands on my knees, still dizzy and nauseous, and wondered if I was going to blow lunch like Les had. Right then it seemed like a great idea.

A series of coughs rose up beside me, and I looked down to see Tony's eyelids flutter open. He tried to sit up, looking around as if wondering where he was, and I stepped out of the way as one of the EMTs came over and pushed him back down. "Hold on there, kid…why don't you take it easy for a minute while I have a look at you, okay?"

As the man knelt beside Tony, I looked past him and found myself staring directly into Darren Lynch's eyes. His scowl deepened, and he glanced past me toward the shop building before turning and walking away.

Before I had time to think much about it, though, one of the firemen came up beside me. "C'mon, buddy," he said, grasping my shoulders and pulling me away. "I got something that's gonna make you feel a lot better." He helped me toward the fire truck, where Les already was seated on the running board wearing an oxygen mask that covered his face. A moment later I was beside him, breathing deeply inside a mask of my own, and my dizziness and nausea began to ease as the last of the fumes cleared from my lungs. We watched as the EMTs worked on Tony and the girl—the same girl who had been with him at Ab's party, I realized offhandedly—and I was relieved to see her regain consciousness before they loaded her on the gurney.

It was about then I noticed Sheriff Hastings and a man wearing a white uniform shirt with a silver badge marching toward us from where they had been talking to the teacher I had pushed down. It turned out the man in white was chief of the Silver Creek Fire Department, and after first asking if we were okay, he spent the next few minutes chewing us out for being so goddamned stupid. I tried to look as meek as I could, avoiding the gaze of the sheriff as he loomed behind him.

Eventually the chief ran out of things to yell at us about and stalked away, and Sheriff Hastings waited until he was out of earshot before speaking. "He's right, you know," the sheriff said, frowning down at us with his thumbs hooked in his gun belt. You both could have died in there." Then his expression softened. "On the other hand, you probably saved the lives of those kids. Nice job, guys."

Les and I exchanged a glance. I couldn't see much of his face inside the mask, but judging from the crinkles at the corners of his eyes I figured he was grinning, so I grinned back.

"I want to talk to you after the medics check you out," Hastings went on. "I need you to tell me everything that happened, as well as anything you may know about why those two kids would try hurt themselves like that. So, stick around…this is probably going to take a while."

As we watched the sheriff walk away, Les elbowed me and then held out a fist. I bumped it with mine before reaching into my jacket pocket for my cell phone, realizing that I needed to think about how to break the news to Mom.

Instead, I thought about how Darren had scowled at the shop building, and the shadowy figure that might or might not have been inside.

THIRTY-FIVE

I WOKE THE NEXT MORNING WITH A HEADACHE, AND AT first I wondered why. Then I remembered all the exhaust fumes Les and I had sucked down the afternoon before. *Probably killed about a zillion brain cells,* I thought, and figured the pounding in my head was from all that gray matter lying around without a proper burial. I imagined Les felt the same way. I reached for my cell phone on the nightstand, expecting a text from Kelly, but then frowned when I saw the battery had died sometime during the night. *Crap.*

By the time I finally made it home around 6:45 the evening before, I was beat. Just the same, I had to sit through nearly an hour of Mom dividing her time between saying how proud she was, lecturing me on how Les and I could have gotten ourselves killed, and making me promise to never, *ever* scare her like that again. But at least the car had taken only minor battle damage (a few scratches, one cracked taillight I was sure I could glue, and a dent in the rear bumper), so thankfully she skipped that part of the parental debrief.

All I had wanted to do was crash, but Mom made me eat some dinner first, though by the time I trudged upstairs I couldn't remember what it was I'd shoveled down. I had just enough gas left in my tank for a shower (I had to shampoo twice to get the smell out of my hair), but before I stretched out, I decided at the last minute to call Kelly to let her know I was okay. I figured she already knew that, since I had not seen her among the teachers, firefighters, and assorted stragglers who were still hanging around after Sheriff Hastings cut us loose. But if she wanted to gush about how wonderful I was (or yell at me—could go either way), who was I to deny her? The call went right to voicemail, though, so I sent her a text instead and then I was out.

The next morning, I showered again and dressed, and then fed Moe while Mom cooked me an omelet, and I was all ready to head out the door when I remembered I had forgotten to put my phone on the charger. *Crap again.* Glancing at my watch, I saw I had barely enough time to pick up Les and Ab, and since I didn't own a car charger, it looked like I would be electronic-less for the day.

Meh, I thought. *There are worse things in life.*

On the way to school, Les and I circled back to our Tim Curry versus Bill Skarsgard as Pennywise argument that we had not settled the afternoon before. Ab kept inserting quips, criticizing first my side and then Les', which made things a lot livelier. I suspected she didn't really care one way or the other, though—she just liked poking the bears. Then, just as we were pulling into the school lot, Les said, "*Dude…* that's like saying the remake of *Battlestar Galactica* was better than the original. Nothing beats a classic, man."

I rolled my eyes, even though I could tell by his smirk that he just messing with me. "Oh, my *gawd…*are you *really* gonna go there?" That sent us down the sci-fi rabbit hole, which carried our argument all the way onto campus. The back-and-forth was so much fun, in fact, that I didn't even notice when Ab's smartass comments stopped.

"Guys," she said after a moment, her voice edged with tension. "*Guys!* Something's wrong."

I looked around, for the first time noticing that kids were clustered in small groups, some talking softly, others holding friends while they cried, but nearly all of them watching us. *No...scratch that*, I realized. They were watching *me*.

By then we had reached the quad, and our steps only carried us a few more feet before we slowed to a halt. I looked around, and felt the smile slowly fade from my face as I tried to figure out what had happened. At first, I thought maybe something new and shocking had come out about Riley's murder, but no...that wasn't it. That wouldn't explain why everyone was staring. Then I noticed the sheriff's department vehicles, a firetruck, and a van marked *Coroner* parked outside the entrance to the gym—not the pool center, but the gym itself—which puzzled me even more.

"Hey..."

As one, we turned to see Vern approaching us, shiny tear tracks standing out against the ebony of his cheeks. He stopped while still a few feet away, as if reluctant to come closer, and cleared his throat nervously. "Um, guys...*Ben*...there's something you should know." He said something else after that, but all I remembered afterward was a name: *Kelly*.

My head snapped back around toward the cluster of emergency vehicles, and before I even realized it, I was sprinting toward where Principal Powell and a bunch of uniformed first responders were gathered by the open side door. Vern called out, "*Ben!*" behind me, but I barely heard him. In seconds I was past the adults, dodging around them while someone yelled, "*Hey!*" and then I was through the door, skidding to a stop just inside.

It took me only seconds to piece together what I was seeing. The bleachers along that side were mostly retracted against the wall, except for the end closest to me, which had stopped before closing completely and stood askew. Something had blocked the accordion framework from scissoring together like the rest, leaving a narrow, darkened gap at the end like the entrance to a cave. A man pointed the lens of a big camera into the opening, the strobe flashing repeatedly as he leaned and bent and craned at different angles in order to capture whatever was inside. The odor of old, burned wiring tainted the air, sour and acrid, and a second man in coveralls stood beside the open panel for the bleacher controls checking things with a voltmeter. I figured the other adults were waiting for him, and had stepped outside to keep out of the way. Then I looked down and noticed the large, irregular pool of blood that had crept out from under the bleachers. It was maybe four feet across and was mostly dry except for a spot near the middle that still looked tacky, glistening under the lights.

Then a deputy was beside me, grabbing me roughly by the upper arm and collar of my jacket. "Get out!" he snarled, starting to drag me back outside.

I shook loose and shoved him violently away, and then turned back, unable to tear my gaze away from the blood. One step more and I would have been standing in it. My mind spun, and I began to feel disoriented. *No way*, I thought. *There had to be some mistake. There's no way this could be happening...*

I must have caught the deputy off guard, and after stumbling back a few steps, he came at me again. "*Okay... you wanna go to jail, tough guy?*"

"Gary!" a woman's voice snapped. "Knock it off! She was the kid's girlfriend." Gary pulled up short, and then the woman was beside me. "*Hey...*" she said in a soothing voice, "it's Ben, right? Ben, you can't be in here. Let's get you outside, okay?"

I looked up, not quite understanding at first because the world had started to get fuzzy. Then I recognized Sergeant Shelton, who I offhandedly remembered was nice, though hard to get a laugh out of.

Since it was all just a big mistake anyway, I allowed her to steer me back outside. "Sheriff?" I heard her call, and I looked up a moment later when a shadow fell over me.

Sheriff Hastings. Rick's Dad. He was cool, too. I wanted to ask him what was going on, but I seemed to have forgotten how to speak.

"I'm so sorry, Ben," he told me.

And that's when things got really strange, because him saying that made everything real. It wasn't a mistake after all. It was horrible... terrifying...crushing. But not a mistake.

Kelly Thatcher was dead.

A big, heavy arm settled across my shoulders and I felt myself being guided away. Part of what the sheriff was saying managed to penetrate the thickening fog—something about my friends waiting—but that was the last halfway clear thing to come through for a while. Not that it mattered. Only the concrete in front of my shoes mattered, because it was all I was able to focus on. People were trying to talk to me, but my ears were ringing and their voices were muffled and indistinct. I could make out tone and inflection—a little, anyway—but the words themselves were not much better than the *wah-wah* sound of the teacher in the Charlie Brown specials. Dimly, I felt hands grasp at my arms, trying to steady or comfort me, but the concrete still had my full attention, so I couldn't tell who they belonged to. I tried pushing the hands away, wishing they would leave me alone so I could think. But thinking was so, *so* hard right then. It shouldn't have been that hard, but it was, and pushing the hands away was even harder. Maybe Kelly could help me to understand—she always made things better—but then I remembered that Kelly was dead, which was why it was so hard to think in the first place. I bet Charlie Brown could think. Good ol' Charlie Brown understood the *wah-wah* language just fine, so he had to be a lot smarter than me. He was a genius and I was stupid and Kelly was dead. Then my vision blurred with tears and it was hard to see. I wiped at my eyes, but they just filled again, so after a while I just gave up and let the tears do whatever the hell they wanted. Kids would see me crying and probably say mean things, but screw it—what was I supposed to do? I needed to think, which was *way* more important right then than not crying, but I couldn't do both at once. Hey…I could walk, though. Walking was good, so I tried that, and then I tried to walk and think, but that didn't work. Next, I tried to walk and not cry, but that didn't work, either. Walking and crying, though…that turned out to be easy, so I did that.

Voices: *Ben!...Hombre…Wolfman!...Oh, Ben…*

How about that? I could hear a little now. But I didn't want to. I was walking and crying, and that was all I could manage right then. Yep, good ol' Ben was maxed out, and Ben needed space. The Wolfman needed to go *lobo solitaro*, just until he got his shit back together. I wanted the grasping hands and the faint voices and the whole goddamned *world* to just leave me the hell alone so I could walk and cry. No…not the whole world. I wanted Mom. I wanted Moe. I wanted Kelly, too, but that option wasn't on the table anymore. Why was that again? Oh, yeah, because Kelly was dead. Kelly was a pool of blood under the bleachers, which is why I couldn't think and why nothing worked right and why I was now *lobo solitaro* because KellywasdeadKellywasdeadKellywasdead…

Slowly, I became aware that someone was clutching my wrist while trying to pry my hand open. Then, as if waking from a nightmare, the world snapped back into focus and I could think again. I looked around, realizing that I was beside my car. Somehow, I had made it from the gym, across the quad, and all the way out to the parking lot. A crowd of fifteen or twenty people had gathered around—had probably followed me—and were now watching silently as Les yanked my keys from my hand. "What are you doing?" I asked. I was probably eighty, maybe eighty-five percent back in the ballgame, though still a little dull from shock.

Les' eyes were wide; his face pale. "What the hell are *you* doing?"

"Going home," I answered. Or maybe I realized it. Anyway, it was a great plan. I didn't want to be at school any more, and heading for home was suddenly the best idea I'd had all day.

"No problem, amigo…but why don't you let *me* drive you, alright?"

He still looked scared, though I wasn't sure why, so I reached out for a quick read of his emotions.

Nothing. Les wasn't feeling anything at all. Weird.

"I'll come too," said Ab.

I turned, noticing for the first time that she was beside me. Tears ran down her cheeks, and I almost reached out to sense her too, but then remembered that I couldn't. I had never been able to read Ab.

Low murmuring rose from all around, and even some snickering that was quickly shushed by others, and then I remembered the crowd. I blushed, embarrassed to be the center of so much attention, but at the same time I was confused. Something was wrong. Something was… missing. After a few seconds, I finally realized what it was:

I couldn't sense anybody!

The realization was enough of a shock to clear all the remaining fog from my mind, and I was suddenly uneasy. For my whole life, the feelings of people around me had always been in the background. It was like living by the sea, where the sound of the waves was a constant presence. Sure, to get a clear read on a single person I had to concentrate, but the general mood around me was always just *there*, like the cool of morning air or the smell of fresh-cut grass. Now, while I could see and hear the people gathered around, it was the same thing for me as watching a movie…like they weren't real.

Maybe I'm just still out of it, I reasoned hopefully, and tried focusing on individuals to kick my gift back in gear.

Cece Ramos, watching with a concerned expression—nothing.

Dozer Vasquez, smirking while he shared a muttered exchange with a guy I didn't know—nothing.

Vern, who glared at Dozer, looking angry—nothing.

My breath came faster as my heart rate increased.

The dude from my biology class—nothing! Miss Gillman, my Geometry teacher—nothing! Jasmine and Monica and Nicole—nothing, nothing, and *nothing!*

I sagged against the car, suddenly sick to my stomach.

"Wolfman?" Ab asked, reaching out to touch my shoulder.

Stricken, I turned my gaze back to my friends. "I…" I began, and then paused to choke back a lump roughly the size of a grapefruit. "I need to get out of here."

Ab nodded, steering me into the back seat and sliding in beside me while Les started the car. I was able to hold everything together while we backed out of the slot, the crowd separating to let us pass. Once we were clear of the parking lot, though, I couldn't anymore, and Ab put an arm around me as I slouched on the bench seat, tears coursing down my cheeks again as I stared at empty space. I wept for Kelly. I wept for the loss of my gift…hoping it was only temporary, but terrified that it might not be. But mostly I wept because life was cruel and brutal and unfair, and nothing would ever, ever be the same again.

THIRTY-SIX

TEEN SUICIDES SPIKE FOLLOWING MURDER OF STAR SWIMMER read the headline, and after skimming the first paragraph, I closed the browser in disgust and tossed my phone to the far end of the couch. "They're *so* full of shit," I muttered. Moe opened one eye, tail thumping the cushion as he lay on the couch with his head in my lap. I patted him absently, grateful for his company.

The article was just the latest attempt by the news to put a bow on things. It had started less than eight hours after Kelly's body was found, with the article *SECOND GIRL FOUND DEAD—DOES A SERIAL KILLER STALK SILVER CREEK HS?*

Tony Cruz and Zoey Markham had still been in the hospital at the time, being treated for carbon monoxide poisoning, so their story didn't come out until a day later. According to that article, *GRIEF OVER CHASE DEATH RESULTS IN ATTEMPTED DOUBLE SUICIDE*, they both confessed to being so sad about Riley that they had decided to end their lives, but regretted it afterward. What a complete pile of crap. The auto shop had *reeked* of patchouli, so I knew they weren't telling the truth, even if no one else did. Did they decide to go with the ending-their-lives thing because they thought no one would believe whatever really happened? Or was it because it got them a ton of attention and sympathy? Either way, they stuck to their story, the rest of the world bought it, and I doubted that anyone would ever know the truth.

The only paragraph the reporter had gotten right was the depiction of Les' and my actions. Well, Les' actions, anyway—our names were listed as Leslie Hawkins and Benjamin Wold. Maybe I should have been grateful for the positive mention, and at any other time I guessed I would have been, but I was still too numb to care. The details were mostly correct, though, and even described us as *brave teens who rescued Cruz and Markham before first responders could arrive on the scene.* There was even a paragraph about how I had rammed my car through the roll-up door to get inside.

That Ben Wold was really something, wasn't he?

Anyway, the news outlets had apparently decided it was all one thing, concluding on their own that Kelly must have been just as depressed as the other two, even though (1) nothing official had been released about her yet, and (2) Riley's death had occurred almost a month before. Didn't anyone else see that as a stretch? As suicide attempts went, a month seemed like a hell of a time lag for impulsive decisions, but maybe that was just me. Nevertheless, since it all happened the same afternoon, the press just lumped Kelly in with Cruz and Markham. How clever of them to wrap things up so neatly. Reporters must really be something, too.

But all of that came afterward.

Someone must have called Mom, because she had already heard the news about Kelly when I got home that morning. After hugging me for a long time and shedding tears of her own, she watched silently as I went upstairs without a word, closed my bedroom door behind me, and then crawled under the covers. I thought I would only nap for an hour or two—just long enough to see if all king's horses and men could put me back together—but when I finally opened my eyes, it was nearly dark out.

Shock can do that to you, I guess.

The cavalry seemed to have done a fairly good job in the meantime, though, because at least my mind was clear again. Sure, there was still a smoking crater where my heart used to be, but maybe they had a night shift for that. I glanced out my window, noting that a steady rain was falling as the gray light faded in the west, but that was fine. My eyelids still felt heavy, and it was always nice to sleep with the sound of rain on the roof.

I let Moe outside, and then made my way through the dark family room to the glow of the kitchen. "Hey," I said dully, watching from the archway as Mom pulled a casserole out of the oven. It smelled like tuna noodle, which had always been one of my favorites. Now, though, the smell just made me queasy, but I didn't mention that since I figured she had made it just for me.

Instead of speaking right away, Mom left the casserole on a stove burner and crossed the floor to hug me again. After half a minute or so, she held me at arm's length to look me over, as if inspecting for damage. "Are you okay, Benny?"

I shrugged. All my wounds were on the inside, but I was nowhere near ready to think about that right then—let alone talk about it—so I didn't.

Mom seemed to sense what I was feeling, and I felt a pang of mild jealousy. Since my gift had gone AWOL that morning, I still could not sense a thing. Offhandedly, I wondered if I was experiencing the same sort of loss that accident victims felt after suddenly going deaf or blind. My jealousy faded almost right away, though, swallowed by an overwhelming numbness that had moved in sometime while I was asleep.

"Dinner's ready," Mom said. "Why don't you sit down?"

"Gotta feed Moe first," I replied, turning toward the darkness of the pantry.

"I can do…"

"It's okay…I've got it," I said, not letting her finish, and I retreated from the light. The kitchen felt too bright and crowded, even with only Mom, and all at once I wished I had not come downstairs. Darkness was better. Darkness didn't leave me feeling so exposed. Maybe if I were lucky, the darkness inside me would expand outward until I merged with the deepening shadows, and then I wouldn't have to answer questions, or think about Kelly, or eat tuna casserole when I didn't feel up to it.

Moe ended up eating only about half of his kibbles before he padded over to sit with his head in my lap. His dark eyes watched me closely, obviously sensing that something was wrong, while Mom and I spent the whole dinner not talking about Kelly. We talked about other things—or at least Mom did, while I replied with the shortest answers I could think of. Talking was just too hard, the memories of Kelly crowding my brain and making words feel thick and awkward in my mouth. I did manage to eat some of her casserole, though not much, and then spread the rest around on my plate, hoping to make it look like I had put away more than I had. At last, I couldn't take it anymore and asked if it was okay if I went back to bed. Mom said yes in spite of the concern I could read in her eyes.

I stayed home from school the next day. Mom tentatively poked her head into my bedroom twenty minutes after I normally would have been downstairs. "Are you getting up, Benny?"

"No," I said, and rolled over. That earned me the concerned look again, but she let it go. Despite sleeping the majority of the previous 24 hours, I still felt impossibly tired. School would have find a way to get along without me. I figured they could manage.

I finally rolled out of bed a little before noon, feeling uneasy after a series of dark, nonstop dreams that I couldn't remember, and my back stiff from lying in bed so long. My exhaustion had been replaced by an irritating restlessness that stuck with me the rest of the day and through the weekend, and I spent my time taking long walks with Moe whenever there was a break in the rain. When there wasn't, the only thing that kept me from climbing the walls was to sit in front of the fireplace, where the warmth and dance of the flames was soothing enough to let me relax with my brain unplugged. By Saturday afternoon I had run out of scrap wood to burn, so Mom made a call, and a couple of hours later a big truck pulled up with two cords of split oak in back. The deliveryman asked where Mom wanted it, and after she had him dump the whole load right in the drive, she said the rest was up to me. I found an old wheelbarrow in the barn, and worked until well after dark schlepping load after load to the carriage house out back, stacking it inside out of the weather. Mom must have figured I needed something to keep me moving, and it turned out to be a good call. By the time I finished, my clothes were soaked through by the intermittent rain, my shoulders and back sore from the repetitive motion and lifting. After a shower and a few bites of leftover casserole, I had a dreamless night and woke the next morning feeling fairly rested.

I probably could have stayed home from school the whole next week if I had wanted to, but that would have left me with too much time for brooding. I also knew that the dread I felt about going back would only get worse the longer I dragged my feet. And anyway, school would be a distraction. My thoughts still wandered as the days crept by, making it hard to concentrate, but at least the memory of that pool of blood by the bleachers—with its glistening, still-tacky spot near the center—was no longer constantly on my mind. Mostly I wondered how Kelly had ended up under the bleachers. The only explanation that made sense to me was that someone or something had *chased* her there, and then retracted the bleachers to crush her. But who…and *why*? The question wouldn't leave me alone, and it drove me crazy.

All my friends did their best to be supportive, repeatedly asking if I needed to talk or if there was anything they could do, but I found it next to impossible to engage with them. Almost none of them seemed to understand that their being there was enough—was all I could take, really—but I couldn't find the words to tell them. I didn't need any psychic ability to see that they felt awkward and hesitant, unsure of what to do, and it put an unspoken distance between us. And since my gift still had not returned, I felt even more isolated. Without it, even surrounded by everyone at lunch, I was alone and adrift. For the first few days, I held out hope that my abilities would come back, but by the end of the week, I decided that I'd better not bet the ranch on it.

At some point, Gina moved into the cafeteria chair where Kelly used to sit. I wasn't sure exactly when that started—maybe Tuesday, maybe Wednesday—but I didn't see that it mattered. I was not consciously noting details like that, not even on Thursday, when Les suddenly stopped sitting with us at lunch. Someone smart probably would have seen the connection there, but not me. The only thing that vaguely registered was that one day the chair beside me was painfully empty, and the next day it wasn't. Gina was there, keeping enough of a physical and emotional distance not to be intrusive, yet still close enough to prod me into eating something now and then, or throw out gentle remarks or questions that kept me at least partway connected to the conversation at the table.

About the only other thing I noticed (and only because it was impossible not to) was that the more care and attention Gina showed me as time went on, the more scowly and withdrawn Darren became. Of course, when it came to moods, Darren was a one-trick pony, and his act had gotten so old and tiresome that I no longer had the patience for it. Maybe that should have worried me, things being what they were, but my give-a-crap factor was at an all-time low.

A conflict raged inside me that I wrestled with every day. The objective part of my brain—what was left of it, anyway—reminded me annoyingly that I still had no concrete idea whether Darren was the cause of things or not. It was the part that realized I had absolutely zero real proof, that I had never witnessed Darren actually *doing* anything, and that all my suspicions were built entirely on his family history and evidence that was purely circumstantial. Even more, part of me still felt sorry for Darren, as I had from the start, instinctively feeling that the only reason he pushed people away was because he had been an outcast for so long and had been hurt too many times. The hours we had spent playing D&D together had shown me there was more to him than the abrasive, disagreeable side that he chose to show the world. I couldn't help but feel that, deep down, there was a regular guy in there who just wanted to be liked and accepted like everyone else.

On the other hand, underneath all the numbness was part of me that smoldered with pain and anger. It *wanted* Darren to be responsible, and some days it was all I could do to not provoke him with sullen glares of my own…daring him to do something, just so I could finally know one way or the other. *Wanna hit me with Voldemort's death curse?* I challenged him inwardly. *Knock yourself out, pal. Bring it, and see what happens.* It would be a relief to finally have someone I could blame and hate.

Every day, that internal tug of war left me exhausted by the time school was over.

As the weeks passed, Gina started spending time at the house. At first, she would only drop by for a few minutes every two or three days to see if I needed anything. Then, during one visit when I asked if she could help me make sense of our geometry homework, she started staying longer. Maybe her heart was just that good, or maybe it was because she had once been so isolated herself, but whatever the reason, she seemed to understand exactly what I needed. On nights when I felt like talking, we would talk—never about Kelly (it was still too soon for me), but about whatever random subject occurred to me at the time. When I didn't, Gina would just sit on the opposite end of the couch; a silent, comforting presence while I stared into the flames. I was still struggling with loss, and while I could not honestly say I had begun to heal yet, Gina at least helped stop some of the internal bleeding, and I was grateful for it. Even Mom remarked several times that Gina was going above and beyond, and that I was lucky to have her for a friend.

The only one who didn't seem to appreciate her was Moe. I could tell that he knew I was hurting, but did not understand why, and it made him wary and protective. When Gina came over, he would make a low warning sound that was not quite a growl, and then stick close by my side while keeping us both under a watchful gaze. It bothered Gina at first, until I pointed out that he would probably act the same way with anyone who wasn't Mom or me. I told her to wait until the next time one of our other friends was around, and she would see it wasn't anything personal.

At last I felt able to think about Kelly's death without being drowned in a flood of emotions, and could finally consider whether Darren had had anything to do with it. The only thing I knew for sure was that Kelly had definitely *not* committed suicide, and the weirdness of it all made her a prime candidate for the growing list of curse victims. At the same time, I had to wonder how that could be. After all, everyone else who had suffered an unexplained accident was someone Darren either didn't like, or with whom he'd had some past conflict—Riley included. As far as I could remember, I had been with Kelly every time she had been around Darren, and I couldn't recall a single angry word ever passing between them. Assuming that Darren was truly responsible, that alone should have kept her off his curse radar, right? So, had some other, unrelated chain of events caused Kelly's death? Or had there actually been something hanging between Kelly and Darren, maybe an incident from their past that I wasn't aware of?

I still wasn't ready yet, and even thinking about it was almost more than I could handle. Worse, without my gift, what could I even do? It was the only advantage I'd had, and without it I was useless. Darren or not, how was I supposed to face someone—*something*—that could kill without leaving a trace behind? Just the same, I realized I couldn't stay on the sidelines forever, not after people had died, and knowing that filled me with a dread so deep it felt bottomless.

Whether I wanted to or not, though, sooner or later I would have to get back to work.

THIRTY-SEVEN

IT WAS THE NIGHT BEFORE KELLY'S FUNERAL, AND I HAD lost track of the hours I had sat in front of the fire that now burned low in the hearth. It was not the bright yellow that came from newly added wood, crackling cheerfully as tongues of flame licked at exposed grain, but the darker glow of logs deeply charred and mostly burned away. It was the part of a fire that I liked best, when the golden light dimmed to shades of darker red. Sometimes, when I looked deeply enough, the flames down between the logs were same dark auburn as Kelly's hair.

I noticed that the ashes under the grate needed cleaning out again, but that could wait until morning. I also noticed that it was time to throw on a couple more logs, but I could give that a few more minutes, too. The fire was the only light in the otherwise dark family room, and I liked it that way. It drew my focus deeper into the red glow, quieting my mind.

I had thought the funeral would have been much sooner, but it had been delayed—first by the coroner's office, where a careful examination determined that there was nothing else to find beyond the fatal trauma, and then by Kelly's mom, who had gone a little off the rails. Wendy insisted that her daughter receive an open-casket funeral, so everyone could look at her one last time when they said goodbye, but there wasn't a single mortuary for miles around that would agree to it. Wendy had cried in my arms when I went to see her, telling me the damage to Kelly's face and body was apparently too great, and all the morticians agreed that it would be impossible to make her appear natural.

I tried not to think about that part.

Personally, I was grateful that things had dragged out so long. It gave me more time to process my own grief, and I was now 95% sure I could get through the service and burial without turning into a wreck. That was good. Much as I didn't want to, I knew that I had to let her go eventually if I ever expected to move forward again, and I hoped the next day would bring some of the closure I needed.

Headlights swept across the front windows and I frowned, wondering what was up. Mom had left a little over ten minutes before for a yoga class—her first in a while—and afterward she and some of her friends planned to stop somewhere for coffee or a bite, so I hadn't expected her back for at least a couple of hours. Maybe she had forgotten something.

Moe raised his head and growled just as I heard footsteps on the front porch, and then I knew it wasn't Mom. I was halfway to the entry hall when the knock came, and I turned on the porch light before opening the door. Gina stood just outside, wearing a long coat that was belted at the waist and her hair sparkling from raindrops that had caught in it. Behind her, the Lynch's old Chevy pickup sat just behind my car, Gina's usual parking place when she came to visit, and it was close enough that I could hear the rain drumming softly on the metal.

"Hey," she said, smiling.

"Hey," I replied, holding open the screen door and trying not to sound as disappointed as I felt. I wasn't in the mood for company, but she had come all that way, so not inviting her in would have been rude. *Hopefully she won't stay long*, I thought.

Gina stepped into the entryway; the night air trapped in the folds of her coat making me shiver as she passed. "I didn't see any lights on, so I almost went back home."

That would have been fine with me, but I didn't say so. And since she did not seem to be expecting an answer, I didn't offer one. I wished that I could sense what she was feeling so I could guess how long she planned to stay, but I was still flying blind, and it annoyed me.

I followed her into the family room, watching while she warmed herself in front of the fire for a minute. The flames glowed red against her legs, and then faded to deep shadow above her waist. "So, what's up?" I asked. "I didn't know anyone would be stopping by, and I was planning to hit the rack soon."

The reluctant host offers a casual remark, hoping his guest will take the hint.

Gina didn't. She took a step back from the fire, turning toward me. The glow from the hearth now illuminated the lower part of her face, and I could see her frown. "You're still losing weight, Ben," she observed instead. "Did you eat today?"

I couldn't remember. "Sure," I told her anyway. "Porterhouse steak, loaded baked potato, and a huge salad."

She made a face. "You suck at lying, you know that?"

There was nothing to do but shrug. "So I've been told."

Gina gave a low laugh, moving to sit on the far end of the couch, and I grit my teeth in frustration. It looked like she planned to stay awhile. Resigned, I dropped back into my spot, stroking Moe's fur as he watched her.

"I..." she began, and then frowned, looking down to inspect her folded hands, "I don't know exactly how to bring this up. So don't get mad, okay?"

"Okay."

She took in a deep breath, and then let it out. "Are you planning to go to the funeral tomorrow?"

I sat back, a little surprised. "Of course," I answered, thinking that it should have gone without saying.

Gina hesitated again. "Are you sure that's such a good idea?"

What the hell kind of question is that? I thought, fighting back irritation. Instead of answering, though, I just gave her a puzzled look.

"Kelly's gone," she went on, "and I know it's been killing you. I can see you slowly coming back to your old self, though, which means you're starting to heal."

"Oh, is that what you think?" There was a flatness to my tone that I didn't bother trying to hide. *Where was this going?*

"Yes," Gina answered, meeting my gaze. "I know this isn't what you want to hear, and I'm sorry. But honestly, what good will it do you to be there? Will that help you to get past this? Or will you just be picking at a scab?"

"Jeez…are you actually *asking* me this?"

"I really think you shouldn't go," she declared, her voice sounding firm. "That's not what you need right now."

I was starting to get angry. "Oh, and *you* know all about what *I* need, is that it?"

She nodded. "Yes. Yes, I think I do."

I glared at the dying flames, trying to keep my temper under control. I was still trying to think of something to say that would keep the discussion from going further south when Gina stepped in front of me, causing me to look up.

"I know *exactly* what you need, Ben…because I need it, too." She opened the front of her coat, allowing it to slide off her shoulders to the floor. Underneath it, she wore only a short nightie of dark satin. Stunned, I was still trying to process what was going on as she grasped

Moe's collar and pulled him off the couch. He retreated with a growl of protest as Gina then straddled my lap, facing me. "Gina, I…" But then her lips were pressed against mine, softly at first, but then with more urgency. Her tongue brushed tentatively against my lips, and then eased into my mouth just before I pulled away, finally catching on. Gina sat back, breathing hard as she crossed her arms in front of her to draw the nightie up and over her head, dropping it to the floor. Beneath it she was naked, and I froze in astonishment as she leaned forward to kiss me again.

I pushed her roughly aside, scrambling to my feet and crossing to the fireplace. I leaned against the mantle, struggling to sort out my feelings and get my breathing under control. "No, Gina," I said after a moment. "This isn't gonna happen."

I never heard her move up behind me, and sucked in a breath as her hands reached beneath my arms to clasp my chest. She pressed herself against me, her breasts full and soft against my ribs. "But *why*, Ben?" she asked breathlessly. "We've both been through so much. Me losing my parents…you losing Kelly. We'd be good for each other. I *need* you. You're all I've thought about since the first day of school."

Her left hand began to drift slowly down my stomach, but I didn't do anything about it. Most of me wanted her to stop, but part of me didn't. Right then, part of me just wanted to lose myself in her lips and body…to forget about how much my soul hurt, even if only for a little while. *And she's a nice girl, right?* I rationalized inwardly. *Even Mom thinks so. And after the shit-show my life has been lately, don't I deserve a break? Would that really be so wrong?*

"It's time for us both to move on, Ben." Her hand had made it to my belt, and was now fumbling with the buckle. "Kelly's gone, and Les and I are over. It's *our* time now."

Images of the night under Kelly's Christmas tree suddenly flooded my mind…

[I love you, Ben…]

…and I reached down to trap her hand. In a heartbeat, all the confusion and momentary desire I felt were swept aside by fresh pain and overwhelming guilt. Sure, I liked Gina…liked her a lot, actually. But that's as far as it went. So yeah, it damned well *would* be wrong, and right then I hated myself for being such weak pile of crap. "Go home, Gina," I said, pulling her hand away and then releasing it. "Just…go home."

She stepped back. "Are you sure?" Then, when I didn't answer, she said, "Alright. Take more time if you need it, but just know that I'm ready whenever you are. We could be so amazing together. Maybe you don't see that yet, but I think you will."

I listened as she got back into her clothes, and then turned to watch her glide into the entry hall, walking back out into the rainy night and leaving the front door open behind her.

I turned back to the fire, searching my memory for anything I might have said or done to give Gina the idea that I wanted to be more than friends, but came up empty. I didn't *think* I had led her on, but then again, my brain hadn't been on top of its game in a while, so I had to admit it was possible. *How do you plan to handle* this *one, genius?* the snide voice in the back of my mind asked, but I told the voice inwardly to shut the hell up. I closed my eyes, gripping the mantle so hard that my hands started to ache.

I felt horrible about what had almost happened. Kelly deserved *so* much better than her boyfriend ending up in someone else's arms the night before she was buried.

I felt horrible about Gina, knowing I had to find some way to let her down easy.

Mostly, though, I felt horrible about how the memory of Gina's lips against mine stuck with me…and how, for just a second there, I had kissed her back.

THIRTY-EIGHT

HEGGS AND SON GARDEN CHAPEL OCCUPIED A BRICK building that had been a good-sized church at some point in the past. Ivy covered the north and east walls, trimmed neatly back from the arched double doors and cedar steeple. Along the west wall, an overhang kept the rain off a gleaming silver hearse that waited to transport Kelly to the cemetery following the service. Located just a couple of miles outside Eureka, it occupied a couple of acres, maybe a little more, that was mostly parking lot bordered by swaths of manicured lawn dotted with redwood and birch trees. Tasteful.

The lot was nearly full when Mom and I arrived, and she pulled her Explorer into a space only five or six slots from the very back. People in dark, formal clothing were getting out of cars and slowly converging on the entrance, and we joined them, exchanging nods or somber hellos with those we recognized. Inside, we passed through a reception area with offices to either side, and then through a second set of doors into the hall itself. Two rows of wide pews were bisected by a central aisleway, with narrower aisles running along the walls on both sides. The walls were painted a light brown color that went well with the dark, heavy beams that supported the peaked ceiling.

The pews were already nearly full of mourners speaking in hushed tones, and after accepting a funeral program from an usher, we looked around for a place to sit. After a moment, I saw Ab and Les waving from the third row back on the left, where they and the rest of our friends were gathered. "There," I murmured to Mom, and she took my arm as we went to join them.

Everyone shifted left to make room for us, and I ended up between Mom and the center aisle. Kelly's casket was positioned up front, surrounded by more flowers than I had ever seen in one place. Behind it was an easel supporting a large framed photo of Kelly in her cheer uniform, smiling radiantly, and I had to swallow back a lump.

The service began a few minutes later, though I was never able to remember much about it afterward. There was a prayer, scripture readings, and a long eulogy that had people wiping tears or weeping softly all around me, but all I could do was think about Kelly while staring at first her photo, and then her casket, and then, when my eyes started to feel hot, the back of the pew in front of me. I don't know how many times I repeated the cycle—photo-casket-pew, photo-casket-pew—but after a long time Mom finally squeezed my hand and I realized that people were getting to their feet.

It was over.

For a moment I felt guilty for not paying more attention to the proceedings. Then I remembered what the whole thing was supposed to be about, and since my thoughts had been full of Kelly all along, I figured it was close enough to the same thing.

Everyone caravanned slowly behind the hearse all the way to Silver Creek Memorial Park, where Kelly's casket was lowered into a grave beside a mound of excavated dirt hidden under sheets of artificial grass. The same man who had delivered her eulogy at the chapel (some sort of reverend, I assumed) spoke again, but I was watching Wendy and Jim. They sat with the rest of Kelly's extended family in three rows of chairs arranged beneath an awning. They were holding hands, and I wondered if losing a second daughter would bring them together again, or drive them further apart. Time would tell, I supposed.

I finally pulled my gaze away when a few of Kelly's cheerleading friends began circulating around, passing out flowers to select people, and I looked up as Jessica handed me a rose. "For her casket," she whispered, and I nodded. A minute or so later I was last in a long line of people who shuffled slowly past, each of us tossing our flower down into the grave. Funny...that was the part I would always remember afterward: the soft, hollow thump of each flower as it struck the polished lid below.

Goodbye, Kelly, I thought.

Goodbye.

"Are you sure I can't fix you a plate, Ben?" Gina asked.

It was the third or fourth time she had asked already, and it was getting annoying. Just the same, I realized that she only wanted to help, so I answered her the same way as every time before: "No, thanks."

"How about something to drink? Water? Or there's this vanilla lemonade that's really good..."

"No. I don't want anything. But thank you."

The graveside service had ended close to two hours before, and afterward everyone had been invited to a reception held at the Silver Creek Community Center. It was only my second funeral ever, and the first had been followed by dinner instead of a reception, but Mom explained that the purpose was to offer sympathy to the family while sharing thoughts and memories with the other mourners. As we were going in, I overheard Les call it a Potato Salad Wake, and despite everything, hearing that made me smile a little for the first time in weeks.

The Thatchers had catered a huge buffet of appetizers and sandwiches for the guests, and most stood around holding plates and drinks
while chatting in small clusters. I sat with the rest of my friends at a
large table set off by itself in one corner, and while everyone else ate and
shared stories about Kelly, I just listened while waiting for a chance to
talk to Wendy and Jim. Gina claimed the chair next to mine, and had
been hovering ever since we arrived. She sat close, occasionally rubbing
my shoulder and asking if I needed anything while slipping "we" comments into the conversation every now and then: *"Ben and I thought
the service was very nice... we'll have to bring flowers to the grave, won't
we, Ben?... No, thank you, we'll probably be leaving soon."* Normally,
comments like that would likely sail right past me unnoticed, but after
what had happened the night before, I was sure noticing them then.
They reminded me that I still had to find a way to set Gina straight on
our status. What I also noticed was the stony expression on Les' face
every time she tossed out something like that. He said nothing, his gaze
flicking back and forth between Gina and me while his frown deepened.
I tried a couple of times to signal that it wasn't me, rolling my eyes when
she wasn't looking and offering a shake of my head, but it didn't look
like he was buying it. *Guess I need to talk to him, too*, I thought.

After a while I began to pick up hints that everyone else was starting
to notice as well—lots of awkward pauses and exchanged glances—and
I decided enough was enough. Luckily, just then I saw Wendy disengage
from the group she had been talking to. She glanced around briefly, as
if making sure everything was going as planned, and then stepped to
an open side door where she leaned against the frame, arms crossed,
staring out into the gray afternoon.

That was my chance.

"Hey, guys," I said, standing suddenly, and conversations broke
off as everyone at the table turned to look at me. "I'm gonna go talk to

Wendy, and then see if my mom is ready to take off. I'll catch you at school, okay?"

Gina quickly gathered her things as if she were coming too, and had half-risen from the chair when Ab caught her by the elbow. "*Gina*. Can I talk to you outside?"

Free at last, I made my way to where Wendy stood alone in the doorway. "Hey," I said. "Everything was really nice today. How are you holding up?"

The woman looked over, offering me a smile that was sad and wistful all at once. "Hello, Ben. Thank you for coming."

She hadn't answered my question, which made me realize it had been a stupid one. I couldn't think of what to say back to her, though, so I just gave her a gentle smile of my own.

"Kelly really loved you…did you know that? She told me so, even though she didn't need to. I could tell. She looked at you in a way I had never seen her look at anyone." Wendy smiled again. "I think she was crazy about you from the moment you moved to town."

Hearing her say that made my heart wrench. "I felt the same way."

"Which reminds me…I have something for you. Can you wait here a second?"

"Sure." I watched as she crossed to a nearby table, picking up her purse and digging through it as she made her way back. She found what she wanted just as she returned to my side, and held out a small, black velvet box that I recognized right away. It held the bracelet I had given Kelly for Christmas.

"It was broken the night Kelly…" Wendy's voice trailed off as she looked away, swallowing a couple of times before meeting my gaze again. "Well, it was broken. Kelly wore it all the time—she was wild about it—and I meant to have it fixed so she could wear it today. It slipped my mind, though, so I thought you might like to have it instead. Something to remember her by."

I hesitated, my eyes suddenly feeling hot again. I wasn't sure if I wanted it, but I could tell by Wendy's expression that my having it was important to her. I reached out, swallowing as she handed the box to me. It felt heavy in my hand—full of memories we'd never had the chance to make. "Thank you."

Wendy hugged me, and she looked like she was about to say more, but just then Jim called to her from not far off and she drifted away. I stared at the box for another long moment, then drew a deep, shuddering breath and dropped it into the pocket of my sport coat.

I needed to get out of there.

The exit right beside me was just as good as any, and I stepped out into the afternoon and followed a sidewalk that ran along the side of the building to the front. Before I even got there, though, I heard angry voices:

"Yes, you *are*! You've been doing it for weeks now, and everyone can see it! He needs some *space*, Gina. Couldn't you have at least waited until Kelly's body was cold before you went swooping in?"

Ab. Her accusation made me stop in my tracks.

"You don't know *anything*!" Gina shot back, sounding on the verge of tears. "I've been trying to be there for him! You're just mad because, deep down, you want him for *yourself*, don't you? Well, you can't have him, you scheming bitch! Do you hear me?"

Oh, crap, I thought, as a pause hung heavily in the air.

"What did you just call me?" Ab asked quietly, a dangerous edge in her tone.

I hurried to the end of the building, rounding the corner and acting as if I was surprised to see them. "Oh, hey," I said, forcing a smile. "Do either of you need a ride? 'Cause I was about to text Mom, and..."

"You *still* suck at lying, Wolfman," Ab snapped, glaring at me. "You heard. Don't even *try* to pretend that you didn't."

I felt my face turn red. She had me. "Look," I began, trying to smooth things over, "it's been a long day, and I'm sure Gina didn't…"

Ab looked incredulous. "You're taking *her* side? After all we've been through…after what she just *called* me?"

"No…no, I'm not taking…"

"Maybe if you ever took a break from playing white knight all the time, you'd see what's going on!" Ab looked furious. "Tell you what, Ben: come talk to me after you pull your head out of your ass!" With that, she turned and stormed back into the building.

I rounded on Gina, but she started yelling before I could say anything. "She's just trying to come between us! Who's been there for you all this time? *I* have! Who's the one who really loves…"

"*Enough!*" I snapped. "Look, I'm *not* your boyfriend, Gina. If I said or did anything to make you think that, I'm sorry, but that's just the way it is. And don't get me wrong…I *really* appreciate what a good friend you've been, and I honestly don't know how I could have gotten through these last few weeks without you. But it's like you're all set to register the China while I'm still way too messed up to think about being with *anybody*! Not yet, and probably not for a while. So, give it a rest, okay?"

Then I saw the hurt and betrayal in her eyes and I felt terrible, wishing I hadn't just blurted it out like that.

Ben Wolf, Captain of the Sensitivity Team.

"Get away from her!"

I turned around, not really surprised to see Darren, his face livid with rage. *Perfect…just perfect*, I thought. He stood just a few feet back from the curb, the Lynch's pickup idling with the passenger door open behind him, and I figured he was there to pick up Gina. One look at his expression, and I half expected to be hit with some sort of curse right then and there—my skin suddenly liquefying and sliding off my bones, maybe, or an anvil falling out of the sky and turning me into a bloody smear on the concrete. Then again, considering the day I was having, that might not be such a bad thing. At least it would put a stop to the constant ache in my chest. There wasn't a whiff of patchouli in the air, though, so I guessed I was out of luck.

I turned back toward Gina, searching for a way to apologize.

"You just don't get it, Ben," Gina spoke before I could say anything. Tears were streaming down her face, although otherwise she looked calm. "Once you do, you'll see I'm right. We're going to be together, just wait and see." Then she walked past me, heading for the truck, and Darren stared dangerously at me for another second or two before turning to follow her.

I watched them drive away, wondering how she could still be so sure of that after the way I had just dumped on her. Finally, I turned back toward the community center's entrance, wondering if I should try to patch things up with Ab right then, or wait until she had cooled off. It was the first time she had ever called me Ben, and I didn't want to think about what that might mean.

Les stood just outside. He stared at me with an expression like he had just taken a bite from an apple and found half a worm left inside. Then he turned and disappeared back through the doors.

Screw this, I thought. Everything around me was a smoldering wreck, and right then I didn't have the first clue how to fix any of it. I texted Mom, letting her know I was outside and ready to go whenever she was, then went to wait beside the Explorer.

Way to go, big guy, I told myself. *Maybe if you work straight through the afternoon, you can have the rest of the world to hating you by dinnertime.*

THIRTY-NINE

IT WAS LATE AFTERNOON WHEN MOM AND I MADE IT back to the house, and after Moe welcomed us home, I went straight upstairs to change out of my suit. My mood was still dark, and after hanging everything up, I took a long shower, letting the heat and water pressure work the tension out of my shoulders and upper back. I felt a little better afterward—enough to work on salvaging part of the day, anyway—and I decided to try right then. I hurried back to my room, then sat on the bed with my towel still around my waist and tapped out a quick text to Ab:

[HEY… I'M SORRY ABOUT EARLIER. I WASN'T TAKING GINA'S SIDE & EVERYTHING CAME OUT ALL WRONG.] I pressed the send button, and then watched the screen until the text status turned from *SENT* to *DELIVERED*.

Good, I thought, feeling slightly less like the world's biggest loser. I kept one eye on my phone while I dressed, hoping to hear the ping of a reply, but my text was still unanswered by the time I finished putting on my shoes. I decided maybe a follow-on would help:

[I H8 HAVING U MAD @ ME. R WE OK?]

SENT...

DELIVERED.

Minutes passed. Still nothing, and my anxiety grew. I tried not to worry, reminding myself that it had only been a short while after all. Maybe Ab had decided to shower, too. Maybe her battery had died. Maybe a hundred different reasons.

Maybe she isn't hovering by her phone, holding her breath until you text her, the voice in my head pointed out. *Maybe Ab has a life, and you aren't the center of her existence. Did that ever occur to you?*

I frowned. My inner voice could be a real dick sometimes. Still, it had a point.

"*Ben...?*" Mom called from downstairs. "*Did you want some dinner? Or did you fill up earlier?*"

"Be right down!" I called back. I hadn't eaten all day, and I realized that I was kind of hungry after all. At least I could take care of that while I waited. "C'mon, Moe," I said, grabbing my phone, and he followed me out into the hall.

By a little after 8:00, I was pacing around the dark family room, pretty sure I had ruined everything. Ab was still ignoring me, even after three additional texts I had sent since dinner:

[CAN WE TALK?]

[I WANT US TO BE OK AGAIN]

[THIS IS KILLING ME. I'M A JERK, AND I'M REALLY, REALLY SORRY]

Nothing. Ab *had* to be super pissed, otherwise she wouldn't have gone radio silent. Would she ever forgive me, or was our friendship over for good? I couldn't believe how badly I had screwed things up. Everything was falling apart—had *fallen* apart—and it was all my fault. I would do anything to fix it, but I had no idea where to begin or even exactly what I had done to push things over the cliff. Someone with half a brain would have figured things out already, but clearly, I wasn't that guy. I doubted the confrontation at the community center was all there was to it. There had to have been more, and that afternoon was probably just the final straw. Still, that was bad enough. I should have taken Ab's side the second Gina called her a scheming bitch. Ab sure as hell would have stood by me if things had been the other way around. She would have gone in with guns blazing and without a second of hesitation, and my wussy-assed attempt to ride the fence and play peacemaker left me ashamed. Ab deserved better than that.

She deserved better than *me*.

Even Les had seen the disaster I had caused, and I winced when I remembered the expression on his face before he turned and went back inside. Les had been nothing but an awesome friend ever since I moved to Windward Cove, yet somehow, I had managed to disgust and betray him, too. How about that? I was batting a thousand on disgust and betrayal lately. It seemed to be the only thing I was good at. I had known all along how hurt Les was about Gina liking me over him, and had noticed—dimly, anyway—how he had been pulling away. But I hadn't done anything about it. The idea had never even crossed my mind, which meant I had been too self-absorbed over my own problems or just too plain stupid to be there for him. Probably both.

Ben Wolf, self-centered douchebag and epic moron.

Let's sum up, shall we, big guy? I thought. Kelly was dead and buried, the result of a threat that I knew good and damn well was out there somewhere, but I hadn't warned her. I hadn't said a single *thing*. If I had, maybe she would have been more careful. Maybe she would have stayed clear of whatever chased her into the gym in the first place. That was on me. For that matter, I had known that something was going on before Riley was killed, too, but I was too dense to figure it out—was *still* too dense, even now—so that was on me, too. I had driven both Ab and Les away; they probably hated me now, and I didn't even want to *think* about how the rest of our friends would feel about me when they found out why. Finally, there was Gina. I had known early on that she had feelings for me, but I hadn't done a thing to stop it. I had allowed her close without setting any boundaries, and now she was convinced that we were the most perfect couple since Mike and Carol Brady. How the hell could I have let that get so out of hand? Then I remembered Darren's escalating sullenness and anger as he watched Gina slowly moving away from him and closer to me. Had my cluelessness put her in danger? Family ties aside, how much longer would he be able to stand that? And how would I be able to live with myself if Gina suffered some strange, unexplained accident, too—or worse, wound up dead?

It was all such a mess. All things considered, I figured I was lucky that Mom and Moe could still stand the sight of me.

I sighed. The real question was what was I supposed to do about it? My gift was gone like a cool breeze, and everything I touched lately had turned to crap. I remembered Mom's joke about running for the border, and suddenly that didn't seem like such a bad idea. After all, my sticking around here was only making things worse. But we wouldn't need to go that far—just far enough so ex-psychic Ben Wolf could start a new life being just as normal as everyone else.

Funny…for months I had been thinking off and on about what to do after high school. Of course, Mom's and my inheritance meant I didn't *have* to do anything, but after all that had happened since last summer, I had started to think how rewarding and fun it would be to investigate hauntings with Ab and Les—Kelly too, after I had finally let her in on my secret. Not that I wanted our own TV show like *Ghost Adventures* or *The Dead Files* or anything, but sorting out real mysteries as a way to help people. Well, so much for that plan. *Hard to do any of that when you're giftless and friendless*, I thought. Now I had to figure out a different path for my life. Hmm…maybe I could work at Disneyland. Now, there was an idea. After all, Disneyland was supposed to be the Happiest Place on Earth, right? Or, better still, I could land a gig at Magic Mountain or Knott's Berry Farm. That way I could go to Disneyland on my days off.

Jeez, will you just…freaking…STOP? I asked myself, and I took a deep breath. None of that was helping things. I was wallowing and feeling sorry for myself. Like Ab said, I needed to pull my head out.

"Ben…"

I turned, noticing Mom standing in the kitchen archway.

"You've been pacing for nearly two hours. Go see her."

I frowned, still shaking off my last train of thought. "See who?"

Mom held up my phone. It was open to my text page.

"You're snooping through my *texts*?" I had never bothered to set up a passcode, but now it looked like maybe I needed to.

She shrugged. "I had to do something to understand what's going on. Getting you to talk has been like pulling teeth since Kelly died, and even when you do say something, I'm lucky to get three syllables." Then she smiled. "But no, I wasn't snooping. I'd never do that. Your phone was open to this page and it lit up when I walked by. But that's not the point. Go see Ab. Right now. You'll feel better."

I hesitated, swallowing. "What if she hates me, Mom?" Tears were suddenly very close.

She gave me a gentle smile. "I think maybe you're not giving her enough credit. Best friends don't hate, Benny. Best friends fight sometimes, but then they get over it and move forward."

I was driving up Main Street, wondering what to say to Ab's Mom or Dad if one of them answered the door. If she had told them how badly I had let her down, that could be an uncomfortable minute or two. Then I noticed the lights were on in Tsunami Joe, and I thought maybe I was in luck. I circled the block so I could park on that side, and just as I was shutting off the ignition, I saw a familiar silhouette exit Chuy's Taqueria.

Les. One of the employees let him out the door, then locked it behind him and turned off the neon *OPEN* sign.

Feeling a surge of hope, I quickly got out and crossed the street, hurrying to catch up. He was walking west—probably headed home. I was eager to make things right between us, and was beginning to hope the night might not turn out so badly after all. "Hey, Les!" I called. "Wait up!"

He turned, regarding me silently as I approached. He wasn't smiling.

"Hey, brother," I began. "I know things went off the rails today, and I just wanted to make sure…"

"Make sure *what*?" he snapped. "Make sure nobody finds out what kind of guy you really are? Well, too bad—the word's already out."

That stunned me, and I felt my own smile fade. "What are you talking about?"

"Oh, *please*…did you think I wouldn't find out? I called Gina earlier to see if she was okay, and she told me everything."

Everything? I thought. *Meaning what*? Then the image of Gina naked in the firelight suddenly filled my mind, and I swallowed. I could only imagine how Les would feel about that.

He must have taken my silence for guilt. "Oh, yeah…she told me all about how she started spending time with you because you needed her. About the way she fell hard for you, and how she thought you were starting to feel the same. But then you just kicked her to the curb like she was nothing. But she didn't need to tell me that part—I was *there*, remember?"

Is that the way Gina really saw it? I thought. If so, then it was no wonder things were such a mess. "No, Les. It wasn't like that. See…"

"What kind of asshole *does* that?" Les went on, ignoring me. I didn't need psychic abilities to tell that he was seething with anger. "Gina's a nice girl! I can get over her dumping me for you—that's life. But I'm not gonna stand by and let you treat her like shit. You used to be a good guy, Ben. What happened? What's *wrong* with you?" He turned away without waiting for an answer, walking fast.

I sprang forward, grabbing his shoulder to turn him around. We needed to talk, and I wasn't about to let him go without telling him that it was all just a big misunderstanding. He spun, batting my hand away, and as it flew free of his shoulder, my knuckles landed a glancing blow to his chin. Two or three heartbeats passed while Les just stared at me, his eyes wide with shock. Then his face clouded with anger.

I never saw it coming. His fist landed on my cheek with the force of a sledgehammer, causing me to stagger backward as lights flashed inside my head. "What the *hell*!" I snarled, suddenly furious. Then everything I had been bottling up inside for weeks exploded outward all at once. All that pain and anger hit me like a rogue wave, sweeping the rational part my mind away as my hands curled into fists. All I needed right then was a target, and if Les wanted to volunteer, that was fine by me!

I stepped forward, swinging.

FORTY

AB CHAMBERS STEPPED BACK TO ADMIRE THE ROWS OF *sparkling glassware. An hour before she had noticed the shelves were dusty, with darker circles in the empty spaces where mugs usually rested. After removing everything to the counter, she wiped down and polished the shelves, and finally re-washed every mug and glass before putting everything back in place.*

Much better.

She had not wanted to go home after the funeral. She was still upset about the fight with first Gina, and then Ben. Mostly Ben. Dad had sensed that she was upset after he came to pick her up, but she had not wanted to talk about it—mostly because she wasn't quite sure how she felt about it herself—and asked him to drop her off at Tsunami Joe instead. She needed time to think, even though being alone after talking about Kelly all afternoon was kind of depressing. Keeping busy helped, though, so she spent her time double-checking the inventory sheet Donna had filled out that morning (she had been off by one bag of sugar), wiping away the sticky residue that always accumulated on the bottles of flavored syrup, and dry-mopping the floors even though they didn't need it. The glassware shelves had been last. The nice clothes she had worn to the funeral were a mess now, of course, but it didn't matter.

The person she really wanted to talk to was Ben, but she couldn't. She was still mad at him. Part of her—well, most of her, if she were being honest with herself—realized that she shouldn't be. After all, he had not actually been taking Gina's side when he tried to intervene. Ab had seen that as clear as day the moment she had cooled off. Wolfman had just tried to turn the temperature down. The problem was he had said everything in the way Ab least wanted to hear right then, and she had gotten her back up about it.

So, what did that mean? That she was staying angry with him on principle? The thought embarrassed her. Yeah, maybe she was. Reading Ben's texts hadn't helped her confusion, either, as on one hand she felt a sort of petty satisfaction that he at least realized she had been hurt, while on the other hand she had to admit, inwardly at least, that she had blown the whole thing out of proportion. Picking up her phone, she reread the last one for the seventh or eighth time:

[THIS IS KILLING ME. I'M A JERK AND I'M REALLY, REALLY SORRY.]

No, Wolfman, you're not a jerk, *Ab thought, setting the phone down again.* You're just being you, and that's nothing to be sorry for.

Ab had never experienced a friendship quite like the one she shared with Ben. Something between them had just clicked right from the start, and during all the months since he had moved to Windward Cove, they had never once fought, or even disagreed about anything that really mattered. Her fascination with ghosts was something he not only accepted, but also had come to share. Considering how many people simply dismissed her as weird, that alone made him stand out. But there was so much more, too: the way they could talk about anything, the way he had opened up to her and Les about his secret abilities, and the way she knew, down to the bottom of her soul, that if she were to call him in the middle of the night and say, "Help," his first words would be, "What can I do?" Friends like that didn't grow on trees.

Sometimes she wondered how different things would be between them if it had not been for Kelly. Ab had felt stirrings of attraction for him almost right from the start, but realized as soon as Ben first set eyes on Kelly that he was a goner. Clearly, Kelly was more Ben's type (which hardly came as a surprise—Kelly was every guy's type), and that was that. Them's the breaks, she had decided at the time, grateful to have found out before her attraction turned into something more.

And that was the part about the fight that bothered her the most: Gina's furious accusation that Ab wanted Ben for herself. Even if that were true (an idea Ab refused to even think about), hearing it came as a shock. Was it obvious…if not to herself, then to other people? Did she feel more than friendship, even best friendship, for him? Or had Gina just been lashing out, assuming that every girl was as obsessed with Ben as she was?

The worst part, though—even worse than being called a scheming bitch—was that Ben heard Gina say it. That was beyond humiliating, especially after the way Ab had planted one on him at New Year's. What on earth had possessed her to do that? Yes, it had seemed like the thing to do at that moment, and had felt more natural than she would have ever imagined. Ab had even thought about it off and on since it happened, smiling at the memory of how nice it had been. Now, though… What an awful mistake. All she could do was hope that he wouldn't think to put two and two together and decide that Ab was chasing after him, too. The last thing she wanted was any awkwardness between them.

Everything was such a wreck.

Ab sighed, knowing that she was just delaying the inevitable, and that she wouldn't feel better until she patched things up with Ben. Taking a seat at a nearby table, she put her feet up comfortably on the chair beside her and was about to send him a text when she caught a whiff of unfamiliar smell—sweet, mixed with a kind of musky spice.

She put her feet back down, sniffing the air while trying to remember if they had brought in some new kind of herbal tea. Then the smell of something burning assailed her, faint at first, but then growing in intensity. Automatically, Ab looked toward the drip coffee machine. The amber light for the top burner had stopped working months before, making it easy to not realize it was on. Ab had lost track of the number of times a carafe of coffee was left up there, eventually evaporating down to a blackened mess scorched to the bottom. But no…that wasn't it. Finally, her gaze fell on an electrical outlet just to the left of the espresso machine, where tendrils of gray-black smoke issued from all six holes to writhe gracefully up the wall. Just as Ab realized what she was seeing, flames blossomed from the outlet, blue at the base and flickering yellow on top. The wall began to catch fire, too, as the outlet cover blackened and started to melt.

Startled, but not really scared, Ab hurried over to grab the fire extinguisher near the end of the service counter, then pulled the pin from the handle and smothered the flames.

Oh, great! *she thought irritably as she surveyed the damage.* The perfect ending to a perfect day. *It was then that she noticed that neither the sweet smell nor the burned odor was dissipating. If anything, both were getting worse as smoke continued to thicken in the air. Turing, she scanned the room and then froze, her eyes widening.*

Flames had emerged from a second electrical outlet, this time adjacent to the archway to the back room. She quickly put out that fire as well, and then hurried to the table for her phone to call 911. She frowned, blinking away the acrid sting of smoke as her phone went dead in her hand, its battery depleted. But that was impossible—it had been fully charged just that morning!

A crackling sound rose behind her and Ab spun, horrified to see twin columns of flame burning bright and hot to either side of the front entrance, both outlets below spitting sparks onto the floor. An animal sound of fear came from her and she ran for the side exit to the alley, where the circuit breaker panel was located across from the ladies' room door. If she could kill the main breaker and cut power to the shop, that would at least prevent any more outlets from catching fire! Just as she reached the mouth of the hall, however, Ab scrambled backward as the panel door blew open with a bang, belching out a ball of blue-green flames that immediately spread to the walls and ceiling. The overhead lights went out, leaving her bathed only in the reddish-yellow glow of the fires.

Coughing in the thickening smoke and her lungs beginning to sear from the heat, Ab went for her only remaining option: the landline behind the service counter. She made it to the counter more by feel than sight, boosting herself up to lie across it on her belly, and reaching over to fumble on the shelf below until her hand closed on the phone's receiver. She put it to her ear, sobbing in terror as she heard only silence instead of a dial tone.

Ab rolled off the counter, seeking the marginally cooler air near the floor, and landed painfully as she looked around desperately for a way out. The almost musical sound of breaking glass came from all around as the pictures on the walls fell victim to the heat, her collection of photos burning in their frames as ominous creaks and groans drifted down from the roof beams above. Raging fires flanked the front entrance to either side, and the way to the alley was a tunnel of flame.

As Ab watched, she thought for a second that a quantity of smoke had been trapped in the superheated air of the hallway, but then she realized that it wasn't smoke at all! Slowly, almost lazily, ragged shreds of darkness drifted together to form a silhouette. Even blinking through smoke and tears, Ab was certain she could make out the figure of a woman—a woman in full skirts and topped by a mane of long, voluminous hair. Totally unaffected by the fire raging all around, the dark figure remained eerily still, seeming to watch her, and it was only then that Ab realized the musky perfume must be patchouli—the scent Ben had described to her.

At that moment, the overhead fire sprinklers belatedly released their spray, pushing down the flames by perhaps a third, but it was already too late. The temperature at that height had grown so hot that most of the droplets turned to steam in midair.

"HELP!" Ab screamed as loudly as she could. But that only resulted in a fit of coughing and gagging as she choked on the intensifying heat, the thickening smoke, and above all, the sickly-sweet odor of patchouli that filled the air.

FORTY-ONE

I SAGGED TO ONE KNEE, SWAYING FOR A MOMENT AS I steadied myself against an awning post. My face had taken so many blows it felt as if it had been shot full of Novocain. My ears rang, I was pretty sure my nose was bleeding, and a cut near my left eyebrow trickled blood down my cheek.

I wasn't winning the fight.

"Stay down," Les warned.

His expression looked more concerned than angry, though, and it made me mad all over again. "Screw *that*," I rasped, finally swaying to my feet. Despite the half dozen solid punches I had managed to land, Les still looked fine, like he could keep going all night. How irritating was that? But it was okay—I needed him standing. It felt good to finally take my feelings out on someone, even if it was one of my best friends, and the pummeling I was receiving in return was only what I deserved. Cosmic justice at its finest. I raised my fists again, trying to look more solid than I felt. "You're the one who wanted this, so let's finish it!"

Les retreated a step, looking bleak. "C'mon, hombre…it's over. Don't make me put you down." Then he swallowed. "Please."

By my count, he had already put me down three times, but what did it matter? I paused for a moment as a wave of dizziness made the world pitch and yaw, then staggered forward again.

Les straightened, raising a hand. "Dude, hold on," he said, looking around. "Do you smell *smoke*?" He turned, and at that moment we both saw the billowing black clouds and firelight coming from the coffee house. "Call 911!" he shouted, already sprinting that way.

It took me a heartbeat or two to process what I was seeing before I followed at a shambling run, digging my phone out of my pocket as I crossed the deserted street. By the time I reached Tsunami Joe, Les already had his jacket off, using it to shield his hands as he strained to pull the front door open.

Locked.

"Nine-one-one, what's your emergency?" asked a calm voice in my ear.

I reported the fire, choking back desperation as I heard Ab scream for help inside. The siren summoning Windward Cove's volunteer fire department began wailing only seconds later, and while I was still trying to figure out what to do next, Les stepped to the knickknack shop next door and picked up a small, wrought-iron bench that sat out front. His big muscles straining, Les lifted the bench over his head, staggering back to the coffee house and heaving it through Tsunami Joe's front window with a crash.

A huge ball of smoke and flames billowed outward, fueled by all the fresh oxygen and nearly engulfing Les. The rest of the window exploded outward with the sudden release of pressure, throwing him backward into the street amid a hail of broken glass. He landed hard on the asphalt, his shirt and hair smoking and bloodied by numerous cuts. He sat up right away, though, so I figured he was mostly okay.

Turning back to the coffee house, I discovered the smoke had momentarily cleared enough for me to see inside, and my heart seized in my chest as I saw Ab lying on the floor near the service counter. She wasn't moving.

Before I could give myself time to think about it, I took three running steps and dove across the window sill, landing on my belly and making my way toward Ab in a scrambling crawl. Embers rained down all around me as the ceiling above creaked and groaned, and the sound of shattering glass and sealed containers bursting from the heat was like a battlefield. I could feel my legs already baking in my jeans, and was glad the bomber jacket Kelly had given me insulated by arms and torso. A cracking sound rose from my left, and I looked over in time to see a large portion of the wall tumble inward, breaking apart as it crashed and scattering bricks, shards of mortar, and dust across the floor. The roof above sagged alarmingly with the sudden lack of support, warning of imminent collapse as larger chunks fell like fiery meteors.

I didn't have much time!

Ab opened her eyes, blinking uncomprehendingly at me when I grabbed her arm, and I scrabbled back toward the window, overjoyed that she was alive. Between dragging Ab behind me and having to either go around or bat aside burning debris along the way, the trip back across the floor took twice as long. Les was waiting at the window by the time we got there, though, and between us we got her outside and across the street just before the fire truck arrived, skidding to a stop in the street.

Les and I sat on the curb, holding Ab between us as we watched Tsunami Joe die.

The firemen were still setting up hoses when the roof caved in, smothering most of the fire and blinding everyone with a cloud of smoke and dust as it landed on the floor below. A second crash followed almost immediately afterward, and when the air was clear again, we could see the entire west wall had come down on top of it. One of the firemen put an oxygen mask on Ab before pulling a radio from his belt to call for an ambulance, and through the face shield I could see tears making shiny tracks through the soot on her cheeks.

"Are you okay?" I asked, still trembling with leftover adrenaline. Ab said something I couldn't make out through the mask, so I leaned over and pressed my ear to the clear plastic. "What's that?" I asked.

What Ab said then turned my blood to ice. All I could do was sit back, staring while the fire department sprayed down the worst of the remaining flames.

Les put a comforting had around the back of my neck. "Dude… what did she say? Is she alright?"

Slowly, I turned to meet his gaze. "Cozanna," I told him. "She said Cozanna."

I barely had time to register the look of confusion on his face when movement up the street behind him caught my eye. A tall figure stood silhouetted against the glow of a street light. Before I could react, it turned and ran into the shadows of a side street, but there was no mistaking the round shoulders and pudgy build.

Darren.

I'll be damned, I thought, feeling a rush of shock, disbelief and certainty all at once. All those months I'd been looking for proof.

Now I had it.

FORTY-TWO

AB WAS SITTING UP BY THE TIME THE AMBULANCE
arrived. The paramedics got out beside one of the firemen, who
pointed toward us, and they unloaded a gurney and a couple of cases
of equipment before heading our way. "Hey, hon…I'm Sarah. How
are you feeling?" asked the driver, directing her question to Ab. She
was a slender, athletic-looking woman with thick, dark hair pulled
back from her face. She probably would have stood a good head
shorter than me had I been standing, but possessed an air of confidence and authority. She helped Ab out of the firefighter's mask
while her partner, a hulking black man built like a pro wrestler, set
up their equipment.

"I'm…okay," Ab rasped softly, followed by a wince. Talking must
have been painful for her. "Listen, I don't need all…you don't need to…"

"I know," Sarah said soothingly, pulling on a pair of disposable
gloves. "But we came all this way, so we might as well look you over
while we're here, right?" Les and I moved aside while she began a cur-
sory inspection of Ab's skin, and when she lifted the short sleeves of

Ab's shirt, I could see how her normal coloring contrasted to the red of areas that had been exposed to the heat. "Well, it looks like you got a little cooked, but the good news is I don't see any blistering. How long were you inside after the fire broke out?"

Ab shook her head, and then looked over at me, and Sarah did too. "Five, maybe six minutes," I answered for her. It was my best guess.

"That had to be scary. What's your name, hon?"

"She's Ab," I spoke up again. "Short for Abigail."

"Cute," Sarah told her, smiling. "Listen, Ab, I'm going to help you stand up, and then I want you to lie back on this gurney. Think you can do that?"

Ab could, and a moment later Sarah had already checked her pulse and temperature while her partner placed a smaller oxygen mask over her nose and mouth, and then took her blood pressure. The two worked together with the casual efficiency of teammates who had done the same thing a thousand times before. Les and I exchanged a worried glance as Sarah hooked her up to a heart rate monitor, but she noticed our concern and said "Nothing to worry about, guys—all part of the act."

It made me feel better.

Ab objected when they raised the gurney and rolled it toward the back of the ambulance, but her words were muffled behind the mask, and I couldn't make them out. "No, hon," Sarah answered, "there's no cleaning up *this* mess tonight. And all the firemen are still busy, so we might as well swing by the hospital and make sure your lungs are okay while they finish here." That appeared to ease Ab's mind, and she relaxed as the paramedics loaded her up.

"Now let's look at you two," Sarah said, turning. Les and I both said we were fine, but she ignored us until she saw for herself, and even took the time to clean and bandage the cut on my forehead. "Now, one of you can ride with us if you want…"

I nodded toward Les, and he nodded back, agreeing.

339

"…and the other can follow," Sarah finished. "Has anyone called her parents yet?"

I flushed, embarrassed that the idea hadn't occurred to me. "I'll take care of it."

Sarah gave me the address of the hospital in Eureka where they were taking her, and I tapped it into my phone. The ambulance pulled away a moment later.

I know that I spoke to her dad for two or three minutes, but I couldn't remember afterward what I said. He kept asking questions, which probably meant I wasn't making much sense. My thoughts had been focused and clear while I was in the thick of things, but now that the scary part was over and I had time to think, I couldn't. The image of Darren running off after nearly killing Ab overwhelmed me with white-hot anger. How could I have been so stupid? The red flags had been there all along, but I kept giving him the benefit of the doubt over and over again. Did Darren have to hold up a neon sign saying, *I'M A PSYCHO* before I got a freaking *clue*?

Well, not any more, I resolved coldly. His hatred for the world, his self-centeredness, and general assholery had hurt and killed people. Right then I decided that Darren Lynch was evil, pure and simple, and if I had my way, the last thing he would ever see would be me taking a bite out of his still-beating heart.

I wanted to jump in the car right away and head for the hospital, but I was trembling with rage by then, so I made myself wait while I called Mom instead. I would later remember that conversation a little better; essentially me telling her that there had been a fire at the coffee house, that Ab was at the hospital but was essentially okay, and that I was going there myself. Mom offered to come too, but I waved her off, saying that Ab's parents would be there, things were getting crowded, and that I would phone or text her later with an update. She was disappointed, which made me feel bad, but the truth was I did not want her to see me before I had time to clean up a little and see for myself how much my face looked like a catcher's mitt.

I walked into the emergency room just in time to see a nurse herding Les away from a closed set of double doors, behind which they must have taken Ab. Les didn't look happy, and the nurse looked absolutely livid, so they must have disagreed on whether he belonged back there. The nurse pointed toward three rows of plastic chairs, maybe two dozen in all, that were crowded in a waiting area with a TV, and I adjusted course to meet him there. He dropped into a chair, still looking angry, and I took one two spaces to his right. Neither of us said anything.

Mr. and Mrs. Chambers arrived a minute or two later, and were immediately ushered in to see Ab, but if either of them noticed us sitting there, they gave no sign of it. The TV was muted, tuned to a late-night infomercial selling some cleaning product, so I ignored it and went back to getting my emotions back under control. Les stared straight ahead, offering no clue what he was thinking, and for the millionth time I wished I still had my gift. If I at least knew what he was feeling, maybe then I could figure out what to say.

Only a single empty seat separated Les and I, but it might as well have been ten miles for the distance that lay between us. My face was tender, and my shoulder ached like a rotten tooth from dragging Ab across the floor. Worst of all, a headache pounded the inside of my skull. I didn't know if it was from tension, all the smoke I'd breathed, or Les using my head for a punching bag, but it was a bad enough to make me nauseous. We both kept coughing off and on, but other than that, the silence that stretched out between us was heavy with words, both said and unsaid. I didn't know if we were okay again or not, but I couldn't think of how to ask, so I stared at the clock above the television instead, watching the second hand sweep its steady three-sixty while I wondered what to do.

After eight minutes and twenty-six seconds, Les finally solved the problem. "I'm sorry, hombre," he said quietly.

A wave of relief washed over me. "I'm sorry too," I said, matching his quiet tone.

"I shouldn't have hit you. You were trying to tell me your side, but I was too mad to listen. That wasn't right."

I nodded. "I messed up a lot of things, too."

A pause.

"Just so you know, if you want to tell me now, I'm all ears."

I thought about it. "I do. But not here. There's a lot you don't know yet, and it'll take some time. Tell you what: let's get through this part first. Once we know Ab's okay, we'll go someplace and talk."

Les nodded. "Okay." Then he cleared his throat nervously. "One thing first, though...are we still friends?"

Relief flooded me again. "To infinity and beyond," I told him, and I was pretty sure I could read the relief in his expression. That, or maybe he just liked Buzz Lightyear. Either way, the tension in the room seemed to drop by half.

"If you think about it," I went on, "it was lucky we were out there pounding on each other. Otherwise, we never would have noticed the fire, and Ab would probably be dead." *Ab and me both*, I amended inwardly. Seeing Les on the street was the only reason I had not been trapped in Tsunami Joe with her.

"Mm," he mused. "In that case, we should probably fight more often."

"Think of all the lives we'd save."

Another pause stretched out between us, though it was a lot more comfortable than the last one.

"Oh...and Les?" I asked after a while.

"Yeah?"

"You hit like a girl."

He snorted, glancing over to look at my face. "I can see that."

We got up when Ab's parents emerged an hour later, and after thanking us for an embarrassingly long time, they let us know that she was going to be fine. The doctor had ordered x-rays of her lungs, just to be sure, and was admitting her overnight for observation, but as far as he could tell there was no permanent damage. We asked if we could see her, but they said Ab needed to be cleaned up after they assigned her a room, so it would probably be better if we waited until she was home. After thanking us again, Mr. and Mrs. Chambers moved off to fill out paperwork at the nurse's station, so there was nothing left for us to do.

By then it was well after midnight, and both of us were hungry, so after sending Mom a text to give her the latest, we got in the car and found an all-night diner a few blocks from the hospital.

"So," Les began, pouring syrup over an enormous stack of pancakes, "you want to tell me your side of the whole Gina thing?"

I told him a lot more than that. Starting from the day Darlene shattered her elbow, when I first picked up the smell of patchouli and that feeling of vindictive satisfaction, through all the other strange occurrences, as well as Gina's increasing level of attraction I had sensed over time, I laid it all out in chronological order. I went through the Lynch family history, after which I pointed out that the victims of each weird event—Brianna, Alan, and Dozer, and all the way up through Cruz and Markham nearly dying in the auto shop—had all been people who had angered Darren, either directly or by picking on Gina. I finished with the events of the last 48 hours (okay, I sort of glossed over the part where Gina took her clothes off, telling him that she "came on pretty strong," but if Les suspected there was more that I wasn't saying, he didn't mention it), and ended with our argument in front of the community center, and finally seeing Darren run off into the shadows right after we pulled Ab from the fire.

"Holy crap," Les said at last. He had abandoned his pancakes some-where along the line, pushing his plate aside with half the stack now lying cold beside him. "So, it's been Darren all along. Who would have thought he had it in him?"

I shrugged. "That's been bugging me for a while. I didn't really want to believe it was him, but I guess even *I* can see the truth if you hit me over the head with it long enough."

Les frowned, still taking it all in. "So, what do we do now?"

All I could do was shake my head. I had absolutely no idea.

FORTY-THREE

A HARD GUST OF WIND ROCKED THE CAR, AS IF TRYING to flip it over, followed by a brief staccato of fat rain drops that slashed down onto the roof and windshield. The sun glowed a dim, sullen red through a narrow band of open sky to the east, between the tops of the hills and the low, thickening clouds that would soon smother it completely. A dark morning, and it was only going to get worse. According to the weather app on my phone, a storm was due to hit late in the afternoon and last through the next couple of days, complete with occasional thunder and lightning.

We had gone to see Ab the afternoon before, but her parents turned us away at the door. "She's still not feeling well, and has been sleeping most of the day," explained her mother.

"We can't thank you enough for everything you did," her dad added, looking apologetic, "but tomorrow really would be better."

Skunked for the time being, we drove over to Pirate Pizza instead and worked our way through a large pepperoni and sausage while deciding our next move. We finally landed on a plan—not a great plan, but the only one we had—and since it had to wait until Monday morning, we finished lunch and went our separate ways.

Les sat beside me, not talking, as we both stared through the windshield. We had gotten to school before anyone else so we would have our pick of parking spots. I had chosen a space near the back where we could watch both the loading zone on the street in case Darren and Gina got a ride, and the gate they used when they walked. As stakeouts went, we were in good position.

Cars and trucks began to trickle in around 7:15 as the first of the early birds arrived, and then increased to a flow just before 7:40 as the lot began to fill in earnest. Kids streamed toward the buildings from the lot or funneled through the pedestrian gates, about half of them under umbrellas while the other half just hurried, head-down, to get out of the weather.

It was 7:52 when Les finally spoke. "There," he said.

I had been watching the side gate, but turned to follow his gaze fifty or sixty yards farther up the sidewalk where Darren and Gina were trudging through the blustery morning. They would be among the last to arrive, and Darren struggled to hold onto a wide, old-fashioned umbrella that the wind kept trying to tear away. The umbrella had seen better days, with two of the ribs bent and a small hole on Darren's side, but it was keeping them mostly dry.

Wordlessly, we got out of the car. Les disappeared into the crowd to my right while I moved through the entrance to the quad, concealing myself in a corner just past the first bank of lockers where I could watch while still remaining mostly hidden.

Darren hung back when Gina caught sight of Monica, scowling as she hurried out from beneath their umbrella to join Monica under hers. The two passed by without noticing me, talking with their heads together, and I stepped out a few seconds later, stopping directly in Darren's path. He was looking down, shaking the water from his umbrella while folding it, and nearly ran into me before he realized I was there. He pulled up short, looking at me with an expression that looked first startled, and then guarded. He moved to brush past, his eyes narrowing in annoyance as I stepped sideways to block him.

"We need to talk," I said.

His scowl deepened as tried going around my other side.

I didn't let him.

A look of panic flashed briefly in his eyes and then he spun, looking as if he was about to bolt for the parking lot, but Les had moved up behind him, barring his way.

"Let me by!"

Les shook his head, his expression stony. "Not happening, Hondo."

Darren retreated warily sideways until his back was against the lockers, while we moved to box him in. "I've got nothing to say," he declared angrily, "to *either* of you!"

"Oh, I think you do, Darren," I said, doing my best to look menacing. The dark bruises Les had decorated my face with probably helped. "I think you have plenty to say. About fires. And *Cozanna*."

The color drained from Darren's face as his wary expression dissolved into shock, and maybe three heartbeats passed before he remembered to speak. "I...I don't know what you're talking about!"

Even without my gift I knew Darren was full of crap. And judging from his expression, he knew that I knew it. But I had anticipated that he would try denial first, and I was ready for it. "You hear that, Les?" I asked blandly, keeping Darren's eyes pinned beneath my gaze. "Darren doesn't know anything."

"Sonofagun. Looks like we got the wrong guy."

I stared into his eyes for a couple of seconds longer, and then abruptly stepped aside, clearing him a path. "Okay...sorry to bother you. C'mon, Les. Looks like we'll have to talk to Sheriff Hastings instead." We turned, starting to walk toward the parking lot. I wished I was able read

Darren's emotions to see if we had rattled him enough. I was beginning to think we hadn't when his voice rose behind us.

"*Wait!* What do you need to see *him* for?"

There it was. I couldn't sense his panic, but I could hear the edge of it in his voice, so we stopped and turned. "Oh, I bet the sheriff would be interested to hear our ideas about how the coffee house caught fire," I told him. "About how Ab landed in the hospital, and all the rest of the weird crap that's being going on around here. So far, he has zero to go on, so even crazy theories might be better than nothing." I paused. "But what do you care? *You* don't know anything." Darren appeared rooted in place, looking scared and uncertain of what to do. I had a feeling he was near the edge, though, so I figured one more nudge might send him over. "Oh," I added, as if in afterthought, "you *are* going to be home later, right?"

His eyes narrowed. "Why?"

I shrugged. "The sheriff will probably ask."

We resumed walking. I held my breath, but after we had taken a dozen steps or so without hearing anything more, I was sure this time we had struck out. "Crap," I muttered to Les. "I guess he didn't buy it."

"It was a long shot, but we had to try something," he replied. "What else did we have?"

I sighed. "Not a thing."

"Wait!" Darren called out again, and I turned, my spirits lifting as he made his way reluctantly toward us.

ROAD ENDS read the sign posted above the barrier fence, which I always thought was only obvious. Someone had spray-painted a skull and crossbones above the lettering since the last time I had been there, though, which I thought was an improvement. The steep grade we had followed east of Windward Cove wound its way up a heavily wooded mountainside for nearly two miles, ending abruptly at a gravel lot that was the trailhead to Hermit Springs. It was more sheltered from the wind up there in the trees, but we were still hammered by the occasional spats of rain. I shut off the engine, and then turned sideways to glare at Darren in the back seat.

He licked his lips. "Why are we here?"

"Just a quiet place to talk," I told him. "The trail's all mud, so I bet nobody will be up here much before May."

"Plus, this far from town, no one can hear you scream," Les added from where he sat beside him.

I was sure (well…pretty sure, anyway) that Les wasn't being serious, but he wasn't smiling, so I didn't either.

Darren paled, sweat beading his forehead and starting to darken his gray T-shirt at the collar. His gaze flicked nervously through his side window toward the edge of the lot, and I would have bet real money he was weighing his chances of being able to make it to the tree line before we caught him.

"Don't even think about it," Les threatened. "I'm in a bad enough mood as it is. If you make me run you down, I'm bringing an ass-whoopin' with me."

Enough of this, I thought, suddenly furious again. "Ab nearly *died* Saturday night," I snapped. "Do you *get* that? She's been nothing but nice to you!"

For a second or two he looked like he was going to deny it again, but then something in his expression crumbled. "I *know*," he said softly, his breathing coming faster as his voice started to hitch. "And I'm suh-*sorry*! I'm…I'm really glad you…you guys got to her in time." Then Darren surprised me by suddenly leaning over, palms to his face, and began to cry in hoarse, ugly sobs.

It was my turn to pause. I shook my head, exchanging a confused glance with Les, but then my anger got the best of me again. *"THEN WHY THE HELL DID YOU SEND COZANNA TO KILL HER?!"*

Darren's sobs slowly trailed off as my words sank in, and at last he lowered his hands. His eyes were red, his face glistening with tears and snot as he looked at me uncomprehendingly. "What?"

Oh, my freaking God, I thought. I was *so* done with his crap. "Ab *knows* it was her! The whole place reeked of her patchouli! Why, Darren? What did Ab ever do to you?"

"No!" he cried, now looking shocked. "You gotta believe me! I'd *never* hurt Ab!"

"Yeah, right! You were *there*! I *saw* you!"

Seconds ticked by with only the sounds the wind and rain outside while Darren stared into my eyes. Finally, he spoke. "Ben…I went there to *warn* her! I didn't send Cozanna. I *can't*. It was *Gina*!" And with that, he buried his face in his hands again, sobbing forcefully enough to make his shoulders shake.

FORTY-FOUR

IT TOOK A LONG TIME FOR DARREN TO GET HIMSELF back under control, but that was fine. I needed time to think. *Gina?* I wondered. *Really?* After all this time, it was hard to wrap my head around the idea. I had been suspecting Darren for so long that it never even occurred to me to consider anyone else. As shocked as I was, though, part of me realized it was possible, and even made an odd sort of sense. But right then was not the time to wrestle with it as Darren began to tell his side of things—haltingly at first, but then in a rush as he seemed relieved to finally get it off his chest:

Darren had not liked his cousin at first. In fact, he had decided he didn't like her even before she moved to Silver Creek. Up until the previous June, he had only been aware in an offhand way that he even had cousins. After all, his grandparents had moved to California before his father was even born, and Dad only spoke to a couple of relatives, and then only once or twice a year. Now, all of a sudden one of them would be moving in to ruin Darren's life.

351

It started with a series of phone calls over the course of a few weeks, both from some law firm in Rome and a bunch of extended family members in that part of New York. They explained that Gina's parents had been killed in a head-on crash, that no one else was able to take her in, and after all, what could be better than a change of scenery to help a young girl move past her grief and start a new life?

Darren would have told all those assholes to go pound sand. It wasn't like any of them had ever helped his family out. And if none of those people wanted her, why should they? It wasn't their problem in the first place, and anyway, there had to be something wrong with the girl, otherwise why would everyone be so eager to ship her off to the other side of the country? But Dad and Mom had called a family meeting to talk it over, and just like always, he got outvoted 2-1. It wasn't fair! What was more, before Darren even had time to get used to the idea, he was being evicted from his bedroom to the basement so Princess Whatshername could take over his space and feel all welcome and comfortable. He felt shoved aside, and his resentment was off the scale. Then his worst fears came true when his parents started gushing over Gina almost as soon as her bus pulled into town. Just like that, he was officially the Forgotten Son. He supposed he should have seen that one coming, though. After all, everybody else hated him, so it was only a matter of time before his parents did, too.

After the first couple of weeks, though, he started to think maybe things wouldn't be so bad after all. It turned out that moving to the basement was actually a good deal. There was a lot more space, Dad built him shelves for all his stuff, and since he was out of everyone's line of sight, the times he got asked to help around the house or yard were cut in half. Gina steered clear of him until his resentment died down, and when he found out she liked board games, they even started spending time together playing a lot of his old favorites that no one else was interested in anymore: Clue, Operation, Sorry!, Connect 4. *He even started teaching her D&D, even though she sucked at it (at least until Ben started playing.)*

The best part, though, was that he finally had someone to talk to. Gina's shyness had made her an outcast just like him, and for the first time Darren knew what it was like to have an ally, and then a real friend. Once they both confessed their mutual loneliness and distrust of people, the floodgates opened and they talked about everything. Coolest of all was when they discovered that their voices carried amazingly well through the old furnace duct that routed air to both the basement and Gina's room directly above. They would have conversations late into the night, confiding their daydreams and fears, what they wished their lives were really like, or just exchanging made-up stories where the other was the main character and always ended up getting exactly what they wanted.

It was near the end of July when Gina finally showed him her Ouija board.

At first, Darren thought it was just another game. After all, you could buy one from Amazon for just a few bucks, and besides, anyone who really believed in that stuff was just plain retarded. But then Gina told him the story of how she had found it the year before in the attic of her old house—a house that had been in the family for generations—and that it had originally belonged to a grandfather of theirs from way back in the day. What really got him interested, though, was when she told him that the spirit inside was the old man's wife, a Gypsy woman named Cozanna, who was their grandmother from over a hundred years before.

Holy shit! Darren's Dad had told him there was Gypsy blood in their family, and the idea that maybe it was true after all—despite all the crap people had given him over the years—was exciting enough to make him want to check it out.

They sat cross-legged on Gina's bed, facing one another with the board resting on their knees between them, and Gina told him to rest the tips of his index and middle fingers as lightly as possible on the planchette. "Cozanna...are you there?" she asked.

At first nothing happened, and Darren's excitement began to fade. It looked like it was just a stupid game after all. But then a sweet, spicy smell crept into the room out of nowhere, and abruptly, the heart-shaped indicator moved! It lurched, only an inch or two at first, and then paused briefly. Then it slowly slid across the polished wood surface until the glass window rested above the word YES. *At once, Darren's heart began thudding heavily in his chest, though he was mostly still skeptical.* "You're pushing it!" *he accused.*

"I'm not." *Gina's voice was serene, and she gazed at him with a knowing smile.*

It was the smile that got him, and he felt an icy prickle run down his back.

To show him that Cozanna was real, Gina first introduced them, and then challenged him to ask her questions that only he knew the answers to.

The name of the dog they had when he was five?

BEAR

How old was he when he learned to ride a bike?

8

The name of his fourth-grade teacher?

PALMER, *came the answer, the planchette sliding from one letter to the next with increased sureness and speed. It was as if Cozanna was becoming more attuned to him with each passing question. Darren asked about more than a dozen bits of information that Gina could not possibly know, and the spirit inside the Ouija board answered correctly every time.*

Every. Single. Time!

He decided to change things up. "So, what...are you?" *he asked.*

DRABARNI

"That's the Romani word for 'one who foretells the future,'" *Gina volunteered.* "I had to Google it. Drabarni can also sometimes mean 'healer' or 'witch.'"

The icy prickle ran down his back again. Darren opened his mouth to ask another question, but then the planchette began to move again of its own accord, spelling out another word: MAMI. *He glanced at Gina.*

"'Grandmother,'" she told him, and she smiled.

Darren began to tremble. Part of him still suspected she was messing with him, but a much bigger part was both scared and convinced beyond all doubt. He was about to remove his fingers when Gina said, "Hold on."

He looked at her, eyebrows raised.

"We have to close the session when we're done."

"How do we do that?"

"You thank her, and then move the planchette down to the bottom of the board where it says Goodbye. *See it?"*

Darren saw, and he did what he was told. Then, suddenly he needed to get out of there, away from the sweet smell and craziness to somewhere he could think. Hurriedly, he retreated to the cool, comforting dimness of the basement, feeling uneasy and vulnerable. It couldn't be real, could it? But some deep part of him knew he was just denying the truth. There was a ghost buried somewhere in the grain of that old, polished wood, and it knew things it had no business knowing. He lay on his bed for a long time, doing his best to not to freak out and waiting—hoping—for the weirdness to pass.

"Hey," came Gina's voice a while later, drifting softly down from the vent above.

"Hey," he replied after a pause.

"Are you okay?"

Darren swallowed. "I guess."

"It's a lot to take in all at once," Gina soothed. "After my first time, I was so scared I didn't touch it for a week. But you get used to it, and Cozanna is really nice."

Darren nodded, and then remembered that Gina couldn't see him. "Okay."

"We can try again. But only when you're ready. Maybe tomorrow?"

"Sure. Maybe."

"Good," she said. *"One thing, though…you can't tell Aunt Roxie or Uncle Tim about this. It's our secret, okay?"*

Darren didn't see that it mattered, but it seemed important to Gina, so he said, "Okay."

"Promise me, Darren."

"I promise."

He ended up not wanting to wait. As soon as he heard his parents go to bed, Darren called out to Gina and invited her down. They sat across from one another at the basement table, communicating with Cozanna long into the night while the exotic scent wrapped them like a hug. The spirit spoke (wrote?) to them mostly in English, but sometimes threw in Romani words or phrases, most of which Gina had long since translated. They ended the session only a couple of hours before dawn, with the planchette spelling out DUCABA TU *before moving down to* GOODBYE.

"We love you, too," Gina whispered. *Then, when she noticed Darren's puzzled gaze, she said, "We're family, remember?"*

As much as he was fascinated by the Ouija board, and grateful to his cousin for letting him in on her secret, it did not take long for Darren to realize that he wasn't Cozanna's favorite. She mostly called him chavo *(Romani for boy or son), and sometimes* dinlow *(idiot) when he said something that annoyed her, while Gina was always* chi sugra *(pretty Gypsy girl.) Still, he didn't really mind. It was amazing, like having access to a magic oracle from one of his fantasy books!*

The scary stuff started in later. Sometimes he would wake in the middle of the night to the sound of Gina's voice drifting down from above. He could never make out the words, like maybe she had placed a towel over her vent to muffle the sound, but he knew she was talking to Cozanna. The tone of her voice would sometimes rise at the end, like she was asking a question, or stay even like she was answering one. Then there would be a pause, and Darren could imagine the planchette moving back and forth across the board as the spirit replied. Sometimes he could make out a word or two if Gina raised her voice a little—a "No!" or "I understand"—and he would wonder what they were talking about…what it was they did not want Darren to hear. And sometimes Gina would laugh, which he found especially creepy. Darren had been hearing just that sort of laugh from girls all his life: conspiratorial and wicked, like they were sharing mean or nasty secrets.

Gina would always be exhausted the next day, sleeping in until well after noon. That worried him. He asked his mother if something might be wrong, but she didn't think so. She said that Gina was still getting over losing her parents, and to let her take the time she needed. But Darren knew that wasn't it, because (1) Gina never talked about her parents— she appeared to not even give them a passing thought—and (2) the more time she and Cozanna spent together, the stronger both of them seemed to become.

Night after night, the pauses between Gina's questions or replies steadily got shorter, and Darren wondered just how fast the planchette had to be moving. If he had not known better, he would have assumed he was overhearing her talk on the phone (which definitely wasn't it—Gina didn't own one), which meant Cozanna had to be spelling things out faster than he could imagine anyone being able to keep up with!

Then a chilling thought struck him: or maybe…just maybe…it was because they didn't need the Ouija board anymore.

It was a couple of weeks before school began when Darren started to become genuinely frightened. It started with sounds from the rooms above late at night, long after even Gina had fallen asleep. Occasional footsteps…doors opening and closing…kitchen drawers sliding out and back. At first he would creep upstairs to investigate, wondering if Mom or Dad had gotten up—or worse, that somebody had broken into the house. But there was never anyone there. The house would be still and silent until he went back down to bed, and then a minute or two later the sounds would resume. After a while, Darren began to catch lingering traces of Cozanna's scent, and he realized that it was her. Somehow, she had grown strong enough to free herself from the Ouija board, and was exploring her surroundings while everyone upstairs was asleep.

Then, objects around the house would mysteriously go missing or be found in weird places. Dad lost his truck keys, only to find them in the cookie jar. Items on the kitchen counters or the living room shelves were rearranged. It exasperated Mom (who was the queen of everything-in-its-place) and it wasn't long before she started blaming Darren and Gina.

That was when things started to get out of hand.

One evening while cooking dinner, Mom called Darren and Gina to the kitchen, and immediately lit into them about how she was sick and tired of their carelessness. It was one of the rare times Roxanne Lynch was angry enough to raise her voice. She had just spent ten minutes looking for the can opener, only to find it in the cabinet with the coffee mugs. "What's *wrong* with the two of you? Why on God's green earth can't you put things back where they belong?"

As she was scolding, Darren noticed movement behind her. A skillet began to slide slowly off the burner in her direction, and he was only just able to jump forward at the last second and reach it before it went over and splashed her with hot oil! As he seized the handle, he caught a faint whiff of Cozanna, the smell barely masked by the heady aroma of fried chicken. The situation died down quickly after that, but later that night, Darren and Gina used the Ouija board to ask Cozanna if she realized she might have seriously hurt Darren's mom.

For a long time the planchette remained still, but at last Cozanna answered: NONE SHALL ABUSE MINE.

"Abuse her what?" *Darren asked, confused.*

"I think she means her family," *Gina replied, smiling.* "She means us."

Darren tried explaining to Cozanna that Mom hadn't been abusing them, begging her to never, never do something like that again, but before he even finished the planchette began to move again, repeating the same four words over and over:

NONE SHALL ABUSE MINE NONE SHALL ABUSE MINE NONE SHALL ABUSE MINE...

"Things only got worse after that," Darren said quietly, and I sensed he was nearing the end. "You know that blue-and-white house just down our street?" he asked me. "The one with the picket fence out front?"

I nodded.

"The guy who lives there had a dog. A mean one. Mostly he kept it out back, but once in a while it would be in the front yard. One morning we were walking past and it charged the fence right at Gina—scared the crap out of her. She freaked and ran partway up the block, thinking it was going to bust right through and get her." Darren cleared his throat, as if the memory made him nervous. "When we came back later, there was blood all over one of the pickets, and we haven't seen the dog since."

Les frowned. "So, you're saying..."

"I think Cozanna killed it—impaled it on the fence. But that's not the scary part. What scared me was when I looked over at Gina and caught her smiling." Darren frowned. "Or I'm *pretty* sure I did, anyway. I only saw it for a second, but I could have sworn it was there. Just a little smile, like she had a secret." Then he shuddered. "I've had nightmares about that bloody picket ever since. Lately, though, the nightmares I have about Gina are worse."

Darren exhaled a long breath, rubbing at his eyes. "I know all you guys think I'm an asshole—that I'm hovering over Gina all the time just because I'm overprotective or whatever. But you're wrong. Yeah, I stick close to Gina to make sure no one hurts her or makes her feel threatened. But I'm not looking out for Gina. I'm looking out for everyone

else. C'mon, guys…you've seen how she's changed, and I swear it's not just because her folks died or because she made some friends. I think…"
He hesitated, looking uncertain as he wet his lips.

Les elbowed him. "You think what?"

Darren shook his head. "No…forget it. You're gonna think it's stupid."

"Tell us anyway."

"Well…it's like somewhere along the line, Cozanna moved out of the Ouija board *and into Gina*."

I sat back, confused and trying to process way too much information at once. "So, what are you saying? That Gina is *possessed*?"

"I didn't think so at first," he confided. "At first, it was like a little piece of Cozanna was just along for the ride sometimes. And it seemed like a *good* thing, you know? Gina was getting more confident—saying what she thought and standing up for herself. The first time I noticed was when we all went to pizza that time…the night those jocks barged in and you and Alan Garrett nearly got into it. Gina told them, '*Why don't you leave us alone?*' and it blew me away. It may be hard for you guys to understand, but that was *huge* for her."

I nodded, remembering. Everyone had been a little surprised.

"I asked Gina about it later, and she told me it was like Cozanna was whispering to her to speak up. You wouldn't *believe* how excited and proud of herself she was for doing it." Darren paused, smiling to himself. "At the time, it made me think of a funny picture I saw once called *The Last Great Act of Defiance*. It showed this teeny-tiny mouse flipping off a bird of prey that was swooping down in him with its talons out.

"Anyway, that was when I really noticed that she was changing, bit by bit. Mostly it made me jealous that I had to share her with all of you, but I knew it was good for her. She started really coming out of her shell, like when she finally felt safe enough to stop hiding under that hoodie all the time. All of it was harder for Gina than you can imagine. Like when she asked you to the Homecoming Dance, Ben. It took her *two weeks* to work herself up to it, and she even threw up a couple of times because she was so nervous. When you said no, I thought it would drive her back into herself, but then she asked *you*, Les, and no one was more surprised than me. And it was all because of Cozanna encouraging her, making her feel safe and supported."

"Sure, great for Gina," Les snapped. "But what about the people who were getting hurt all around you? Do you think all of that was *worth it*?"

Darren paled. "I guess I didn't put two and two together at first. Or maybe I didn't *want* to. It's easy to tell yourself it's all just coincidence when the truth is that scary. But after a while I couldn't ignore it any-more, and that's when I found out just how much Cozanna had crept into her. I tried talking to Gina about it, but she yelled at me—actually *yelled* at me—saying that Cozanna was only protecting her because I wouldn't. She said that if I wasn't on her side, then we weren't friends anymore and I could spend the rest of my life alone for all she cared." Tears welled in Darren's eyes again. "I couldn't take that. She's all I have."

I couldn't help but feel sorry for him. I didn't want to, but there you go.

"But you need to know that Cozanna isn't with her all the time. I can tell, because when she is, Gina acts like her—sure of herself, demanding, short-tempered. She'll even use Romani words now and then without realizing it. Other times, it's like Cozanna is only partway there, and I think that may be when she's off roaming by herself. Gina is more normal then, like Monica or Ab.

"But then there are times when Cozanna leaves her completely, which is why I can't give up on her. It only happens every few days, and then only for three or four hours at a time, but when Cozanna is completely gone, Gina is back to her old self. Quiet...shy...sweet. She's the Gina I miss. Sometimes she can't remember things that happened when Cozanna was totally in charge, and I think those memory gaps scare her. When I ask, she just says that Cozanna went home to sleep."

"*Home?*"

Darren nodded. "The Ouija board. I think she has to go back there to recharge…ground herself…whatever. When she goes there, Gina is Gina again, and I love her. But when Cozanna is back, even partway, *watch out.* She's always watching over Gina—and me too, sometimes—and bad things happen to anyone who makes her angry. *That's* why I try to keep people away. Do you understand?"

The inside of the car was silent for a long time after that. I thought about the birds attacking Brianna. The disco ball falling at the Homecoming Dance. The lighting rig that nearly took out Cece Ramos.

It all made sense.

Finally, I cleared my throat. "Okay. I think we're done here. For now, anyway. I'll drive you back to school."

"Can you drop me at home instead?" Darren asked quietly. "I don't feel so good. I'll ask Mom or Dad to pick Gina up."

"Sure."

None of us had anything more to say during the drive to Silver Creek. Darren got out when I pulled up to the curb in front of his house, shutting the car door behind him without a word while Les came around to slide into the shotgun seat.

"Do you believe him?" he asked, watching Darren walk away.

"I don't know. You?"

Les shrugged.

"That meltdown of his was pretty convincing," I said, thinking aloud, "and a lot of his story fits with what Ab dug up and the stuff that's been happening."

Les snorted. "Yeah, or maybe he was crying because he was scared, and made it all up to throw Gina under the bus and let her take the blame."

I nodded, shifting the transmission into drive and pulling away from the curb. That could be it, too.

"So, what do we do now?"

In the rearview mirror, I watched Darren trudge onto the porch and disappear inside before I answered. "We need to find out if he's telling the truth."

"How? Do you have a plan?"

It was more of an idea than a plan, and already I was wishing it had never occurred to me. I couldn't see any other option, though, and a sense of dread settled over me that was nearly overwhelming. "There might be one thing," I admitted finally. "But I need to think it over first. And it probably won't even work."

"Is it something I can help with?"

"No, I don't think so."

Les settled back in his seat. "Okay. Let me know if you change your mind. I'm just glad *you* have an idea—I'm fresh out."

I sighed. Yeah, I had an idea all right.

I just didn't know if I had it in me to try it.

FORTY-FIVE

WE AGREED THAT THE FIRST THING WE NEEDED TO DO was to bring Ab up to speed, so we headed back toward Windward Cove. "Let's hit Hovey's on the way," Les suggested.

I glanced at my watch, frowning. "So early? It's not even 11:00 yet."

"And I've been living off my own fat since breakfast," he insisted. "Besides, I bet Ab could use a burger *way* more than a bunch of get-well flowers."

He had a point. Besides, if we showed up with lunch, we would stand a much better chance of getting past the front door.

That turned out not to be a problem. As we pulled up to the Chambers' house, we could see Ab's mom and dad loading suitcases into the back of their car while she watched from the front window. Her parents waved as they backed out of the driveway, first to her and then to us, then disappeared up the street.

Ab opened the front door as we mounted the porch steps, shivering in the cold wind that swirled past her. She was barefoot, wearing sweatpants and a Marvin the Martian T-shirt, and she had to push hard against the door to close it again once we were inside.

I felt suddenly awkward. The guilt that had been festering inside me ever since our argument was like a lead weight in my stomach. Before I could say anything, though, Ab stepped over wordlessly and wrapped me in a tight hug. She held it for a long time, and the relief it brought was like stepping from darkness into sunshine. There were a dozen things I had had been meaning to tell her over the last couple of days, everything from *I was so stupid* to *I'll never let you down like that again*, but right then I couldn't remember any of them. At last, I settled for whispering "I'm sorry," hoping she understood everything I meant by it.

"Me too," she whispered back, and I knew that she did.

Releasing me, she turned to hug Les while he held his arms out carefully, our sack of food in one hand and a drink carrier with milkshakes in the other. "Somebody's feeling better!" he said, grinning down at her.

"I'm so glad to see you guys," she said, stepping back and wiping absently at a tear that slid down one cheek. I noticed that her skin was still a little red, and there were circles under her eyes, but otherwise she looked okay. "Thank you both *so* much for getting me out of there. I would have died if it weren't for you, and I've never been so scared in my life." Then she focused on me again. "I have a lot to tell you. We're not dealing with curses at *all*, Wolfman! It's…"

"A ghost," I finished for her, which made her eyebrows arch. "We have a lot to tell you, too."

"*We*? So Les knows everything now? Good. That will save time."

"But food first," he declared. "We brought burgers and fries—just what you need before tackling the things that go bump."

"You guys are the best!"

We followed her to the kitchen and took seats at the table. The first thing Ab did was remove the lid from her chocolate shake, dip a wad of French fries in it, and then cram them in her mouth. "*Sho* good," she said while chewing.

"So where are your folks headed?" Les asked.

She swallowed before answering. "Mendocino. It's where they first met eighteen years ago, and they go back this time every year. They almost cancelled the trip, but I told them I was fine and that they should go."

We had brought Ab's favorite burger—double patties, double cheese, and topped with a mound of pastrami. While she worked her way through it, she told us everything that happened that night at the coffee house, from the moment she first smelled patchouli, to fires breaking out everywhere, and most of all, the shadow figure that watched her from the blazing hallway.

That triggered a memory of my own. "I think I saw Cozanna once, too."

"Really? When?"

"That day in the auto shop," I told her. The air was so full of exhaust I could barely see, but at one point I thought I could make out a shadow maybe ten or fifteen feet ahead. I figured it was Les, but then he hollered over from the other side of the room. When I turned back, the shadow was gone."

"How come you didn't say anything?"

I shrugged. "I guess I forgot. We were pretty busy, remember? And then the next day, well..." I let my voice trail off, not wanting to talk about it.

"So how did you guys get me out?" Ab asked, switching subjects. "I really don't remember much until the lady from the ambulance got there. And is that how your face got all banged up?"

"It was all the same night," I said evasively, and then allowed Les to take over. He didn't mention our fight either, and I was glad to keep that part just between us. After going through how we carried her away from the building, he turned it back over to me, and I described seeing Darren run off into the darkness. We continued going back and forth, telling Ab how we had confronted him that morning and everything he had confessed to us.

Ab was quiet for a minute or so afterward. Her food was long gone, and she sucked at what was left of her milkshake, looking thoughtful. "I'm stuck on the part about Cozanna moving from the spirit board into Gina. Assuming Darren didn't make the whole story up, that complicates things."

"How do you mean?" I asked.

"There are all kinds of ways you can get rid of spirits inside a house: salt or brick dust at the doors and windows, or tar water, or sometimes you can just declare that it isn't their home anymore and they're not welcome. But how do you get rid of a ghost haunting an object or person? Especially one as powerful as Cozanna?"

"Easy," Les said. "We just get rid of the board, right? Smash it, burn it, whatever. Darren said she has to go back now and then to recharge, so if we wipe out her home base, she'll eventually run out of juice, won't she?"

"Yeah, but what if she's inside Gina at the time?" Ab argued. "What will that do? Hurt her? Maybe even kill her? If everything has been all Cozanna and not Gina, we can't risk it. Darren said that when the ghost is sleeping, Gina is her old self again—our friend. We can't hurt her, guys."

Neither of us could argue with that.

"The way I see it, we need to figure out two things," Ab went on. "First, we need to know the right way to destroy a spirit board. Second, we need to find a way to get the ghost out of Gina before we do it."

Les and I both nodded, but I knew there was something that had to be done before either of those things. We needed to find out if Darren's story was even true.

That part was up to me.

FORTY-SIX

IT WAS A LITTLE AFTER 11 P.M. WHEN MOE AND I PARKED
a block away from the high school and walked the remaining distance to campus. Only a few of the neighborhood houses were still
showing lights, so probably no one would have noticed if we parked
in the lot, but there was no sense risking it. The wind was still gusting, but at least the rain had taken a break, which was good. If my
plan worked, the next few minutes were going to be bad enough
without us getting drenched, too.

I had almost chickened out. Twenty minutes before I had been
standing in front of my open closet, thinking about what I planned to
try with my insides tied up in knots.

When Mom and I first moved to Windward Cove, I had discovered my Aunt Claire's diary hidden in my room. It had acted as a sort
of catalyst as soon as I touched it, enabling me to experience visions of
her past that were so realistic it was as if I was there. Over time, my gift
grew to the point where I no longer needed it, but holding an object

that had soaked up so many of my aunt's feelings and memories was what first opened that door.

My hands were sweating when I reached into the pocket of my sport coat and pulled out the box containing Kelly's bracelet. Funny…it had only been a couple of days since Wendy had given it to me, but it felt like a lot longer. I hesitated, on the verge of putting it back, shutting the closet door, and forgetting the whole idea. Then I shook the feeling off, calling for Moe and heading downstairs to the car before I could talk myself out of it.

Moe scampered around the deserted parking lot, excited to be outside and exploring new territory while I crossed toward the narrow strip of asphalt that led to the auto shop. Weaving my way around the deeper puddles, I tried to remember where Kelly had been standing the last time I had seen her. When I figured I was close enough, I slowed to a stop and pulled the box from my jacket pocket. The dark velvet was warm from my body heat as I opened it, gazing down to where the glow from the street lights caused the delicate gold and silver strands to wink on their bed of white satin.

Last chance to back out, my inner voice reminded me.

No, I thought. This needed to get done.

Taking a breath, I tipped the bracelet into my left palm, snapping the box closed and returning it to my pocket. A tingling sensation ran from my scalp all the way down my back. I didn't know if it had anything to do with my gift, or if it was just because I was a little freaked out, but I didn't give myself time to overthink it. Closing my eyes, I forced myself to relax, opening my mind to whatever might be out there.

Maybe a dozen seconds ticked by.

Then, without warning, a vision slammed into my head as suddenly as a sniper's bullet!

"They're both pretty amazing, aren't they?"

"Yes, they are."

I open my eyes.

Kelly is beside Jessica Tanner only three or four paces to my left. They stand with their arms crossed against the evening chill, gazing over to where Les and I are still talking to Sheriff Hastings. I have never seen myself in a vision before, and it's surreal.

The sun has already set, so I guess it must be 5:30 or a little later. A light, misty fog has crept in, gliding across the parking lot and between the school buildings, and creating orbs that glow softly around the streetlights. Fifteen or twenty students and a handful of teachers still linger at the edge of the asphalt, talking quietly while watching the firefighters pack up the last of their equipment. The crowd is starting to disperse, though, with people moving off by twos and threes now that the last of the excitement seems to be over.

"Whoops…I need to get home," Jessica announces after checking the time on her cell phone. "How much longer do you plan to hang out?"

"Just until the guys finish up. I want to make sure Ben is okay. Then I'm going to yell at him for risking his life like that, right before I kiss his face off."

Jessica laughs. "I wish I could stay and do the same to Les, but I'm late already. See you tomorrow, okay?"

"Bye."

Jessica turns toward the lot, and then frowns. "Isn't that your friend? The new girl?"

"Where?" Kelly asks, turning, and I do the same.

"Over there…heading toward the quad."

A slender shadow has detached itself from a cluster of others, making its solitary way through the fog. The shadow finally crosses a pool of yellow cast by a security light, just before disappearing through the entrance, and we all see that Jessica is right. Definitely Gina.

A grim sort of anger settles over me.

"Where's she going? After everything that's happened, you wouldn't catch me here alone after dark for anything."

"Maybe she needs the girl's room," Kelly answers, then glances quickly over her shoulder to confirm that Les and I are still tied up. "Actually, that's not a bad idea. I'll go too."

Jessica heads for her car. "'Kay. See ya."

My heart sinks as Kelly sets off after Gina, hurrying through the fog, and I have to jog the first few steps in order to catch up. As we enter the shadows between the school buildings, we can just make out Gina on the far side of the quad maybe a hundred yards ahead. Sure enough, she pushes futilely on the door to the restroom on that side, then steps back and looks around when she finds it locked. Then Gina hurries off to try somewhere else, disappearing from Kelly's and my field of vision as she is blocked by the building to our right. Kelly increases our pace to a trot, then pauses at the edge of the quad seconds later, scanning the darkness.

There, I think, catching sight of Gina walking in the direction of the gym. Looking ahead of her, I can just make out a rectangle of deeper shadow on the west wall. It's one of the side doors, still standing open from when the basketball team evacuated at the sound of the fire alarm. Kelly frowns, hurrying after her and rapidly closing the distance as she takes us diagonally across the quad. She slows momentarily, casting her gaze nervously toward the pool center on the south side, its outer doors still covered by crime scene tape left by the sheriff's department. Then she picks up the pace again.

Dread wells up inside me. "No-no-no-no-NO!" I cry out. I know I'm being stupid—this has already happened, and there isn't a thing I can do—but I can't help it. "Please don't go!" Opening myself to this vision tops the charts as the absolute worst idea I have ever had, and for a second, I consider abandoning it right here. I already know how things are going to end, and the last thing I want to do is watch it happen. But I stay by Kelly's side anyway, partly to make sure there isn't some surprise detail

I may need to know later, but mostly because something inside me can't let her die alone.

The soles of Kelly's cross-trainers are nearly silent on the concrete as we approach, and she looks as if she's about to call out to Gina—probably so she won't startle her. Then we catch a fragment of whispered sentence:

"...wasn't supposed to happen! He could have been hurt..."

Kelly's brow furrows as her steps slow to a halt. She is probably wondering why Gina is talking to herself, I realize, as well as who she's referring to. I suspect it's me, and I have a feeling that Kelly suspects it, too.

But there isn't time to think beyond that as Gina disappears into the darkness of the gym. Kelly follows, now moving silently on purpose and wearing an expression of wary curiosity. She pauses just inside as our eyes adjust, and I see that the green glow from the exit signs posted above the doors provides just enough light to see.

Gina is more than halfway across the basketball court, headed diagonally toward the girls' locker room in the far corner. She is still whispering to herself, and the acoustics of the space carry her words more clearly: "No...not him! I want him, and you have to promise he'll be safe!"

Kelly glances around the deserted gymnasium, as if wondering if she has missed someone else in the darkness.

"No, I will not give him up!" Gina shouts suddenly. "And no, I don't care! You loved a raklo *once!"*

The sudden outburst catches Kelly by surprise. She sucks in a gasp, and then quickly darts into the deeper shadows beneath the bleachers when Gina pauses, half-turning.

"Is someone there?"

I don't follow Kelly, but continue standing where I can watch them both. I can just make her out, remaining still as she watches Gina through the narrow, lateral spaces between the bleacher seats.

"No, he isn't Romani," Gina insists, taking up her solitary conversation again. "But you don't know him like I do."

A long pause.

"Alright then," Gina says at last, sounding more relaxed. "It's settled." She turns and continues across the floor.

Her steps must be carrying her out of Kelly's narrow field of vision, and I watch as she worms her way further into the metal accordion framework in order to keep Gina in sight. Just then I hear the unmistakable sound of an empty soda can clattering across the floor, and I realize Kelly must have kicked it in the darkness.

Gina whirls. "Who's there? I can hear you!"

My chest constricts, and all at once it's hard to breathe. I watch as Kelly freezes, as if trying to decide what to do, while I fight back a sudden need to be sick.

Then Gina suddenly throws her head back, flinging her arms wide. As I watch in horror, what looks like tendrils of black smoke emerge from her eyes, nose, and mouth, curling upward with a lazy, almost sensuous grace. Gina staggers slightly to one side as the last of it leaves her, and the smoke coalesces into the shape of a woman floating ten feet above the floor.

Cozanna.

A savage wind makes the banners above billow and flap as the shadow figure swirls through the air, circling the gym's interior, and then it flies right toward me, passing through my chest and out my back without slowing. Cold like the wind off a glacier all but makes my heart stop, and I nearly gag on the scent of patchouli. But I know instinctively that the ghost is unaware of me and this is not an attack—I was just in the way. I hear a metallic squeal and snap behind me, and I spin around just in time to see the metal door for the bleacher control panel being torn off its hinges. Then I hear the click-click! *of switches being thrown, followed by the whir of electric motors coming to life somewhere in the blackness behind Kelly. Slowly, the steel framework all around her begins to change shape, the web of heavy bars scissoring and folding in on themselves as the bleachers retract toward the wall!*

The door to the outside slams, shutting us in.

Kelly screams as she begins to duck and weave back toward me, desperately trying to reach the narrowing gap that looks like the closing mouth of a predator. At the last moment I squeeze my eyes shut, unable to watch the end.

Kelly screams again, this time in agony.

But it's hard to hear her, because I'm screaming, too.

When the vision faded a few moments later, I found myself back outside, leaning with one hand resting against the locked gym door and the other still clutching Kelly's bracelet. My hair was wet, and it occurred to me that the rain had started again at some point. But I no longer cared. Moe was pawing at my leg, and I could sense his concern and confusion. Dimly, I realized that my gift had returned in full force—even more so—which probably should have made me happy and relieved, but I was just too numb right then. I turned to place my back against the door, and then slid down until I sat on the wet concrete.

Moe crawled halfway onto my lap, licking my face, and I put my arms around him, grateful for his comfort. We sat together in the rain and wind for a long time.

I wasn't sure how long it would take me to get over what I had just seen, but I knew it would be a while. Or maybe never. Kelly's screams still echoed in my mind, but what I remembered most right then was what happened after her screams finally stopped.

I had heard footsteps, and turned to see Gina stroll over to watch the pool of Kelly's blood creep out from beneath the bleachers, looking black in the dim light.

"*Thank you, Cozanna,*" Gina had murmured.

And she smiled a secret smile.

FORTY-SEVEN

LES AND I WERE ON STAKEOUT DUTY AGAIN.

Both he and Ab had been irritated with me at first when I called them after midnight. I must not have been thinking straight so soon after my vision, because it only occurred to me later that I could have waited until morning. They got over it right away, though, as soon as I told them everything I had seen and what I meant to do about it.

They were both in. Ab would be all over the internet, tracking down a foolproof way of getting rid of a spirit board (assuming there was one), while Les would back me up on a stealth mission. If everything went according to plan, we would meet up back at Ab's place afterward to decide our next move.

It was just after 7:00 in the morning when Les and I drove up a residential street one block east of the Lynch house. When I figured we had gone far enough, I turned left into a connecting alley and came to a stop just short of the next intersection, parking behind a rusty van that sat on three flat tires and one that was mostly there. Moe stood up in the back seat, tail wagging, but then lay back down on his blanket with a sigh of disappointment when neither of us got out.

A short, chain link fence surrounded the house on our left. No lights were showing behind the curtains, and a realtor's *For Sale* sign leaned drunkenly in the overgrown yard, looking like it had been there a while. Les smiled grimly when we exchanged a glance. From where we sat, we could see through the fence and diagonally across the lawn to the Lynch place sixty or seventy yards down. Both the front porch and the garage out back were in our line of sight, while my car sat mostly concealed behind the corner of the deserted house.

Perfect.

At 7:18, Darren and Gina came out the front door, turning right and walking away from us on their way to school. At a guess, I figured we had just over seven and a half hours before they would be back, so we settled in to wait. People from the houses to either side drove away not long after, presumably headed for work. Hopefully, Tim and Roxanne would leave at some point, too, and that would be our chance. In the meantime, there was nothing to do but keep an eye on the house while time crawled by with the speed of a crippled snail.

The morning went from gray to gold and then back again as high, broken clouds drifted overhead. Forty minutes later, we watched as Tim strolled into view from behind the house, carrying a travel mug as he made his way to the garage and pulled the double doors open. Fluorescent lights came on a few seconds later, followed by the faint sound of music. A customer's pickup truck sat on jack stands just inside, both front wheels off, and Tim sat down on a short, rolling stool. It looked like he was working on the brakes, but he was too far away and I couldn't tell for sure.

"Brake job," Les said softly a second or two later, as if reading my mind. I nodded silently, even though it didn't matter.

By 8:45, he had already moved over to work on the passenger side when Roxanne emerged to bring him a second travel mug, and then returned to the house carrying the first.

At 10:03, a FedEx truck pulled into the driveway, and we watched Tim help the deliveryman unload several boxes of auto parts. While signing for the order, Tim said something that made the driver laugh, and they exchanged a friendly wave before he got back into the truck and drove away.

Stakeouts on TV were a lot more interesting.

Nothing else happened for a while except for a couple of passing cars, and at 10:55 Les rummaged around in the paper sack that sat between us. I had packed a bunch of food before leaving the house that morning, along with some sodas and bottles of water, and Les pulled out a Pepsi and a ham sandwich. He handed me a turkey and cheese even though I hadn't asked for it, and I even tried a bite, but my insides were still in knots and I couldn't eat it. I passed the sandwich to Moe and sipped at a water instead.

At 11:14, a postal truck pulled up and delivered the Lynch's mail. Seven minutes later, Roxanne came out to retrieve it, and then went back inside. Tim had disappeared further back into the garage long before, so maybe the truck needed rear brakes, too.

More time passed.

"So, what's it like having your superpowers back?"

The unexpected question broke the silence, startling me. I didn't feel much like talking—the vision from the gym was still too fresh, even in the light of day. But I could sense Les' concern, and I knew he was trying to make me feel better. The least I could do was be a good sport about it, so I tried to figure out the best way to answer. "It's sort of like that scene in *The Wizard of Oz*," I said at last, "when Dorothy first drops into Munchkinland. Until then, the movie was drab black and white, remember? Then she steps outside into Oz and everything is in bright color. It's kind of like that. For me, the world just has a lot more going on. Does that make sense?"

He let that sink in. "Yeah, I guess it does. You must be glad."

I shrugged. "Maybe I'll feel glad later."

That put a damper on the mood, and I was sorry about that, but Les continued anyway. "You know, sometimes I wonder what it must be like. You know…to be you."

"To me it just feels normal."

"Well, sure. But it must be pretty great just the same."

I paused, considering the idea. "I never really thought about it, but mostly it is, I guess. Being able to sense people's feelings is a definite plus, and if I pay attention, it can keep me from saying the wrong thing. And those flashes I get sometimes—suddenly knowing where to find lost things, or that something is about to happen. That can be a big help, too." I smiled in spite of my dark mood. "When I was little, I used to pretend it made me part Jedi."

Les chuckled.

"But it's not all good," I went on. "When people are feeling really dark, or angry, or depressed, it can be hard to shut it out and even harder to keep it from affecting me. And those sudden flashes? Those are great until I see something I wish I hadn't. When I started having visions last summer, at first they scared the crap out of me—and depending on what I see, they still can." That made me think about Kelly again, but I shoved the thought aside. "Anyway, it's a mix. You have to take the good with the bad."

"Don't we all?" Les' gaze then shifted as he caught movement through the windshield. "Hey…looks we may be in business."

It was just after noon. Roxanne stood in the drive, calling out toward the garage while wearing a long coat. Tim emerged a few seconds later, looking apologetic and wiping his hands on a rag. He closed the garage doors, and then trotted to the house while his wife went to their truck and sat in the passenger side. Tim emerged less than five minutes later wearing a clean shirt, got in beside her, and they drove off toward downtown.

"You're up, hombre."

I shook my head. "Let's give them another five. Just in case one of them forgot something and they come back."

The minutes ticked by with us still in the clear, so I finally got out and made my way toward the Lynch house with my school backpack over one shoulder. I tried to look casual, like maybe I was just out for a stroll, and I glanced around carefully to see if anyone was watching me. As far as I could tell, no one was.

I turned into their driveway, moving more quickly since I had no idea how soon they would be back. For all I knew, Mr. and Mrs. Lynch might be running a quick errand, or going to lunch, or taking off to vacation in the Bahamas. Whichever it was, I just wanted to be in and out of there as soon as possible. If they came back before I was done, Les was on lookout and would text me.

Trying the front door would have left me in full view of the street, so I didn't. Instead, I moved quickly along the side of the house, trying the windows to see if one would open, but none did. The back door was locked, so I circled around to the far side, now beginning to feel anxious. I really didn't want to break in, but I would if I had to. That would suck—I liked Roxanne and Tim.

Nothing would open on that side either, and I had almost decided I was out of luck when I remembered the basement. Looking down, I saw the row of narrow windows that ran along the foundation. The third one I tried was unlocked! It was hinged to swing inward and up, so I pushed it open and stuck my head inside.

It took a few seconds for my eyes to adjust, and I saw I was just above Darren's old console TV. Quickly, I tossed in my backpack, and then turned around to wiggle in feet first on my belly. Reaching around blindly with my right foot, I felt the pile of old wires and game systems piled on top. I gently pushed some of it aside to clear space for my foot, and then eased the rest of the way inside. Balancing on one leg, I swung the window closed and then hopped to the floor.

Okay so far.

After pushing the wires back over my foothold, I snagged my pack before trotting upstairs to the kitchen, blinking in the sudden brightness. Moving past the entryway, I turned down the hall that led to the back of the house, passed their only bathroom, and opened the first door I came to.

A queen-sized bed and long bureau took up most of the floor space. The bed was made, knickknacks and a jewelry box were arranged neatly on the bureau, and framed school photos of Darren at various ages, along with a couple of more recent ones of Gina, hung on the wall. Tim and Roxanne's room.

Closing the door behind me, I continued to the only other one in the hall, which was just before an archway that opened to the mud/laundry room and door to the back porch.

Gina's room was tiny, with barely enough space for a twin bed, chest of drawers, a small writing desk, and an old steamer trunk crammed into the far corner. I had been in the house for only four or five minutes, but already my anxiety meter was in the yellow zone and climbing toward the red. Whether that was my gift sending me a premonition that the Lynches would be back soon, or me just wrestling with nervousness and guilt, was anyone's guess.

I closed the door behind me, and was crossing to the desk when my phone vibrated in my jacket pocket. It was a text from Les, and he had included Ab. [FIND IT YET?]

[No] I texted back.

[HURRY UP! I'M AS NERVOUS AS A HOOKER IN CHURCH]

"Join the club," I murmured, putting my phone away.

I went through Gina's desk, careful to leave everything exactly the way I found it.

Nothing.

Her closet was next. A few clothes hung on the bar, and there were moving boxes and totes both on the shelf above, and stacked in one corner. I started with the ones on the shelf, going through each in turn before returning it to the space where it had been before. Then I went through the boxes in the corner, bringing them out one by one and stacking them on top of each other so when I put them back, they would be in the same order. Still nothing.

I was running out of places to look.

I checked under the bed, glanced up to ensure nothing was hidden in the slats, and then ran my hands all around between the mattress and box spring. Strike three.

That left only the steamer trunk.

I swung the lid up to find it crammed full of folded clothes on one side, books and some odds and ends on the other. I took everything out, stacking it in sequence on the bed so I could put it all back that way, and my heart sank when I reached the bottom.

Where did she keep the damn thing?

I was in the middle of putting everything back when my phone buzzed again, and I paused to look at Les' text:

[GET OUT!!!]

I listened, and my heart beat faster when I heard the sound of an approaching engine, followed by the crunch of tires on gravel.

Oh shit oh shit oh shit!

Hands shaking, I fumbled to cram my phone back in my jacket pocket, missed on the first try, and then managed to shove it mostly in. I put everything back as quickly as I could, and was about to close the trunk when I noticed something pasted to the underside of the lid. It was an old handbill, and I had seen it before:

By Limited Engagement: 14th-27th May 1922
Archibald Lynch and his Mystical Spirit Board
Purveyor of wisdom and vessel of ancient knowledge!
Past—Present—Future
Why trust chance? Let benevolent spirits guide you
to success!
Money! Luck! Love! Fate!
By Appointment Only
Inquire at the Evans Hotel, Baltimore

Just then a glint of metal centered above the handbill caught my eye—a tiny round button. I pressed it, and a concealed inner panel swung downward.

There it was!

Lined with wine-colored silk, the hidden compartment held the spirit board securely in an indentation that had been custom built into the top of the lid. Tucked next to it was the planchette in a similar niche, with both secured in place by swivel tabs like on the back of a picture frame. The grain of the board was so dark it was nearly black, with elegant lettering of silver inlay, and all of it so highly polished that it glowed even in the dim light.

Quickly, I opened my backpack and rotated the tabs to release the board. In the two or three seconds it took to transfer the board to my pack, evil images flashed across my mind in incredible detail, one after another:

...A man I don't recognize, pinned against a wall by multiple kitchen knives, coughing up red, foamy stuff as he bleeds out onto the floor...

...A girl in a restroom stall swarmed by rats—maybe twenty or thirty of them—screaming as she tries to tear one away that has latched itself to her cheek...

...Riley Chase, clawing helplessly at the bottom of the pool while the shadow figure of Cozanna Lynch crushes her down against it...

The images stopped as soon as I let go. Horrified, and not wanting to see any more, I held the opening of my pack against the underside of the lid and tipped the planchette into it with the end of one finger. Closing the secret panel, I swung down the lid of the trunk just as I heard the back door open!

I rose quickly to my feet, whirling around in terror when I heard a soft thump. *Busted!* I thought, half expecting to see Tim and Roxanne glaring at me from the bedroom door. Then I exhaled a sigh, realizing that they were still in the mudroom, and it was only the clump of their footsteps on the hardwood. I held my breath as they passed Gina's door, listening to more of their footsteps and the rustle of plastic shopping bags.

"...just so *expensive*," Roxanne was saying. "I'll see if I can get an extra shift or two at Hovey's, otherwise we'll be eating beans and rice..."

The sounds faded as they moved down the hall.

After waiting a few seconds more, I opened Gina's door a crack and put my eye to it. The hallway was deserted, and I could hear the murmur of the voices from the kitchen. I stepped out into the hallway, eased the door shut behind me, and then made my way silently out the back.

FORTY-EIGHT

"CAN I SEE IT?"

Ab's eyes shone with excitement, so I slid my backpack across the kitchen table to let her dig it out for herself. No way was I going to touch it again.

She unzipped the canvas and withdrew the spirit board gingerly, as if she were handling a precious, fragile antique.

Well, at least she got the antique part right.

"It's *beautiful*," she breathed, running her palm across the polished grain, "and smooth as glass, too! I can't even feel a seam between the wood and the inlay of the lettering. I bet Cozanna's husband spent a *ton* of money on this."

I didn't share her enthusiasm. I had seen some of the memories stored inside, so it looked butt-ugly to me. But there was no sense ruining it for Ab, so I just shrugged.

Les pulled my backpack over and fished out the planchette to inspect it. It was made of the same wood, though stained lighter for contrast, with a trio of legs on the underside that were tipped in felt. I noticed a tiny, empty hole in the center of the glass indicator window and idly wondered how and when the pointer had been lost…and if it actually had been a nail from Cozanna's coffin. Then I decided I didn't care. I just wanted it gone, and the ghost with it. "So how do we destroy it?" I asked.

Ab set the board down, and then went to retrieve a sheet of notes she had left on the counter. Les placed the planchette on top and gave it a gentle flick with his finger, and we both watched as it slid effortlessly to the far side of the board. Like Ab said: smooth.

"Like a lot of paranormal stuff, nobody seems to agree on a single way to do it, or whether or not the phenomenon is even real," Ab began, sitting back down. "You run a search for *destroy a Ouija board*, and a ton of articles come up, but most of the hits you get are personal accounts from people who claim to have accidentally opened a portal for a spirit or demon that ended up terrorizing them…sometimes even ruining their lives. One of the most common stories involves a demon named Zozo, who sometimes impersonates other spirits to trick people into inviting him over from the other side. Or there was this other story from back in the nineties about a bunch of students in Bolivia who were playing with a board, and ended up in the hospital being treated for things like mental agitation, confusion, and even trance states. That's *one* side of the belief scale—the people who really take spirit boards seriously and consider them dangerous.

"On the other side, you've got the nonbelievers," she went on. "The ones who think everything paranormal is so much crap. According to a lot of psychologists, the movement of the planchette is actually something called *ideomotor phenomenon*…basically that the people around the board are unconsciously moving it themselves."

Les looked impatient. "Is there a point coming any time soon?"

"Yeah," I agreed. "We already *know* this board is haunted. How do we get rid of it so Cozanna can't come back?"

"My *point*," Ab said, shooting Les an annoyed look, "is that the ways people recommend getting rid of a spirit board are all over the scale, too. The nonbelievers say just toss it in your recycling bin. The hardcores tell you to break it into five pieces, put them into five holes laid out in the shape of a pentagram, and then douse them with holy water before you cover them over." She frowned. "That last one seems a little too Hollywood for me, but there you go."

"Okay," I said, "so different people suggest different ways. Why do I have a feeling you've already picked one out?"

The hint of a smile touched her lips. "Because I have. I read a paper published back in the nineteen-sixties by a professor of parapsychology from some university I never heard of in the Midwest. He may be dead by now for all I know, but he was one of those guys with lots of letters after his name—PhD, ThD, EdS, stuff like that—so he seemed legit. According to him, you need to break the board into four pieces, place them into holes dug at all four corners of a crossroads, and then cover the pieces completely with salt before filling in the holes. He didn't say what to do with the planchette, other than to not bury it with any other part of the board." She shrugged. "His method sounds as good as any— and better than most—so that's what I think we should do. I even have a hammer, shovel, and four boxes of salt all ready to go."

"If that's what you think, then it's good enough for me." I looked at Les, who agreed with a nod. "Now comes the hard part...how do we make sure Cozanna isn't inside Gina when we do it?"

That launched us into a brainstorming session that went on for hours. It even included going upstairs to Ab's computer to search for any rituals we might use to banish Cozanna back to the board, or at least get her out of Gina, but that turned out to be a bust. It was after dark and we were back down in the kitchen by the time we finally settled on a plan. We decided to go with simple: get Gina alone somewhere and threaten to smash the board unless Cozanna left her. Then, as soon as she was clear, we'd smash it anyway.

What could go wrong?

Only everything.

"I think you should be the one to bring her to us," Ab said, looking at me. "You're the one she's been crushing on, so…" Her voice trailed off, interrupted by the sudden ringing of her cell phone. She picked it up, glanced distractedly at the screen and then frowned, her brow furrowing.

"What's wrong?" I asked. "Who's calling?"

She raised her gaze to meet mine. "*You* are."

FORTY-NINE

AB TURNED THE SCREEN TO FACE ME, AND I READ
WOLFMAN on the caller ID.

Automatically, my hand went to my jacket pocket, and the bottom seemed to drop out of my stomach when I found it empty. Then I remembered the soft thump I had heard just as Tim and Roxanne got home—the thump I thought was a footstep. I reached out for Ab's phone, then answered and touched the button for the speaker. "Hello…?"

"Guess what *you* lost," Gina said with fake cheerfulness, and then her tone switched to disappointment. "I *knew* you'd be with her. Why, Ben? We could be so perfect together, but you just won't admit it. And why are you *stealing* from me?" She sounded hurt.

"Am I speaking to Gina…or Cozanna?"

She didn't answer right away, so the question must have caught her off guard. "It doesn't matter," she said at last.

"It matters a lot. Gina is our friend, and she's awesome. Cozanna… not so much."

"Bring it back, Ben," she pleaded. "*Please.* Return the board, and then *be* with me so we can put all of this behind us. Give me just one chance, and I'll prove I can make you happy—way happier that Ab or even Kelly ever could. But I need the Ouija board back. Cozanna will forgive you if I ask her to, and once we're finally together, she can watch over *both* of us."

The thought chilled me. Even if I wanted to be with Gina, the idea of Cozanna always lurking around, dealing out vengeance on anyone she thought was a threat, made my insides twist. "I can't do that," I told her.

"Last chance," Gina said, her voice losing the pleading tone. "We've been patient with you, but our patience has run out. Now, where is it?"

We. Our. I shuddered. "It's someplace safe. Somewhere you'll never find it."

"It belongs to us, and you're *going* to give it back. *Now.*"

"Why should I?" I challenged. "So you can keep on killing people?"

"No," she answered. "You'll give it back so we *don't* kill your mother."

Cold like an Arctic wind washed over me, and all at once it was impossible to breathe.

"Go home, *raklo.* Not Ab...not Les...just you. Bring the board. We're leaving for your house now, and you'd better pray you get there first." Then there was a muted beep as she ended the call.

Slowly, I handed Ab her phone. "I have to go," I said, my voice sounding surprisingly calm. I wasn't, though. Not even close. But the last thing I could afford to do right then was panic. It would take Gina at least fifteen minutes to reach my house, while I could be there in half that.

Fifteen minutes to get Mom clear *and* figure out a plan. I hoped it would be enough.

Ab and Les looked at one another, and then rose to their feet. "Okay," Les said, stuffing the board and planchette back into my pack, and then held it out. "We don't have a choice."

I shook my head. "She's not getting it back. The plan is still on. I just need to get Mom somewhere safe first."

"So call her!" Ab said, handing the phone back. "Tell her to get out of there!"

I tried, but the call immediately went to voicemail. I looked back at her, shaking my head again.

"Wolfman…"

"This doesn't change anything." I glanced down at Moe. He gazed back solemnly, muscles tensing as he rose to his feet, clearly sensing that something was wrong. I knew he would try to defend me if I was attacked, just like he did the night he lunged at Tony Cruz. But Cruz was a bug compared to Cozanna. "Keep Moe here, okay? I don't want him to get hurt."

"*What*?" exclaimed Ab. "What are you talking about? Just give her back the spirit board and we'll think of something else!"

"Guys…there *is* nothing else!" I exploded. "C'mon, do you honestly think any of us will be safe if we hand it over? Cozanna won't let us live after this. She *can't*. We know her secret, so it's tonight or never. Just go find a crossroads and get everything ready, okay? Like you said, we don't have a choice. I'll just have to figure something out."

"And if you don't?" Ab pressed.

Then I'm probably screwed, I thought. But I didn't say it. "We need to roll."

"Okay," Les agreed reluctantly. "But I'd feel better if we were closer by, just in case you need us."

"Where, then?"

He thought about it. "The dock. It's less than a quarter mile from your drive. There's that maintenance road that crosses Main Street just before it ends, and no one will be there this time of night."

"Fine. I'll drop you there." I shoved Ab's phone into my pocket. "If I can get Cozanna out of Gina, I'll text you. If not, I'll find some way to bring her to the crossroads. Just be ready either way."

They nodded, and we grabbed Ab's tools and salt by the front door before running outside to the car.

FIFTY

THE NIGHT AIR WAS COLD AND EERILY CALM WHEN I scrambled out of the driver's seat and ran to the house. Throwing open the front door, I shouted "*MOOOM!*"

"*What*, Ben?" came her voice from the kitchen. She sounded annoyed.

I hurried to find her. She stood drinking a glass of water by the sink, dressed in one of her yoga outfits and a retired pair of running shoes, obviously back from class. I glanced at my watch, relieved to see I still had five or six minutes left before I expected Gina. Plenty of time, but I still needed to hurry. I still needed a plan, too, I reminded myself, but first things first. "Mom, you need to get out of here. You need to get out of here *now!*"

She frowned. "What? Why? I just got home, and…"

I took the glass from her and set it on the counter. "There's no time to explain," I said, taking her arm and trying to pull her away. "Just trust me, okay?"

She shook herself free. "Hold up! What's going on? I'm tired and I want to shower."

I knew she wasn't going to budge without some sort of explanation, so I closed my eyes, taking a deep breath while trying to slow my heart rate by willpower alone. "There's a ghost, Mom. Like the one last summer that made you sick, only stronger. A *lot* stronger. It's what killed Riley in the swimming pool, and Kelly too, and now it's coming *here*. I'll give you all the details later, but right now we need to move!"

I sensed Mom's emotions shift from annoyance to confusion tinged with fear. It was enough to get her going, though, and she allowed me to lead her hurriedly out of the kitchen. Then we froze halfway across the family room when headlights swept across the front windows, the rumble of a big engine coming through the open door as someone pulled up to the porch.

I knew the sound. It was the Lynch's pickup truck. *How did she get here so fast?* I wondered. She must have blown through every stop sign and broken every speed limit along the way.

Truck doors slammed, and a few seconds later Gina strolled into the room to confront us, Darren looming behind her. "Oh, *hi*," she said with exaggerated sweetness, and then smiled. I reached out with my gift, sensing a mixture of anger and betrayal from Darren; triumphant satisfaction from Gina. But there was a third source of emotion, too, and it was all rage. *There you are, Cozanna*, I thought.

Mom looked at me. "*This* is your ghost?" Her emotions shifted back to annoyance. "Will someone *please* tell me what's going on?"

"Your son is a thief, Connie," Gina told her. "Did you know? He broke into our house today and took something that doesn't belong to him."

Mom looked at me again. "Is that true?"

"Not now, Mom," I said, my gaze still fixed on Gina. I needed to think!

"It *is* true," Gina told her. "He took something that has been in our family for a long, long time. An heirloom, I guess you'd say, and we want it back."

There it was again: *our…we*. But something told me that didn't include Darren.

"If Ben gives it back now, then no harm done," Gina went on. "There will be some fallout, but we'll deal with that later. Just give us what we came for, and we promise to leave."

Mom took a few seconds to digest what she had said, and then she turned to me. "Ben, I'll ask you this just once: do you have Gina and Darren's property?"

"No," I told her. And it was the truth—Les and Ab had it.

Mom nodded, and then turned back to Gina. "Ben says he doesn't have it, so there must be some sort of misunderstanding. I'll call your aunt and uncle tomorrow, and we'll straighten this whole thing out."

"Ben's lying."

Anger flared hot in Mom, but she kept her voice level. "Go home. Both of you."

"We're not going anywhere until he gives back what he stole."

Oh, crap, I thought, knowing what was coming. Like that old Jim Croce song Mom sometimes played, you don't tug on Superman's cape, you don't spit in the wind, you don't pull the mask off the ol' Lone Ranger, and you never, *ever* challenge Connie Wolf in her own home.

Things were about to get real.

"Who the *hell* to you think you are?" Mom began, her cheeks flushed with anger.

Gina suddenly threw her head back, flinging her arms wide. Blackness poured from her eyes, nose, and mouth, and as soon as it came together to form the shadow figure, Cozanna tore a circle around the room like a hurricane, blowing out every window as she passed. The black figure swooped in behind Mom, seizing her hair to pull her head back while her other arm encircled Mom's throat, choking her.

"*THIS is who we are!*" Gina screamed, all pretense of niceness gone.

"STOP!" I shouted. "You win! Let my mom go and I'll get it for you!"

Seconds passed before anyone reacted.

Her eyes narrowed in suspicion. "Where is it?"

Mom was still choking and struggling. "It's nowhere *you'll* ever find unless you let my mom go," I answered. "*Now.*"

Gina thought about it, and then nodded to the shadow figure. Mom sucked in a gasp, so I knew she was okay, at least for now. "Where is it?"

"In the basement," I lied. "Stuffed into a crack in the wall. Go see for yourself."

"No, *you* show me," she ordered.

"Okay, okay," I said, raising my hands and doing my best to look defeated. I hoped it would work—I had never tried the defeated look before.

"Keep an eye on the mother," Gina commanded, although if she was speaking to Cozanna or Darren, I couldn't be sure. Just the same, Darren stepped closer to Mom. None of it mattered, though. I had rolled the dice, and now everything would depend on how the next minute or so played out.

I led Gina back through the archway to the kitchen, and then opened the door to the basement. The light from the kitchen overhead only penetrated down the first few steps of the wood staircase before being swallowed up by blackness. Just like at their house, there were windows at ground level, but it was night outside so they didn't help. Reaching inside, I made a show of yanking the string-pull for the basement light several times. "Crap," I muttered, trying to sound exasperated. "Not again." But the basement light didn't work. It never had.

I felt Gina's palm thud against my back. "Hurry up!"

I shot her a glare over my shoulder, and then reached onto a shelf just inside where we kept a flashlight. It was a heavy, four-cell Maglite with a metal housing, left over from when we first moved in and had to wait weeks for an electrician to restore power to the house. I clicked it on, and it cast a circle of white at my feet. The light was unsteady because my hand was shaking, but I figured that that only helped. "Come on, then."

Gina hesitated, but when I started down the stairs without her, she reluctantly followed.

After only a few steps, the cellar stairs opened up as we descended below the subfloor, and only the right-hand side continued with a railing. The left was open to empty space. "There," I said, stopping about halfway down, and I pointed the flashlight at a random spot on the mortared stones of the back wall. "See?"

"No…" she said uncertainly, stopping a couple of risers behind me.

"*There*," I insisted, continuing to point. "In that great big crack."

Curious, Gina descended another step, and then I had her. Turning suddenly, I shoved her as hard as I could out over the side without a railing, for a split second seeing her face register shock as she plummeted into darkness. Her scream echoed behind me as I pounded up the stairs, and just as I was close to the top, a familiar sub-zero wind ripped through me as Cozanna swirled down the stairs after her!

Three steps later and I was back in the kitchen, where I paused long enough to slam the door and twist the lock, just as an enraged scream rose from behind it: "*Ka xlia ma pe tute!*"

I didn't know what that meant, but I wasn't sticking around to find out.

FIFTY-ONE

LES GRUNTED, SLAMMING THE SHOVEL INTO THE FINAL *hole before stomping it down into the saturated earth below. He pulled back on the handle, and there was a sucking sound just before the mud let go. He lifted it out, and then tossed the shovel aside, deciding it was good enough. Each of the four holes was about ten inches across and between twelve and sixteen inches deep—plenty big to hold a quarter of the spirit board.*

Blotting sweat from his brow with a sleeve, he called over to Ab. "Anything?"

She stood on the opposite corner of the small intersection, silhouetted in moonlight. As he watched, light blossomed in her hand as she checked his cell phone. "Not yet."

Beside her, the spirit board leaned against a rock the size of a bowling ball, the hammer and boxes of salt beside it. Everything was ready.

His boots were heavy with mud, and he stamped both feet several times, wiping them on the wet asphalt as he crossed over to join her. "What do you think is taking so long?" he asked. Of course, the part of him that wasn't scared silly knew it hadn't been long at all. The pickup truck had turned onto Ben and Connie's drive only a few minutes before, and they had watched silently as the headlights zigzagged their way slowly up the grade, flickering behind the trees.

The crossroads was only twenty or thirty feet from the end of Main Street, where the pavement ended at the Windward Cove dock. Moonlight reflected on the water, clearly showing the dark outlines of half a dozen fishing boats that rocked gently at their moorings. The rumble of the truck engine had faded away soon after the lights disappeared over the crest, and after that the only sound they could hear was the lapping of the waves against the shore.

"What's taking so long?" he repeated.

His cell phone glowed in her hands again as Ab checked for a text, and then went dark. She shifted her weight nervously from one foot to the other, but didn't answer him.

FIFTY-TWO

I RAN FULL SPEED INTO THE FAMILY ROOM TOWARD Darren, raising the flashlight as if I were going to hit him with it. His eyes widened in fear as he retreated a step or two, hands up to ward me off, but at the last second I half-turned, lowering my shoulder and driving it into his gut. He had been standing behind the sofa, and my hit sent him ass-over-teakettle over the back and onto the rug between the sofa and the coffee table, knocking the wind from him.

Recovering quickly, I grabbed Mom's hand just as the sound of the basement door exploding into the kitchen reached our ears. I risked a glance behind us just in time to see pieces of the door fly across the room in splintered chunks.

We needed to get out of there!

In seconds we were out the front door, dodging around the Lynchs' pickup, and I released Mom's hand just before we made it to the station wagon. Stuffing the Maglite into my back pocket, I ran around the front of the car and dove behind the wheel just as Mom got in the passenger seat. Digging the key out, I stabbed it into the ignition and started the engine just as three silhouettes appeared on the front porch, backlit by the glow from inside. I stomped on the accelerator, and the old Ford leaped forward, spitting mud from the back tires as I jerked the wheel to the left, guiding the car in a circle around Mom's Explorer and toward the drive down to the road.

Just as I was about to congratulate myself for our escape, a loud *BOOM!* came from the back as an something hit us with the force of a charging rhino! The car fishtailed almost out of control as the back and left rear windows of the cargo area shattered inward. Mom cried out while I overcorrected, almost flipping us over, but then I got the car back under control just as I glanced through the rearview mirror. Behind us, I saw the shadow figure of Cozanna swirl back into Gina as she and Darren climbed into their truck.

Not good.

The drive was muddy and slick from the recent rains, forcing me to slow as we navigated our way down. Gina and Darren must not have been nearly as worried, though, as their headlights glared through the shattered back window much sooner than I expected. I had to slow even more when we reached the Y that split the road between our drive and the one that led up to the inn. I had just swung around the left-hand turn when the truck hit us a glancing blow, driving both our right wheels over the edge! Metal shrieked as the pickup shouldered past, overshooting us as it skidded downhill with its brake lights glaring. I pressed the accelerator again, and the engine roared in response, but nothing else. The car had grounded out along its centerline, and the wheels were no longer on the ground! We continued to slide sideways, the world beyond the windshield beginning to tilt, and I realized we were about to go over the edge!

"Come on!" I shouted, throwing my door open and scrambling clear as Mom scooted across the bench seat after me. Turning, I could see her eyes widen in terror just as the car reached its tipping point. Desperately, I leaned inside and grasped her wrist, yanking her free just as the old car tumbled down the hillside. It rolled and bounced several times, finally coming to rest near the bottom, headlights still shining. The engine sputtered, and then died for the final time as steam rose from under the hood.

There wasn't time to worry about it, though, as I looked down the drive to see that the Lynchs' pickup truck had stopped nose first against the hillside at the next hairpin turn. The engine had stalled, and the starter whined as Darren tried to get it going again. "Listen," I told Mom, turning her shoulders to face me. "Les and Ab are down near the dock. You need to get there. Tell them to be ready and wait for my text."

"Ready for *what*?" she asked, eyes wide with terror.

"There isn't time! Just go!"

Mom hesitated for only a second, then turned and raced down the hill. After only a few strides, her body found its rhythm, and she sprinted past the stalled pickup at a smooth, graceful pace. Just then the truck's engine came back to life, the backup lights flaring as Darren reversed onto the pavement.

Reaching into my back pocket, I pulled out the Maglite and clicked it on, the pool of light standing out like a beacon. Gina must have seen it, because almost immediately the passenger door of the truck flew open and she jumped out. "After her, *dinlow*!" she cried. "Run her down!"

Fear for Mom washed over me, but only for a second. We were in the woods, she could go places the truck couldn't, and there was no *way* Darren would ever catch her on foot. I watched the Chevy roar downhill while Gina turned and began to make her way back up the drive toward me.

Good, I thought, smiling in the darkness. That was exactly what I wanted.

Because finally, I had a plan.

FIFTY-THREE

LES AND AB EXCHANGED A LOOK AS THE SOUND OF AN *engine drifted down the hillside. There was the faint sound of a crash, causing Ab to gasp, but before there was time to think, a pair of head-lights appeared at the crest and began to wind their way down. Seconds later, a second pair appeared, moving faster as if in pursuit.*

Ab's hand crept into his and he squeezed it, hoping to be reassuring.

After the first couple of turns, Les could see that the headlights of the second vehicle sat higher up than the first. "Gina's chasing Ben," he said. "He must be trying to bring her here." Ab moved closer to him, and he could feel her trembling against his arm.

"Careful, Wolfman," she whispered.

The lead car slowed about halfway down the grade to navigate a particularly sharp turn, and they heard the screech of metal against metal as the pursuing headlights first caught up, and then rocketed past. Les frowned. How could that be? The drive wasn't wide enough for two cars!

The taillights of Gina's truck glared red as she came to a halt further down the drive, but Ben's car had already stopped. A moment later, Ben's taillights began to chase one another in circles as the car rolled over the edge. Ab screamed as Ben's car tumbled to the bottom, finally coming to rest only fifteen or twenty feet up from the road.

They stood frozen in shock for two or three heartbeats before Ab released his hand. She tensed like she was about to run toward the wreck, but Les held on tight. "Look," he said, holding her back. "Up on the road."

A solitary beam of light shone in the darkness. They heard Gina shout something from below where the pickup was stopped, and then the truck reversed briefly before heading downhill again.

Gina had not been alone, he realized. Darren, probably.

Above her, the lone light swung back and forth as it moved upward and to the left, and Les realized it was a flashlight. Ben was on the run.

"Dude," he murmured. "What are you doing?"

FIFTY-FOUR

BLUE-WHITE MOONLIGHT SLANTED THROUGH THE
trees, dappling the ground in front of me. It was bright enough to see
even without the flashlight, but that wasn't why I kept it on.

I wanted Gina to see it.

I waited until I was sure she was following, and then sprinted uphill,
wanting to put some distance between us. I wasn't worried that she
would get lost—there was only one way in or out.

At first, I was terrified that she would just send Cozanna after me.
That would have been the smart play. After all, it would have been the
easiest thing in the world for the ghost to overtake me, tie my body
into some kind of Boy Scout knot, and then just wait for Gina to catch
up. But she didn't, and the only reason I could think of was that Gina
was nervous. She was in the woods at night, not knowing where I was
headed or what I was up to, and I imagined Cozanna stuck close to
provide protection and reassurance.

Lucky me.

I was gasping by the time I reached the top (gawd...Mom did this for *fun*?) and broke out into the open. Before me sprawled the outline of the Windward Inn, black and brooding against a backdrop of stars. Ducking under the chain that stretched across the drive, I sprinted the remaining distance, past the crumbling fountain and onto the night-darkened porch. There was a window just to the left of the wide double doors, and I started ripping away the boards that covered it. Nails that had been in place for decades complained like bitter old women as I tore them free, while splinters from the unfinished planks dug into my hands. I gritted my teeth, though, ignoring the pain. There would be time enough to worry about my hands later.

Assuming there *was* a later.

"I seeee yooooou!" Gina called out playfully behind me, and I looked back to see she was already past the barrier chain.

Crap!

My original plan had been to break just one of the cross-hatched window panes so I could unlock the sash and raise it, but now there wasn't time. Instead, I used the flashlight like a club, smashing through glass and wooden framework alike until there was a hole big enough for me. Even through all the impacts and abuse, the Maglite never wavered or even flickered, and I offered silent thanks to the people who had made it. I ducked, squeezing sideways through the opening, and winced as a jagged shard I had missed in the frame slashed a deep cut into my left cheek, an inch or so below my eye. I felt a trickle of blood, but that was just one more thing to worry about later. At least I was through.

I crossed the lobby at a run, taking the stairs to the second floor two at a time. Visions and presences from all over the hotel pressed in around me, but I shoved them all aside. Reaching the first landing, I paused with my hand on the banister post, breathing hard...sweating... waiting.

I didn't have long to wait.

With a sound like a cannon going off, the double front doors suddenly burst inward, forcefully enough to send them both bouncing off the walls. As it swung back, the right-hand door separated from first the top hinge, and then the bottom. It dropped like a boxer after a knockout punch, sending dust up from the floor as it landed with a loud clatter.

Seconds later, Gina crossed the threshold, just as I saw the last remnants of Cozanna swirl back inside her. Glancing around, she caught sight of me at once. "Stop running, Ben!" she called out, sounding confident. "Do you really think there's anywhere to hide where we won't find you?"

Certain that she had seen me, I dashed up the stairs.

FIFTY-FIVE

CONNIE WOLF SPRINTED DOWNHILL, LISTENING TO THE *sound of the truck behind her. Each time it seemed as if Darren had caught up, the sound of the engine almost at her heels and her shadow sharply defined in the glare of the headlights, she would reach another of the driveway's hairpin turns. She would leap across and down the final fifteen or twenty feet, cutting the corner, while the truck was forced to slow and creep around the turn, giving her time to regain some distance.*

At last, she made it down to the road and turned right, opening her stride to run even faster on the level, moonlit asphalt. The mouth of the drive was fifty yards behind her when the truck turned to follow, throwing her shadow long ahead of her as the headlights found her again.

Her advantage gone, Connie drifted to the left, leaping across the shallow ditch beside the road and climbing awkwardly over the old, barbed wire fence that surrounded the open field just beyond. One of the barbs bit cruelly into her left hand as she crossed, but then she was clear, running through high grass as her shoes squelched and splashed in the damp earth.

Darren tried to follow, the truck's engine roaring as it jumped the ditch, breaking through the old fence and slewing sluggishly as the offroad tires sank in the muck. It proceeded only another thirty or forty feet before getting bogged down and coming to a halt.

Connie paused, breathing hard as she saw Darren exit the truck, squatting beside the front wheels to twist the manual hub locks, readying the Chevy for four-wheel drive. That gave her some time, though not a lot, so she climbed back over the fence and returned to the road, sprinting down toward the dock. Each footfall felt lighter as the mud fell from her shoes, and her heart felt lighter, too, as she left the glow of the headlights further and further behind her.

Then the truck's engine snarled again, the beams from the headlights swaying and bouncing as it slowly worked its way free of the mud, breaking through the fence again and finally lurching back onto the road.

The dock was only a hundred yards ahead, so Connie put her head down, increasing her pace to give it everything she had.

FIFTY-SIX

NEARLY A QUARTER MILE UP THE ROAD, LES AND AB watched the pickup truck emerge from the drive, turning downhill to wash them in the glow of its high-beams. It leapt forward, and then a moment later swerved suddenly, ending up in the open field to their right.

"What the hell?" Les asked.

Less than a minute later, though, it started moving again, engine revving and headlights swaying and tilting as it fought its way back onto the pavement. It accelerated again, and as the headlights drew within fifty yards, Les saw something he never expected—the silhouette of someone running ahead of the truck toward them!

Then Ab was sprinting up the road. Without hesitating, he followed her, watching as she dodged left within ten feet of the front bumper, tackling the figure out of the way just before the truck flew past!

Les had just enough time to dive to the right to avoid being hit himself, and then turned to watch brake lights blaze red. Tires screeching, the truck slid entirely through the intersection, the combination of wet pavement *and mud-filled treads allowing it to skid at nearly full speed to the dock. There was a loud crunch of metal as it hit the first dock piling on the left, and then the entire back end flew upward and left, somersaulting over the cab as the truck flipped into the cove. It landed on its roof with a great splash, sinking until only the wheels were above the surface of the water, still spinning.*

Scrambling to his feet, Les ran down to the wrecked truck. Wading in past the headlights that still glowed steadily, he took a deep breath and ducked under.

The water was dark and bitterly cold. Through the driver's side window, he could see Darren hanging upside down from his seatbelt in the glow of the instrument lights. Blood ran from a deep gash on his forehead where he had struck the steering wheel. Dazedly, he tugged at the door handle as water began filling the cab.

Les tried the door from the outside, only then noticing that the sleeve of Darren's shirt had hooked itself over the post for the door lock during the crash, pressing it down. He pounded on the glass, pointing to the corner of the window, but Darren just looked at him blankly, not understanding.

By then the water had crept up to Darren's forehead and Les screamed under water, pounding on the glass and pointing, trying to make him understand. Just then the lights flickered and died as the battery shorted out, and he could only make out shadows in the moonlight.

Darren struggled briefly when the water rose above his head, and then he went still.

FIFTY-SEVEN

GINA KEPT CALLING OUT TO ME—MOSTLY IN ENGLISH, but sometimes in Romani—but I ignored her as I finally made it to the third floor. The echoes from the dark, deserted hallways below made it hard to tell, but from the sound of her voice, I figured she was maybe a flight and a half below me on the stairs. That was good, but I still had to make it to the end of the hall before she reached the top.

It was going to be close.

Nearly all the doors on that floor were standing open, the cracks between the boarded-over windows allowing just enough moonlight to filter in and throw dim rectangles of light into the hall. I sprinted to the far end, gasping for air and my heart trying to batter its way out of my chest, until I finally skidded to a stop in front of my goal:

Suite 324.

I didn't have time to hesitate. Twisting the knob, I opened the door just enough to toss the flashlight inside, and then immediately pulled it closed again before darting across the hall into the shadows of the opposite suite. Thumps and clatters sounded from the room as the spirit of Frank Delgiacco reacted to the intrusion, the glow from the crack under the door wavering as he threw the flashlight around in fury.

I retreated further back into the shadows, trying to get my breathing under control so it wouldn't give me away. Sweat ran from my forehead, stinging my eyes as I waited for Gina. Time passed, the seconds dragging by with agonizing sluggishness. The glow from under the door was as obvious as a neon sign in the darkness—how could she not see it? Or had I gambled wrong? Had Cozanna sensed the other spirit and warned Gina off? If she had, I was as good as dead—trapped in a room three stories up.

Nowhere to go.

I was wondering if I should try the window anyway and hope to survive the fall when Gina finally stepped into my field of vision, pausing just outside the closed door. "What are you *doing* in there?" she called out, laughing. She turned the knob, releasing a wedge of light into the hallway as she stepped inside.

Then she screamed.

From where I stood, I could see the shadow figure of Frank Delgiacco fly across the room to her, picking up Gina and flinging her against the north wall. She crumpled to the floor like a rag doll, unmoving, just as blackness emerged from her and formed itself into Cozanna.

The door to 324 slammed shut.

My cue to leave!

Loud crashes and impacts rose from behind me, sounding as if the battling spirits were tearing the room apart as I ran down the hall. Stopping at the top of the stairwell, I pulled out Ab's phone, found Les' text string from that morning, and typed a single word…

[NOW]

…before pressing send. The text status read *SENDING* for five or six seconds before changing to *No SIGNAL. Crap!* I looked at the indicator. Zero bars.

Darting into the suite across the hall, I crossed to the boarded over window and waved the phone around close to the glass. I forced myself to move slowly while staring at the indicator, and was on the verge of running out to try somewhere else when *there it was!* A quarter bar! I hit send again, trying to hold still and terrified that my trembling alone would move the phone out of the weak signal.

SENDING…

"*C'mon,*" I whispered. "*Pleasepleaseplease…*"

…SENT…

DELIVERED.

FIFTY-EIGHT

LES SHIVERED VIOLENTLY AS HE CLUTCHED MOE'S BLAN-
ket around him, nearly too frozen to think, let alone speak.

Ab had called 911 while Connie ran to retrieve the blanket from the
wrecked station wagon. She shut off the lights while she was there, and
the car was too far back in the brush to be easily visible in the darkness.
He was glad the two of them were there to figure things out. He was too
cold, too tired, and mostly too numb from shock.

He had never watched anyone die before.

Ab was partway through giving Connie a hurried, shortened version
of Cozanna's story when his phone lit up, buzzing in her hand.

"Now, Les!" she cried, reading the text.

Now? he wondered briefly, and then he remembered. Shambling over
to the spirit board, he dropped to his knees and braced it against the rock.
The blanket fell from his shoulders as he raised the hammer, then brought
it down as hard as he could.

FIFTY-NINE

A PRIMAL SCREAM ECHOED DOWN THE HALL, SO SUD-
den and deafening that it made me cry out.

For a second, I assumed it had come from Gina, but then I knew
it hadn't. It sounded like a woman, yet at the same time it *didn't*...as
if whatever gave voice to that scream had not been human for a long
time. It pierced the darkness like a dagger, making my skin break out
in gooseflesh while my heart seemed to lock up in my chest. Then the
sound died away...as if fading off into the distance.

The hall was silent.

For a moment, I was overwhelmed by panic, and I was almost to
the top of the stairs before my brain took charge again. I managed to
stop myself before heading down as I suddenly remembered something
Darren had said:

[*...when Cozanna is completely gone, Gina is back to her old self.
Quiet...shy...sweet. She's the Gina I miss...*]

Trembling, I turned my head to look back down the hall. Dim light
still shone from beneath the door to Suite 324.

416

I drew a shuddering breath, torn between going back and bolting down the stairs.

Dude...seriously? the voice in the back of my head spoke up. *Get the hell out!*

Every cell in my body wanted to. In fact, it took all the willpower I had just to stand in place. Then I thought back to the painfully shy girl from the first day of school, and my insides twisted with pity. Gina was hurt. She might even be dying.

So what? the voice insisted. *She killed Kelly and Riley! She hurt a lot of others, too. Why should* you *care what happens to her?*

Maybe I shouldn't. Then again, maybe when all the bad things happened, Cozanna was calling the shots.

So, you're ready to die, too? Because that's what will probably happen if you go back there. If one ghost doesn't get you, the other one will!"

Yeah, maybe.

My heart jackhammered the inside of my chest while I thought it over. "*Damn* it," I whispered at last, and then I headed back down the hall.

I'm stupid that way sometimes.

I tried to move silently, but fear made my footfalls seem impossibly loud to me. I winced at every little creak in the floor, making me feel about as stealthy as your average marching band in the Macy's Thanksgiving Parade. At last, I made it to the door, and then paused to reach out with my gift to test the emotions inside.

Nothing.

I straightened, frowning. That was strange. I had expected to pick up Frank Delgiacco's brooding, violent menace. Or Cozanna's all-consuming rage. But there was nothing. Nothing at all. Had my gift decided to pack up and go to Florida again? It didn't feel that way, but I couldn't be sure.

Gingerly, I twisted the knob and pushed the door open, then immediately scooted back a few steps to see what would happen.

Still nothing.

Gina lay crumpled on the floor where I had last seen her. By the glow of the flashlight, I could see she was breathing, which was good. But it also meant I had no choice but to go in and get her.

I wasn't crazy about that idea at all.

Crap.

Shaking with terror, I took two tentative steps into the room. Then, when nothing happened, I rushed over to pick her up, and then retreated to the door as quickly as I could. Turning, I swept the room with my gift one final time, starting to feel a little more confident.

Psychically speaking, Suite 324 was empty. A line from some old movie—*nobody here but us chickens*—occurred to me, but it didn't seem funny right then. Exhaling a grateful sigh, I made my way back down the hall at a trot, not wanting to press my luck any further than I already had.

It was a good thing Gina was so small, as I was able to carry her all the way to the front porch before I had to set her down and rest. It also gave me time to put together a theory on what must have happened. We had assumed that Cozanna only used the spirit board as sort of a recharging station—that its destruction would cause her to weaken over time until she faded away. But an essential part of her must have been permanently bonded to it, and breaking the board had broken her, too. That was lucky. Luckier still was that it had taken her so long to deal with the other ghost. I didn't want to think about what might have happened if she'd had time to circle back to me. Most likely I would have ended up just one more in a long line of grisly victims, while Cozanna continued onward through the decades, vengefully guarding her family line. I thought about all the people she had hurt or killed, wondering how many more there might have been if we hadn't stopped her.

But there would be plenty of time to think about that later. I needed to get moving. Gathering Gina into my arms, I began my slow trek to the house, breathing in the frigid air while the moon and stars looked down indifferently from the dark winter sky.

EPILOG I

THERE WERE SOME LOOSE ENDS TO TIE UP, BOTH THAT night and during the days and weeks that followed, but not as many as I would have thought.

I learned later that when Sheriff Hastings questioned Ab and Les about what they had been doing at the crossroads, they simply told the truth: they had gone there to destroy a haunted Ouija board. The sheriff listened politely, but other than inspecting one of the holes they had filled in, he didn't ask for details. Apparently, he wasn't much of a believer. Naturally, he was far more interested in Les' account about how he had tried to save Darren, but the boy had been too dazed by the crash to understand that all he had to do was unlock his door. Les' statement went into the official report, and his heroics even made the news.

The part about the Ouija board didn't.

Mom had it even easier. She explained that she had been out running, which was true, and that she had seen the truck skid through the intersection and wreck against the dock piling, which was also true. She backed up Les' story about trying to save Darren, and a couple of days later the incident was described in the local paper as TEEN JOYRIDE ENDS IN TRAGEDY.

While all that was going on, I managed to load Gina into the back of Mom's explorer, and even found my phone in her jacket pocket. Ducking inside just long enough to wash and bandage the cut on my cheek, I called Les while grabbing Mom's keys. When Ab picked up, we brought one another up to date on everything that had happened while I drove Gina to the emergency room.

We were five minutes from Eureka when I heard her stir in the back seat. "Ben?" she asked drowsily. "What am I doing here?"

I took a quick read of her emotions, but sensed only confusion. "You don't know?" I asked suspiciously, glancing at her in the rearview mirror. Confused or not, there was no way I was going to trust her.

Gina shook her head.

"What's the last thing you remember?"

She frowned, appearing to think hard. "We argued…after Kelly's funeral. But I don't remember what it was about."

"That was *days* go, Gina. You don't remem…" My voice trailed off when I saw her head slump forward, unconscious again.

Hmm.

A security guard helped me get Gina into the ER, and a couple of nurses wearing scrubs wheeled her back on a gurney. As I watched the double doors swing closed, I offhandedly remembered they were the same doors Ab had been wheeled through just three nights before. Funny how random things like that occur to you.

When the nurse at the desk asked what happened, I told her I had found her on our property. I told her uncle Tim the same thing when I called him a few minutes later. I knew he was bound to ask what she had been doing there to begin with, so I asked *him* first, and he told me he didn't know. He apologized for any trouble Gina might have caused, and even thanked me for taking her to the hospital, saying that he and Roxanne would be right there.

I guessed they hadn't heard about Darren yet.

I tried telling myself that, technically speaking, I had not said anything that wasn't true. But that was BS and I knew it. I had misled him, and felt horrible about it, but I had to face the fact that he wouldn't have believed the truth even if I told him. Even so, I realized that I might have to come clean later, depending on what Gina eventually recalled, but I decided I would deal with that when the time came.

It turned out I didn't need to worry. Gina stuck to her story about not remembering anything since Kelly's funeral reception, but whether she was telling the truth, or just leaving out everything else to keep from being questioned, was anyone's guess. I saw her two weeks later at Darren's funeral. We didn't speak, and the only emotion I could read from her was grief, so I didn't learn anything new. Most of my friends showed up to support her, but I was the only one of us who was just there for Darren. Warming up to the guy had always been hard, but still, I had always felt a little sorry for him, and I still did. All he had wanted was a friend, and part of me wished I had done better.

That was the last I saw of Gina. She never came back to school, and just three weeks later I heard that the Lynch family had moved away. I spoke to their next-door neighbor and learned that Roxanne's brother had offered Tim a job in the service department of his heavy equipment dealership in Arizona. Following the loss of Darren, the family had needed a change, so they packed up a rented moving truck and hit the road.

I never got my D&D stuff back, but that was okay. I didn't feel much like playing anymore.

A week or so later I received a postcard in the mail. The picture on the front was of a lizard wearing a cowboy hat, sitting next to a frozen Margarita and with the words *Greetings from Wyatt, AZ!* across the top. According to Google, Wyatt was located a little northwest of Kingman in the Mojave Desert—population just over 6,500 as of the last census. Other than my name and address, the postcard bore only a single sentence…

[I still think about you]

…in Gina's handwriting. There was no return address, and while she might have just forgotten to add it, my guess was she figured I wouldn't send a reply anyway. She was probably right.

It was late in the afternoon on the third Sunday of April when I finally got around to the last of it. The day was clear and warm, with a light offshore breeze that smelled of wildflowers and eucalyptus, and I decided it was finally time. I loaded up Moe and drove to Silver Creek in the Explorer (*my* Explorer now—Mom had given it to me after our old station wagon had been hauled to the junkyard, explaining with a wink that she liked the color of her new red one better). After a brief stop at the sporting goods store to buy a pocket knife, we continued to Silver Creek Memorial Park.

The gravel lot was empty when we parked, so I felt safe enough to let Moe trot along beside me despite the *No Dogs Allowed* sign posted near the gate. We arrived at Kelly's grave a few minutes later, and after another quick look around to make sure no one was watching, I knelt, carefully cutting and prying out a small square from the grass at the base of her headstone. Reaching into my pocket, I pulled out the velvet box containing her bracelet, opened it, and tipped the broken silver and gold strands into the hole. It was hers after all, and it felt right that she should have it back. I replaced the square of sod on top of it, tamped it into place, and then just sat there awhile, remembering. I had not allowed myself to do much of that since those long evenings in front of the fireplace, and it was nice to finally be able to think about Kelly without my thoughts turning dark.

One errand down, one to go.

We drove back home, though instead of taking the right-hand fork to the house, we continued up to the inn. Les had helped me re-mount the door Cozanna had blown off its hinges, and a sheet of plywood now covered the window I had smashed, but otherwise the place looked the same. Funny…part of me sort of expected the old hotel to look different—or at least *feel* different—after that last night, but I guessed that was just me.

That, or maybe hotels got over stuff faster than I did.

Grabbing my backpack from behind the driver's seat, I followed Moe around back to the edge of the cliffs. The afternoon was waning by then, with the lower arc of the sun already dipping into the Pacific and changing the sky to shades of orange and pale rose. I would have come earlier in the day, but after checking the tide charts online, I waited until I was sure it was headed out.

Unzipping my pack, I reached inside and withdrew the planchette. Ab and Les had forgotten all about it the night everything had gone down. But since Professor Whatshisname had only specified to not bury it with any other piece of the spirit board, I figured it didn't matter. Tossing my pack aside, I turned the heart-shaped indicator over in my hands for a long moment, thinking about everything that had happened and glad that the evil memories it contained were faint enough to ignore now that Cozanna was gone. At last, I drew back my arm and threw it as hard as I could, watching the planchette sail like a Frisbee out from the cliffs, arcing downward to drop into the restless waves below with a tiny splash.

I lowered myself to the ground, sitting cross-legged at the edge of the cliff with the wind ruffling my hair. Moe ambled over a moment later to lay down beside me with his head in my lap. Together, we watched the tide carry the planchette west toward the horizon. When we couldn't see it anymore, we watched the sunset instead.

As sunsets go, it was a nice one.

Finally, I realized that it was time to go home, and that Mom was probably wondering where we were. But we stayed put for a moment longer, watching a black spot out over the ocean glide north against the backdrop of shimmering water. It was a bird—either a seagull or a pelican; it was too far away to tell for sure—skimming a foot or so above the waves, as if enjoying the last flight of the day.

I wondered how long it would be before I felt that good again. *Probably a while yet,* I decided after thinking about it.

But I would get there.

EPILOG II

THE NEW GIRL PAUSED AFTER EXITING THE LUNCH LINE, *glancing around tentatively until seeing an empty table near the outside doors. Eyes down, she scuttled toward it, feeling all but invisible under her hood.*

Invisible was good. Invisible was safe.

Laughter rang out from the far side of the cafeteria, and she looked warily over as she walked, suspicious that it was directed at her. It wasn't, though—just a cluster of boys making fun of a fat kid—and she turned her head back just as she collided with two girls coming in, knocking her tray to the floor.

"Watch it!" one of them snapped angrily. "You almost spilled on me!"

She didn't know what either of them looked like—she couldn't bring herself to raise her eyes that far—but the one who yelled was wearing a WHS Dust Devils T-shirt. Instead, she looked sadly at her spilled lunch, trying not to cry. She had not had breakfast and was very hungry.

"Clumsy bitch!" said the other, which made the new girl angry enough to glare after them as they made their way toward the lunch line. The two

glared back at her over their shoulders, exchanging whispers she was glad she couldn't hear.

She was the only one who noticed the empty chair that slid by itself into their path, chrome legs silent on the waxed linoleum. They stumbled over it, going down hard in a tangle, and one of them—the girl who had called her a clumsy bitch—began to shriek. Her right wrist was bent at an odd angle, clearly broken. Kids from the surrounding tables rushed to gather around them, abandoning their lunches, and the new girl idly plucked half a sandwich from someone's tray as she headed for the doors. Turkey, she noted, deciding that maybe she wasn't that hungry after all. The sandwich would do nicely.

"Thank you, Frank," Gina murmured as she stepped out into the desert sunshine.

And she smiled a secret smile.